IN FULL FORCE

In Full
FORCE
BADGES OF BECKER COUNTY

KATHY
ALTMAN

IN FULL FORCE

For more information on Kathy Altman and her books, sign up for her newsletter or visit her website: www.kathyaltman.com.

For Joyce Lamb,
romance champion and treasured friend.

- 1 -

CHARITY BISHOP'S PULSE BUCKED and her breath shuddered in and out of her lungs as she gazed down at the man she straddled. Torso heaving, hips twisting, he tried his damnedest to tip her sideways. *Oh, no, you don't.* What was it with men, anyway, and always having to be on top?

She squeezed her thighs tighter. He groaned, and muttered an oath.

With a frustrated sigh, Charity stretched through the gloom, rocking forward over a scrawny hind end. She shook her head, snagged the man's wrists, and pulled them around to his lower back. Seriously. Was there anything more pathetic than a woman whose only opportunity to ride a man came when she needed to fit him with a pair of handcuffs?

And not even the fun, fur-lined kind. More like the your-ass-is-going-to-jail-so-I-hope-you're-into-strip-searches kind.

Not that she had cause for a strip search. Nor the desire for any kind of hanky-panky here — the idea itself was enough to make her belly yearn for a ginger ale. The sour stench of stale cigarettes and beer muscled aside the sweet, sage-laced smell of a Montana prairie after dark and Charity's stomach roiled. She relaxed her jaw and breathed in through her mouth as she patted him down.

He was clean.

So to speak.

She winced at the cold damp soaking through the knees of her pants and lifted into a squat. Right on cue, the man beneath her started to retch. Great. Perfect. The county was steadily hacking away at their budget and all three deputies shared janitorial duties. With her luck, tomorrow would be her day to clean out the holding cells.

"Upsy-daisy." Tugging hard on the cuffs, she coaxed the drunk to his feet. The moment she'd shaken him awake, he'd bolted from the pickup. He hadn't given her much of a chase, but her heart kicked like a two-year-old throwing a tantrum. Time to get serious about cutting back on the coffee.

The drunk swayed beside her, mumbling, squinting toward the truck. Fretting over what she'd find in the cab, no doubt. She sighed, scooped up her flashlight, and gave her collar a push. She'd stash him in her SUV along with the pickup's driver, then conduct a search. Another pursuit and her over-caffeinated heart just might explode.

The instant she opened the rear door of her Tahoe, the first drunk started screaming.

"I ain't done nothin,'" he yelled, thrashing along the length of the seat until he reached the open door. He tried to spit at her, couldn't get his cheeks working and dribbled sputum down the front of his grubby denim jacket. "You got nothin' on me. I'm innocent!"

She couldn't remember a time she'd ever believed that. By now his desperate denial of guilt had become part of their arrest ritual, like the token foot chase and the resigned rummage through his empty beer can collection.

Still she couldn't help asking, "So why'd you run?"

"Everyone runs from the cops, you stupid bitch."

"Sweet talk me all you want, but you're still going to jail."

"What for?"

"Seriously? You smell like you took a bath in a beer keg, and you were driving like you had both hands over your eyes."

"Fuck you."

The guy in her grip chortled and Charity set her jaw. "Nope," she gritted. "That'd be incest."

After kicking the door shut with her foot—somehow the jerk managed to pull his head back in time—Charity hustled drunk number two around to the other side. She shoved him in, gave an approving grunt when he intercepted the second batch of spit, slammed the door shut, and straightened. Eyes closed, she turned away and counted to ten, then tugged a pair of latex gloves from her equipment belt and marched over to the pickup.

The truck had skidded to a stop three feet from a cottonwood with a trunk as wide as a tractor tire. Her asshole brother and his drinking buddy were lucky to be going to jail instead of the morgue. She scowled at the battered pickup. The driver's side door sagged open, the interior light flickering wearily. *Stand back, I'm going in.*

Her shoulder mic crackled and she froze.

Crap. The night dispatcher knew Hank Bishop and what he was capable of, which meant she'd be pissed at Charity for not checking in. Charity put her hand to her mic and thumbed the volume up, but the sultry female voice that could have ruled the phone sex industry didn't transmit the expected rebuke.

"All units, we have a one-eight-seven on Richland Road. Please respond."

Charity sucked in a breath and pressed push-to-talk. "Dispatch, this is Unit Four. Could you ten-twenty-two?"

"You heard me right, Charity. One-eight-seven. Unit Three's on location."

"Ten-four." Charity stared in the direction of the river. After two days of April rain, the muddy water tumbled as madly as the inside of her belly.

Homicide. She'd been with the Becker County Sheriff's Department for six years and only once had she worked a murder. Even then she'd hovered on the periphery, covering shifts for the investigators and offering clerical support. Now the sheriff was on leave, which put the undersheriff, who happened to be Charity, in charge. Her heart gave an anxious kick and she peeled off her gloves. Becker County, Montana was a small town; chances were she knew the victim. She angled her chin toward her radio.

"Unit Four responding. ETA twenty minutes." Why did she have to be on the opposite side of the county? She'd have to send someone else to work her brother's accident scene.

Fifteen seconds later, she was strapped into her seat and turning the key. She switched off the takedown lights and tossed her hat aside. Behind her, Hank started in with a slurred monologue of worn-out curses, threats, and pleas. He knew he was facing time. Not only did he have three DUIs under his belt, but he was supposed to be driving the Buick, already fitted with a court-ordered ignition interlock. She figured two years, minimum.

A burst of static from the radio. Charity's fingers curled around the gear shift and she shot a warning glance at the rearview mirror. "I'm needed out on Richland Road. Either of you gives me any trouble, I'll pull over and cuff you to a tree."

"You can't do that." Hank kicked the back of her seat. "There's bears out here. I'll sue!"

"You could use the money for tires. I bet that old pickup of yours doesn't even know what a tread is."

"Fuck you."

She sighed. Next he'd start harping about how a sister should look out for a brother. Never mind he was ten years older. Never mind she couldn't remember him once looking out for her.

"Not very original, are you, Hank?" She shifted into drive and ground her boot into the accelerator. Hank slammed back against the seat, hollering a garbled protest, while his buddy started whining about the half-empty bottle of beer he'd left in the truck. Charity smiled grimly.

Twenty-three minutes later she turned into the parking lot of the Becker County Veterinary Clinic. Arriving late at the scene? Not a great way to take lead of a homicide investigation. But she'd had to pull over twice to let drunk number two out to puke.

Deputy Coroner Riley Morrissey, or "Mo," had been busy. The lot was lit up like an outdoor court prepped for a game of midnight basketball. Someone had turned on the clinic's floodlights, and they merged into the collection of headlights, emergency lights, and spotlights, all illuminating the body sprawled on the dull asphalt.

The body of a woman.

A helpless dismay seared the inside of Charity's chest. Dealing with the occasional traffic accident victim and household fatality was bad enough. But homicide...

With a quick exhale, she plucked her hat from the passenger seat and pushed out of the SUV. She didn't have to worry about Hank; despite her driving, he was fast asleep in the back seat, snoring loudly enough to rattle the paint off the chassis. Meanwhile his less-hostile, spew-happy partner-in-crime had started singing a garbled version of Pat Benatar's "Hit Me with Your Best Shot."

A member of the sheriff's posse, or reserve unit, nodded as he passed by, walking backward while unreeling a bright strip of *Do Not Cross* tape. Charity scanned the vehicles in the lot. Besides Mo's squad vehicle, the twin to her Tahoe, she noted an ambulance, a half dozen pickup trucks belonging either to members of the volunteer rescue squad or the sheriff's posse, a battered compact no one other than the owner of the local paper would bother to claim, a minivan Charity didn't recognize, and a two-seater convertible the bright white of a celebrity's smile. She frowned. She knew that car.

A muffled, staccato sound finally registered. Dogs, barking inside the clinic. The barks faded behind a desultory clatter as two paramedics took their time offloading a stretcher from the back of the ambulance. No need to hurry when they were headed to the morgue.

Charity ducked under the flimsy yellow barrier.

The dead woman lay on her left side, left arm extended and cushioning her head, right arm bent behind her back. A long, off-white, expensive-looking coat hid her torso and upper legs. Beneath the coat she wore jeans and a three-inch pair of brown leather heels that cost more money than Charity took home in a month. She knew that because in a moment of madness she'd looked them up online, after Sarah had shown them off at the fire house's annual pancake breakfast two weeks earlier. One look at the price and Charity had cringed. The boots were gorgeous, but not worth maxing out her credit card.

Her throat locked as she stared down at the woman sprawled at her feet. There was no mistaking that hair — a thick, glossy, enviable mass the color of polished pennies. Definitely Sarah Huffman. Single, smart, and successful, she'd been an agent with Tarrant Properties for years. She couldn't have been more than thirty-five years old.

Charity's gaze traveled to the purple-edged stripe of red that banded the woman's throat. *Who did this to you?* No answer but the emergency lights that clicked and whirred, tinting the coat red, then blue, then red, then blue.

She crouched and scanned for signs of blood or other trauma. Hopefully Mo had asked Dispatch to contact the sheriff. And where was Dix? She needed her lead detective on site. Now.

"Strangled. Better than drowning. But not by much, I'm thinking."

Charity let loose a quiet sigh. She knew that doomsday voice. Whenever she heard it she couldn't help thinking of Eeyore. Only Eeyore was a damned sight more cheerful. Fingers digging into her knees, she peered up at Phil Smiley—owner, editor and head reporter of the *Becker County Herald*.

"I doubt she'd agree with you." Her gaze dropped to Smiley's hands. "What are you doing inside the barrier? With that?"

He gestured with the camera. "Deputy Morrissey forgot his. I'd already got plenty of shots of... Anyway, you can have the memory card when I'm done. Long as I get a pic or two for the morning edition. I'm just trying to help out here."

He adopted an injured expression, but Charity didn't bite. She reached beneath her jacket and slid a pen free of her shirt pocket, then turned back to the body. Carefully she lifted away Sarah's hair to get a closer look at the bruising. A flurry of superficial scratches marked both sides of the throat, above the ligature line.

Charity swallowed. *Fingernails.* Despite Sarah's tidy appearance, she'd struggled.

"Guess you're wishing the sheriff was here."

Slowly Charity stood, replaced the pen, and slipped both thumbs into her rig. Smiley was right. At the same time, in some tragic, twisted way, this homicide would give her a chance to prove what she could manage on her own. Maybe help the town discover a female sheriff wouldn't be such a bad thing after all.

"He'll be here soon enough." She turned and headed for Mo.

The department's part-time coroner stood beside his unit, a notepad in one hand and a wad of paper towels in the other. In front of him a petite brunette wavered on high heels and brushed at the front of her leather jacket with her own fistful of towels. Charity winced. Looked like tonight was puke night. Chances were *someone* would be disinfecting their —

Crap. She halted. The face on the other side of all those dark curls finally registered. She knew she'd recognized that convertible. It belonged to Justine Langford. Justine West Langford.

Grady's sister.

Cold dread hit Charity's stomach. *Please let her be nothing more than a witness.*

The moment she acknowledged the thought, it shamed her. The day she let bias affect her job was the day she gave up being a law enforcement officer. And a law enforcement officer was all she'd ever wanted to be.

Mo shot her an it's-about-time look, but behind the irritation in his baby blues lurked an unmistakable edginess. She noted the sad cast to his mouth and remembered — once upon a time, Mo had dated the victim, which meant he'd have his own issues to deal with.

This just kept getting better and better.

Mo gestured in Charity's direction. "This is Deputy Sheriff Bishop, Mrs. Langford. She'll head the investigation until the sheriff arrives."

Justine gazed at Charity through red-rimmed, tormented eyes. Navy eyes, like her brother's. Charity looked away and waved over one of the paramedics. When she looked back, she aimed her gaze at Justine's quivering chin.

"Can I get you anything, Mrs. Langford? Water, maybe?" No response. The paramedic jogged over, and Charity touched Justine on the shoulder. "How about you let Yolanda take a look at you? Just to make sure you're all right."

Numbly Grady's sister turned to follow the paramedic to the ambulance. Her gaze landed on the body and she slapped a hand over her eyes.

"Cover her," she begged in a high-pitched, breathy voice. "For God's sake, can't you cover her?"

Mo moved to block her view. "No disrespect, Mrs. Langford, but we have to finish working the scene. I promise we'll take care of her as soon as we can." He gestured for the paramedic to take his place, then he and Charity watched Justine Langford wobble away.

"She's half-loaded." Mo held the soiled paper towels way out in front of him as he headed for the back of his SUV.

Charity exhaled. If Justine had been driving, that meant another DUI. Not good. Not good at all. This did not bode well for the socialite's reliability as a witness.

She turned toward the empty single-lane highway. On the other side of the aging pavement, something made a scraping sound. A rattle of displaced pebbles. Awareness tickled the back of her neck, and every muscle locked. She squinted into the night, straining to see past the borders of the crime scene to the shadows that lurked beyond the reach of the lights.

Was he out there? Watching them labor over his handiwork? Enjoying the shock and grief and horror he'd spawned?

Charity tipped her head and listened. Nothing. But she didn't have to be trained in law enforcement to know there were times criminals felt compelled to return to the scene of the crime, to witness firsthand the aftermath, to revel in challenging the police.

Unless the killer had never left the parking lot.

"Think he's out there?"

Charity cursed herself for flinching. She offered Mo a shrug. "Remind me to check across the road for tire tracks. Maybe he panicked and left the scene in a hurry. And we should search the ditches. Fifty yards in each direction."

"You got it. Could be a she, you know."

"Could be." Charity led him back to his Chevy and opened the top drawer of his heavy-duty kit cabinet. Bandages and crumpled evidence bags. The next drawer contained a tangle of zip ties. The next, a jumble of gas receipts and accident forms. With a huff of disgust, Charity pushed the door shut. "You've got to straighten this up, Mo. How do you find anything?"

Scowling, he nudged her aside. "What are you looking for?"

She leaned around him, held up her hands and waggled her fingers.

"Coming right up." He lifted the plastic bag of puked-on paper towels, revealing a box of latex gloves in the corner. He snagged a pair and with a smug flourish, presented them to Charity.

"Thank you." She peered over his shoulder, checking that Smiley was steering clear of her crime scene as she worked her hands into the latex. "So what's the story?"

"Mrs. Langford was first on the scene. She was passing by, saw something, pulled in for a closer look, spewed her dinner plus three or four cocktails, and called nine-one-one."

"What time?"

He pulled out his notepad. "Twenty-two thirty-seven."

Just past ten thirty. "Time of death?"

With a roll of his eyes he offered up the usual disclaimer. "I'm a coroner, not a medical examiner. The ME in Great Falls has to do his thing before we know for sure."

"But if you had to guess..."

After shoving his notepad back into his belt, he pulled out the drawer with the zip ties, scooped them out and replaced them with the box of gloves. "She died about two hours ago. Ligature strangulation. The marks slant upward at the back of her neck. Not wire—her skin's not broken." His fingers were stiff as he straightened the strips of black plastic. "No obvious signs of molestation."

Charity opened drawers until she found the first aid kit and tucked the loose bandages from the top drawer inside. "Could she have been killed somewhere else and dumped here?"

"Always a possibility. But there's scuff marks on the pavement nearby, and the heels of her boots are all scratched up."

Pushing aside the image his words induced, Charity moved away from the SUV and looked from the road back to where the body lay. "Mrs. Langford mention which way she was headed when she spotted the body?"

"East."

Interesting. "Where would she be going this time of night? Headed out of town?"

Mo slammed the tailgate closed. "Didn't get that much out of her. She's pretty upset."

"And you?"

A pause. "I'll be fine once we catch the son of a bitch who did this."

Charity gave his arm a quick squeeze. "How about next of kin?"

"Sarah's parents live in Virginia. Okay if I handle notification?" At her nod, Mo cleared his throat. "Looks like they're done with our witness. You want to run her in, or have her wait?"

"The kindest thing would be to get her to the station. I don't think either of us should leave, though." She nodded her head at the men and women grouped around the back of the ambulance. The man who'd strung the caution tape was a trained volunteer who served with the sheriff's reserves.

"I'll get Tim to take her back and keep her company. While he's at it, he can take care of booking my brother and his buddy. By the way, what happened to your camera?"

Color seeped into his face. She'd bet that under that surfer-blond hair, even his scalp was scarlet.

He dropped his head and took his time adjusting his rig. "I, uh, must have left it somewhere."

"You'd better find it before the sheriff gets back."

"You gonna call him?"

Crap. Her hands went to her hips. "You mean you didn't?"

His head came up and he didn't bother hiding his smirk. "You're the undersheriff. I'm just a lowly deputy."

"Thanks a lot, Mo. I'll remember that the next time you're looking to trade shifts for the sake of a hot date." Ignoring his pained expression, Charity watched with approval as across the lot Yolanda steered Justine away from the ghoulish Phil Smiley.

Charity gestured to Mo and they started back toward their victim. "Heard anything from Dix?" Only a few bystanders had parked on the side of the road to watch the excitement, but with police scanners a household item in these parts, it wouldn't take long for others to gather. They had to get this scene worked before they lost any more manpower to crowd control.

"He's on his way."

As soon as Charity called him, the sheriff would be, too. So much for his long-awaited fishing trip. Any trout playing hard-to-get with the sheriff's pole would have to stay in the Gallatin River.

She stopped, lifted her hat, and scrubbed her fingers through her hair as Mo walked on. If Justine Langford proved to be anything more than a witness, yet another male would be on his way back to Becker County. The Grady West she remembered wouldn't sit on his thumbs while his sister faced criminal prosecution.

Would he bring his wife and child?

Charity rolled her shoulders up and back. Seriously, what did she care? What was past was past. She'd moved on. Grady had moved on. She hiked her chin and trailed Mo to Sarah Huffman's lifeless body.

Besides. Some things just couldn't be undone.

* * *

GRADY WEST STRODE ACROSS the poorly lit parking lot of the Becker County courthouse, gaze locked on the innocuous beige door that separated him from the family he'd seen maybe a handful of times since he'd left town twelve years earlier. He knew his parents were inside — he'd parked his rental car beside a gleaming Mercedes sporting the IMADOC vanity plate. His father had claimed a space reserved for sheriff's office employees.

Good ol' Dad.

Grady straightened his tie. He should have stopped at the house and changed his suit before rushing here from the airport. Especially now that he knew his parents hadn't been home.

He grimaced. No doubt Drs. Hampton and Roberta West were raising quite a ruckus on the other side of the courthouse door. Justine had asked him not to contact their parents, which meant someone else had clued them in.

Dammit, he wasn't ready for this. For any of it. Returning to Becker County, making nice with his mother and father, finding some way to sort out Justine and her troubles. He'd been out of the loop a long time. But not long enough.

Hell. The sudden heaviness of shame slowed his stride. Grady hesitated at the edge of the lot, next to an SUV made doubly brown by the fresh mud spattered across its paint. His parents weren't getting any younger. His sister needed him. Besides, he'd never managed to ditch the feeling he'd let Justine down by moving away. Answering her call for help was the least he could do.

He exhaled, his thoughts settling on the other woman who'd ruled his brain the past few hours. Charity Bishop. He hadn't seen her since that god-awful night after high school graduation. And now she'd arrested his sister. For murder.

Didn't bode well for a cheery reunion.

He jerked at the cuffs of his jacket and stepped up onto the concrete path. The overpriced ham sandwich he'd forced down his throat at the airport lay heavy in his gut. Justine hadn't exactly been coherent over the phone, but Grady had heard enough of the pieces to allow him to put together one hell of an outrageous puzzle.

Disturbing the peace, he could understand. When they were still married, Justine and her husband had regularly entertained their neighbors with their disagreements, producing about the same number of decibels as a subway train passing ten feet away. Sadly enough, Grady could even buy that his sister had been picked up for driving under the influence. But murder?

As he reached for the door handle, he froze, and squeezed his eyes shut. *Oh, Jesus. Don't let it be a hit and run.* He pulled in a breath, held it, felt it burn inside his lungs. He yanked open the door.

At the end of a short corridor, he found a layout not unlike an emergency room waiting area, with rows of battered plastic chairs on one side, reception area behind glass on the other, outdated posters scattered across the walls, and rusted rings on the floor mapping the rearrangement of furniture. In the corner, a soda machine gave off a quiet, continuous hum.

Besides the positions of the chairs, not much had changed.

"What are you doing here?" a female voice demanded.

Including this.

"I came to help," Grady said, and held out his arms. "How are you, Mother?"

She didn't answer, stepping out of his hug as fast as her three-inch heels would allow. He caught a whiff of her signature scent — the finest bourbon money could buy — and noticed a few extra lines had sidled onto her face. He shifted his shoulders up and around, but they wouldn't settle back into place.

Lately his son Matt had been pestering him about needing more time with his grandparents. Seemed Grady had been right to put him off.

His mother patted the hair gathered at the back of her head and gave Grady the once-over. "Where's Matthew?"

"I left him with Valerie."

"Was that wise?"

"Wiser than yanking him out of school so he could visit his aunt in the pokey."

An amused, muffled sound wafted from behind the thick glass window. His mother yanked at the hem of her blouse. "That woman will let him stay up all night and eat cold pizza for breakfast."

And yet two more reasons for his preteen son to hope Grady took his time getting back to Seattle.

"'That woman' is his mother," Grady said. "He'll be fine." He hoped. Valerie didn't seem to have much time for their son anymore, and it was ironic as hell, considering Matt had made it clear he'd rather live with her. Grady extended his hand to his other parent. "Dad."

His father had money, smarts, charm, and a solid reputation as an orthopedic surgeon. What he wasn't smug about? A son who'd snubbed medical school, a divorcée daughter who continued to reject his hand-picked candidates for spouse number two, and a wife who exceeded her husband's height by a solid three inches. When she managed to stand upright.

Oh, yeah. Hampton West was a bitter man. He clasped Grady's hand and squeezed hard. Too hard. Surgeon's roulette, Grady liked to call it. Because one of these days someone would squeeze even harder in return and shatter the good doctor's livelihood.

Then Grady looked closer. His father's eyes were red-rimmed and dazed, like he hadn't been sleeping. "You okay, Dad?"

"I had to get him over here from the hospital. He was working late." His mother pursed her lips. "Again."

Christ. "Neither one of you should have been driving tonight."

His father swayed, and promptly sat. "How'd you know about your sister, anyway?"

"Justine called me."

"Why would she do that?" His mother looked like she'd caught the housekeeper bringing in the groceries through the front door.

"Maybe she thought I could help."

His father made a flicking motion. "If you're that determined to be useful, why don't you get someone to tell us why they haven't released her?"

"No one's talked to you yet?"

"And while you're at it, apply some of that crisis management training you're so proud of and put a gag on the local paper. That damned Phil Smiley—"

"That's what you're worried about? The press?"

His mother, sought after more for her talents as a hostess than a psychiatrist, gave a throaty huff of anger and rifled in the outside pocket of her handbag for the mints she always carried. "You don't have to live here. We do. We all know who's behind this, don't we?" She tossed back a handful of mints as though they were aspirin. "Keeping us waiting here on purpose," she seethed. "Making sure the entire county knows exactly where we are. Arresting Justine for no better reason than to promote a run for sheriff."

"We haven't arrested Mrs. Langford. At this point she's a witness only."

Grady's stomach dipped. *That voice.* He'd never forgotten that voice. Huskier, after twelve years. An even stronger a reminder of his grandfather's favorite drink—heated rum and honey, with a splash of lemon.

His father struggled to his feet. His mother frowned, wavering as she pivoted on too-high heels. Grady turned more slowly, memories of the sass he'd heard spoken in that voice tempting his lips into a smile.

He resisted the temptation. He needed answers, not a rehashing of the past. Still, when Grady met Charity's cool hazel gaze, every nerve in his body quivered as if strummed. He had to admit, there were some moments in the past he wouldn't mind reliving.

And some he'd give anything to undo.

Charity stood before him in a long-sleeved, mud-brown uniform, same pretty face, same pale skin, same wicked curves. She'd exchanged her curly ropes of butter-colored hair for a short, wispy cut, and the bridge of her nose sported a telltale bump. He wanted to ask her about the injury, about her job, longed to pull her close and hear the lusty laugh that once upon a time had never failed to pull him back from the edge.

But that fairy tale was long since over. And even though she'd forgiven him, or once claimed she did, one glance at the jut of her chin made it clear she'd never forget.

Didn't matter. Grady had come to help his sister, not make nice with an ex-girlfriend. Despite the gravity of the situation, though, he couldn't help feeling smug that Charity had no choice but to see him. Ten years too late, but still. This time there'd be no blowing him off over the phone.

"Charity." He offered a grim nod. Then his mother's words worked their way to the front of his brain. *Arresting Justine for no better reason than to promote a run for sheriff.* He narrowed his gaze on that pale, no-nonsense face.

Charity was running for sheriff, and a high-profile case had just dropped into her lap. Complete with a convenient suspect. One whose brother had once managed to get Charity arrested.

Shit.

2

CHARITY KNEW EXACTLY WHAT Grady West was thinking and it took every last ounce of her willpower not to reach for her Taser. So he figured she'd toss his sister under the bus for the sake of a little payback, did he? Nice. At least she wouldn't have to worry about conflict of interest. The suspicion in his eyes made it clear there was no interest.

She tucked both thumbs into her rig, narrowed her eyes, and treated her high school sweetheart to her most intimidating cop face. Crap, crap, crap, crap, crap. Twelve years. Twelve years and the jerk still had the ability to knock her off balance. To heat her belly with a slow, liquid curl of need. Could the timing be any worse? She had a lot to prove, to the department, to the community, even to his smug-ass family. With Grady around dredging up feelings best left buried, she'd wind up trying to prove something to him. She couldn't afford the distraction.

And she resented the hell out of him for being one.

Dark brown eyebrows jacked over the same navy eyes that had rattled her when she'd first seen Justine at the crime scene. He'd caught her staring.

Shaking off the shock of seeing him again, she jerked a nod in return.

"Grady." Her jaw ached, as if saying his name had exercised long-unused muscles. She lifted her chin, took in an extended breath, and noticed the color of Hampton West's face had deepened from brick to magenta. Seemed he'd been trying to get her attention.

"I asked you a question," he thundered. "What do you mean, 'at this point she's a witness?'" He was glowering at her, hands on hips, neck thrust forward. "What the hell does that mean?"

"It means we're still trying to figure out what happened."

"She told you what happened." Hampton West was so spun up, he actually lifted up onto his toes when he spit the word "told."

Charity nodded. "We need to corroborate her version of events."

"Are you calling my daughter a liar?"

Charity gritted her teeth. *Think overwrought father. Think public servant.*

Think of the hours of paperwork one knee to the groin would generate.

"A murder has been committed," she told him. "We'd be doing this community a disservice if we failed to conduct a thorough investigation."

Roberta West dropped her designer bag on the chair behind her and crossed her arms, the peach silk of her blouse making angry *shush*-ing sounds as she moved. "Is my daughter under arrest or not?"

"Dr. West, your daughter found the body. She's a key witness, and she's agreed to give us a statement."

"You've had more than enough time to get her statement." The woman's hand flew to her mouth when she almost spit out a mint. "She's in shock. She needs her rest. We're taking her home."

"We shouldn't be much longer." Charity blinked up at the standard government-issue, black-rimmed, slightly off-center clock on the wall. Half past one in the morning. Was it too much to hope that Brenda June had packed an extra sandwich? Or a Valium? "If you're tired of waiting, we'd be happy to drive Mrs. Langford home after the interview."

Hampton West had made his unsteady way over to the soda machine in the corner. Dear Lord, were both of Grady's parents drunk? Had *everyone* been drinking tonight?

The surgeon swung back to face the room, a bottle of ginger ale in his hand. "Of course we're tired of waiting, but we're not going anywhere." He sounded like he suspected that once they set foot outside the building, Charity would toss his daughter behind bars and swallow the key. She might at that, if Brenda June didn't come through with that sandwich.

"You let me know the instant the sheriff gets here," he continued, and pointed the bottle at Charity, not realizing he'd already removed the cap. Soda splashed onto the floor. "You understand me?"

Enough already. "What I don't think you understand, Dr. West, is that I can have you — all of you — barred from the courthouse. Now if you think that's in Justine's best interests then by all means, continue to make an ass of yourself."

A snort sounded on the other side of the glass. Grady's mother gasped in outrage while his father pushed his soda into Grady's hands and grabbed for his phone.

How many blistering messages had Hampton West already left for Sheriff Pratt? Charity bit back a sigh and turned to Grady. "Justine contacted you. We need to talk."

*   *   *

IGNORING HIS PARENTS' PROTESTS, Grady followed Charity to a door marked AUTHORIZED PERSONNEL ONLY, where she held up a badge to the camera in the corner above their heads. A buzzer sounded, and she gestured him through. A chair squealed and groaned as a dipstick-skinny woman, sporting a buzz cut, crimson lip color, and a bright-orange, oversized sweater, swiveled away from an array of monitors to watch them pass. She aimed an exaggerated wink at Grady, and he walked right into Charity.

His hands shot up and out and his fingers closed around her upper arms. She still smelled like honeysuckle. The scent, coupled with the supple warmth beneath his palms, kicked off an erotic carnival of memories. His breathing went shallow, and every muscle in his body tightened.

Judging by the stone-faced glare Charity aimed over her shoulder, her memories were not as agreeable. He dropped his hands in the same instant she shrugged free of his grip.

18

"Sorry about that." And he was. Because he really wanted to touch her again, which meant he was forgetting the reason he was here in the first place.

Justine? The sister you flew six hundred miles to rescue?

A few long strides caught him up again to Charity, who'd stopped outside a room at the end of the hall. Table, two chairs, a whiteboard bearing the smudged streaks of a permanent marker. He motioned with his jaw at the room next to it.

"Justine in there?"

Charity nodded.

"She all right?"

"Physically she's fine. Hungover, but fine."

"Can I talk to her?"

"Not yet."

Right. Not until he'd provided his version of the phone calls. He raised a hand and squeezed the back of his neck. "Who died?"

Charity shoved her hands into her pockets. "A local real estate agent. She'd been in town less than five years. And she didn't die, she was murdered."

Her voice caught on the word "die." Typical Charity Bishop. Harsh words, marshmallow heart.

"I'm sorry to hear it," he said sincerely.

He gave her a moment by surveying the space, looking from the dispatcher's station with its semicircle of monitors to the battered file cabinets and glassed-in bulletin boards lining the wall he faced. To his left, the hallway ended in a wide metal door sandwiched between a water fountain and a tall, wall-mounted lockbox. The lower half of the door was riddled with scratches, dents, and scuffmarks. Had to be the entrance to the holding cells.

Where they'd be holding Justine, once they'd finished grilling her?

He jerked back to Charity. "Used to be Sheriff Pratt and one deputy."

"We have four deputies now." Static blurted from her radio and she slapped a hand to her shoulder to dial it down. Impatience had already replaced distress. "Three of us work the day shift and pull nights when we need to. The posse fills in when we're shorthanded."

"And you have a dispatcher."

"Two, actually." She gestured behind him, at the desk manned by the woman who'd winked at him. "Brenda June and her sister Trudy. Night and day."

"As in shifts, or personalities?"

"As in both."

He braced his arms across his chest and leaned a shoulder against the wall. "You seem to be in your element here."

"You seem to be surprised." She paused. "But that wasn't a compliment, was it?"

"It wasn't an insult."

"I'm a checkmark on a list. I get it." Yanking her hands free of her pockets, she swung toward the wall space between the interview rooms and plucked a dark blue folder free of a plastic holder attached to the wall. She kept her head bent as she flipped through the pages. "You're reassuring yourself that Justine's in good hands. Don't worry, she is. We're a great team. We'll make sure justice is done."

"Spoken like a true politician."

She stiffened, then surprised him by making a face. "At least you didn't say comic book hero."

"Not hero. Heroine. Like Wonder Woman. Big hair, big—"

"Let's leave my hair out of this." She was frowning as she flapped the folder at the interview room, but he hadn't missed that telltale twitch to her lips. "Have a seat," she said.

"I was going to say 'crime fighting opportunities.'"

"I'm sure you were. Deputy Morrissey will be right with you."

"I thought you had questions."

"We do." She hugged the folder to her chest. "A deputy will be in to ask them."

"You're a deputy."

Another third party snort. They both turned. A flash of orange and a grinding squeal was followed by a thump and a low-pitched curse as the dispatcher Brenda June tried—and failed—to hide the fact that she'd been eavesdropping. Charity clenched her teeth.

Grady straightened away from the wall. "What if I have questions?"

"When you're the one wearing the uniform, you can ask all the questions you want."

He eyed her patch-happy shirt, tucked into a pair of pants sporting a gold stripe down the seam. She filled out both oh-so-nicely. And he was an ass for noticing. "You really think my sister's capable of murder?"

"I already explained —"

"That she's a witness. Right. So why treat me like I inherited some kind of killing gene?"

For one glimmering instant the detachment disappeared from her eyes. It happened so fast Grady didn't have time to decide what had taken its place. Frustration? Sadness? Regret?

She took a deliberate step back. "I have a job to do. The sooner you let me get back to it, the sooner we'll all have some answers."

"There's nothing you can tell me. Nothing at all?"

Charity's eyes narrowed. "You expect me to compromise the investigation why? Because once upon a time I wore your letterman jacket? Because you dropped everything and hustled out here from Seattle? Or because your last name is West?"

Grady inhaled. She was right. He was out of line. But he needed to know what the hell was going on. "How about because we're friends."

"We were friends once. Now we're barely acquaintances."

She jerked her chin at the room behind him, and this time Grady took the hint. His mother was right; they needed to get his sister back home. No doubt she was exhausted, and more than a little freaked out. He scraped a chair out from under the table and sat down to wait.

Half an hour later he was back in the lobby with two teed-off parents and a headache the size of Yellowstone National Park.

Justine had called him twice. Each time he'd assumed she was calling from the sheriff's office, but it turned out that first call had been made from the crime scene. The police wanted to know why. So did Grady, but they wouldn't let him see his sister.

The relief he'd welcomed half an hour earlier had gathered into a cold ball of dread, weighing heavy in his gut, chilling him from the inside out. When Charity returned to the lobby, Grady stood, but no one else stirred. His mother had long since passed out on his father's shoulder. Not that his father would have gotten up, anyway.

Grady eyed the rigid line of Charity's shoulders, and his fingers fisted inside his pants pockets. Whatever she had to say, it wouldn't be good.

She aimed her words at his tie. "You can all go home now," she said quietly. "We won't be releasing Mrs. Langford this morning."

His father blasted up out of his chair and his mother fell forward, ready to somersault onto the floor. Both Grady and Charity lunged forward, but Charity got there first. His mother woke, sputtering and slapping at Charity's hands. Grady wedged himself in between the two women while his father picked up the nearest chair and slammed it back down with a rattling crash.

"Give me one good reason! One good reason for keeping my daughter here!"

"For God's sake, Dad."

"Calm down, Dr. West."

"Calm down! Calm down? You tell me why I can't take my daughter home, and you tell me now."

Charity widened her stance and emptied her expression. "You can't take her home because she just confessed to the murder of Sarah Huffman."

*   *   *

IF CHARITY DIDN'T HAVE a confessed killer to question, Dix and Mo waiting for her in the break room, and a boob-high pile of paperwork to finish, she'd strip naked and crouch in the corner of the shower and sob while the water ran from hot to cold, cliché be damned.

But she didn't have the time, and the department didn't have a shower. Well, unless she counted the one in lockup.

Not.

Tears prodded the backs of her eyes. With the heels of her hands, she prodded right back. This time yesterday, Sarah Huffman had been alive and well.

Hell, five hours ago, she'd been alive and well. Someone had choked the life out of her and left her lying in a parking lot. Had she had any inkling at all of the danger she'd been in?

Charity stood in front of the bathroom mirror, chin to chest, eyes clenched shut. She shoved at the mental image of Sarah Huffman's body, only to have it replaced by Grady West's face.

Crap, crap, crap, crap, crap. She didn't need this. Didn't need him. Didn't need the mocking tilt of his mouth or the dark blue tease of his eyes or the loose, lean length of him she'd once upon a time spent hours and hours wandering, like an idle tourist without a map.

She pictured his mouth again and willed away a shudder. What she was feeling had nothing to do with Grady West. It was her. Her and her undersexed body craving the sensations they'd once shared. The sweaty, honest, boneless-as-a-marathon-runner-at-the-finish-line kind of sex they'd always enjoyed.

And that was with the teenaged Grady. What would sex be like with the all-grown-up-and-in-his-hunky-prime version?

The bathroom door opened and the dispatcher sidled in, checking over her shoulder all the while, as if one of the guys might sneak a peek.

Charity slapped the faucet on. "I'm not naked in here, Brenda June."

"Course not." Brenda June set the latch. "I just didn't want anyone to see you blubbering."

The soap clattered into the sink. "What's that supposed to mean?"

"I grew up in Becker County, blondie. I remember. You and Grady West were the talk of the town — the soccer-playing valedictorian with all the money and manners hooking up with the brash blonde with more looks than pedigree. Now, years later, he's back and, well — who could blame you for feeling nostalgic?"

Charity grunted. Nostalgic. That was one way to put it. She yanked a paper towel free of the dispenser.

"And then you're forced to arrest his sister? For murder? No wonder you're hiding out in here. I say, go ahead and wallow."

"I'm not hiding or wallowing, Dispatch, I'm washing my hands. Yes, I regret having to arrest Justine. More than that, I regret that Sarah Huffman is dead. As for the rest of it, how pathetic do you think I am? Seriously, I have better things to do with my time than pine for a married man."

"Pine?" Brenda June shoved the sleeves of her pumpkin-colored sweater up past her skinny elbows. When she dropped her arms, the fabric coasted right back down again. "First of all, babycakes, I don't think anyone uses that word any more. Second of all, I don't know who your snitch is, but you might want to rethink their Christmas bonus. Grady West is divorced."

"Divorced?" Charity turned away from the mirror.

Divorced. Smugness wriggled its way in first. *Guess I'm not so easy to replace, after all.* Seconds later shame struck, hot and stinging, like her soul had been spanked. Charity thought of the child, of what he or she must have been through. She balled up the paper towel and flung it at the trash can. "Doesn't matter."

"Has been, for a couple of years." Brenda June took Charity's place at the sink and leaned toward her reflection. She checked her teeth and ran her palm over her hair. "So. That whole arson thing. Is that why you two broke up?" At Charity's gasp of disbelief, she shrugged. "What can I say? I'm a history buff."

My ass. "What are you up to, Brenda June?"

The dispatcher moved to the door and paused, thin fingers resting on the tarnished brass knob. "Just wondering if you remember why you two called it quits. 'Cause maybe things have changed."

"You can't be serious."

"You wish I hadn't told you about the divorce, right? It's easier when there's no decision to make."

"Cut the crap, Brenda June. I'm not looking for romance, and even if I were, it wouldn't be with him." Charity plucked the plastic air freshener thingie off the window sill, saw it was empty, and dropped it into the trash. She dusted her palms and frowned at Brenda June. "Does the phrase 'conflict of interest' mean anything to you?" That was only the tippy-top of a crap-load of reasons she and Grady would never manage a sequel, even supposing she wanted one, which she didn't.

She may as well have been talking to the bathroom sink.

"I'm surprised you didn't notice the absence of a ring," Brenda June said idly. "You being an investigator, and all."

"I wasn't looking. I have bigger things on my mind, and I'm not eighteen anymore. Besides, what are you, his pimp? The man has a life in Seattle. He's not sticking around."

"He might if you ask him to."

Oh, for — "One more word and I'll tell the sheriff we need to set up a coffee mess in the lobby. For the dispatchers to manage." She leaned over the sink and washed her hands again.

Brenda June refused to be drowned out. "You do that, and I'll... I'll tell Mo you think he's hot."

Charity shrugged. "Mo believes every woman thinks he's hot. But the second you do that, I'll tell the sheriff you think *he's* hot."

The color in Brenda June's cheeks rivaled the color on her mouth. "You wouldn't." At Charity's raised eyebrows, the other woman fumbled with the doorknob. "Fine." She was halfway through the door when she turned back and stretched her bright mouth into a smile. "But surely while Grady is here you two could manage to be friends." The door rattled shut behind her.

How about because we're friends? Grady's words echoed in the tiny space.

Charity clicked her tongue against her teeth and scowled in the mirror. She and Grady had about as much chance of being friends as the camera-toting Phil Smiley had of acing sensitivity training.

Justine's indictment wouldn't change how the West family felt about Charity, and neither would an acquittal. Up until Justine's arrest, the Wests had regarded the Bishops with disgust and disdain. Recent events made it obvious those feelings had graduated to out-and-out loathing. Good thing Charity didn't give a damn what any of them thought.

Except she did, because she had an election to win.

In the mirror flashed the image of Grady's face and the grim disappointment she'd put there.

Good thing he didn't get a vote.

*   *   *

"WHAT DO YOU MEAN, she didn't do it?" Charity frowned at Detective Dixon Ironmaker, who scooped another forkful of banana fudge cheesecake into his mouth. "She confessed!"

Dix chewed and swallowed. "Yet could not tell us how she did it. Or why. We asked for details and she asked for a lawyer."

Mo trapped his tie with one hand and used the other to snag another slab of cheesecake. "She can't remember the details because she was drunk off her ass."

"If she was drunk off her ass, how'd she manage to overpower a woman four inches taller and thirty pounds heavier?" Dix asked.

Mo licked his fingers and shrugged. "So they were both drunk."

"I don't think so." Dix shook his head.

Charity pushed her cheesecake away and tipped forward, bracing her arms on the table. "Based on what?"

Dix reached for his coffee mug. "She is a smart woman. Why kill someone, stay to call nine-one-one, then pretend to have found the body?"

"Happens all the time." Charity slapped the table and swung her legs over the bench seat. "A criminal with more pride than sense finds a way to be part of the investigation, either to find out how much we know or to revel in not getting caught."

"Or..." Mo drew out the word. "She did it because she was drunk off her ass."

Dix looked at Mo. "When can we expect the ME's report?"

"The man said by lunch tomorrow."

Brenda June appeared in the break room doorway, lips as red as the cherry halves she'd pressed into the top of the cheesecake. She passed around a frown. "Shouldn't at least two of you be on your way home to bed?"

When Mo let that go without making an X-rated suggestion, Charity knew he was still thinking about Sarah Huffman. She ignored Brenda June and started clearing the table. No way she was calling it quits before everyone else. Besides, she wanted to go home about as much as she wanted to wander back to lockup and kiss her brother and his buddy good night. She had plenty to keep her busy here. Once she left the building, she wouldn't be able to stop from thinking about Grady West, what they once had together, and how he'd ruined it by setting her up.

No. That wasn't fair. They would never have made it as a couple anyway. He'd just accelerated the process.

Like gas on a fire.

"Listen, blondie." Brenda June scowled at the untouched wedge on Charity's plate. "Do you have any idea what goes into making one of my cheesecakes?"

"Too much," Charity muttered.

"Excuse me?"

"Why can't it ever just be plain?"

"Because you already have too much vanilla in your life. What's wrong with a little flavor?"

"Vanilla is a flavor."

Dix scrubbed his napkin across his mouth and glanced at Mo. "What did she blow?"

Charity blinked. Damn, she was tired, because it took a few seconds to realize he was talking about Justine and the breathalyzer. She struggled to focus on all the bad things Grady West had done when they were together, but still her mind lingered on bad-naughty instead of bad-thoughtless. She swallowed a groan and snatched up the plastic wrap.

"Point-one-five." Mo's lips twisted in disgust. "That was after baptizing herself in puke. Twice."

Brenda June scowled at him. "Mind your manners. People are trying to eat." She perched her bony behind on the bench. "More cheesecake, Dixon?"

Dix shook his head while Mo and Charity exchanged a look. Dix had one hell of a sweet tooth. Only Brenda June, aka his sugar dealer, could get away with using his given name.

"Enchanted cheesecake," Charity whispered.

"Magic oven," Mo whispered back.

Charity gasped out a laugh. Mo was going to get himself slapped.

Brenda June snapped her backbone straight and eyed Mo and Charity with suspicion. "Why don't you two go home and get some sleep?"

"Maybe we will." The prospect of sliding between cool sheets made Charity light-headed. When Grady's face flashed across her brain she wanted to kick her own ass. "Justine will fill in her lawyer tomorrow, and then we'll all know why she did it."

"If she did it." Dix drank the rest of his coffee and frowned down into the mug, as if waiting for more brew to magically appear.

"Oh, come on, Dix." Mo slapped his palms against the tabletop and pushed himself upright. "You said yourself she's not an idiot. She could have stayed at the scene to throw us off."

"Don't forget that first call to her brother." Charity ignored a kick of guilt as she folded and refolded a dishcloth. "Which she made before she called nine-one-one. Not the action of someone with nothing to hide."

"Or maybe she had never found a dead body before, and panicked." Dix scratched his jaw. "That leather necklace we found is not something Justine Langford would wear."

"Maybe it was already there before the murder," Mo suggested.

Dix jerked his chin in denial. "No weathering, and the clasp was broken."

"That doesn't mean it belonged to Sarah's killer," Charity said.

"Tell me this, Charity." Dix cocked his head. "Can you be completely unbiased here?"

Her breath left her lungs with a searing whoosh, as if she'd fallen out of a tree and landed flat on her back. She pushed away from the sink, glowering at Dix. "I can't believe you just asked me that."

Mo ran a hand through his hair, swung around and peered at his reflection in the door of the microwave. "Come on, vanilla. How many times have you brought Justine in for driving under the influence, then had to deal with Hampton West making sure his precious little pie-eyed princess got off scot-free? And we heard about that thing you had with Grady West."

"That thing?" Charity jerked away from the table, the stainless steel forks she'd collected rattling in her fist. She glared at Brenda June.

The dispatcher hunched her shoulders and busied herself wrapping up the remains of the cheesecake.

"He was my boyfriend in high school," Charity said. "We were kids. And yes, I can be impartial."

Mo smirked. "I don't know, vanilla. You sound pretty heated for 'impartial.'"

"You know damned well it's because you're winding me up. And if you call me 'vanilla' one more time, I'll get Big Mike to hold you down while I shave your head."

Mo paled. "Why are we even arguing? The woman confessed."

Brenda June harrumphed. "You don't think her lawyer's going to try to talk her out of that confession? Claim it was coerced?"

"He'll have a hard time making that stick," Mo said. "We'd barely started questioning her."

Dix grunted as he got to his feet. "Which could mean she is protecting someone."

Charity gave him the side-eye. "Or wants us to think she is."

*   *   *

CHARITY WAS HALFWAY THROUGH the parking lot, trying to remember if she had enough milk at home for a bowl of cereal, when she noticed the shadow hovering near her car. Her heart bounced and her right hand slid to her holster. Twenty-hour workday and serious calorie deprivation aside, she should have expected this.

Then she realized the shadow was too tall to belong to baby brother Lucas. Too tall and too —

Grady.

Her stomach slid down to her toes. She stopped, shoved her hands deep into the pockets of her duty jacket, and tipped her head.

"You do realize it's not the smartest thing in the world to stalk a police officer. In the middle of the night. In the parking lot right outside the station."

He moved forward, stepping into the underachieving beam of a floodlight. He'd changed out of the suit. In jeans, turtleneck, and worn leather jacket, he looked more like the Grady who had teased her dreams for years. Only, in her dreams his posture hadn't been rifle-barrel rigid.

And they'd been standing a lot closer.

Charity braced herself against an inconvenient shudder. "Why are you here?"

"You think she did it."

"So does Justine. Which might explain the confession."

"I don't believe this," he growled. "You actually think she could have—"

"Why would I think anything else? What with the DUIs and the shoplifting and the public scenes she was famous for?"

He moved closer, the light making his dark hair gleam. "None of that makes her a killer. There's a difference between stealing a lipstick and committing murder."

"It's called progression. You gotta start somewhere."

He leaned back against her car. "So you're done? You're taking the word of a woman who was wasted when she claimed she killed her best friend?"

Charity bent her head and scrabbled in her pockets for her keys. "I'm not doing this. I'm not discussing this with you. I'm not explaining myself to you. You have to go. Now."

"Dammit, Charity, you're not—"

"Who is it you're really angry with?" She threw her head back and stared up at him. "Me? Justine? Or yourself?"

"You going to let me finish a fucking sentence so I can tell you?" The leather of Grady's jacket whispered and creaked as he lifted his hands to his hips. He looked away, exhaled, and shifted his gaze back to meet hers. "I need to know she's all right."

A sudden sadness, hot and bitter, bristled behind Charity's eyes. Did Justine know how lucky she was to have someone like Grady on her side?

"She's my sister," he said simply, but the dare in his eyes proved he knew the words weren't simple at all.

"You can see for yourself tomorrow. Visiting hours are eight to four."

"That's it?"

"That's an eight-hour window."

His eyes narrowed and he pushed away from the car. "I mean, is that all you're going to tell me?"

She picked through her keys, one by one, gratified when she found only four she didn't recognize. "Bring her a change of clothes."

He gave a frustrated groan and Charity stifled a whimper. Good Lord, would every sound he made conjure up memories of sex?

"I need more." He moved quickly, snagging her arm. "Did she give you a reason? A motive?"

"This is an active investigation. I can't answer your questions." *Not that I have any answers to give.* Beneath the padded nylon of her jacket, Charity's skin burned. Her fingers fisted around her keys. "Now let go, before you really piss me off."

He didn't let go. Instead his grip tightened and he pulled her closer. *Oh, no, you don't.* She braced a hand against his chest. He relaxed his hold and inhaled, the zippered edges of his jacket scraping against her wrist. The stroke of chilled metal sent heat sparking up her arm and tingling across the tips of her breasts. She shuddered, and stared through the gloom at the back of her hand. The furious throbbing behind his shirt had her mesmerized.

"I have to go," she said.

She didn't move.

Spring nights in Montana were chilly. Which explained the vapor that spilled from her mouth when she spoke. It also explained the rigid state of her nipples. She wouldn't, *couldn't* let the reason be anything else.

"This isn't helping your sister," she gritted.

He released her and backed up a step, jaw rigid. Then he surprised her with a wry half smile. "Guess I should count myself lucky you didn't break out your nightstick."

"It's called a blackjack," she said. "Though in situations like these, my weapon of choice is a Taser." She refrained from telling him this wasn't the first time he'd tempted her to use it.

"I'll keep that in mind."

"You do that." She inhaled, wishing the butterflies fluttering against the wall of her chest would drop dead. "I won't pretend to know what you're going through. Yes, I have a sibling in jail, and yes, he's facing time, but there's no doubt my brother is guilty. Plus he's no stranger to prison."

"And he's not charged with murder."

"There is that. What I'm trying to say is, I understand your frustration. You have my word that if your sister doesn't belong in jail, she won't be there long."

He studied her, shoulders rising and falling as he grabbed and released a mammoth breath. He nodded, and looked down while he palmed his neck. When he looked back up, some of the bleakness had faded from his eyes. "I'm in town for Justine," he said quietly. "But I hope you and I get a chance to talk while I'm here."

We are talking hovered on her lips, but she knew what he meant. He wanted to clear the air. Shame poked at the thought of the phone calls she'd never returned.

She took a sideways step toward her car. "Even if I had the time, that wouldn't be advisable."

One eyebrow lifted. She knew that look. He was all but calling her chicken.

Hurried footsteps scraped across the pavement. "There you are, you ungrateful bitch!"

Charity spun to her right. *Here we go.* She slapped her hands to her belt and widened her stance.

Although she'd expected this visit hours ago, she'd never figured she'd welcome it.

3

YOU RELEASE HIM THIS instant!" The woman marching toward them wore a faded plaid bathrobe over a thin cotton dress and ragged jeans. One end of the robe's belt bobbed along the pavement behind her. A fluorescent-green scrunchie held her thin, gray hair in a ponytail on top of her head, like something out of an eighties exercise video. Her face was flushed crimson with anger, and she kept reaching for the burly, baby-faced man at her side, as if assuring herself she wasn't facing the big, bad deputy all on her own.

"Mom," Charity said evenly. "Lucas."

Her brother scowled and opened his mouth, ready to do battle.

Charity shook her head. "Hank stays in jail." She breathed in through her mouth. A wonder that after all these years, she hadn't gotten used to the smell of stale sweat and cigarettes. "He's charged with felony gun theft."

While she and Dix had questioned Justine, Mo had handled the search of Hank's truck and found a loaded nine millimeter Glock. The problem wasn't that the idiot had been driving a loaded weapon around without a permit—Montana law required a concealed weapons permit for personal carry only. Nope, problem was, the pistol had been reported stolen.

Her mother fisted her hands in the lapels of her bathrobe. "Well, you'd just better uncharge him, priss, or I'll make sure this entire pisspot of a town knows what you're up to with the sheriff."

Charity threw out an arm but Grady pushed right past it. At least he wasn't dumb enough to try to shield her.

"Mrs. Bishop. Lucas." He didn't offer his hand, but shot Charity's brother a meaningful look. "You might want to take your mother home, man. This isn't the time or the place."

"This isn't any of your fuckin' business, *man*."

"Who the hell are you?" Charity's mother squinted through the early morning dark at Grady.

"He's nothin.'" Lucas was shorter than Grady but twice as wide. He shoved at the sleeves of his sweatshirt and flexed his hands.

Perfect. Just perfect. "Stay out of this," Charity snapped at Grady and turned to her brother. "Take her home. Please. Before I lock her up for being a public nuisance."

"Go ahead! Arrest me! I dare you!" Eve Bishop drew out the word "dare" so long, she staggered sideways. "I'll make sure everyone knows you're the sheriff's whore."

Charity barely refrained from slapping a hand to her forehead. She had to admit that trumped the last rumor her mother had started—that Charity had been boinking the owner of the grocery store so he'd refuse her mother cigarettes whenever she tried to use her government benefits card to buy them.

"That's enough." This time Grady didn't let Charity push him behind her. "Your daughter is no more a whore than you are an astronaut." He jabbed a finger at Lucas. "And you get your mother out of here before you both end up in jail and there's nobody left to come up with bail."

It had been a long time since anyone had risen to Charity's defense. The sharp ache in her throat could attest to that. But she needed a protector like Mo needed an ego boost. And Grady had no idea who she was anymore.

Anyway, there'd be no bail. Hank was headed to city jail in the morning.

She popped out from behind Grady and saw all kinds of mean working its way onto Lucas's face. Her muscles bunched.

Lucas glowered at Grady. "I told you to mind your own goddamned business."

Eve Bishop hummed a gotcha. "I know you. You used to date our priss. Threw her over and went off to college. So, what, you found out she'd been doing the rest of the soccer team?"

Grady grunted a warning and Charity gritted her teeth. If she didn't clear this parking lot — and quickly — she'd have yet another mountain of paperwork to scale.

Charity glared at her mother. "Either go home, or get banned from visiting Hank. Yes, I can do that. And I will, if you're still here by the time I count to one. One."

A confused silence. Her mother scratched her neck while Lucas curled and uncurled his fingers. Charity reached under her jacket for her radio. Mother and son looked at her, then at each other. They mumbled a hurried conference, scowled a dirty double whammy at Charity and Grady then left, trailing curses, and the raggedy belt to Eve Bishop's bathrobe.

A mocking chorus of crickets rolled into the silence. Somewhere nearby metal clanged — a raccoon checking out a trashcan.

"So." Grady zipped up his jacket. "The families haven't changed."

"Yes, they have. They're worse." Charity faced him. "Astronaut, huh?"

"Got my point across, didn't it?"

"I don't know whether to thank you or knock you on your ass." The surprised sound of his laugh triggered a throb of wistfulness. Before said wistfulness could get her into any more trouble, she jabbed a finger at his chest. "I could have handled that on my own. You. Stay away from me." She spun away and headed for her car. He was right behind her.

"I deserve the thanks, but I'll settle for the ass-knocking thing if you'll answer one question. What happened to your nose?"

She yanked open the driver's side door and dropped into the front seat of her Camry. "I stuck it where it didn't belong." She slammed the door.

Grady leaned down and rapped on the window.

Charity lowered it, but only because she had more to say. "You'll only make things worse for your sister if you don't leave me alone."

"That the only reason you want me to stay away?"

"Isn't it enough?"

"Way I remember it, with the two of us it was never enough."

Her belly lifted, then dropped, and a spiny heat tickled the inside of her chest. Then fury struck, and the heat flared into a scorching resentment. "You son of a bitch. You're trying to play me."

He frowned.

Charity gave a rasping laugh. "I'm not the same needy, insecure teenager you nearly screwed out of a future, West." *Liar, liar.* "And your juvenile innuendos? Don't do a thing for me." *Pants on fire.*

She snatched at her seatbelt. "I have a murder to solve and a campaign to run. So stay the hell out of my way."

"Your problem, Bishop, is that you were always in your own way." Grady slapped the car twice and stepped back. "Seems that much hasn't changed, either."

*   *   *

CHARITY WAS TWO MILES from her house when she turned her car around and headed back toward the county seat. As hungry as she was, and as much as she looked forward to wrapping herself in her electric blanket and pretending she might actually manage some sleep, she couldn't resist the compulsion to check out a place she hadn't visited in years.

It wasn't sentimentality. It was the need to lay a ghost to rest.

Three minutes later, she gave a disbelieving squawk and her fingers tightened on the steering wheel. The ghost had beat her to the punch. His rental car sat in the parking lot.

Charity hesitated, letting the SUV's engine idle, even as her heartbeat pulsed faster. After half a dozen shallow breaths, she lifted her foot off the brake and pulled into the nearest space.

She'd wanted closure. Seemed she'd be getting it in person.

The cold mobbed her as she hopped out of the SUV. She tugged the collar of her jacket up around her neck and followed the sidewalk past the one-story brick library to the small, walled-in garden in the back. Moonlight streamed through the leaf-fringed branches of middle-aged oaks, brightening the spaces neglected by the streetlights. A tall, shadowed figure stood by the circular fountain, one foot propped on the rounded rim. The hushed burble of the water nearly masked his grunt of surprise.

"I thought for sure once you saw my car, you'd burn rubber on your way out."

Charity didn't respond. Slowly she walked the ring of paving stones, touching a leaf here, a bud there, ridiculously saddened by how much the greenery had grown. She finished her circuit, stopping an arm's length away from Grady.

She clutched at the hem of her jacket. "I haven't always been in my own way," she said. "We were in each other's way."

"I know." He straightened. "I said that out of frustration."

He'd always been straightforward with her. Scratch that. He'd mostly been straightforward with her. She'd missed that.

She pressed her teeth into the inside of her lower lip and resisted the urge to take a step back. Not from him, but from the memory of the crazy, intense teen love they'd shared. "You didn't want me to join the force, and I didn't want you to leave town."

Something chittered in a tree across the lot and Grady turned his head toward the sound. "Is this the part where we take turns assuring each other it all turned out for the best?"

"You're mad because I won't discuss Justine with you."

"I'm pissed because there's nothing I can do for her."

This time Charity had to resist taking a step forward. "Yes, there is. You can be there for her. Considering you just traveled several hundred miles at a moment's notice, I'd say you're off to a pretty great start." She dropped down onto the edge of the fountain. "Speaking of which, aren't you exhausted?"

With a short, sharp exhale, he scrubbed his fingers through his hair and settled beside her. "You know I'm not looking forward to going home."

"Yeah," she said softly. "I do." She tipped her head back and stared up at the moon through the layers of oak leaves. "So absence hasn't made the heart grow fonder?" When he remained silent, the vagueness of her words registered. "Of your parents, I mean."

His chuckle carried an edge. "Are we going to talk about why we're both here?"

Charity caught her breath. Here in their spot, he meant. In high school, finding time to be alone together had been a challenge. Their schedules had been very different, and after school Grady always had soccer practice or some charity or volunteer event to go to, while Charity was due at her job washing cars at the auction yard. When they did find time to see each other, they had to be sneaky about it, because though Charity's mother didn't pay much attention to what her child was up to, Grady's mother did. They'd taken turns inventing research projects that demanded late nights at the library, and out here in the seclusion of the meditation garden that Grady's mother herself had spearheaded a committee to create, they could relax, and talk, and joke, and make out, and plan.

Oh, how they'd planned.

A hollow ache spread through Charity's insides as she scooted around to face him, shifting backward at the same time. She dipped her fingers in the fountain and gasped at the frigid snap of the water. "Seeing you again today..." Her lungs pulsed. "I thought it was time for some closure."

"And here I was, hoping for a chance to reconnect."

She curled her damp fingers into her palm, hating herself for the flash of hope that warmed her chest. "I'm sorry I didn't take your phone calls."

"I wanted to apologize."

"I wanted to forget."

"Fair enough." He slapped his hands to his knees and pushed upright. "You're right. I'm beat. I'll see you in the morning." He hesitated, then held out his hand.

She didn't need help getting up, but there was no way she could refuse his gesture without appearing rude. Thank God. Because, heaven help her, she'd been dying to touch him again.

Charity put her hand in his and allowed him to pull her to her feet. The warm solidness of his grip stoked her feminine side, long neglected thanks to her job. They faced each other, listening to the other's breaths, surrounded by the faint scents of hyacinths and fresh mulch, remembering a similar spring night long ago that had echoed with shouts and accusations. Grady didn't tug her close, but he didn't release her hand, either.

"Hey." Gently he jiggled her fingers. "Whatever happened to that freshman who used to follow you around? The skinny math whiz who won that trip to Las Vegas, then missed his flight?"

She had to swallow before she could answer. "Tater Boggs." Dear Lord, her palm was sweating like a glass of iced tea on a summer day. Still she couldn't bring herself to separate from his touch. "I haven't thought about him in forever. Last I heard he was out in California, making big bucks writing apps."

Grady huffed a laugh that actually sounded genuine. "Every day he bought fries to go with his lunch. Didn't matter if he'd packed peanut butter and jelly or leftover lasagna. He could fit a dozen fries in his mouth before he started to choke. We're talking steak fries here, not the fast food, matchstick kind." Grady shook his head. "Sounds like he could probably buy his own French fry factory now. Good for him."

The earnest sincerity in his voice reminded her of why she'd fallen for him in the first place.

Oh, hell, no. She could not afford to be thinking like this.

She retrieved her hand. "Get some sleep. You've had a long day."

After a moment he nodded, and motioned for her to precede him. He followed her to the SUV, and waited while she climbed in. When she reached to close the door, he held it open.

"You were looking for closure. Did you get it?"

No was the truthful answer, but if she gave it to him, he might consider it a challenge. She refused to consider why saying *yes* was not an option.

"Good luck with your parents," she said, and yanked the door shut.

*   *   *

GRADY TURNED OFF THE engine and stared across a brightly lit expanse of marble statuary surrounded by topiaries so tortured and twisted they looked like a psychotic's version of balloon animals. On the far side of this bizarre, evergreen zoo sprawled his parents' four-level brick home. The house looked down on the Teton River — much like its occupants looked down on the other residents of Becker County — and was lit up like a nineteenth century lighthouse guiding river travelers through the fog.

He gave a soundless snort. No doubt a hundred years ago his family would have guided those river travelers right into the rocks. But only after making sure they had enough local labor to tote the spoils up the riverbank.

The front door swung open, and his mother leaned against the doorframe. Waiting. The light behind her emphasized the sharp edges of her fragile form. Grady sighed. A stranger might consider her pose a sign of fond impatience. Grady knew better. She needed help staying upright.

For one fierce, brief, insane moment, Grady wished he could camp out at Charity's instead.

The engine scolded him with a muffled *tik tik tik,* and he scrubbed a hand over his face. Damn, he was bitter. How bitter hadn't registered until he'd been sucked back into the family dynamic. *You're not the one in control here,* Charity had said at the station. And she had it right. He hadn't felt in control since the moment Valerie had told him she was pregnant.

Even less in control since the first time his son had announced he hated him.

Grady exhaled. He had to shake this resentment. It wouldn't do anyone any good, least of all his sister.

Sitting out here freezing his ass off wouldn't help, either.

His mother pushed away from the doorjamb as he approached. She adjusted her heavy, satin-trimmed dressing gown, a far cry from the thin, ratty bathrobe Mrs. Bishop had worn. But her disapproving expression was a perfect match. "Figured you'd gone to a motel."

"I will if you'd prefer it."

She considered, then lifted a thin shoulder and stepped aside. "Peyton waited up."

A slim teen with red-rimmed eyes, pale skin, and dark hair as straight as her mother's was curly turned the corner into the hallway, and Grady blinked. He'd seen her three months earlier when Justine had brought the kids out to the Pacific coast for a long weekend. Still it seemed his fifteen-year-old niece had grown two inches.

"Uncle Grady." She wrapped her arms around his waist and squeezed.

Grady watched his mother shut the door behind them and, in an elegant zigzag, drift away toward the living room. He set his bag on the floor and pressed a kiss to the top of Peyton's head. "How you doing, cupcake?"

"She didn't do it. You don't believe she did it, do you?" Peyton looked up at him, chin pressing into his chest.

He shook his head.

Peyton's eyes went liquid. "Then why'd she confess?"

"I'll ask her when I see her."

"When are you going to see her?"

Grady lifted an arm away, retrieved his phone, and glanced at the screen. "In less than five hours."

"I'm going with you."

"Let's get to bed, then." He gave her a final squeeze and retrieved his bag. He called after her as she headed up the stairs. "Drew up, too?"

"Yeah, he's around here somewhere. See you in the morning."

"It is morning," he said, but she was already gone. He followed his mother down the hall and paused in the living room doorway. "Which bedroom shall I take?"

Roberta turned from the liquor-laden credenza. "The first one you come across with an empty bed."

Damn. Even wearing her your-sister-is-a-killer attitude, Charity had been more welcoming.

She'd felt something, back there in the library garden. Some of their old magic. Her fingers had trembled. Had she felt his tremble, too?

For God's sake, let it go. They were far from the kids they used to be.

He chose a small guestroom in the "east wing." Before he'd left home, his bedroom had been on the other side of the house. After

Justine's divorce, she'd moved herself and her kids into that section, the "west wing," and Drew had claimed Grady's old room. Just as well. Too many less-than-friendly memories over there.

He shrugged out of his jacket, dropped it on the designer-clad bed and unzipped his bag. The door opened behind him and he turned, expecting to see Peyton. But it was Drew who stepped into the room. Grady went still, arrested by the pained confusion shadowing the eighteen-year-old's face.

"Uncle Grady," Drew choked.

Some vague masculine instinct stopped Grady from pulling his nephew into a hug. Instead he offered his hand.

Though Drew's grip was firm, his fingers shook, and when he spoke his voice followed suit. "I have to get Mom out."

"We'll work on that first thing. We're meeting with the family lawyer—"

"You don't understand. She doesn't need a lawyer. She needs me to tell the truth."

"What truth?"

Drew swallowed, and squared his shoulders. "I'm the reason she's in jail."

*   *   *

DREW FELT BETTER JUST saying the words but his uncle looked like he wanted to hurl.

Uncle Grady rubbed his hand across his mouth, backed up, and sat down hard on the bed. "What does that mean, exactly? That you're the reason she's in jail?"

Drew itched to fold his arms across his chest. But that would make him look defensive, so he buried his hands deep inside the pockets of his jeans instead.

"I was there first. I'm the one who...found her."

"You found Sarah Huffman. Dead. In the vet's parking lot."

Drew nodded, fighting hard against the lava-like surge of emotion that threatened to spill out of his eyes. Judas Priest, he'd never forget his confusion when he'd pulled in and seen that minivan instead of Sarah's Audi, or the instant he'd seen her lying on the ground and he'd known, he'd *known,* even before staring at the spooky flat shine of her eyes...

"Then you called your mother."

Drew choked out a half laugh, half sob. "I'm not proud of that."

"Hey. Anyone criticizes your reaction, you ask when's the last time they found a dead body."

"She's not just a dead body."

"Christ. I know. I'm sorry. What the hell happened? Why were you out there in the first place?"

"I got a text. Around eight. From Sarah. I was at Ethan's, shooting pool with the guys. The message said...wait, I'll show you." Drew slid his cell from his pocket and pulled up the text. His uncle took the cell and frowned down at the screen.

Need help. Pls come. Just u. 11pm vet clinic.

Drew gestured. "I couldn't ignore something like that, could I? And yeah, even though it's like some pathetic frickin' slasher movie cliché, to meet someone in an empty parking lot in the middle of the night—" He shrugged, as slowly as he could, using the time to swallow the burning mass of regret that clogged his throat. "What was I supposed to do?" he whispered.

He waited for his uncle to growl something like "Take someone with you, dumbass," but instead he handed back the cell. Which made Drew feel a hell of a lot less like a loser, since he could tell his uncle would rather have kept it.

Uncle Grady stood. He walked to the window and back, his motions slow and jagged, like his grandfather after a nap in his recliner. "Why would Sarah contact you instead of your mother?" He said it like he didn't expect an answer and Drew hated himself for feeling relieved.

His uncle turned. "What'd you do then?"

"Nothing, until 10:30. Then I told the guys I had to leave. Said I had a date."

"Wait a minute. You were hanging out at 10:30? On a school night?"

"News flash. I'm not twelve anymore."

His uncle dipped his chin and held up a hand, conceding the point. "Go on."

Drew's palms started to sweat and he was suddenly craving something cold and wet, something made with tooth-eating acid and enough sugar to fuel a busload of first-graders for a week. Hell, maybe all he really needed was a healthy belch or two to drive the panic from his gut.

"Mind if we talk in my room? I need a drink." He caught a glimpse of his uncle's face before he turned and opened the door. Talk about panic. Drew wanted to smile but his lips wouldn't cooperate.

"What kind of drink?"

But Drew was already well on his way to the opposite side of the house. Two minutes later he opened his bedroom door and ushered his uncle inside, grabbed two sodas from the mini fridge and tossed one to his guest. Uncle Grady's expression was as sheepish as it was relieved.

"Thanks." He looked around Drew's own personal "man cave," at the hand-striped wood floor and the leather furniture culled from the family room, at the sports wall holding the standard swimsuit posters and trophies as well as skateboards and an electronic dartboard and even the grille from a 1954 Corvette — the missing teeth replaced by Drew himself. His uncle tipped his can and pronounced his verdict. "Sweet."

Verdict. Judas Priest. Drew popped open his can of soda and took a swig. The rush of wet eased his thirst but it didn't do anything for the misery simmering beneath his skin. His uncle raised an eyebrow and Drew sighed, slumped down onto the side of his bed.

"When I was about seven or eight years old I got up really early one Saturday morning and wandered outside. I was headed down to the water when I noticed something waddling along the riverbank. I kept staring and staring but the sun wasn't all the way up and for the life of me I couldn't figure out what the thing was. Finally I realized it was a possum, but there was something wrong with it, 'cause it kind of…rippled. Then it clicked. I was watching a bunch of baby possums, clinging to their mother's back. She was moving them, or carrying them somewhere, or something."

Another swig, and he couldn't help wishing it was something a hell of a lot stronger than soda. Something that could numb his memory of the night before. He leaned forward, and let the soda can dangle between his legs.

"That's the way it was when I found Sarah. I pulled into the parking lot and saw this pile of clothes and I thought *what the hell?* I got out of the car and walked over and stared and stared and finally it clicked. It was a woman. It was Sarah. And she was dead."

He didn't remember releasing his grip on the soda can but all at once he had both palms pressed against his eyes. He couldn't hold back the tears anymore, couldn't stem the emotion that punched and kicked and banged against the walls of his chest since the moment he'd discovered Sarah's body.

"I-I panicked," he choked. He felt the bed dip beside him, felt the sturdy warmth of his uncle's arm around his shoulders. "I knew I needed to call 9–1–1 but I was afraid she'd killed herself and it was my fault and I couldn't stand it. Then I saw sh-she'd been strangled and...I called Mom."

"Why would you think it was your fault?"

He hesitated. Of course it had to come out. *Man up, dude.* He wiped his eyes on his shirt sleeve and stood. "Thing is, she wanted to call it quits."

His uncle rose more slowly. "She wanted to...kill herself?"

"No, I mean she wanted to bust up." He dropped his gaze and caved to the urge to cross his arms. His fingers dug into his biceps. "We have...had...a thing."

He figured he should probably feel shame. All he felt was loss.

"I wouldn't have hurt her. Not for anything. I didn't love her, but I cared about her. A lot. She was smart and sexy and honest and...when I was with her I didn't feel any pressure, you know? All we wanted was just to enjoy each other." He could feel his cheeks heating and wished he'd kept his soda so he could press the can to his forehead. "I thought maybe she was going to tell me she was pregnant," he whispered.

"That's why you didn't call the police." Uncle Grady put a hand on his shoulder. "You know what this means, don't you?"

"Yeah. Means I have a motive."

The hand on his shoulder tightened. "Good thing you saved that text. I'll go wake your grandfather. We need to make some calls."

"Wait." Drew ran a hand through his hair. "There's one more thing and it's...not good. Sarah...she called it quits because she wanted to see someone else."

"Someone in particular?"

"Yeah." Drew swallowed. "My father."

His uncle stared, then blasted out a hard, disbelieving laugh. "Son of a bitch."

"Uncle Grady? No one except me knows she was already dead when I got there."

"That's where you're wrong, kid." His uncle gripped the doorknob, so tightly the metal squeaked beneath his fingers. "The killer knows."

*   *   *

CHARITY DIDN'T HAVE THE ugliest car in Becker County, though she figured her fifteen-year-old sedan placed somewhere in the top twenty. Still it was hers, and it was paid for, and she couldn't bring herself to care much about the faded paint or the punch in the bumper or even the missing wheel covers. Besides, she usually drove the department SUV.

Maybe she didn't spend a lot of time behind the wheel of her Camry, but she depended on her. Valued her. Loved her.

Which was why, when she staggered out of her house the morning after Sarah's murder, having spent three long, frustrating, pensive hours flirting with sleep, now intent on divorcing her brain from its Grady-induced fog by going for a run, she took one look at her driveway and yelped.

Or more accurately, she took one look at what was *in* her driveway, and yelped.

She stumbled down the porch steps and ran to her car, her cross-trainers slipping and sliding over the frosted grass. "Clarabelle," she breathed.

The Camry waited in the sun-brushed morning, as silent and faithful and patient as ever. With a brand new tilt to the right.

Charity clapped her hands to her cheeks and circled the disaster that used to be her car. Someone had been maliciously thorough. He—or she—or they—had slashed three of the four tires, splashed the hood and all four doors with flamingo-colored paint, and bent both windshield wipers so the arms extended from the car at awkward angles. The anonymous asshole had gouged out sections of the grille, plastered bumper stickers over the back window, and judging from the crumpled bag that lay a few feet from the driveway, subjected Clarabelle's gas tank to a sugar high. Never mind the sugar would do nothing more than clog up the filter.

Lucas. If not her brother, then that pair of teenage hellions determined to tag every Dumpster, public bench, and fire hydrant in town. Except this was personal. Spiteful. If the teens were responsible, their methods had escalated.

Lucas was a better bet.

Anger swelled in Charity's throat, and she turned in an agitated circle. What she needed was to kick someone's ass. What she'd have to settle for was giving Mo a call. Then she'd have to take her own pictures, since Mo probably hadn't reclaimed his camera.

Suck it up, Deputy. She wrapped her arms around her waist, drew in a breath, and peered closer at the stickers on the back window.

MY KID MADE HONOR ROLL AT SAN QUENTIN.

SQUIRRELS ARE NATURE'S SPEED BUMPS.

And the eternally classy, *MY OTHER RIDE IS YOUR MOTHER.*

Okay. Maybe not Lucas, after all.

The morning chill seeped through Charity's sweats and she shivered. She patted Clarabelle's trunk and headed inside to call Mo, hating that part of her welcomed the excuse for skipping her run. Hating even more that she'd entertained the idea, even for a millisecond, of tracking down Grady instead.

Half an hour later, she was back out in the yard, her confidence bolstered by her uniform, and her determination to secure justice for Clarabelle fueled with fury, two handfuls of chocolate-covered almonds, and a freshly-brewed mug of the coffee she'd banned herself from drinking. She was considering going back inside and putting some of that coffee in a cup to carry with her to work when a car swung into the driveway and jerked to a stop behind the Camry. When Charity recognized the driver, she barely managed to hide her grimace.

Kate Young. Next to Justine Langford, she'd been Sarah Huffman's closest friend. Even from outside Kate's car, Charity could hear the whimpering. Double crap. Could this morning get any better?

The strawberry blonde pushed out of her Volvo and launched herself at Charity. Charity hugged her back, fighting a natural rush of sympathy tears as Kate's slim body trembled against hers.

"I was hoping you'd be here," Kate gasped. "I stopped at Smart Mart for gas, and they told me. Sarah...I can't believe it. I can't believe she's gone."

"I know. I'm sorry."

Kate leaned out of the hug and gestured with a balled-up tissue. "I was supposed to sub today, but I called and said I couldn't make it." She jammed the tissue against her nose and shook her head. "As if the kids care about cross-pollination anyway. Oh, God. Who would do such a thing? Who would want to hurt Sarah?"

"We don't know. But we'll find out."

"It couldn't have been Justine. I know you have her in custody, but Justine would never hurt a fly, let alone — " She reached out and gripped Charity's arm. "Who did it? Do you know who did it? Do you have any leads?" When Charity hesitated, Kate's hand flexed and dropped away.

Charity barely resisted rubbing her arm where the teacher's nails had dug in.

"I'm sorry," Kate choked. "Of course you can't say anything. And here I am keeping you when you're obviously on your way to work. Find them, Charity. Find whoever did this terrible thing." She produced a fresh tissue, blew her nose, and finally noticed Charity's tortured car. Her red-rimmed eyes went wide. "What happened here?"

"The vandals paid a visit to my side of the county."

"Your poor car." Kate stared down at the bag that had once held five pounds of sugar. At least the distraction had stemmed her tears. "Do you need a ride?"

"Thanks, but I'm all set." Charity realized Kate was still shaking. "How about you? Feel up to driving?"

"I can make it home. Once I get there, I'm going to chug a monster glass of wine and go to bed. I didn't get a lot of sleep last night."

Charity's curiosity must have shown on her face, since Kate offered up a self-conscious shrug. "I was at a sleepover. For two, if you know what I mean." A pause. "Allison is sixteen, you know. Old enough to be home alone." The uncertain defiance in Kate's face made it clear she was second-guessing that decision.

Charity lifted her hands, palms out. "No judgment here."

Kate wasn't paying attention. "To think I was...you know...while Sarah was...*God.*"

Charity was rubbing the distraught woman's back when Mo pulled up. "I have to go," she said, probably too quickly.

Mo gave Kate a solemn nod as she backed out of the driveway. He turned and gave Clarabelle the once-over, shook his head, and reached for his notebook.

Ten minutes later, Charity dropped into Mo's passenger seat and buckled herself in. Mo slid in beside her and started up the shiny black BMW. She used to give him hell for living in Montana and not owning a truck, until he had the nerve to start giving her hell back.

"I talked to Sarah's family," he said. "They should be here this afternoon."

"Let's hope the ME's done by the time they arrive."

"I'll make sure of it." Mo rubbed his chin, the rasp of fingers over razor stubble echoing inside the car. "Brenda June called. Dix is looking for us."

"Does that man never sleep?" Charity turned her head without lifting it from the back of the seat. "Or did his wife lock him out of the house again?"

"You know Dix. Keeps things close to his chest."

49

Unlike Charity's entire family, who preferred to scream their personal business at an unsuspecting public. She turned her head and looked forward again, and winced at the sight of Clarabelle through Mo's spotless windshield.

"Hey." Mo shifted in his seat. "What Dix said, about you being objective?"

Charity shrugged. "He was right to bring it up. I have a history with the family."

"I have a history with the deceased." He watched her closely as he fastened his seatbelt. "He never questioned me."

"Dix might not know you dated Sarah. Anyway, it's not the same. Grady and I were together all through high school."

"If I were to ask you what happened —"

"I'd threaten you with Big Mike again." Her gaze roved the pristine, leather-clad interior. "How do you even afford this car?"

"I save my money instead of blowing it all on chocolate." He reached over and squeezed her hand. "Don't worry, we'll get your car fixed up so she's good as new."

"Clarabelle was never new. She was better than new."

Mo made some kind of grunting noise that was probably supposed to be comforting but came out sounding smug. He patted his polished rosewood dash and eased the BMW into gear.

* * *

DIX WAS PACING IN front of Brenda June's window when Charity and Mo walked in. The lead detective was a tall, lithe man with skin the color of peanut brittle and gleaming black hair he kept a little too long to be regulation. Charity fought a wince when he turned toward them. The stains of sleeplessness under his eyes were worse than ever.

She thought she had crap to deal with. At least she didn't live with someone who nagged her daily to quit the force, move to the city, and sell condos.

Dix drained his coffee mug. "About time you two got here. We had someone come in first thing. A witness."

Mo perked up. "What kind of witness?"

"The kind who can place Drew Langford at the vet's before eleven last night."

Charity's insides clutched, as if tensing for a punch. *Oh, no.* She swallowed. "That's almost an hour before Justine called nine-one-one."

So she had been protecting someone.

Her son.

Don't jump to conclusions.

There had to be another explanation. Drew Langford was just a kid. What possible reason could he have for hurting Sarah Huffman? Then she remembered the leather necklace they'd found beneath Sarah's body. The kind of necklace a man would wear.

She resisted the urge to sag against the wall. "We need that coroner's report," she ground out.

Mo's baby blues had gone lethal. "Want me to bring him in?"

Before she could answer, they were interrupted by an approaching cluster of footsteps. They turned to see a pale-faced Drew Langford and his father Scott walking toward them, followed by Grady and Owen Quinn, the family lawyer. The four men looked like pall bearers on their way to a funeral.

An ache crept into Charity's throat.

Quinn offered the deputies a neutral smile. "That won't be necessary."

*   *   *

CHEST TIGHT, JAW LOCKED, Grady watched Charity thank Drew for coming in. For giving himself up, is what she meant. The attorney had made it clear that at the very least, Drew faced charges of failure to report a death, and interference in the investigation of a murder.

The lingering taste of a hastily gulped glass of orange juice went sour in Grady's mouth. This was all so damned unreal. What the hell was happening with his family? His nephew was just a kid. When they'd visited after Christmas, Drew had practically danced a jig when he'd unwrapped the dive watch Grady had bought him.

Except he wasn't a kid. Not anymore. His eighteenth birthday had come and gone. Legally, Drew was an adult.

Grady swallowed against a sudden rise of bile.

Montana was fighting to abolish the death penalty, but Drew could still get life without parole.

4

THE NOW-FAMILIAR BUZZING sounded again. Both male deputies escorted Drew, Scott, and Owen Quinn into the back.

Grady started forward, but Charity stopped him with an outstretched arm.

"We'll need to get the okay from Drew before any friends or family members can sit in on the interview."

Interview? You mean interrogation. Grady gritted his teeth, grinding the words into nothingness. It wouldn't do any good to take his frustration out on her. She was only doing her job. Still it annoyed the hell out of him that she could be so matter-of-fact with two members of his family in custody.

"You're welcome to wait," she continued. "It might be a while. I have a feeling Drew's father will be right out to keep you company."

"What about Justine?"

"We'll let you know something when we can."

"Not good enough." He stabbed a finger at the door. "Inside one of those rundown straitjacket rooms back there, my nephew is about to describe how he discovered the body of Sarah Huffman. His version of events proves Justine wasn't on the scene until later. When Drew called her from the parking lot, he interrupted some sob story she was giving the bartender at Sweeney's. Doesn't that add up to letting her go?"

"So Drew found Sarah's body, panicked, and called Justine. How do you know she was at Sweeney's?"

"My father has been on the phone all night, scaring up alibis."

"Perfect," Charity muttered. She turned and rapped on the glass, signaling she wanted in. "I get it. You're worried, and I can't imagine what Peyton's going through. But we have your sister's confession."

"Which she provided under duress in an attempt to protect her son."

"Did she have a reason to?"

"Hell, no. Talk to Drew. You'll see."

The fact that they were having this conversation made Grady feel…outside of himself. Like he'd stepped into a movie. Without a script. And his role called for an actor who could speak Swahili. With an Australian accent.

Charity peered up at him, head tilted, seeming to try to read him. Once upon a time they'd never had to second guess each other — they'd been unfailingly honest for the sole, searing reason that no one else in their lives had ever considered not lying.

Coolly Grady returned her stare, doing his best to ignore the familiar shape of her lips, the tips of her hair curving against her neck, the damned fine fit of her butt-ugly uniform. Still, the image would serve him well when he finally managed to swing that hand job he'd been aching for since the moment he'd seen her again.

Shit. What had happened to family first? His lips twisted as he wrenched his brain out of primal mode.

The way she held herself made it clear she didn't trust him. Well, guess what? He wasn't sure he trusted her, either. Though he did have to give her credit for being civil.

No, not civil. Professional.

Was it weird, that it made him proud?

The door opened behind her. Charity didn't turn, didn't seem to realize they had company.

"Justine will be here a while," she said, voice as crisp as the creases in her pants. She gestured at the tote he'd placed in a chair. "Is that for her?"

Grady retrieved the bag. Charity held out her hand.

"I want to see her," he said.

"We'll need to talk to her again, once we've interviewed Drew. I'll try to set up a visit in the meantime." She took the bag, curling her fingers around the handle. "But just because you decided to play knight in shining armor last night does not mean I'll bend any rules for you."

Dammit, had he asked her to bend any rules? Never mind he would have, if she'd given him the chance.

"Last night? What happened last night?" The skinny woman who liked to eavesdrop poked her head over Charity's shoulder. He blinked. Hadn't her hair been blond the day before? Now her buzz cut was a vibrant orange, and she wore purple dangly earrings that bookended a wicked smile. "Do share."

Charity rolled her eyes. "None of your business, Dispatch."

But the older woman darted out into the waiting room, leaving Charity to hold the door. She looked Grady up and down. "Spill it, handsome. Your goods for mine. A bit of intel for a slab of the best cheesecake this side of—"

"Brenda June." Charity's voice sliced into the older woman's words. "This is not the time."

Brenda June pursed her lips and marched back through the door, chin held high.

Charity offered him an expressionless nod. "We'll get back to you." She turned to follow Brenda June.

Before she could let go of the door, a deep, chiding voice rolled down the hallway. "Since when do we conduct our interviews in the waiting room?" A sixtyish bald man with a linebacker's shoulders and a stern expression strode into the room. Thick hands rose to his hips as he transferred his scowl from Charity to Grady and back again. "Don't you have something better to do, Deputy? Like investigate a homicide?"

Charity disappeared.

Sheriff Clarkson Pratt thrust out a hand. "Grady West. Been a hell of a long time."

"How are you, Sheriff?"

"About as tired as you look." Pratt snatched off the black-framed glasses that suggested nerd while the rest of him shouted badass. He massaged the bridge of his nose, then slid his glasses back into place. "I'm sorry for your trouble, son."

Grady's automatic "thanks" lodged in his throat. Yeah, he was on edge, but Justine and Drew were both alive. No doubt Sarah Huffman's family would give anything to be in his shoes right now. And no way would he let himself believe Drew would end up anywhere else but right back at home with his mother and his sister, where he belonged.

Tension hijacked the space between his shoulder blades. Dammit, he missed his son. He'd tried to catch Matt before he left for school, but no one had answered the phone. Grady needed to hear his kid's voice.

Sheriff Pratt had always had a lot more savvy than he liked to let on. "How's your boy?"

"Inherited the soccer gene." Grady couldn't help a grin. "Considering the state of his bed every morning, he's even playing in his sleep." He stopped smiling. "The divorce was hard on him."

"Acting out?" Pratt stroked a wiry goatee peppered with gray, understanding in his eyes.

Acting out and pulling in. Almost a year since the split, and the kid was more remote than ever. Grady's fingers twitched as he registered the weight of the phone in his jacket pocket. He could call the school office and ask them to pull Matt from class. He'd loathe being the center of attention, though.

Grady shrugged. "You know what they say. Eleven is the new sixteen."

The big man snorted. "That were true, he'd have himself his own Charity Bishop by now, hanging onto his arm and every word that popped out of his mouth."

"Think you've got that backward." The teenage version of himself had never been able to get enough of his girlfriend. Her strength. Her passion. Her raunchy sense of humor. The yielding softness of her body.

All those luxury vacations his parents had dragged him and Justine on? Skiing in Aspen and summers in France and spring break in Tahoe? Being with Charity had won out over any of those. She had been his favorite retreat. His best and only escape. Until he got greedy. The moment he'd asked for a commitment was the moment things had started going to shit.

Grady exhaled. "God, we were young."

"You're not exactly geriatric now." The sheriff dropped his chin and peered at him over his glasses. "You realize you're a conflict of interest."

Yeah, well. Lots of conflict, little interest. On her part, anyway.

Grady blew out a breath. How many times would he have to remind himself why he was here? "The last thing I want to do is get in the way of her job," he said. "The sooner you find out who did this, the better. If you can use my help, you've got it."

Pratt eyed the empty chairs around them. "Seems you already did help. How'd you manage to keep your folks away?"

"Told them Phil Smiley would be here, camera in hand. They prefer to pitch their fits when the paparazzi aren't looking."

Grady finally recognized that the muffled static he was hearing was coming from the other side of the glass. Someone was on the radio. Pratt jabbed a thumb over his shoulder. "I need to get back there and do my job. But when all this is over, I wouldn't mind the chance to catch up over some barbecue. You been to Jerzy's since he added on?"

Grady fought the urge to ask *are you fucking kidding me?* With everything that was going on, the old man wanted to set a date to score some ribs and shoot the shit? There, of all places?

"I've stopped in once or twice over the years," Grady finally said. For both his sake and Matt's, he didn't often make the trip back to Becker County.

"Jerzy said he almost gave up the place after the fire. Glad someone talked him out of it."

Grady didn't let himself react. Seemed the sheriff was still doing most of his fishing on dry land. "Hard to imagine Becker County without Jerzy's Shake Shack."

"Man does make the best damned chocolate malt this side of the Mississippi." The sheriff offered his hand again. "Just trying to put you at ease, son. We'll do everything we can to get this business taken care of, as soon as possible."

"I appreciate that." So Pratt could read his mind, after all. Good thing Charity didn't have the same talent.

The buzzer sounded as Pratt reached for the door. Obviously the dispatcher had been keeping an eye out for him. The lawman looked back over a brawny shoulder. "One last thing."

"Sheriff?"

"About Charity. You need to steer clear. 'Less you want her to lose the one thing that keeps her going." At Grady's raised eyebrow, the sheriff tapped his badge. "The job."

*   *   *

CHARITY FINALLY MANAGED TO distract Brenda June from that knight-in-shining-armor comment by suggesting she make a run to the store for the sheriff's favorite amaretto-flavored creamer. Next Charity searched Justine's overnight bag, then asked Mo to man the radio while she delivered it.

The Becker County Sheriff's Department had fewer employees than the nearest fast food restaurant and still needed more office space. Sheriff Pratt and his crew occupied one half of what used to be a bowling alley, which explained the persistent smell of cigarettes and sweaty feet. Crammed into the other half were offices for the County Commissioner, the Treasurer, the Commissioner of Revenue and a local judge who presided over municipal cases when he wasn't at his bait and tackle shop waxing poetic about streamer flies and surgeon knots.

Each half of the building needed more room. Neither had room to give, which meant Charity had had no choice but to park Justine Langford in their only vacant holding cell smack dab in the center between Hank's and the cell that housed his drinking buddy. Charity would have given anything to put Justine somewhere else, but short of getting her a room at the motel, there *was* nowhere else. And considering their operating budget barely covered the cost of toilet paper, she'd have been skinned alive for spending that kind of money. Thankfully the night shift — usually their fourth deputy, Flunker Beazley, who watched *The Golden Girls* reruns while cleaning and recleaning the contents of the department's weapons locker—had reported no unusual activity on the part of their guests, other than the normal shouts of innocence and threats to sue.

Charity made her way to lockup, grateful she didn't have to pass Hank's cell to get to Justine's. Didn't solve the problem of the smell, though. One of them, maybe even all three of them, had been sick during the night. Charity breathed through her mouth and prayed the puke fest was over.

After rapping a heads-up on the steel door that opened into the six-by-eight room assigned to Justine, Charity unlocked the door and stepped inside. Slowly Justine rose from her sitting position on the bed, which was a halfway-decent twin mattress topping a one-piece metal platform. Justine's glare made it clear the accommodations had been less than comfortable.

"Are you kidding me?" The brunette had always carried an attitude five times bigger than she was. She jabbed a finger at the wall shared by Hank's cell. "Putting me next door to that lowlife? When he wasn't throwing up, he was snoring, and when he wasn't snoring, he was shouting horrible things." She swiped the back of her hand under her nose. Her gaze glinted with the sharp, polished purpose of a knife. "Your name came up a lot."

Charity couldn't help a laugh.

A muffled thumping echoed through the wall. "That you, little sister? Get me the fuck out of here."

Charity ignored him. "If we had somewhere else to put you, that's where you'd be. I'm sorry you got stuck with him, but I'm not the reason you're here."

Bit by bit, the bitter seeped out of Justine's face. Fear crept in behind it. Her hands shook as she gathered her wild hair at the nape of her neck. She held it there, watching warily as Charity set the overnight bag on the narrow bed.

"Where's the orange jumpsuit?"

"You haven't been formally charged with anything, Mrs. Langford."

"Oh, please. We both know you have no respect for me so go ahead and call me Justine."

The pounding got louder. Hank had started kicking the wall. "You hear me, bitch? Let. Me. Out. Keep ignoring me, and I promise, I will fuck you up."

Justine's lips twitched. "Brothers."

Charity couldn't help smiling back.

"But you will, right?" Justine whispered. "Charge me. I did confess."

"We have seventy-two hours to figure it out." Charity backed toward the door. "Your lawyer is here. I'll come back and get you in a few."

Justine shook her head. "I already told you I changed my mind. I don't want to see him." She stared down at the zippered bag. "Is anyone else here?"

Charity wanted to tell her Drew was in the station so she could gauge Justine's reaction, but she knew better than to do it outside of the interview room. "Your brother is waiting to see you."

Relief flickered across the brunette's features. Still her hands shook as she unzipped the bag and studied the contents, though her posture remained rigid, elbows tight against her ribs.

Crap. Maybe she really was protecting her son. Even as regret pinched at Charity's heart, she had to wonder if Drew Langford realized how lucky he was to have a mother willing to sacrifice her freedom for his sake.

Quite a contrast to Charity's own mother. Once when Charity was in the second or third grade, Eve Bishop had forgotten a pan of bacon on the stove and the kitchen had caught fire. Her mother had fled the house with a pack of cigarettes and a stack of lottery tickets, leaving Charity to find her own way out. Eve had blamed the fire on her daughter, and a red-faced fireman had given Charity a stern lecture on kitchen safety.

Her brother's muted groans brought Charity back to the present. Hank began to describe in great detail the bowel movement he was enjoying.

Justine slapped her palms to her ears. "When will you be back for me?"

"Soon." Charity turned toward the door.

"Wait."

Charity stopped, and made a face at the doorway. Damn it, if Justine was about to tell her something important, then Charity had screwed up royally by not bringing along someone else to hear it.

"Would you take that thing with you?"

Charity swung back around. Justine was frowning down at the breakfast tray she'd barely touched. Charity picked up the tray.

"You still in love with my brother?" Surprisingly, Justine didn't take time to gloat. "I heard all about it. How you went wild after Grady left for college. Stayed wild, too, till you decided to run for sheriff."

Charity's fingers clamped tightly on the tray. Hank started to howl like a gray wolf baying at the moon.

"Wild runs in the family," she said. She backed up two steps and pushed the heavy door shut, unable to prevent herself from enjoying the satisfying clang.

*   *   *

CHARITY'S LIPS MASHED TOGETHER as she strode away from her brother's howls. No surprise that Grady's family had talked about her. Everybody in town had talked about her. She'd heard it all before. Good Lord, she'd have been drooling onto a straitjacket for years now if she hadn't learned how to ignore gossip.

Besides, Justine was angry, nauseated, and frightened, more for her son than for herself. Charity would put money on it. Time to hear Drew's side of the story.

She carried the tray to the break room, noticing as she walked past reception that Pratt was still talking with Grady. Seriously? Once she took care of Justine's tray, she'd have to break that up. If they made Drew wait any longer, his lawyer would pitch a fit.

She tried not to dwell on what they might be discussing. Or who. She'd done enough dwelling for one day, thank you very much.

In the station's tiny kitchen, Mo leaned against the counter, munching on an apple, while Dix poured himself a cup of coffee. A familiar fondness sapped the tension from Charity's shoulders. As always, Mo's short blond hair was combed and in control, while

Dix's hair looked like his four-year-old nephew had been racing toy cars through it.

Mo took a breather from his apple. "Sheriff ready?"

"Not yet." Charity narrowed her eyes at Dix, who was adding waaaay too much sugar to his coffee. Especially since he took it black. "You okay, Dix?"

His hand jerked and sugar sprayed the counter. "*Kakêpâtis,*" he muttered. He'd used that word before.

Moron, Charity thought it meant. She decided not to ask who he was talking about.

With a shake of his head, Mo tossed what was left of his apple into the trash. "Easy, Detective. You're about as jumpy as the Langford kid."

Charity pulled a mug from the cabinet. No way she could get through this day without another dose of caffeine. "How is Drew?"

Dix's spoon clattered into the sink. "How would you be if someone murdered your girlfriend and you were the one who found the body?"

A taut silence ensued, broken only by the sound of Dix's palm brushing across the countertop as he swept the sugar into his hand. He took his time emptying it into the sink.

When Dix turned, Charity offered a bright smile. "You want to handle the interview?"

Dix blew at his coffee before taking a sip, avoiding her gaze. "You are the lead." The hint of bleak in his tone gave him away, and it had nothing to do with Mo.

Charity gave up on the smile and filled her own mug. Dixon Ironmaker was a good man. He was honest, hardworking, and loyal to a fault. Why couldn't his wife appreciate what she had?

Why don't you mind your own business?

She and Mo had speculated about Dix's wife and whether she suffered from depression. It would explain a lot. It would also mean Charity should be offering compassion instead of censure.

Sheriff Pratt strode into the room, avoiding Charity's gaze as he brandished the Sarah Huffman case file.

"Okay, people. We have two West family members in custody and four others breathing down our necks. Let's do this right so we don't have to call in the state. Talk to me."

Charity, Mo, and Dix took turns filling him in on what was already in the file: Justine's nine-one-one call and subsequent confession, the crime scene details, the witness who reported seeing Drew, and the teen's admission to finding the body *before* he knew he'd been busted.

"Anyone check out the witness?"

Dix nodded. "She's solid. A middle-aged woman who runs a small computer services firm. She was on her way to a technology conference out of town when she spotted Drew Langford."

The sheriff grunted. "What do we know about the kid?"

"Just turned eighteen," Mo said. "Senior in high school with better-than-average grades, star soccer player, no juvenile record."

"The posse is working in shifts, keeping the scene secure and searching for the murder weapon." Charity frowned down into her coffee. Days like this, she could almost understand the lure of alcohol-induced oblivion, but the price for that oblivion was too damned high.

Pratt tugged at his goatee. "Got a warrant to search the Wests' home?"

Charity nodded. "Already signed off by Judge Purl. Said he's waiting to hear all about your fishing trip, by the way."

"You mean he wants to gloat over the fact that I didn't catch squat." Pratt turned his scowl on them all. "Any idea what kind of weapon we're looking for?"

"Not the leather necklace we found." Mo motioned with his chin at the photos in the file the sheriff held. "What we're looking for is a pair of thin straps, maybe an eighth of an inch diameter each. One of the straps has a thicker segment, extending a couple inches."

"Like a decoration, you mean?" Pratt squinted. "An eighth of an inch is too thin for a purse strap. Boot laces, maybe?"

Mo scratched his jaw. "Or some kind of woman's belt. Hey, how about a leash?"

The sheriff stared. "For what, a toy poodle?"

Red exploded in Mo's cheeks. "She was found outside the vet's," he muttered.

With a loud, deliberate slurp of his coffee, Dix reclaimed their attention. "Could be a necklace or a lanyard made out of coated wire. Or a paracord bracelet, which is woven from parachute cord. You can unwind it and use it as a rope."

The sheriff raised an eyebrow.

Dix shook his head. "Nothing like that found on Mrs. Langford."

"What about the victim's vehicle?" the sheriff asked.

"Her personal car is an Audi sedan. The A8." Mo spoke quickly, without checking his notes. "She wasn't driving it last night, though. Transmission problems, according to Muscoe's. They gave her a minivan while they're working on her car."

"The A8?" Pratt raised his eyebrows. "That's an expensive vehicle. Find anything in the van?"

"No, sir." Dix tipped his mug toward the folder, as if to say *it's in there.* "We searched it last night. We tagged a few items, but Muscoe's did a thorough job of cleaning it before they loaned it out. Nor did we find anything in Mrs. Langford's convertible."

We? Charity bit at the inside of her cheek. She hadn't gotten much sleep, but it sounded like Dix hadn't gotten any. Meanwhile she'd been mooning around behind the library.

She gulped at her coffee.

"And Sarah Huffman's residence?" Pratt tucked the file under his arm.

"Townhouse in Norwood Estates. One of the regulators has been keeping watch. I'll take a team when we're done here." Dix hesitated. "I have heard rumors."

Mo's head came up. "What kind of rumors?"

"The kind that hints at shady property deals," Dix said grimly.

The sheriff nodded. "Everyone keep that in mind during the interviews."

"After we're done with those, I'd like to drop in on the ME," Mo said. "Sarah was five-eight. The angle of strangulation indicates the killer is a few inches taller."

"Which would eliminate Justine," Charity said, and earned a stone-faced glance from the sheriff.

"Unless the killer had Sarah on her knees," Dix said.

"Check out the body, see if her knees are missing any skin. Check her pants for marks as well." Pratt made a shooing motion at Mo. "Go now. Don't come back until you have the ME's report."

Mo didn't give the boss a chance to change his mind. With a jerk of his cleft chin, he was gone.

Charity lifted her now-lukewarm coffee to her lips, but before she could take a sip, the sheriff wiggled his fingers in a *hand it over* gesture. Reluctantly she surrendered her mug. Why had she ever confessed she was trying to cut back?

"You and Dix handle the interviews," Pratt said. "While you're doing that, I'll get someone to check alibis. I already have the county commissioner riding my six for a statement, so I need to work one up. Don't forget to ask young Mr. Langford if he owns one of those rope bracelets. Oh, and Deputy Bishop? Come see me when you're done."

Charity nodded, her stomach tightening as she walked out. She stopped Dix outside the interview room. "Hey, what's with all the weird looks and innuendos?" When he frowned, she gave the sleeve of his uniform shirt a tug. "You know what I mean. I'm getting the hairy eyeball from both you and Pratt. Want to tell me why?"

He didn't respond, simply watched her.

"Don't pull that silent Cree warrior bull with me, Dixon Ironmaker. Give."

His chest rose and fell with a soundless sigh. "We both know what has the sheriff worried. My issue is personal. We can talk later."

Personal. Dix never told her anything personal. Her stomach muscles twitched, and she was tempted to beg him to tell her and get it over with. But you couldn't push Dix any more than you could push a chain.

She hugged Sarah's file to her chest. "Just tell me you and I are okay."

Something unsettling passed across his harsh but handsome face. He smoothed it away, but not before she'd realized that whatever he had to say, she wouldn't enjoy hearing it.

"Stop call me 'Dixon' and you and I will be fine." Dix reached for the door handle. "Let's find out whether Drew Langford will be."

* * *

THE DOOR OPENED AND Drew jumped. Two deputies came in, the hot blonde he'd heard his grandparents arguing about before they'd left for work that morning, and the tall, fierce-faced cop the kids in school called Chief. Never in earshot, though. Drew sat up straighter, praying he wouldn't humiliate himself by spewing. Or worse.

Where was the other dude? The blond surfer type? He'd been cool, and hadn't made Drew feel anywhere near as lowlife as these two did.

In clipped voices the deputies greeted Drew and Owen Quinn, the family lawyer. They each pulled out a chair on the other side of the table, neither reacting when the metal legs screeched and scraped over the worn tile floor. They sat.

Two against two.

Drew didn't care much for Quinn—the dude rarely cracked a smile and always seemed to be watching his mom. Still he was damned glad to have someone on his side.

"I'm Deputy Bishop and this is Sheriff's Detective Ironmaker. Ready to talk about what brought you in this morning?"

Drew glanced at his reflection in the two-way mirror. Who was watching from the other side? Were they high-fiving each other for catching a killer? Placing bets on how much time he'd get? Or maybe his mom was back there, still trying to convince them she was capable of murder. A woman who'd cried for an hour after finding three hummingbirds lying dead beneath the feeder their orange tabby had staked out.

"We've been ready." Quinn's voice was smooth, his posture relaxed, but that one cocked eyebrow carried more disapproval than Drew's mom had ever managed with her face screwed up in a frown and both hands on her hips.

"I'd like it noted that my client came forward of his own free will to offer his account of the events of last evening. He recognizes he was remiss in not contacting the police earlier."

"Remiss." Deputy Bishop turned her steady gaze on Drew. "Is that the word you'd use, Drew?"

He resisted the urge to shift in his seat and tried not to move his arms since he had what felt like a game day's worth of sweat trapped in his pits.

His gulp was embarrassingly loud. "You guys know my mom is innocent, right?"

"That's why you're here," Chief said, in a deep, quiet voice the soccer team could use for their haunted house fundraiser. Anyone hearing that voice coming out of the dark would piss their pants. "To help figure that out."

"Well, the word isn't 'remiss,' it's 'scared,'" Drew said, the grit in his throat making his voice unrecognizable. Shame soured his stomach. "I was scared and sad and angry. Instead of doing the right thing, I ran."

Deputy Bishop continued to watch him and he was shocked as hell to see encouragement instead of disapproval in her eyes. Probably some good cop bad cop bullshit. Still he held onto her gaze like a lifeline.

He told her everything he'd told Uncle Grady. To his surprise Quinn let him talk. On TV, lawyers were always advising their clients to shut it. Quinn interrupted only once, and that was because Drew got choked up. He always did, whenever he thought of how badly he'd let Sarah down. When he finally finished his story, the lawyer produced Drew's phone and pushed it across the table.

"The text message is intact."

"Thank you." Deputy Bishop set it on the folder she had yet to open. "You said you told your father and your uncle about your affair with Sarah Huffman." Deputy Bishop tapped a finger on his phone. "Did anyone else know?"

"I told my mom, when she drove out to the vet's office."

"And how did she react?"

"She hurked all over the parking lot."

"And your father?"

"He, uh…Sarah broke up with me so she could be with him."

No better word to describe the silence than shocked. Drew kept his face as stone-still as possible while Deputy Bishop shot Chief a quick side-eye. "But he didn't know about your affair until you told him?" she asked.

"No. At first he didn't believe me. Then he got angry."

"How angry?"

Good going, dumbass. "Not violent angry. Embarrassed angry. My dad wouldn't hurt anyone."

Chief leaned forward. Drew knew he should meet his gaze, but he couldn't bring himself to look away from the strong, copper-colored hands clasped on the table. "Anyone else know?"

Drew shook his head.

"Anything else you want to tell us?"

He looked up then. "I'm worried about Allison."

Chief frowned. "Allison?"

"Allison Young." He shifted his gaze to Deputy Bishop. "You're friends with her mom. Kate."

She nodded. "Why are you worried?"

"We used to go together. Then we broke up and" — beneath the table he scrubbed his palms along the thighs of his jeans" — I started seeing Sarah."

"And Allison didn't like that." Deputy Bishop said it slowly.

Drew shook his head. Judas Priest, was he going to get *everyone* in his life in trouble? "She never knew. I mean, I never would have told her."

"Did you still love her?"

"No, it's because of what she said when we split." His left leg started to bounce. "She was all hysterical and stuff. Said she'd hurt herself if she ever found out I was seeing someone else."

"She used those exact words? That she'd hurt herself?"

His fingers dug into his thighs, and he swallowed again. "Kill," he muttered. "She said she'd kill herself. I can't stop thinking about it. What if she finds out about Sarah?"

*   *   *

CHARITY'S MIND RACED AS she swallowed her concern. What if Allison already knew? What if her threat to hurt herself didn't have the effect she'd hoped for, so she'd taken it one step further? One huge, gigantic, mammoth step, yeah, but still a possibility.

"You were right to tell us. We'll talk with Mrs. Young and make sure Allison gets the attention she needs," Charity said.

Drew's leg slowed. "Good. That'd be good."

Charity picked up the phone and traced a finger over the flame design on the case, biting the inside of her lip. If anything happened to Allison Young, Drew would blame himself. An emotional burden like that would zap the joy right out of his life. Given Justine's standard state of inebriation and her ex-husband's apparent preoccupation with Sarah Huffman, the teen would have to bear it on his own. Like Grady, who'd received more censure than support from his own parents.

Her fingers convulsed around the phone. Drew reminded her of Grady. Was that why she couldn't believe he was guilty? Why she'd already accepted she wouldn't relax until they'd cleared him of all suspicion?

Dear Lord, maybe Dix was right. Maybe she wasn't capable of being objective. She felt him watching her, but didn't dare turn her head.

Owen Quinn gave his throat a slow, deliberate clearing. "Is my client free to go?"

Charity swallowed a sigh. If only.

More obnoxious scraping as Dix stood. "You know the answer to that."

Her coworker's face remained impassive, but Charity could feel the impatience vibrating in the air around them. Dix was anxious to compare notes. She understood, because she was reeling herself.

Drew and Sarah. Who'd have thought?

Sarah Huffman hadn't been thinking, that much was clear. Had Justine known about the affair, despite what Drew claimed? Talk about a motive for murder. An even stronger motive when you factored in that not only Justine's son, but her ex-husband was sleeping with her best friend. She had more than enough reason to hold a grudge.

Charity put down the phone and pulled a clear plastic envelope from her breast pocket. She slid it across the table. "Recognize this?"

Drew eyed the coil of leather and its one ornament, a turquoise cat's eye marble. He swallowed thickly. "Yeah," he rasped. "Sarah gave that to me."

Dix leaned forward, and braced his palms on the table. "So why do we have it?"

"I don't know." Drew's gaze flicked back and forth, from Dix to Charity and back again. "I lost it a while ago."

"How long's a while?" Charity asked quietly.

"I don't know," he said again. "About a month?" He pushed a hand through his hair. "She was going to break up with me. Maybe she took it back?" All at once his face went slack. "Is that what they used to kill her?"

Charity scooped up the necklace, folder, and phone, and got to her feet. "We'll check back in a little while. Anything you need in the meantime?"

"Some coffee would be nice."

Dix grunted, not even looking at Owen Quinn. "We were talking to Mr. Langford."

Drew managed a shaky smile. "Could I get some water?"

Charity was halfway out the door Dix held open for her when Drew called out.

"Deputy Bishop?"

She turned.

He stood with his shoulders level, hands fisted at his sides, like a soldier braced for a dressing down. "How much trouble am I in? For running, I mean?"

She had a feeling he didn't so much run as fail to reject bad advice from his mother, though the distinction wouldn't make much difference in court.

"It's up to the prosecutor whether or not she'll press charges," Charity said. "Failure to report a death is a misdemeanor. It's possible you could get jail time up to one year, a fine of up to one thousand dollars, or both. Might be more if the prosecutor decides to tack on obstruction of justice."

Drew nodded, looking almost relieved. "Sarah deserved better."

Charity knew he was talking of his own actions as much as he was talking of the murder. "About your mom—" She hesitated. "Mothers can be fierce when their children are threatened." She saw it firsthand every time Hank or Lucas got mixed up with the police.

"She thinks I did it." Drew's eyes looked haunted. "Why else would she confess?"

Quickly Quinn stood, turned his back to Charity, and spoke in a murmur to Drew.

Preparing to shut his client down. She let fly one last question. "You don't believe your mother is guilty?"

"How can she be? She was...Grandfather said she had an alibi."

She saw Drew work it out, saw the moment he realized his mother could have left the bar long enough to kill Sarah and make it back in time to get his call.

Indignation piped red into his cheeks. "Just because she could have done it doesn't mean she did. Even if she did kill Sarah, which she never would—she'd never kill anyone—why would she lure me out there with a text and try to pin it on me, only to turn around and take the blame?"

The kid had a point.

"So, Detective." Quinn adjusted his tie. "How about you bring us those drinks you promised?"

Outside in the hallway Charity rubbed her forehead. "We need to talk to Allison."

Dix grunted his agreement. "I'll check with the sheriff, see how he wants to handle it. You do realize we have probable cause to hold Drew?"

She rubbed harder. "I know."

"You putting Mrs. Langford in the box next?"

Charity dropped her hand and nodded. "We'll do Scott Langford last."

"Better make sure those two don't catch sight of each other."

"Right. I don't feel like breaking up any fights today."

"I heard you almost had one out in the parking lot last night." When she bristled, Dix backed off. "I will talk to the sheriff, then call Kate Young."

Charity nodded and turned away, hesitated, and turned back. She fingered the button on the left cuff of her uniform shirt. "Dix?"

He must have heard something in her voice, something that made him nervous, because he crossed his arms over his chest. "Yeah?" he asked warily.

"Justine didn't kill Sarah."

He shrugged. "Never thought she did."

"Despite what Sarah did to her?"

"We did our due diligence. Talked to Big Mike. Checked the security footage from the bar. She had the time to leave, but she did not."

"Maybe she hired someone."

"Maybe. But that is not what she confessed to." He unfolded his arms. "Either she knows what happened or she does not. I know an easy way to find out."

"I'm listening."

"Tell her that her son is here."

*   *   *

TEN MINUTES LATER, WITH drinks delivered to Drew and his lawyer, and Justine delivered to interview room two, Charity met up with Dix in the hallway. "She refused to let Quinn sit in on the interview."

"She does not want him to talk her out of it."

"So let's see if we can. Ready?" Again Charity walked into the room ahead of Dix.

He paused in the doorway behind her and spoke over his shoulder at the fire extinguisher on the opposite wall. "The kid asked for a glass of water. Get it for him, would you?"

"Kid?" Justine grabbed the edge of the table. "Drew? Is he here? Do you have my son in custody?"

Dix winced, muttered something that sounded like an apology, and left the room. So far, so good.

Charity sat, and leaned forward over the scuff-marked table. "We're prepared to accept your confession, Mrs. Langford."

Justine blinked. "You are?"

"We need just a few more details. I realize this might be upsetting for you, but do you think you can walk me through what happened with Sarah last night?"

"Again? It's...I can't..." Justine waved her hands. "It's all a blur."

Charity shook her head and offered a flat, tight-lipped smile, as if in sympathy. She lowered her voice, and leaned in further. "You don't remember anything? The bar? Meeting Sarah in the clinic parking lot? Drew's phone call?"

Justine tugged at her left earlobe as her gaze skittered around the room. "I'd been drinking."

Charity hummed in understanding. "You're sober now, right?"

With an unconvincing smirk, Justine tossed back her lustrous black hair. "I've been locked away in a cell all night, and someone forgot to stock the mini-bar. So yes, I think it's safe to say I'm sober."

"But you don't remember meeting Sarah Huffman last night?" Charity frowned, flipped open her folder, and started scribbling. "Just as well we didn't bother your lawyer," she muttered.

"Wait." Justine pressed the heels of her hands to her eyes. "Wait. I think...yes, I do recall pulling into the lot." She dropped her hands. "It's hazy, but I do remember seeing Sarah there."

"Do you remember who arranged the meeting?"

Justine shook her head.

"When you first pulled in, did Sarah remain in her Audi, or did she get out and approach your car?"

"She...when I got there, she was standing by her car."

Charity resisted the urge to drop her pen and sit back in smug celebration. "Standing by the Audi, or leaning up against it?"

"Standing beside it. With her arms wrapped around herself because she was cold."

Charity tapped her pen. "Did you argue?"

"I don't know," Justine whispered.

"Do you remember how she died?"

"She was...I...strangled her."

"With your bare hands?"

"No. No, of course not." Justine's fingers shook as she brushed them back and forth at the base of her own throat. "She had a—" She stopped, and swallowed. "I used... something."

"Something like this?" Charity slid a clear, flat plastic bag out from under the folder and pushed it across the table. Justine stared at the dark green terrycloth belt coiled inside.

"Do you remember using this to strangle your best friend?"

One slim, quivering hand hovered over the evidence bag. Tears glazed Justine's eyes. "I didn't mean to kill her," she said, voice tormented and raw.

Charity fought a surge of sympathy. Sympathy didn't get the job done. "We need to know. Is this what you used?"

"Yes."

Charity closed her eyes for a moment, then jerked a nod. She shut the folder, slapped the bag on top of it, and pushed to her feet.

Justine blinked. "That's it?"

"That's it."

"What happens now?"

"Now we find out if the prosecuting attorney wants to file charges against you for providing a false confession."

Justine popped upright. "But I'm guilty! I am. Me. No one else. I just told you how I...." Her voice trailed off as her frantic gaze finally registered the certainty in Charity's expression. Justine's shoulders drooped, and her face sagged. "How did you know?"

"Sarah didn't drive her Audi last night. Her car's in the shop. They set her up with a loaner." Charity plucked at the evidence bag cradled in her arm. "And this isn't what killed her."

Justine sighed. "Can I see my son?"

"It may be a while." Charity paused. "Would you like me to bring your brother back to sit with you?"

Justine nodded listlessly. As Charity opened the door, Justine spoke behind her. "Make sure it's *my* brother," she said, her tone weary. "Don't bring me yours by mistake."

Charity couldn't help a snort. She stepped out into the hallway, threw her head back, and stared up at the dirty-yellow water stains on the ceiling tiles. Despite her best intentions, she was starting to like Justine Langford.

*   *   *

GRADY PACED THE AIRLESS waiting room, resisting the urge to make a break for the chilly sunshine. The moment he stepped outside they'd come looking for him, and no way would he miss his chance to see Justine. Make sure she was okay. Let her know he cared.

He was tired of straining to hear the muffled voices beyond reception and of ignoring the static of the police radio and the *thunk* of metal catching metal as doors opened or closed.

Two days, two relatives in custody. Hell, if he had to come back tomorrow, would there be a third?

A sudden wave of weariness had him leaning back against the nearest wall. He shoved his hands in his pockets and closed his eyes. Besides sweat and antiseptic and stale nicotine and…muffins?…he smelled coffee and wanted to beg a cup, if only to give his hands something to do. If he sucked down any more caffeine, though, he wouldn't sleep for a week. Everyone else in the family was in the same shape. They'd sat up all night with Owen Quinn, speculating, strategizing, arguing. Even his parents had stuck to coffee, realizing they wouldn't get any rest before starting their rounds at the hospital.

His dad had looked worse than ever but refused to go to bed.

Grady grimaced as he thought about Peyton. She had to be upset he'd left her behind. Her grandparents' ranting had dragged her out of bed and she'd begged to be part of the discussion. He'd refused, not wanting her to hear what his less-than-tactful parents might say about Drew's relationship with Sarah. Luckily Quinn had backed him up, and Peyton had stomped out of the room. Hours later, when Grady had gone upstairs to shower and change, he'd found her asleep at the top of the steps and swore when he realized how much she must have heard. He'd carried her to bed and asked his mother to call the school with an excuse.

Maybe he should buy flowers on the way home. Something with a lot of pink. She liked pink.

A door clicked open and Grady jerked away from the wall. Charity hovered in the doorway, her expression carefully neutral. Half a dozen strides and he stood in front of her, alarm crowding the air from his lungs.

"Your sister would like to see you. If you'll follow me?"

He hung back, as pissed at Charity as his niece was sure to be at him. "This is the way it's going to be? Pretending we're nothing more than casual acquaintances?"

Her gaze skimmed his suit. "Who's pretending?"

Grady watched the frost creep into her hazel eyes and gave a sharp exhale that was almost a laugh. She was, he realized. She was pretending there wasn't anything left between them. When he could still clearly picture her snuggling into his letterman jacket on the bleachers beside him, laughing against his neck as flakes of snow swirled around them; scrunching her face and shoving a palm across their table at the diner as he tried to coax her into taking a bite of his black bean soup; squeezing her own sweat-slick breasts with trembling hands as breathless moans ripped from her throat while she rode his cock.

Deputy Bishop cleared her throat, splayed all eight fingers over the stiff polished leather of her belt and swung impatiently toward the door. But not soon enough to hide the place on her neck where her pulse punched at her skin.

Grady allowed himself a small smile. No matter the reason, no matter that it didn't, couldn't, change anything, the ache in his chest loosened its grip.

5

CHARITY TURNED BACK AROUND in time to catch his smile. "I don't find anything funny about this," she said stiffly.

The dispatcher slid into view, like the sun peeping out from behind a cloud. "You'll have to excuse her," Brenda June said, earrings swinging a cheerful rhythm. "She's had a rough day." She patted Charity's shoulder. "I heard about Clarabelle. You have my deepest sympathy."

Grady sobered. "Who's Clarabelle?"

"Never mind."

Brenda June shook her head at him, signaling either *none of your business* or *nothing to worry about*. He barely knew the woman but was fairly certain she meant the latter.

"You want me to call Muscoe's?" the dispatcher asked Charity.

"Mo already did."

"J.T. Muscoe's still working on cars?" Grady squinted at Charity. "Wait, you named your car Clarabelle?"

"So what?" Scorn twisted Charity's lips as she glanced downward. "You named your—"

"Christ, Charity."

"I was going to say soccer balls."

Brenda June perched her chin on Charity's shoulder, crimson lips curved, gaze avid. "You named your balls?"

A tall, skinny dude in navy uniform pants and a gleaming black leather jacket came up behind the dispatcher, shaking his head as he dropped a stack of papers on the counter. Grady gave him a shrug as if to say, *Women. What can you do?* Brenda June never looked around, her gaze locked on Grady. When the other guy walked away, he was still shaking his head.

"So, what'd you name them?" Brenda June demanded.

Charity shifted her scowl to Grady. "Do you want to see your sister, or do you want to stand here trading juvenile jokes with our dispatcher?"

"I want to see her," came a strident voice.

Hell. Grady turned in the doorway.

His father strode into the room, jaw slanted at his usual I-dare-you-to-defy-me angle. Abruptly Charity straightened and swung toward him, nearly catching Brenda June's nose with the back of her head.

"Dr. West," Charity said crisply. "I'll tell Mrs. Langford you're here."

"I'll tell her myself."

"I need you to wait until I've checked with your daughter. Please sit down."

Right on cue, his father's already flushed face turned even redder. "You were ready to take him back." He never looked at Grady, just jerked a thumb in his direction. "Take me instead."

Charity nodded coolly. "I will. As soon as she okays it." She glanced at Grady. "You ready?"

"I'm her father, dammit!"

"For God's sake, Dad, take it easy. Grab a seat."

His father shook off Grady's grip. "Is Clarkson here?"

"Yes, Sheriff Pratt is in his office," Charity said.

"Then I'll see him."

Charity nodded once. "I'll tell him you're here."

Grady would have laughed out loud if he wasn't afraid it would kick his father's blood pressure straight into the stratosphere.

Hampton West's eyes collapsed into condescending slits. "You're not doing yourself any favors here, Charity Bishop."

And that's when Grady heard the quaver in his father's voice. His dad was scared out of his mind.

"Deputy Bishop. And what I'm doing, Dr. West, is my job."

"Dad." Grady grabbed his father's arm again and this time refused to let go. "I'll tell her you're here. I'll make it quick. You want to help her? Show her we're going to be fine, no matter what."

After a few tense moments, the muscles under Grady's hand went soft. Resentment, followed by resignation, chased the fury from his father's face.

Grady guided him to the nearest chair. "I'll be right back."

As he turned, he met Charity's gaze. The rueful tilt to her mouth asked, *why'd we both get stuck with assholes for parents?*

Then she did an about-face and headed for wherever they were holding Justine. Grady hung behind to sneak a word with the dispatcher.

"Who's Mo?" he asked quietly.

"Tell me what you named your balls."

Grady watched Charity, the view as enticing from the back as it was from the front. He sighed. "Jake and Elwood."

She blinked. "The Blues Brothers?" She clapped a hand over her mouth.

"Made sense at the time."

"What'd you name the star attraction, the Bluesmobile?" She flashed a grin. "With a sense of humor like that, you might actually have a chance. But can you wow her in the sack?"

He gritted his teeth. "Want to tell me about Mo?"

"Deputy Riley Morrissey. The brother Charity should have had." She winked and stepped aside. "Head on back, handsome."

* * *

DIX HAD DONE SOME juggling with their visitors. They only had two interview rooms, and with Justine in one and Drew in the other, the detective had been forced to stash Scott Langford in the office shared by the regulators. Charity delivered Grady to Justine and Hampton West's message to the sheriff, verified he'd talked to the prosecuting attorney and they could release Justine, then joined Dix outside the interview room where Drew and his lawyer waited.

"Ready to tackle Scott Langford?" she asked.

"He will not make it easy for us."

"Easy? Where's the fun in that?" She opened the door to the interview room, interrupting Quinn as he discussed the arraignment process with Drew.

A process she hoped they'd never see.

"Mr. Quinn? A moment, please?"

Quinn stepped out into the hallway and closed the door behind him. The man couldn't have gotten much more sleep than she had yet still looked as fresh and crisp as if he'd just finished getting ready for his day.

"We're not charging Justine," she told him. The naked relief that flickered in his eyes triggered a burn at the back of her own. *Going soft, Deputy Bishop?* She cleared her throat and motioned with her chin at the door behind him. "I can give you two more minutes with Drew, then we'll need you to sit in on Scott Langford's interview."

"I'll be right with you."

When she turned, she saw that Dix was watching her with an unsettling intensity. "One Langford down, one to go?" he drawled.

"You don't want the kid to be guilty, either."

"No. Then again, I am not personally vested."

The fact that she couldn't deny it pissed her off, big time. "Bite me, Ironmaker," she said sourly.

"Deputy Bishop!"

Sheriff Pratt's deep voice vibrated with disapproval. *Crap.* She set her shoulders and turned and met the equally disapproving gaze of Grady's father. At this rate she wouldn't have to worry about campaigning for sheriff, because she'd no longer be working for the department.

"Dr. West would like to see his daughter," Pratt snapped.

"She's in two," Charity said meekly.

Justine had agreed to see her father. Reluctantly, but she had agreed.

The sheriff pointed the way and Dr. West disappeared into the room. Charity caught a glimpse of Grady holding his sister's hand and she couldn't help thinking of the night before, when he'd seemed so reluctant to let hers go.

"Talked to Scott Langford yet?" Pratt folded his arms across his chest and glowered at her over the top of his black-rimmed glasses.

His bald head gleamed under the fluorescent lights. Hampton West had made the sheriff sweat and now Pratt was paying it forward.

Charity did her best to shake off the sentiment and keep her expression a snark-free zone. "We're headed that way now."

"Then I suggest you get to it. And may I also suggest you watch your language when you're in uniform?"

What he meant was, when a bigwig like Hampton West was around to hear it. Dix opened his mouth to comment.

Pratt held up a hand. "I don't care who says it's okay. Respect the badge and it'll respect you."

A prickling heat surged into Charity's cheeks. "Yes, sir."

"Heard anything from Deputy Morrissey?"

"Not yet," she said.

"Come see me when you're done." Pratt stomped off.

Dix gave a low whistle. "Keep that up, and even your own mentor will vote against you."

Instead of laughing, she went still. "Is that it, Dix? The election? Is that what's bothering you?"

The disgust in his expression was answer enough. "We talked about this. Why can't you accept that I do not want to be sheriff?"

"I've seen the way you eye his badge. Or is it his manly chest you're —"

"Bite me, Bishop."

*   *   *

SCOTT LANGFORD WAS AN avid outdoorsman with perpetually sun-reddened skin and a heavily creased neck. His eyes were shadowed, but the belligerent set of his jaw and the way his gaze raked Charity when she walked into the office — he practically fell out of his chair checking out her ass — made it easy to skimp on the pity. He made it even easier by refusing to provide an alibi when Dix asked where he'd been between the hours of eight and midnight. Charity reminded him they were trying to not only solve his girlfriend's homicide, but clear his son of the crime. Didn't matter. He wouldn't say where he'd been or who he'd been with, though his sly expression made Charity suspect his alibi was of the female persuasion.

His reluctance to name his companion was eerily reminiscent of Kate's, but Charity hoped to hell that was coincidental. Kate and Justine were close — surely Kate wouldn't have slept with her best friend's ex.

Charity hustled Scott Langford out of the building only to learn she needn't have worried — Justine had already been released and was on her way home with her father and her brother. Good. Perfect. She found Quinn and let him know his client — one of them, anyway — had left. The combination of gratification and disappointment on his face looked too damned familiar. He went to sit with Drew while Charity fled to the break room, desperate for a caffeine fix before her mystery meeting with the sheriff.

Three interviews and only nine-thirty. No wonder she was hungry. With mug in one hand, Pop-Tart in the other, and murder file tucked up against her armpit, she headed for Pratt's office. He wasn't in. She perched on the edge of a chair, resisted the urge to slouch down and close her eyes, and tried not to regret missing out on one last glimpse of Grady.

Even as she acknowledged those last five words sounded like the title of a crappy-ass country song, she wondered why she'd want to torture herself, why she'd want to add to the agitated hours she'd already spent in bed remembering the heated stroke of his hands, the relentless play of his fingers, the needy rasp of his breathing, the exquisite glide of his cock —

When she spotted movement outside the window, Charity fanned herself with the frosted Pop-Tart and craned her neck. Pratt paced along the sidewalk, staring down at his phone. Okay, well, she might as well do something constructive while she waited. She set her coffee and pastry on the bookshelf beside her, flipped open the murder file, and began to read.

Minutes later, Pratt barged into his office and Charity surged to her feet. He held her gaze as he rounded his desk, blindly picked up a stack of case folders, and let them slap back down. The man liked to make noise when he was mad.

She was in the mood to make a little noise of her own, but she knew better than to show her ass when Clarkson Pratt had a bug up his.

"At least you didn't make me chase you down," he grumbled, and reached for the stapler.

Charity frowned. "What do you mean chase me down? Where would I go?"

"Nowhere." *Chucka, chucka.* Staples dropped to his desk as his hand flexed. "Nowhere is exactly where you're going if you don't start getting results. I had fifteen voicemail messages from Hampton West when I got up this morning." *Chucka, chucka, chucka.* "*Fifteen.* You think the Wests don't trust you now? Wait'll they decide you're making eyes at their son again. You want to win this election? You need to stay away from your ex."

Charity dropped the folder on her chair and stepped closer. "There is so much wrong with what you just said, I don't even know where to begin. What exactly did Dr. West say when he was in here?"

Chucka, chucka.

She slapped her hands down on his desk and leaned in. His eyes widened, and he thrust the stapler up out of reach, like a kid with a toy he didn't want taken away. Somehow she resisted the urge to slap the damned thing out of his hand.

"Screw the election," she gritted. "How about we solve the case so we can give Sarah Huffman the justice she deserves? And by the way, the Wests are never going to trust me, and they're never going to vote for me. No one on their social calendar will vote for me. Hell, no one who works at the hospital will vote for me. I'm okay with that. What I'm not okay with is your implication that I'm less interested in doing my job than I am in doing Grady West."

"Watch it, Deputy. I am your superior."

"You're also grumpier than a horny teenage boy with two broken wrists." Brenda June elbowed her way into the office, carrying the top of a cardboard box that doubled as a tray. "Coffee, fruit, blueberry muffins, cream cheese." She set the food down on his desk and thrust out a handful of napkins. "Eat. We'll all feel better."

The sheriff set aside the stapler. "Coffee will do."

After an indignant Brenda June flounced out of the room, Pratt yanked off his glasses and rubbed the bridge of his nose. "You think the kid did it?"

With a shake of her head, Charity straightened. "If he killed her, it was because she ended their affair and it made him angry or desperate. He's neither. He's sad that she's dead and upset about finding the body, but what disturbs him most is what Allison Young might do when she finds out they were involved."

The sheriff sat back and clamped his arms across his chest. "So who looks good for it?"

"You tell me." Charity plucked a muffin from the tray on his desk. "We're missing a little something called evidence. My instinct is to concentrate on the Wests and Scott Langford. When you talked to Hampton West, did he offer any alibis?"

"He was working late at the hospital. Not unusual, according to the staff who corroborated his story. Roberta was home helping her granddaughter with her homework, and Justine was at Sweeney's, recovering from a bad day at the office."

Charity paused in the act of peeling the paper from her muffin. "She works from home."

"She's a freelance bookkeeper with her parents as her biggest clients."

"Point taken." She moved the folder off the chair and sat. "We also need to question Sarah's coworkers, see if there are any jealous lovers or disgruntled clients lurking in the background. I hope to get a better picture when I talk to her parents. Dix is processing the townhouse now."

Slowly Pratt stood. He picked up a handful of napkins, rounded his desk, and handed them to Charity. When she offered him half the muffin, he shook his head. "Did you mean it when you said 'screw the election?'"

Trying to follow this conversation was giving Charity a headache. And why was she eating a muffin when she already had a Pop-Tart set aside? "I want to be sheriff almost as much as you want me to be sheriff. I get it, you know." She set the muffin on the bookshelf beside the half-eaten Pop-Tart and brushed her palms together. "You understand what discrimination feels like. Even Dix hasn't faced the opposition you have. But the job has to come first."

"The job that's supposed to include more than fieldwork and paperwork?" With a grunt, he moved back around his desk and dropped into his chair. "When was the last time you attended a community event? Or hung out at Jerzy's or the café, instead of taking your food to go? You expect to get elected sheriff, you have to let people see you out there. You have to mingle." He picked up the stapler and pointed it at her. "Show the community you've changed. They don't see you, they're going to think you don't care, and they'll elect big-mouthed Bloom. What happens then?"

Then she was fucked all over again. She retrieved her mug and swigged lukewarm coffee. "I won't know until it happens."

Sweat gleamed on his forehead as he picked at the staple jammed inside the *chucka* machine. "Tell me you can handle it."

"Handle what?"

"Grady West."

Her chest squeezed hotly, and the tepid coffee turned greasy in her belly. "I didn't expect this," she said. "Not from you."

"Cut the bullshit. I was there, remember? You were crying so hard I knew if I followed regs and cuffed your arms behind your back I'd end up with snot all over my backseat."

"That was a long time ago." She stood, tucked the file under her arm and gathered her one-woman picnic. First Brenda June brought up the fire, and now Pratt was bringing up the arrest. Two separate incidents, but both had Grady in common. The first had made her feel closer to him. The second had made her break up with him.

"Yeah, it was a long time ago." The sheriff waved a careless hand. "So was The Funk Brothers' breakup. Doesn't mean the pain is gone."

"I forgave him. I'm a law enforcement officer now, not a lovesick little girl."

"You're an investigator with emotional ties to the family of the suspect you're investigating. Forgiving is not forgetting."

He had a point. And, it seemed, an agenda.

Charity stalked to the door and turned back to make her own point. Plus her hands were full and she couldn't let herself out. "You don't seem to have a problem with me arresting my own family."

"You don't like your own family."

Another good point. She tipped her head. "Are you asking me to step aside?"

He took his time getting to his feet. "I'm asking you to tell me you can handle this."

"Well, then." She spread her feet in a no-nonsense stance that would probably look more intimidating if she wasn't clutching a Pop-Tart. "I can handle this."

Good Lord, let it be true.

"That's good," he said. "'Cause you'll be handling most of it on your own."

Coffee sloshed in her cup as her hand jerked. "What does that mean?" Oh, crap. "Are you retiring *now?*"

He shook his head.

"Then what?"

"Dix is quitting the force."

*   *   *

THIS TIME CHARITY WAS the one tracking Brenda June to the bathroom. The dispatcher stood staring at her reflection in the mirror while water gushed from the tap. Charity turned it off, leaned into the nearest stall, grabbed a handful of toilet paper, and shoved it at Brenda June. "Your mascara's running."

Dispatch accepted the wad of tissue but kept her gaze on the mirror, tipping her chin left and then right. "I'm thinking about letting my hair grow out. What do you think?"

"I think if you let it grow out, it'll be longer. Did you know about Dix?"

Brenda June went limp, and the reflection of her eyes turned sympathetic. "He wanted to tell you himself."

"He didn't."

"He's a man."

Charity swallowed, but it did nothing to ease the stinging in her chest. "Do you know why he's leaving?"

"He didn't say." Brenda June turned and patted her on the shoulder. "The only reason I know he's leaving in the first place is because I handled his paperwork."

"I'll bet his wife's behind it." Charity leaned back against the sink beside Dispatch, and together they stared morosely at the "Wash your hands or you will get sick and no one will have sex with you" sign on the faded turquoise door of the stall facing them.

"In the end, it's his decision," Brenda June said gently. "Dix has been with us longer than you have, so as hard as this is for you, imagine how he's feeling."

Did a so-called friend who refused to let you wallow in self-pity serve any purpose other than to make you feel worse? "You're supposed to coax me away from the edge, not shove me toward it." Charity pushed off from the sink and leaned into the stall again, this time grabbing a handful of tissue for herself. "Damn it, I'm going to miss that man."

"Me, too. We all will. As soon as things calm down around here, we'll start planning a kick-butt going away party."

With a choked laugh, Charity scrubbed at her face. "I have a strong feeling things are going to get worse before they get better."

Brenda June turned back to the mirror and dabbed at the black smears under her eyes. "You're only allowed to feel sorry for yourself for one more minute, and then you have to go back to feeling sorry for me."

Charity sighed. Sentimental, Dispatch was not. Except when it came to Sheriff Clarkson Pratt.

"So what do you think?" Brenda June plucked at her stunted strands of hair. "Let it grow out?"

Charity linked her hands behind her head and walked around the dispatcher, considering her from every angle. "Since when do you care what anyone else thinks?"

"I'm a woman. Of course I care what other people think. That's the problem." Her chin jutted. "My hair is too short and everyone forgets I'm a woman."

87

"Everyone?" Charity lowered her hands to her hips. "Or someone in particular?"

Brenda June rearranged the tissue in her hands, sniffed, and dropped her face into the pile of scented three-ply, which would have been one-ply if she and Charity hadn't agreed to take turns buying their own bathroom supplies. When Brenda June spoke, her voice was muffled by a cushiony, cloud-like softness. "The election's in a few months, and after that he'll retire, and what'll he do then? There won't be anyone around to remind him to take his medicine or pay his electric bill or bake him coconut key lime and mango cheesecake decorated with those tiny umbrellas. Not the pink ones, though. He hates the pink ones." She started to sob.

Charity wanted to laugh, cry, and knock two heads together at the same time. She smoothed her palm up and down the other woman's narrow back. Brenda June's spine felt knobby beneath her knit sweater. "You've been in love with Clarkson Pratt for ten years now and his wife's been dead the last two. Why don't you ask him out?"

"He's my boss. And he thinks I'm too young."

"Did he say that?"

"He didn't have to." She lifted her head and stared miserably into the mirror. "Remember when Big Mike asked me out? Clarkson said dating out of your age bracket was like using a frayed four-weight to catch an Alaskan salmon."

Charity snagged another batch of tissues and nudged Brenda June to throw away the sodden mess she continued to clutch. "What does that even mean?"

"Who knows, but it can't be good." She fluttered her fingers near her mouth. "His lip was all tangled when he said it."

"Maybe he was jealous."

The dispatcher blew her nose. "Why hasn't he said anything?"

"Why haven't you?"

Brenda June peered in the mirror again, wiping her face with the fresh wad of tissue. "Why should I listen to a woman who's given her high school sweetheart the cold shoulder for twelve years because he once pissed her off?"

"Pissed me off? He did a hell of a lot more than—" Belatedly Charity registered the gleam in the other woman's red-rimmed eyes. Drawing a breath, she brushed at the front of her uniform shirt, attacking imaginary crumbs—or maybe not so imaginary, considering all the snacking she'd been doing—and giving her pulse time to decelerate. "Nice try, Brenda June. And I did talk to him back then."

"How many times?"

"Once."

"To tell him...?"

"That I wasn't talking to him."

Brenda June sighed. "Good thing I'm too tired to kick your butt." She opened the door and frowned at Charity over her shoulder. "I don't get it. Trudy said you and Grady were inseparable during high school. With a history like that, it's a wonder you two aren't interested in trying again."

"We let each other down." Charity offered a feeble shrug. "We did it so thoroughly that once was enough."

*   *   *

CHARITY STARED DOWN AT the bright red box in her hand. The label wavered in and out of focus and she sighed. Did she even have the energy to stir eggs and oil into a brownie mix? If she made coffee first, then yeah. She shouldn't have either, but after the crap day she'd had, sleep was pretty much off the table, anyway.

Following that disaster of a meeting with Pratt, she'd been desperate to get out of the office to resume the investigation and remind herself why she loved the job. Her first stop had been Kate's place, but the teacher hadn't been around to answer questions.

Charity slid the box of brownie mix back onto the counter and wandered over to the fridge. She stared at the naked surfer magnet Mo had brought her back from San Diego—a souvenir she'd enjoy more if the surfer were male.

Since Scott and Sarah had already been hooking up, it didn't make sense that the real estate agent would break up with her teenaged lover to cultivate a relationship with his father. Unless

Sarah had hoped for a commitment, or Scott had asked her to. Yet during his interview, Scott had made it clear the relationship was casual. Either Sarah shook off Drew for his own good, or because she had yet another lover in the wings — maybe someone she wanted on a more-than-casual basis. Charity hoped Kate could suggest a name or two. Right after she coughed up the name of her own lover.

Or…what if Drew had told Sarah about Allison Young's threat and Sarah had backed off rather than provide the girl a reason to hurt herself? Or what if Drew had lied, and he was the one who'd called it quits? If Sarah refused to go along with that, would Drew have been desperate enough to kill her?

Crap. Could Sarah have been blackmailing Drew? Charity needed to check with Mo, see if he'd discovered anything irregular with Sarah's accounts. Though deposits could be gifts from Scott. Charity chewed on the inside of her cheek. Had Sarah used Drew as a means of getting to his father? Had she been trying to hook a sugar daddy, or was this some convoluted plot to get back at Justine for some reason?

Charity made a face at the model-thin naked surfer girl and yanked open the refrigerator door. A little too hard — the jars lined up under the egg compartment made a clinking, rattling fuss. She snatched up two eggs and shut the door. More rattling — did she really need three jars of olives? She rubbed her nose with the back of her hand. What she did need was to find out what Scott had been up to the night of the murder. It seemed far-fetched that he'd kill his lover and let his own son take the fall.

She set aside the eggs and consulted the box. Vegetable oil. Did she even have any? Her phone blasted the opening notes to the *Hawaii Five-0* theme song and she jumped. Served her right for allowing Brenda June to pick her own ringtone. She hustled over to the basket on the table by the front door and scooped up her phone.

"You just pulled a double shift," Charity said. "Shouldn't you be sleeping?"

"I had an epiphany. For Morrissey's birthday next month? Peanut butter and jelly cheesecake."

"Oh, dear Lord." Charity wandered back to the kitchen in search of vegetable oil.

"I still have a jar of the boysenberry preserves Trudy put up last year." Brenda June made a pensive humming noise. "Or do you think he'd prefer huckleberry?"

Charity squinted at the pale gold dregs of oil in the bottom of the plastic bottle. Thank God she only needed a quarter cup. "Why would you do that to an innocent cheesecake?"

Brenda June sniffed. "Mo will like it."

"Mo has no taste."

"Says the woman who thinks adding colored marshmallows to a breakfast cereal makes it gourmet."

Charity hovered at the sink and made a face at her reflection in the window—careless hair, faded tee, saggy jammie pants. She stuck her tongue out at herself. "Presentation is everything."

"Says the woman who spends as much time on her makeup as Dix spends on his hair."

"Why so mean?"

"Why so sensitive?"

Charity turned her back to the window and leaned against the beveled strip of counter that rimmed the sink. "I'm sorry about Pratt."

"I didn't call to talk about him." Brenda June's weighty sigh sounded like she'd huffed it through puckered lips. "Okay, I did, but I've changed my mind. Tell me what's up with you."

"I lied to him."

Silence on the other end of the phone. Charity waited, peering down at the unpolished toes that peeked out of her flip-flops. She waited some more.

Finally Brenda June huffed air through her nose in a world-weary laugh. "Spill it, babycakes."

Charity pushed away from the sink and poked at the eggs waiting on the counter. "He's worried I won't win the election."

"He said that?"

"He didn't have to. This thing with Grady—"

Brenda June chuckled with satisfaction. "So you admit there's a thing."

"There was a thing."

"And how big was this thing?"

Charity gasped a laugh, spun toward the oven and jabbed at the "On" button. "Brenda June."

"Sorry. Go ahead. How did you lie?"

After squinting at the back of the box, Charity pressed buttons until the target temperature read three hundred twenty-five. "I told him I wouldn't leave the department if I didn't win. That I'd stay and work with Bloom."

"So you're not staying?"

Charity flinched at the piercing outrage in her friend's voice. "I...can't."

"Why can't you? 'Cause you're afraid he'll talk us into buying decaf for the coffee mess? 'Cause anyone named Oliver triggers painful *Brady Bunch* memories? Or did you have a mad, passionate love affair, and now you're—" Brenda June gulped. "Oh, good grief," she whispered. "That's it, isn't it?"

"'Fraid so. Though I wouldn't call two nights an affair. Okay, maybe it was three."

"But...he's married."

"He wasn't at the time." Charity unearthed a square pan from the cabinet next to the sink and clanged it onto the counter. "And thanks a whole hell of a lot for thinking I'd mess around with someone's husband."

"Wait. The man's been married for what, three, four years? Where's the problem?" Brenda June made a squeaking sound. "You don't still have feelings for him."

"Lord, no."

"Good. Because Grady West—"

"Has nothing to do with this." With a jerk of her hip, Charity bumped a drawer closed and tapped a wooden spoon at the air above the brownie mix. Nope, no magic here. The brownies remained unmade. She set the spoon aside and braced a hand on the counter. "Grady has nothing to do with anything. But I can't imagine Bloom taking me seriously. The man has seen me naked."

Brenda June snorted. "Do you really think that matters after all this time?"

"I'm not sure I want to stay and find out."

"If you're leaving, you should point your car west. I hear Seattle's lovely this time of year."

"Nice try, Dispatch. Good night."

A husky chuckle sounded through the line. "G'night, blondie."

With a smile, Charity set aside her phone, even as her brain continued to sift through the events of the day.

Since Kate hadn't been around, Charity had joined Dix at Sarah's town house. There they'd avoided talking about his departure while unearthing evidence of multiple lovers in the forms of various articles of men's clothing and a collection of handwritten notes ranging from sweet to smoldering. Nothing, though, that would lead them to a killer. Then Sarah's parents arrived, and the ensuing question-and-answer session was more emotional than enlightening. Halfway through the interview, Sarah's mother started hyperventilating. Her husband panicked and slapped her, which kicked off a loud argument and a nosebleed when she slapped him back.

Afterward Dix interviewed Hampton and Roberta West while Charity followed up with Sarah's coworkers. Neither of her fellow real estate agents had much to offer besides speculation about the future of Tarrant Properties and a coupon for waiving closing costs on a thirty-year mortgage. The owner, Keith Tarrant, had been out of the office. Of course no one knew anything about any unethical transactions.

Back at the station, Charity finally confronted Dix about his plans to leave. Her suspicions had been correct. He'd told her his wife couldn't handle living in the country anymore.

"She says it is too quiet and boring, and she's miserable. It's my fault, so I have to fix it," Dix had said. "I have an apartment lined up four blocks from the station. She will be happier in the city."

"What about you?"

"I will do anything she needs to get better."

"Except sell real estate."

"Except that."

Charity had tried but failed to smile. "When are you leaving?"

"Thirty days."

"You couldn't tell me?"

He'd looked away.

"I'll miss you, too," she'd whispered.

They'd hugged, him stiffly, her fervently, while a frigid misery sliced through her chest.

So, yes. Crap day indeed. They'd spent the next several hours conducting interviews, analyzing forensic evidence, writing reports, and spit-balling theories over leftover muffins and some god-awful herbal tea Brenda June had disinterred from the deep, dark recesses of the supply closet.

Hence the current need for coffee. And brownies. Since Charity had skipped dinner, she fully intended to fortify those brownies with chocolate chips. Lots and lots of chocolate chips.

The sound of the doorbell interrupted her semisweet fantasy. With a resigned sigh she slid the bag of chocolate chips back onto the shelf. Saved from a self-induced carb coma. Still...she frowned up at her blueberry waffle wall clock. Who'd be visiting at ten o'clock at night?

No one with good intentions, that was for certain. Maybe the sheriff wanted to deliver part two of his no-room-for-lust-in-law-enforcement lecture. Or maybe Lucas hoped to deliver more threats while gloating over what he'd done to Clarabelle.

She put the eggs back in the fridge. On her way out of the kitchen, she snagged her Sig Sauer from its holster and peered down the darkened hallway toward the front door. Yellow light from the old-fashioned fixture spilled over broad shoulders and neatly trimmed, dark brown hair.

She should have known.

6

WHO IS IT?" SHE called out anyway, and could have kicked herself for not putting more pissed off in her tone.

"It's the plumber. I've come to fix the sink."

With a soundless snort and a depressingly giddy tumble in her belly, Charity relaxed her grip on her pistol and opened the door. "You're smarter than this."

"I would have gone around back, but I didn't want to get shot." His gaze locked on to her service weapon as cool night air swirled around them. "Looks like it wouldn't have made a difference."

"Why are you here?"

"I missed the housewarming." He started forward. When she didn't step back, he asked, "You going to let me in?"

"Considering how much I value my career? No."

Grady nodded at her pistol. "Can you at least put that thing away?"

"I like to leave my options open." She cocked her head. "I repeat. Why are you here?"

"Peace offering." He leaned sideways, reaching for something he'd propped against the siding. He cleared his throat as he thrust it at her.

A high-end box of chocolates. Nuts and chews only. The man was diabolical.

"Peace offering, huh?" Charity shook her head, even as a shiver rattled her bones. Her toes curled into her flip-flops. Why wasn't he wearing a jacket? "More like bribe."

"Whatever works."

"This won't."

"You're very suspicious."

"Keeps me alive."

Grady's face went stark. It pushed her back a step, and he was in.

She heaved a breath and shut the door. "I'm not discussing the case with you."

He tossed the box of candy onto the sofa. "Are you enjoying this? Being the one who gets to call the shots?"

"Absolutely," Charity said, and she could see from his face that he'd expected her to deny it.

"I remember you saying you'd forgiven me," he said.

"And that was true." Without looking at him, she stalked toward the corner cabinet. Well, shuffled, really—what else could she manage in flip-flops? "How could I not? We both made mistakes."

"You refused to see me when I came back to visit."

"You've been back maybe seven times in twelve years." Her cheeks heated when she realized how that might sound.

"But who's counting?" Grady moved closer, and his gaze narrowed on her blush. "You don't want to talk about the past. I get it. But how can either of us get that closure you mentioned if we don't?"

Crap. Might as well get it all out there. Maybe then they could move past…well, the past…and he could finally see her as a deputy sheriff instead of an ex-girlfriend. Maybe then she could concentrate on her job. You know, that thing that paid her bills and made her feel useful?

That thing that had saved her life, in more ways than one.

Charity opened the top drawer of the cabinet and placed her weapon inside, then turned back to Grady. She barely resisted folding her arms. "I didn't want to see you, or rehash what happened because I wasn't sure I could stop myself from doing one of two things—kicking your ass or crying all over your shirt. Either way I'd end up embarrassing us both."

She still might.

He quirked an eyebrow. "If you wanted to kick my ass after forgiving me, I can only imagine what you wanted to do beforehand."

"It involved a car battery and nipple clamps," Charity said with a straight face. At his gratifying wince, she jerked a shoulder. "It took some time to get over you — to get over us — but I did, and you did, and now it's ancient history."

"Is it?" Grady gave his head a shake. "Two weeks after two state troopers are killed in the line of duty, you announced your plan to sign up for the police academy. How was I supposed to react? We had an agreement. After graduation, you leave town with me."

"You were headed for college. It wouldn't have worked."

"We'll never know, will we?"

"*I* know." She moved her arms behind her back and gripped the edge of the cabinet. "Because rather than respect my decision, you tried to keep me out of the academy by getting me arrested."

Grady's gaze remained somber, but his mouth twitched. "It didn't take much to convince you to slash my mother's tires."

"I was all for discouraging her from drinking and driving. It made sense at the time. What didn't make sense was you disappearing when the sheriff showed up."

Grady exhaled, and pushed his fingers deep into the back pockets of his jeans. "You must have hated me."

"I couldn't believe you set me up," she whispered. "I trusted you with my dreams, and you used them to screw me over."

He flinched. That he still carried remnants of remorse both softened and satisfied her. At the same time, she refused to consider how easily those lingering feelings could lure her right back into an emotional nightmare.

Charity let her arms drop to her sides. Her shoulders ached. "Still, when Pratt was putting the cuffs on me, I saw your face. Your relief outweighed your guilt, and that's when I knew you'd done it to keep me safe. You were so determined to get me out of town, you were willing to risk everything we had. Everything we were to each other. Misguided or not, that kind of devotion scared the hell out of me."

"That's why you called it quits?" Grady took a step closer, and stroked a finger down her cheek. "Because I loved you too much?"

"I thought I knew what fear meant. The way I grew up...." Her shrug was anything but elegant. "Then you pulled that stupid-ass stunt and I panicked. Oh, I hated you, all right. But not for playing me. For escaping Becker County. And I hated myself even more for being too chicken to go with you."

He looked startled. "If you had to do it over again?"

"I'd do the same thing. Only for different reasons." Charity edged away from the cabinet, and from Grady. "The people we were, the things we wanted...it would have ended badly, no matter what."

"I'll say it again." Grady tracked her escape attempt with his body. "We don't know that."

She pushed distance into her eyes. "What ifs will get us nowhere. How about we concentrate on Sarah Huffman's murder instead?"

He hesitated, then offered a crisp nod. "Right. So tell me about Drew."

"I said 'we,' but I meant 'me.' Let me concentrate on my job while you—"

"What? Sit on my ass all day? Play Cribbage with Peyton while Justine and my parents drink themselves to oblivion and you and your sheriff's posse build a case against Drew?"

Charity hauled in a breath, slowly filling her lungs with air. "If you're implying we'd sacrifice someone for the sake of a conviction, then you can go straight to hell. The box of chocolates, however, stays here."

*   *   *

GRADY DIDN'T CATCH WORD one of her response. He'd gone into lockdown. His heart, his lungs, even his brain had stopped working, and all he could do was stare. *Christ.* She'd been waving that gun around, and even after she'd put it away, he hadn't paid much attention to what she was wearing.

Then she'd inhaled.

The clingy, long-sleeved tee she wore over plaid pajama bottoms was nothing like her bulky uniform shirt. It clung to her tits like soap suds to wet skin, and son of a bitch, didn't that spark an image guaranteed to have his dick spring to attention. When she exhaled, the power kicked back on, and the left side of his brain started tabulating the odds of getting her into bed while the right side loitered around images of sweat-slick, ivory flesh writhing beneath him. Not realizing that both sides of his brain were otherwise occupied, Charity kept pushing out the words. He knew because he saw her mouth moving, and there was a throaty humming in the background.

Grady started to sweat.

He didn't remember doing it, but somehow he'd managed to peel his gaze off Charity's chest and angle his body away as he pretended an interest in a group of framed photos on the wall. It didn't stop him from picturing her naked and it didn't keep his dick from thickening. In desperation, he pictured Clarkson Pratt in his tighty-whiteys. Instantly his junk recoiled. *Thank you, Jesus.* At least he wouldn't be walking around with a permanent zipper imprint.

Slowly he turned to face her again. "What?"

She stopped mid-syllable and stared. "What do you mean, *what?* Didn't you hear anything I just said?"

He shrugged and hid a smile as pique reddened her cheeks. He waved a hand at the four photos, a seasonal series of the flowering cherry that had fronted the courthouse for as long as he could remember. "Did you take these?"

Charity's posture lost a little of its rigidity, and she shook her head. "Dix did. Detective Ironmaker. Beautiful, aren't they?" She saw something in his face she must not have liked because she scowled. "I'm not the enemy, Grady."

"So let me help with the case. Drew's future is at stake. I need you to let me help him."

"I need you to leave me alone so I can do my job. If Drew is innocent, we'll prove it."

"That right there. That 'if.' That's what worries me."

Charity's expression hardened. "I'm not doing this with you. I have a murder to solve, a murder you have rather a large stake in, and all you're doing is distracting me."

"Maybe I'm trying to distract myself." Grady scrubbed the back of his neck. "You're short-staffed. Use me."

As soon as he said the last two words, his groin tightened all over again. *Dammit.*

"You want to help? Stay out of it." Charity marched back to the front door and yanked it wide. A white-winged moth fluttered around the circular light fixture. Charity turned off the light, plunging the narrow hallway into darkness. "Good night, Grady."

"You should get a storm door."

"You should get going."

He should. It was late, and she needed her sleep. Still he found himself wanting to linger, to explore the whys and wherefores behind the woman she'd become. She'd gotten curvier. More confident. Instead of Ivory soap, she smelled like apples and gun oil.

He hitched a thumb over his shoulder, toward the sofa. "Can we sit for a while? Drink some coffee? Eat some chocolate? Catch up?"

"It's late," she said.

He doubted she was referring to bedtime. "But we finally have a chance to talk without the risk of being interrupted by psychotic family members or curious coworkers. Speaking of which, I should apologize. The way my father spoke to you today..."

"He's scared. The badge makes me an easy target. I may not like it, but I won't judge him for it. Who knows how I'd act under the same circumstances?"

"That's generous." She'd done a lot of growing up. He wasn't sure he could say the same about himself. "So...chocolate?"

Charity shut the door. "Fifteen minutes. And you'll have to make do with ice water."

"Make do? It's my favorite."

Grady didn't know how they'd made it from polar icecap to polite in a matter of minutes, but soon they were settled on the sofa with the box of chocolates and a tentative truce between them.

Charity eyed him over the top of a heavy, ridged glass that looked like the kind diners used for milkshakes. His own glass had a faded picture of the Trix rabbit on it. He'd yet to notice anything in the house that matched.

He liked that. Valerie had insisted on coordinating everything. Their bath towels had matched their bed sheets had matched the sticky paper lining the kitchen shelves.

"So." Charity tipped her glass at him, seeming to scramble for something to say. "You're a high finance guy."

"I work in finance. After staring at numbers all day, I may get dizzy, but I'm rarely high."

Her smile was reluctant. "I guess that's one thing we can thank our parents for. Saving us from addiction—to cigarettes and alcohol, anyway. I can't seem to give up caffeine. Chocolate-covered almonds, either. What's your vice?"

* * *

CHARITY SAW IT IN his eyes, and her pulse started to thump. He was going to say something inappropriate. Something dark and dangerous and wildly sexy—

"SpongeBob SquarePants."

She blinked.

"That goofy little dimply guy who has a pet snail and hangs out with a pink starfish?" That swaggering gleam in his eyes had returned, backlit by his anxiety for Drew. "Whenever it's on, I can't look away. Sad, right?"

"That's one word for it." Dear Lord, she had to get this man out of here. He'd exchanged his business suit for a well-worn pair of jeans and a navy V-neck sweater that matched his eyes, and the way he sprawled against the corner of the sofa, one arm along the back, legs spread, package an enticing bulge, made her want to crawl across the cushions, straddle his lap and...do things.

She gulped at her water, choked a little, tried to recall what the hell they'd been talking about. Finance. Right.

"You're a stockbroker?"

"Financial planner. Weird, since I always hated math, but I took a tax course in college and..." He shrugged.

"It all added up?"

He rolled his eyes.

"Figures you'd end up running your own business," she said. "You never did take orders very well."

"Depended on who was giving 'em and how hard they were breathing at the time."

Charity's face flashed hot. The challenge in his gaze told her he knew more than embarrassment had inspired the flush, but the rush of arousal was tempered with sadness. Their easy banter brought back too many painful memories. And sooner or later — sooner would be better, since she had to get some sleep — he'd steer the conversation back to the case, and she'd be forced to kick him out.

Grady's gaze turned solemn. "Are you going to ask me?"

"About?"

"My ex-wife. My divorce. My son."

Oh, hell, no. She stood. "I don't need to know any of that. We're not trying to bond here, West. Let's not make this personal."

"Oh, we're way beyond personal, Bishop. You know all about my nephew's love life, you know my ex-brother-in-law is allergic to monogamy, and about two minutes ago you wanted my tongue in your mouth."

He knew damned well she'd wanted a lot more than that. "True."

His jaw muscles worked. "What is wrong with you?"

"What do you mean? I'm agreeing with you."

"Cut it the hell out." Grady surged to his feet and rounded the coffee table.

She scowled at him, tempted to go for her pistol again.

"Every time I get a good fury worked up," he said, "you say something to defuse it."

"You're mad because I'm not letting you be mad?"

"I'm not mad, I'm unsettled."

He didn't look unsettled as he moved toward her. He looked determined.

102

And good enough to eat.

"I'm trained to defuse tricky situations," Charity burst out, more to remind herself than to warn him.

He kept right on coming. He stopped a few feet away, and cocked his head. "You want to hear about the whole single father thing?"

"Why? You think if I feel sorry for you, I'll let you grope me?"

"I think 'cop a feel' is more appropriate."

What was next, handcuff jokes? And didn't that spark a mental image. Before her own imagination could work against her, she strode to the front door and fumbled for the switch to turn the light back on.

Grady followed her outside, lingering in the doorway long enough to turn the porch light off again. He gazed down at her through the sudden shadows, expression masked as her eyes adjusted to the dark. When her vision steadied, it was her pulse that went all rickety. The intensity of his gaze, the way he stood with his fingers in his back pockets, the increasingly ragged rhythm of his breathing took her back to the last moments of their first few dates, a neighbor's car idling at the curb while Grady stared at Charity's mouth and she stared back, wondering when he'd find the nerve to kiss her.

Until he was old enough to drive, Grady had paid an older man who lived down the street to drive them to the movies or to Jerzy's or along the dark back roads of Becker County because his parents would never have agreed to let their precious progeny date someone like Charity Bishop.

And oh, dear Lord, had they gone ballistic once they'd figured it out.

A screech owl sounded off in a series of hoots growing closer and closer together, like the last few frenzied bounces of a rubber ball dropped on concrete. The after-dark chill drifted onto the porch. Charity shuddered. Her bare toes curled, and within the lacy confines of her bra, her nipples beaded. She found herself leaning toward Grady's chest and the solid promise of heat. A pair of headlights swept the porch, for an instant revealing the stark need on his face. A need that was no doubt mirrored on hers.

Need for an ex-boyfriend whose family may or may not be implicated in a murder investigation.

With a silent gasp, Charity shoved an arm back through the doorway and slapped at the porch light. A yellow shine shoved at the shadows.

"You need to go," she managed. She backed up against the wrought iron banister that bordered the steps and followed the downward slant with her hip until she landed in the yard. "Thank you for the chocolates."

Slowly Grady followed her down the steps, hands still in his pockets. "No good-night kiss?"

"What do you think?"

"I think you can't blame a guy for trying."

"You can when there's an ulterior motive."

"No ulterior motive. Just complications." He angled his head. "If not a kiss, then how about a joke? For old times' sake?"

"I don't think so."

"Run out of new material? Or have you lost your sense of humor?"

"Fine. You asked for it."

"I asked for a kiss, too."

Charity rolled her eyes and thought for a moment. "A man bought a new range of Olympic condoms. 'There are three colors,' he told his wife. 'Gold, silver, and bronze.' She asked him what color he was going to wear that night. 'Gold, of course,' he answered proudly. 'Why don't you wear silver?' she said. 'It would be nice if you came second for a change.'"

Grady chuckled, and the sound launched a sparkling warmth that tumbled through her veins.

He sobered. "Macintosh," he said.

"I'm sorry?"

He pulled his hands free of his pockets. Before she could back away, he closed the distance between them, reached out, and slid his fingers gently through the tips of her hair. "You smell like Macintosh apples."

Charity started backing toward the driveway, leading him toward his rental car like one big, giant breadcrumb. Her flip-flops slapped a wary rhythm against the bottom of her feet. "Those complications you mentioned? I don't have time for those. Especially your brand. More than one person around here believes I can't work on this case and remain objective."

"That include you?"

"Funny."

"I wasn't trying to be." Grady trailed after her. The light spilling from the windows of the house next door lent a roguish gleam to his gaze. "Aren't you curious? If it's still the same between us?"

She wanted to say no. Knew she had to say no. But her gaze remained fixed on his mouth, and her lips trembled.

The deep, knowing chuckle that rumbled out of his chest set off a humming in her blood. He moved closer, and she continued to back away until she came up against a tree. The tree. The only tree in her front yard.

The perfect excuse to stop running. Charity pressed her back to the massive trunk, her breath coming faster, her palms slick as they scraped over bark. Okay, so she was curious. Scratch that. She ached with curiosity. The overpowering instinct that it would be like it always had been between them—disorienting and fierce and uninhibited and hotter than a rifle barrel after an hour's target practice—made her panties go damp and her thighs loose.

Closer, she begged silently. But he stood firm, damn him. She pushed her shoulders back and tipped her pelvis forward, her breath practically ripping out of her throat as she imagined him fucking her against the tree.

Down, girl. They were negotiating a kiss. Nothing more. She wasn't even sure he'd get to that.

"You let me trap you on purpose," Grady said softly. "So you can blame me later. I'm not playing that game. You want a kiss? Come and get it."

Charity almost whimpered aloud at his take-charge tone. When they'd started dating in high school, she'd been the more sexually experienced. He'd never judged her, had actually been so turned on by her boldness—in and out of bed—that he'd been more than content to let her take the lead. She'd been all over that. She'd never been able to get enough of him.

He was right. Assertiveness was arousing. By the time her eyes locked with his, the heat of long-hidden lust had flashed across every nerve ending in her body, and her lungs vibrated with an urgent need for oxygen. Grady was right about the game playing, too. They both deserved better. With him she'd always been candid, always told him exactly what she'd felt, what she'd needed.

Except for that fiasco with his mother's car, when he'd had her arrested. Then she'd veiled the pain of his betrayal with an it's-just-as-well-because-we-had-no-future speech. It had hurt like hell delivering the eulogy for something that was far from dead. But she'd always known, from the moment he'd sent the first smile her way, that an ending was inevitable. A small part of her had been grateful he'd provided the perfect out.

Charity licked her lips now and watched his eyes flame and his arms press against his sides. He refused to budge. One eyebrow lifted into an arrogant arch.

He'd gotten smart over the years, and she was about to do something very, very dumb.

The petty side of her wanted to make a break for the house and leave his sorry ass out in the cold. The self-respecting side of her had never managed to refuse a dare. Which he very well knew. The excitement that blazed through her was something she hadn't felt in…well, in a dozen years.

She lurched forward, taking three steps before settling her hands on Grady's chest. He inhaled, muscles tensing beneath her palms. Power. Warmth. The smell of — Her eyes stretched open. He'd always smelled like rain. Was it her imagination, or did he smell more like the ocean now? Salt and sunshine. Seagulls and sand.

For some reason it pissed her off.

He cupped her elbows, slid his hands up her arms and over her shoulders, splayed his fingers in her hair and tipped her head back. "Your expression is making me nervous," he said gruffly. "I don't know whether you're about to kiss me or chew on me."

"Can't I do both?" Charity clapped her hands to his head and pulled. Their mouths collided. Opened. Fused. A hot, heady rush of delight had her moaning into his mouth. *There you are.*

His lips were firm and demanding, his taste both exotic and familiar, satisfying and at the same time stoking a riotous craving she'd thought tamed long ago. His ragged breath warmed her face, and his skin beneath her palms was smooth — he'd shaved before coming over, and that tiny detail was more seductive than the taste of chocolate on his lips.

With a rumbling groan, Grady changed the angle of the kiss, his fingers urgent on her scalp and his tongue wasting no time getting naughty with hers. She wriggled even tighter against the muscled hardness of his chest, and his hands skimmed down to her ass and pulled her flush against the thick length of his rigid cock.

Oh, dear Lord. Bolts of white-hot lightning zinged all the way down to her toes, and Charity was gripped by one long, relentless, bone-shaking shudder. She broke free of his mouth and dropped her face against his neck, sucking in the scents of sea and sweat, desperate to ease the burn of too little air.

Of too much sensation.

She'd forgotten. God help her, she'd forgotten. His kiss was intense and electric, and guaranteed to drive her insensible with need. Why had she thought this was a good idea?

Because you weren't thinking at all.

Grady's hands glided up her back and his arms tightened as he hugged her. She let her own hands trail down his chest. One palmed his heart while the other grabbed a fistful of his sweater.

"You okay?" he murmured.

"Wow," she managed. Regret surged. A hot, aching slide of nostalgia that pricked at the backs of her eyes. More. She wanted more. More cuddling. More kissing. More time.

More Grady.

Charity parted her lips and touched her tongue to his skin. He jumped, then growled, low in his throat. A reckless joy sparked and shimmered beneath her skin, heating her from the inside out. His body shifted, his hands finding her shoulders and squeezing, as if warning her to brace for impact. She licked her lips in anticipation of his greedy mouth on hers and lifted her chin.

Footsteps on pavement. The deliberate clearing of a throat.

Not again.

Charity squeezed her eyes shut, muscles locked as she braced for the ugly bluster of her brother's voice. Except Lucas wouldn't keep his distance. He'd charge in and start swinging. She opened her eyes as Grady stepped away from her. The consternation on his face made her belly go hollow. Slowly, cautiously, she turned.

Crap on a cracker.

Sheriff Clarkson Pratt stood in her driveway, arms crossed, head tilted at an oh-yeah-you're-fucked angle. "Deputy Bishop. Please tell me you're experimenting with some newfangled interrogation technique."

*   *   *

CHARITY WATCHED THE TAILLIGHTS of Grady's rented sedan flash an apology before disappearing around a curve. Reluctantly she turned back to her boss, her chilled feet slipping and sliding in flip-flops damp with dew. The screech owl hooted again, this time the sound more mocking than mysterious. Charity opened her mouth, but Pratt didn't wait for the words.

"What the hell were you thinking?" he demanded. "Wait. Don't answer that. Because we both know you weren't." He snatched his ball cap off his head and smacked it against the thigh of his baggy jeans. Now that he'd steered her over into the porch light, the five-o'clock shadow that darkened his jaw and the fury that set fire to his eyes was visible.

"You're a damned fine cop and a solid investigator. You're in charge of your first murder case, and it involves the most prominent family in three counties. On top of that, you have a decent chance of being elected sheriff at thirty. Thirty. Yet here you are, willing to give all that up so you can enjoy some goddamned hanky-panky with your high school squeeze?"

Before the sheriff's untimely arrival, the lights in the house next door had gone out as her neighbors settled into bed. Now a light reappeared in the bedroom window overlooking Charity's driveway.

She winced and gestured toward her front door. "Maybe we should —"

"I'm not finished. When you go down, you'll take the entire Becker County Sheriff's Department down with you. That doesn't seem to matter to you. Explain it to me. Why are you so hell-bent on going down?" Pratt made a choking sound, and dragged a hand across his face. "That didn't come out right. But you know what I mean."

Yeah, she was happy to let that one go. Charity gripped the balustrade behind her and leaned back against her hands. "I wasn't planning on sleeping with him. He came over to offer to help with the investigation."

"How is that better? Either way you're screwed."

"You said it yourself. We're understaffed. We could use the help."

"Not from a civilian. He's feeding you that line of bullshit because he can't keep his hands off you. And vice versa, it seems."

"I'm sorry you're disappointed." He had every right to be. She wasn't happy with herself, either. Especially since her regret wasn't all about the risk to her job.

Part of it came from the squandered opportunity to feel Grady up. Like a few hours after a breakfast buffet, when you struggle to understand why you hadn't snagged just one more cinnamon roll. Her palms still tingled with the need to cup his muscled ass, to stroke the gratifying solidity of his—

"At least you're not offering excuses." Pratt took his time settling his hat back on his head. "I'm not blind. I know it hasn't been easy for you, having him here. But he's not here to stay. You and your career are, as long as you can refrain from…interrogating…Grady West. You deserve to be sheriff, Charity. You've worked hard for this."

The judgment in Pratt's voice had given way to concern. She sank down onto the cold concrete steps as his words finally penetrated the fog of her naked-Grady fantasies. Her boss was right. It wasn't only her job at stake here.

Cold seeped through the seat of her jammies, restoring reason and ushering in shame. She shivered, and tipped her head back.

"Did something happen?" she asked. At his blank stare, she got to her feet. "Why are you here?" Third time tonight she'd asked that question. Somehow she doubted Pratt's reason was the same as Grady's.

I missed the housewarming.

They'd missed a lot. And after he left, they'd miss a lot more. They each had lives to return to. Eventually Grady would get on a plane, and Charity would get back to the election. They could give each other a lot of pleasure in the meantime. Did they have to miss out on that, too?

"Yes," Pratt said.

She faltered. "What?"

"Yes. Something happened. But you're right. It's late. You need your sleep. We'll talk about it later."

Charity hugged herself as he strode toward the pickup he'd parked along the curb. What the hell? She was halfway up the steps when the idea popped.

Had he wanted to discuss Brenda June?

After ten minutes of staring through her bedroom window at the tree that was now guaranteed to play a central role in her nighttime fantasies, Charity brushed her teeth and set the alarm for an ungodly hour—not ungodly enough to allow time for a jog before work, so there was that. She shuffled into the kitchen, put away the brownie mix, and flicked off the light above the sink. And froze.

Movement. She'd seen movement in her back yard. She blinked. Hadn't she?

She gripped the edge of the sink, bent closer to the window, and stared hard at the shadows pressing against the weathered-board fence and the scraggly tree line that separated her house from the two-story rental behind her. Nothing. But someone was out there. She could feel it.

Outrage sent her lunging at the back door. As her fingers clutched the knob, common sense kicked in. She indulged in a few calming breaths, followed by a dash to the hall to retrieve her pistol and an LED flashlight. She turned the living room light off and the bedroom light on. Hopefully whoever was out there would believe she was getting ready for bed. She tucked her phone in the waistband of her jammies. She could call for backup now, but what if it was only Pratt circling back to see whether Grady had circled back?

The next thought set spurs to Charity's pulse. Maybe Grady had returned, and any moment now she'd hear a discreet knock on the back door. The last thing she needed was the humiliation of summoning her fellow cops to what might turn out to be a booty call. Her campaign wouldn't survive it.

And if she had to send Grady away again, she wouldn't survive it.

Still she waited, breath locked in her lungs, ears straining toward the back door. Nothing. Didn't make sense anyway, since whatever she'd seen had been moving away from the house. Maybe waiting for all the lights to go out?

Then she realized. The motion sensor lights hadn't come on. Not the first time the suckers had failed her, but…

She swiveled toward the front. Had the asshole vandal returned, this time with plans to target her Tahoe, which she'd just had washed and waxed?

Oh, hell no.

With a muttered promise of vengeance to Clarabelle and a violent roll of her shoulders, Charity kicked off her flip-flops and slipped quietly outside.

The chill of the dewy grass seared the soles of her feet and she swore, but hunting down her shoes would have taken precious time. She slunk around the side of the house, weapon pointed at the ground, shoulders rigid, gaze roving for any telltale sign of movement. Nothing but the gentle shiver of tall, leggy shrubs ruffled by the wind. No sound but the whispering jangle of leaves and the *whump whump whump* of her own heart.

Just shy of the back corner of the house, she stopped and peered into the back yard, bare except for a rusted pole supporting a birdfeeder and a ramshackle shed that marked the left rear corner of the property. Her right foot found a mud puddle. Cold spiked up through her leg and torso and sliced into her heart. She shuddered. Screw the shoes. Why the hell hadn't she snagged her coat?

She dried the bottom of her foot against her jammie pants and craned her neck. *There.* Was that a shadow near the shed? She blinked again. Maybe it was time for a little LED action.

And maybe she'd better announce herself so she didn't end up with buckshot in her ass. Wouldn't be the first time her idiot neighbor had gone all covert mission on the raccoons who enjoyed tipping over his trashcans.

She stalked the shed. A snuffling sound drifted her way and she almost lowered her weapon. Perfect. She was about to break bad on a possum digging for worms.

"Police," she called out anyway and thumbed on the light. "Step away from the shed, with your hands where I can see them."

More snuffling. She took the corner wide and swore. So much for instinct.

No possum, no raccoon. The noisemaker was a cat. A fat orange tabby that came flying at her face, claws in shred mode. As Charity ducked, she lost her grip on the flashlight. In the tumbling yellow beam she caught a glimpse of a pale face before the human body it belonged to darted away. *Fuck.* She dislodged the hissing cat from her shoulder, snatched up the light, and gave chase, but the shadow was damned fast. Charity found herself in the middle of a night-shrouded street, gun in hand, feet cold and stinging, and no earthly clue whether she'd run off a vandal or a killer.

She slapped a hand to her waist.

To top it all off, she'd lost her phone.

* * *

BY SEVEN THE FOLLOWING morning Charity was at Kate's door, hoping to catch the teacher before she left for school and hating that her own grump factor was at an all-time high. However, little to no sleep combined with self-loathing for letting her intruder escape, a set of cat scratches that stung like hell, and a sad lack of brownies for breakfast was enough to put even Sunshine Barbie in a foul mood.

Mo was sure to be equally cranky. He'd been on call last night, which meant he'd caught her call for assistance. For a solid fifteen minutes he'd lectured her on the meaning of "teamwork." Then he'd bitched for ten more because she hadn't made coffee.

He'd be even more pissed if he found out about the two visitors she hadn't copped to.

Kate answered her door in yoga pants and a pea-green tee that claimed "Life is good." She held a knife coated with peanut butter.

"Charity." Frowning, Kate eyed Charity's uniform. "Everything okay?"

"I have some questions about Sarah. Got a few minutes?"

"Of course." Kate waved her inside. "They didn't call me in today, and I just about cried with relief. Any more field trips and they might have to put me on Prozac, though I do have to go to the hospital tonight." She led Charity back to the kitchen and gestured at the sandwich fixings on the island. "We can talk while I finish making Allison's lunch. Care for some coffee or juice?"

"No, thanks, but what do you mean, you have to go to the hospital?"

"I've been working there three or four evenings a week." Kate flushed. "Things are a little tight, you know?"

Charity nodded and gave the other woman a moment by taking in the light turquoise walls, bright-white, glass-front cabinets, and silver-edged counters. A cardinal-red fruit basket, toaster, mixer, and canister set provided deliberate but happy accents. Charity silently apologized to her own careless kitchen.

"Listen," she said. "I know Detective Ironmaker talked to you about what Allison said to Drew. Is everything okay?"

"I signed her up for some counseling sessions." Kate reached for an open jar of grape jelly. "But really, I don't believe she meant what she said. She's a teenager. Melodrama is what they do." She scooped some jelly onto a peanut-butter-smeared slice of bread and pointed at its twin, also slathered with peanut butter. "Keeps the sandwich from getting soggy, did you know that?"

"I'll keep it in mind." Charity settled onto a stool, the one farthest away from the cloying smell of the nut butter. "I need to ask how you feel about Sarah's affair with Drew."

The knife went still in the middle of a diagonal cut. Kate exhaled, finished cutting, and carefully set the knife aside. "I'd be lying if I said I wasn't upset. My best friend was sleeping with my daughter's boyfriend." She reached for the plastic wrap, meeting Charity's gaze head-on. "What bothers me more is that Sarah never told me, even after Drew and Allison broke up. I thought we were closer than that. Anyway you know—you knew—Sarah. She always got what she wanted, and apparently she wanted Drew. Allison says she and Drew never had sex, so of course he's not going to pass up the chance to hook up with someone like Sarah."

"That's very understanding of you."

"Not understanding. Practical. Allison made it easy by handling it well."

"Kate. She threatened to hurt herself."

"Charity. How many teens are you raising?"

A pang twisted deep in her chest. "Point taken." Charity picked up a kitchenware catalog and started idly thumbing through the pages. "So you had no idea what was going on?"

"I knew Sarah was in a relationship she didn't want to talk about." Kate busied herself wrapping Allison's sandwich. "I assumed she was sleeping with a married man. And I'm not talking about Scott Langford. He was divorced when she took up with him."

Charity held one of the catalog's thin pages mid-turn. "You knew Sarah was sleeping with Justine's ex?"

"I did. I didn't expect it to last. It never does. Did, I mean. Yes, I found it disturbing that she was sleeping with father and son, but it wasn't my business."

Charity ignored a creepy-crawly sensation and shifted on the stool. "When you stopped by my house yesterday morning, you said you were tired because you'd spent the night with someone. I need a name."

Kate fumbled a handful of carrot chips. "I'd rather not. It's complicated. Wait. Why do I need to give you an alibi?"

"It's a standard question. Please don't take it personally."

"Kind of hard not to. Anyway, I'd heard you arrested Drew. Are you telling me you don't think he did it?"

Charity's phone—the phone she'd circled the shed on her hands and knees in the dark looking for, only to have Mo show up and ask dryly why she didn't just call herself from the landline — blasted the default ringtone. Her pulse bounced as she plucked her cell free of the case attached to her duty belt and with one glance confirmed her suspicion. Grady. She thumbed the Ignore button and tucked her phone away.

"Drew came forward to clear his mother, not to confess," Charity said, and turned her attention back to a set of ceramic ice cream sundae dishes made to look like waffle cones. "We're still investigating."

Kate ripped open a package of chocolate chip cookies. "Can I get back to you? You have to understand, it's not just me involved."

"Which means it's not just yourself you're establishing an alibi for."

"My…partner…doesn't need an alibi any more than I do."

This was starting to sound an awful lot like the conversation they'd had with Scott Langford. Charity reached out, hovered a hand over the package of cookies, and raised an eyebrow at Kate. Kate made a careless gesture, and Charity helped herself.

"He didn't want to give us your name, either." Charity ate half the cookie with one bite.

Kate's eyes went wide. "You already know who it was?"

"Not because he told us. I guessed."

"And your guess would be…"

"Scott Langford."

Kate gasped and backed up until she collided with the fridge. Something small — a magnet? — clattered to the floor. "I'm not Sarah. Like I said before, she got what she wanted, and didn't care who she hurt to get it. She meant a lot to me, though. I admired her life-is-short outlook. But I cannot believe you just accused me of sleeping with her boyfriend."

"Boyfriend" seemed a bit of an exaggeration. "I'm sorry if I offended you. Scott's hiding something, and I thought it might be you." Charity winced, and slapped the catalog shut. What the hell? She was leaking details like a wide-eyed rookie hoping to impress her commanding officer.

"I get it." Kate pushed away from the fridge, snatched up her daughter's polka-dot lunch tote, and yanked the zipper closed.

"You think I slept with Scott because Sarah slept with Drew." She shuddered, then shocked the hell out of Charity by flashing a rueful smile. "At least give me some credit. If I were going to plot vengeance, I'd make sure my evil plan didn't include sleeping with a man who calls women 'chicks' and smells like drugstore cologne."

The kitchen echoed with the strains of *Hawaii Five-0*. Charity apologized, and this time took the call.

"Brenda June," she said. "What's up?"

"Give me sixty seconds to explain."

Not Brenda June. Grady.

- 7 -

CHARITY'S HAND FELL TO her side, and her thumb hovered over End.

"Char. Please."

He said it loudly enough for Kate to hear. Kate's eyes went wide, and Charity swore under her breath. As soon as she got back to the station, she'd shoot Grady West and pin the crime on her traitorous dispatcher. She slid off the stool and stalked into the dining room.

"This is not a good time," she whispered furiously.

"Sorry about last night. Pratt made it clear he wasn't leaving 'til I did."

"You did the right thing."

"It didn't feel right."

It did when you were kissing me.

"Except for the kissing," he murmured.

Dear Lord. Charity attempted a casual laugh, but it came out lugging all kinds of awkward. She distracted herself by deciding to hunt down the source of the homey scent that filled the room. She headed for the grouping of candles on the sideboard.

"At least this time you tried to defend me to Pratt before disappearing," she said, as briskly as she could manage.

After a handful of heartbeats, Grady sighed. "How much trouble did I get you into?"

"I handled it." She sniffed at the candles. Nothing.

"Char."

"Don't call me that," she snapped. She felt Kate's gaze between her shoulder blades and lowered her voice. "You need to let me do my job."

"That translate to leaving you alone?"

"Stay off my case, Grady." She moved toward a candy dish on the window sill.

"Good one. Not happening, though."

At the window she leaned over and took a whiff of the potpourri in the dish. Nope, not that, either. "I can arrest you for obstruction."

"I look forward to a thorough frisk."

A liquid heaviness settled between her hips. "I'm hanging up now."

"No calling it quits over the phone. Let me buy you lunch. An apology, for getting you into trouble with Pratt."

"There's nothing to quit. I never said I'd work with you. I have my orders. You're off limits."

Grady gave a husky chuckle. "Pratt knows better than to tell you something is off limits. That's exactly when you decide to go for it."

"Not this time, West." She pressed End and turned.

Kate eyed her like a fresh-from-the-jailhouse Hank eyed a six-pack of beer. "He wants to work with you?"

"Not going to happen. What smells so good in here?"

Kate nodded at the light fixture that hovered over the table. "Scented light bulbs. They work best when the light's on." Her smile wobbled. "A Christmas gift from Sarah."

Cinnamon and pine. That explained it. Charity followed Kate back into the kitchen. "Just to be clear, you and your mystery man were together all of Tuesday evening?"

"From eight o'clock on. You and Grady were an item, weren't you?"

Charity sighed. Kate had arrived in Becker County about the same time as Sarah Huffman, so she wasn't familiar with this particular pathetic piece of Charity's history. Charity would just as soon keep it that way. It wasn't as if she and Kate were close.

"It was a long time ago."

"Think you might get back together?"

"No," Charity said a little too firmly, judging by the hurt on Kate's face. She swallowed her impatience. "In the first place, we're barely acquaintances anymore, let alone friends. In the second place, his family is involved in a murder investigation. And third, he lives in Seattle. If I ever moved it wouldn't be to a city — "

"Where it rains nine months of the year?"

"I was going to mention the rampant homelessness and six-dollar coffee, but the rain thing works, too."

Kate rounded the island and squeezed Charity's arm. "I'm glad," she said. "We need you here. You can do better than Grady West, I hope you know. That family is nothing but one big wine barrel of self-absorbed addicts."

Charity stepped back, gently pulling her arm free. It was all she could do to keep from leaping to Grady's defense.

Oh, what the hell.

"Not all of them," she said. "I don't think you should lump Grady and the kids in with the rest. Or is there something about Drew I should know?"

Kate shrugged. "I never saw any sign of drug use. I wouldn't have trusted Allison with him if I had."

"Did you? Trust him?"

A trace of something not quite right crept into Kate's expression. Doubt? Uneasiness?

Charity gripped her equipment belt. "So you didn't trust him."

Kate toyed with the zipper on Allison's lunch tote. "I just wondered how serious he could be about her, with her being two years younger, and all."

"What about Peyton? Any evidence of drug use?"

"None that I know of." Kate sighed. "I suppose I was talking about Justine and her folks before."

"Yet you're friends with Justine."

"No one knows your faults better than your friends."

"What about Scott? Is he a self-absorbed addict?"

"How would I know? I already told you, he's not the man I'm screwing."

119

"Mom, for God's sake." Kate's daughter, a sixteen-year-old with her mother's athletic build and strawberry-blond hair, growled in disgust as she stumbled into the room and over to the refrigerator. She was dressed for school, in jeans and a lime-green sweater, but her eyes were heavy-lidded and her movements sluggish as she poured a glass of juice.

Charity could relate. She'd started missing her own bed the moment she rolled out of it.

"Allison, you remember Charity Bishop."

Allison swallowed a mouthful of juice and nodded. The teen didn't balk at finding a deputy in her kitchen. Either she had nothing to hide, or she had one hell of a poker face. Or maybe she really was still half-asleep.

Kate busied herself cleaning off the island. "Grab a granola bar, Allison. We have to be on our way or you'll be late."

Charity watched with regret as Kate shoved the package of cookies into a cabinet.

Allison ignored her mother. She set her empty glass in the sink and swung toward Charity. "Did you find out who killed Ms. Huffman?"

"We're working on it."

"Do you think Drew did it?"

"Do you?"

Allison poked out her chin. "He cheated on me. Who knows what else he's capable of?"

Charity exchanged glances with Kate. "I understood he ended things with you before he started a relationship with Sarah."

"You can cheat with your thoughts, though, right? Peyton said he had all kinds of thoughts about Sarah while he was with me. Only he was too chickenshit to tell me."

"Language," Kate scolded. "And we don't need to drag Drew's sister into this. Now go get your backpack."

"What kinds of thoughts?" Charity asked, and pretended not to hear Kate's exasperated exhale.

"He was obsessed with her. Couldn't wait to do her. Peyton tried to talk him out of breaking up with me because she knew how sad I'd be, but that woman had him totally wrapped. That's when

Peyton and I—" Allison stopped, looked down, and fiddled with the hem of her shirt.

"That's when you what?" No response. "How did Peyton know how Drew felt about Sarah?"

"She heard him on the phone."

Kate snatched up her keys and rattled them for effect. "You know how bad it looks when a teacher's kid is late to school?"

"As bad as that outfit you're wearing?"

But Charity could hear the affection in Allison's voice and damn, there went that pang again.

"Worse." Kate gave her daughter a push and slung her purse over her shoulder. "Charity, I'm sorry, but you'll have to excuse us. She gets another tardy and we'll both end up in the principal's office."

"Just one more question. What can you tell me about Sarah's employer?"

"Not much more than what everyone already knows. Keith Tarrant's a rich property developer with more muscles than ethics."

"Was Sarah involved with him?"

"She was when she first started working there. I don't think it lasted long."

"Do you know why not?"

Kate threw up her hands. "You'd have to ask Sarah," she said, and immediately paled.

They stood frozen in an awkward silence until Allison came back down the stairs, dragging her backpack, letting it thump from one step to the next. Kate headed for the door.

Charity followed. "Did Sarah ever mention any problems at work?"

Kate shut and locked the front door behind them. "The usual. Bad economy. Unreasonable clients. Long hours. Can't you ask Keith Tarrant these questions?"

Charity followed them down the steps and over to Kate's Jeep. "He's next on my list."

Kate aimed a speculative glance over her shoulder. "If he asks you out, you should say yes. It'll do you good to blow off some steam."

"Keith Tarrant?" Where the hell had that come from? "If he asks me out, I doubt I'll be able to keep from laughing. Besides, I don't have time to blow off steam."

"Maybe it's better that way. Because you're right. Sarah is important. And so is that election we need you to win. Favoritism won't do you any, well, favors." Kate climbed into the Jeep, shut the door, and lowered her window. "Anyway, there's always the good ol' vibrator. You have one, right?"

"Mom." Allison put a hand to her face and slunk down into her seat. Kate arched an eyebrow at Charity and backed toward the road.

Disturbed, Charity watched them go. Did Kate really think she'd let anything get in the way of finding justice for Sarah? She headed down the driveway, thought of last night's kiss, and winced.

Before crossing the road to her SUV, she hesitated, and stared at an azalea with blooms as deep purple as the jelly Kate had smeared on her daughter's sandwich. While watching the bees hover then drop, hover then drop, in a slow-motion, buzzing bounce, she pondered the sentence Allison had stopped herself from finishing. *That's when Peyton and I…*

She needed to talk to Peyton. And wouldn't that take finesse — the teen would clam right up if she thought Charity wanted her to deliver up her brother or her best friend. Grady could help. The teen might confide something to a doting uncle she'd never admit to a parent.

But what if Peyton's involvement was more direct? How could Charity ask Grady to help win his nephew's freedom if the price was his niece's?

* * *

GRADY STARED DOWN AT the dispatcher's phone. *Not this time, West.* Charity had sounded like she meant it. Like she was breaking up with him all over again.

Dammit, he'd screwed up. He shouldn't have left her last night. That look Pratt had given him, like he'd single-handedly ruined his protégée's life… Grady had left because he hadn't wanted to make things worse. And yeah, Charity had asked him outright to go.

Didn't mean he should have listened.

"What happened? What she'd say?" Brenda June peered around his shoulder at her cell, as if the text of the conversation might appear on the screen.

Grady handed back her zebra-striped phone. "She doesn't want my help. Even if she did, Pratt wouldn't let her have it."

"He might after last night."

"Last night only made things worse." The guilt on her face clued him in. Something cold and slithery crawled into his gut. "Did something happen after I left?"

"Someone was lurking in her back yard. She wasn't able to make an ID."

Dammit, he knew he shouldn't have left. "Any guesses?"

"She suspects whoever vandalized her car came back for an encore performance." With a bony hand, the dispatcher patted his arm. "Stop kicking yourself. The sheriff was there, and he didn't notice anything, either. Besides, Charity can take care of herself."

The thought that someone could have been hiding in the bushes while he and Charity were getting hot and heavy bugged the hell out of him. It was bad enough they'd had Pratt as an audience. If word got out, and she lost the election because Grady was thinking with his dick, he'd never forgive himself. And chances were she wouldn't, either.

Which meant what? Keeping his hands to himself? Or making damned sure they didn't have an audience the next time things got complicated?

A hotter-than-hellfire fantasy was over before it started when a door banged shut and a pair of high heels clattered along the hallway. Justine hurried into the waiting room, cheeks flushed from the cold, hair bouncing on her shoulders, jacket and skirt slightly askew. She paused to dump her purse in the nearest chair then marched up to Grady and punched him in the bicep.

"Thanks a whole hell of a lot for taking off without me."

He rubbed his arm, grateful she smelled of toothpaste rather than booze. "We had a late night. I figured you needed your sleep."

"I need to see my son."

Brenda June backed toward the door leading to her domain. "I'll come get you when he's finished his breakfast. Shouldn't be more than fifteen minutes."

Grady thanked Brenda June, but Justine remained silent, arms wrapped around her waist. He put an arm around her, and his heart squeezed. She'd been steadily losing weight since the divorce, and her suit jacket bunched where she hugged herself.

His cell rang, and after a startled moment, he pulled away from his sister and fumbled in his jacket pocket. "It's Matt." He excused himself and lifted the phone to his ear. "Hey, bud. What's up?"

"Not much."

Grady couldn't help a grin as he heard Matt's usual pained tones at having to offer up even those two words. "You get my text last night?"

Matt sighed heavily. "The one this morning, too."

Grady let go of his smile when he glanced at the clock on the wall. "You're calling from school?" That didn't bode well. His son wasn't one for casual conversation. Or hell, any kind of conversation at all.

"I didn't go today," Matt said.

"You're sick?" Grady asked, and Justine moved closer, forehead creased with concern.

"Nope."

Grady blew out a breath. This was getting him nowhere fast. "Put your mom on, buddy."

"I can't."

"Why not?"

"She's not here."

Dammit. Valerie had promised she'd never leave Matt alone in the condo. "Where is she?"

"Seattle."

Grady stilled. That hadn't sounded like sarcasm. He closed his eyes and reminded himself to breathe. "You say that," he said carefully, "as if you're not in Seattle."

"I'm not. I'm at the airport."

"Which airport?"

"Which one did you fly into?" Matt's tone was one big duh.

"You're at Great Falls? Here in Montana?"

"Yep."

Son of a bitch. "Does your mom know where you are?"

"She put me on the plane."

Grady's fingers tightened on the phone. Of course she did. If Matt were running away, he sure as hell wouldn't run to his father.

What the hell had Valerie been thinking? She must have put the kid on a six a.m. flight. Alone. And those six little words, *She put me on the plane,* had carried a shitload of uncertainty.

Worry clutched at Grady's gut. There was no excuse for making their kid travel across two states on his own. Anger spurted. The horror on Justine's face reinforced his rage, but he'd have to deal with his ex-wife later.

"Wait for me by baggage claim," Grady said grimly into the phone. "No wandering, buddy, okay?"

"I'm still on the plane. They said they have to hold me at the gate 'til someone comes to get me. Mom told them you would."

Grady did his best to swallow the savage from his voice. "I'm on my way."

*   *   *

KEITH TARRANT MAY NOT have earned the right to use the letters MD after his name, but he was seriously loaded, which did earn him the right to build a house on Pill Hill. Two doors down from the West mansion, as a matter of fact. The Tudor style home, complete with steep, ski-lodge rooflines and dark wood timbers crisscrossing cream-colored stucco had always been Charity's favorite in Becker County. She finally had an excuse to see the inside. Considering the circumstances, she couldn't have cared less.

Her Oakley assault boots carried her up a flagstone walk hugged by neat beds of mulch sprouting uniform rows of monkey grass. Nothing but green and brown. Seriously, would a little color kill the guy? Then again, the green seemed appropriate. Charity had never met Tarrant, but she knew his reputation. Apparently his ethics were inversely proportional to the amount of money he'd raked in over the years.

In other words, he was a rich asshole.

Sarah's former employer answered the door wearing Homer Simpson pajamas and a severe case of bedhead. Okay, not what she'd expected. She'd have apologized for waking him if he hadn't been cradling a half-empty glass of orange juice against his chest. From somewhere behind him came the muted sounds of a television show with an exceptionally cheesy laugh track.

"Mr. Tarrant? I'm Deputy Sheriff Charity Bishop."

His gaze lowered to her badge. And lingered in the general area. Screw any kind of apology.

"I know who you are," he said. "I'm not talking without my lawyer present."

Charity did her best to keep her smile from turning feral. Though he'd have to actually look at her face to see it. "I'm not here to arrest you, Mr. Tarrant. I'm hoping you'll agree to answer a few questions about Sarah Huffman. May I come in?"

Instead of answering, he tipped back his head, chugged his juice. When he wiped his mouth with the back of his free hand and let loose a burp, Charity suspected he'd dosed himself with more than vitamin C. Grieving the loss of a star employee? Or a lover?

"I understood you already had a suspect in custody," Tarrant muttered.

"Who told you that?"

"I can't help you." He pushed at the door.

Charity talked quickly. "You do realize that if we find out you knew something pertinent to the case and refused to share it, you could be charged with obstructing a peace officer? Would you really rather spend six months in the county jail than answer a few questions?"

"Threats, Deputy?" Tarrant asked softly, all trace of sleepiness stripped from his voice. "Sure that's the way to go?"

He met her eyes then, and she saw his were colder than the tippy-toppiest peak of the Bitterroot Mountain range. She shifted position in an attempt to disguise a shudder, but the shine in his eyes told her she'd failed.

"I need help recreating Sarah's day," Charity told him, in as neutral a tone as she could manage. "Can you tell me if she had any appointments?"

"We're done here," he said.

"How about you and Sarah? Were you done?" Ignoring the rapidly shrinking space between the door and the frame, she added, "By the way, who is your lawyer, Mr. Tarrant?"

A pause. His head reappeared in the doorway, speculation glimmering in his eyes. "Owen Quinn."

What a surprise. Owen Quinn, lawyer for the loaded.

"I see." Charity glanced to her left, at the extravagant landscaping two doors down. "The Wests let you onto Pill Hill so what they say goes, is that it?"

She didn't get the rise she'd hoped for. Instead she got a flicker of what looked like sympathy in his eyes.

"Money talks, Deputy." He shrugged. "Not our fault you'll never learn the language."

Charity was still crafting her brilliant comeback when he shut the door in her face.

*   *   *

THE DRIVE TO THE airport was a blur—a blur that by all rights should have earned Grady a speeding ticket and maybe even an obscene gesture or two—but it still took too damned long to get there. Matt had said he wouldn't be waiting alone, but Grady knew his kid. He was contrary enough to try ditching his escort.

Once inside the airport, Grady didn't collect any one-finger salutes, but he did get a lot of half-curious, half-exasperated looks as he rushed through the hallways, dodging tourists, glass-encased grizzlies, water fountains, ATMs, and sculpted buffalo. He fidgeted as he waited in line at the ticket counter for the boarding pass that would get him through security. The agent gave him the stink-eye, but Grady didn't bother offering excuses. He snatched up the boarding pass and hauled ass.

Matt stood next to the check-in counter, both hands in his pockets, right shoulder sagging beneath the weight of a black duffel bag. The instant Grady spotted him, his heart crawled back down out of his throat, and wet relief burned the backs of his eyes. When Matt's gaze landed on Grady, his left shoulder went lax, matching the downward slope of his right. At the same time the corners of his mouth went up, if only for an instant. The kid even managed a nod, though it was as rigid as the sand-colored bristles of the military cut he'd insisted on at the beginning of the school year. A side effect of too many hours playing *Call of Duty,* Grady suspected.

Matt's hug was equally stiff. For once Grady didn't mind. His son was safe.

"Sorry about all this, buddy." He had to raise his voice to be heard over the typical airport soundtrack — the excited babble of travelers lining up for access to the Jetway, the mechanical mumbling of the loudspeaker, the low-pitched thrum of baggage wheels on linoleum. "I don't know what your mom was thinking." He winced. He knew better than to play the blame game. He tried again. "I would have been here if I'd known you were coming."

"No, you wouldn't. 'Cause when she called to let you know, you'd have talked her out of sending me. You want to keep an eye on me, but at the same time you don't want me to have any fun." He pushed his shoulders back. "And stop calling me buddy. My name is Matt. I'm not in diapers anymore."

Right.

"I didn't want to stay with Mrs. K.," Matt burst out. "She's always cooking cabbage and her apartment reeks. She only lets me use my laptop for like, fifteen minutes the entire day. And since I miss Grandma and Grandpa and Drew and Peyton and Aunt Justine, I told Mom she should send me here."

No surprise that Matt mentioned missing everyone but his father. Grady took a moment to mourn the loss of the little boy who'd once followed him from room to room. "Why were you going to stay with Mrs. K.?" he asked carefully, when what he really wanted to know was *What the hell was wrong with your mother that she couldn't look after you for one lousy week?*

"Puddly wanted to take Mom on a trip. Wherever they went they don't allow…" He hesitated, then finished with "…anyone under eighteen."

Grady knew better than to free his smile. Maybe he should stop thinking of Matt as a kid, too. Could that be part of their problem? He gave a silent snort. As if being blamed for the divorce wasn't problem enough.

Grady stepped out of the way of a baggage cart. "Any idea where your mom and Pud—uh, Preston went?"

Matt shook his head. No surprise there. Grady was done wishing his ex would value their son more than she valued her privacy.

Grady gestured toward the duffel bag. "That all you got?"

A curt nod. Matt was adjusting the strap when he peered up at Grady. "Didn't she tell you about the trip? Or were you just testing me?"

"Why would I test you?"

"To see if I was telling the truth."

"I didn't think I needed to worry about that with you."

Matt paused then muttered, "You don't."

Hallelujah. Finally Grady had managed to say the right thing. "I didn't get to talk to her. Her phone went right to voicemail. I'll catch her later." He knew she was deliberately putting him off, hoping time would defuse his anger. Screw that. He was fucking furious, and not two hours or two days or even two goddamned months would ease the temper pounding through his veins.

Grady guided Matt down the escalator and toward the nearest set of doors. "It's not that I don't want you here. But what about school? And soccer?"

"I don't mind missing school. And they won't kick me off the team. They need me."

"You'll mind when you have to spend your entire summer trapped behind that same desk you're trying so hard to avoid."

"Seriously? I just got here and you're already trying to get rid of me?"

They stopped at the crosswalk between the airport and the parking structure, and Grady shook his head. "Nice try, hambone. You've got exams coming up. You know you can't miss those."

"You're right, I can't. Not even a little."

Grady chuckled. Traffic cleared, and they joined the throng bustling across the pavement.

"I haven't hung with Drew since Christmas. Think he'll be as excited to see me as I am to see him?"

Grady grabbed at the back of his neck. He didn't look forward to explaining where Matt's cousin was and why. "You bet," he managed. "Everyone is. What you have to understand is that they're all going through a stressful time right now. They're bound to be a little...distracted."

"Distracted I can handle. Distracted I'm used to."

Grady forced a blank expression, even as a familiar frustration burned in his chest. "I'm sorry, were you saying something?"

Matt rolled his eyes.

Grady gave him a light punch to the shoulder. "Listen. It is important to keep in touch with family. It's also important to stay in school and the truth is, this isn't a good time for you to be here."

"So why did we bother to leave the frickin' airport if you're gonna turn around and put me right back on a plane?"

Grady waited until they were alone in the elevator before answering. "Let's get one thing straight. I'm not sending you back alone. Your mother has more confidence in the airlines than I do." He didn't miss the relief in his son's eyes and bit back the acid taste of resentment. "Let's try a compromise. How about you stay one week?"

"Then what?"

"Then if I'm not ready to leave, I'll take you back to Seattle myself."

"Mom won't like that."

"What if I give your coach a call? See if you can stay with him until I get back, in case your mom's not available? You enjoyed hanging with his family that time I had to go to Boston, right?"

The elevator dinged, and the doors dragged open. Matt stepped off the curb and turned and walked backward, steered in the right direction by the jab of Grady's chin.

"I don't want to go back," Matt said. "I want to stay here."

"I just said—"

"I mean I want to stay."

"Matt. We're not moving to Montana."

"I didn't mean both of us."

Jesus. A hot, tingling pain radiated outward from Grady's chest; was this what a heart attack felt like? He didn't stop, didn't even slow as he scanned the faded yellow numbers at the bottom of each parking space. When he spotted the rental car, he fumbled for his keys and pressed the unlock button on the fob. A pair of beeps echoed in the chilly gloom.

Grady cleared his throat and pressed another button to open the trunk. "How about we talk about this over breakfast? I know a great place for waffles. And hot chocolate. You know, the kind piled high with whipped cream?" For God's sake, he sounded like he was talking to a three-year-old. Judging by the disgust on Matt's face, he was thinking the same thing.

"Whatever." Matt tossed his duffel bag into the trunk and stomped toward the front passenger door.

Exactly. Grady would do whatever it took to make sure his son never knew what it felt like to come in a distant fourth behind money, meds, and social dominion.

Whatever.

* * *

CHARITY ARRIVED AT THE courthouse midmorning to find Grady gone and Brenda June conveniently away from her desk, no doubt so Charity wouldn't have a chance to scold her about letting Grady use her cell phone.

You can run, Dispatch, but you can't hide.

According to the in-out board, Dix and Mo were at the West house executing the search warrant. Charity heard voices in one of the interview rooms, knocked, and opened the door to find Justine talking earnestly with her son. When their heads swung around, Drew looked exhausted, Justine downright hostile. The offer of coffee and soda didn't win Charity any points. The mention of Brenda June's cheesecake didn't help either, though Charity suspected that may have had more to do with the ginger tahini flavor than the fact that she was the one who offered it.

Next she went on a reluctant search for the sheriff. When she found him, he repeated the lecture Mo had given her the night before. He also threatened her with a pay cut if she didn't get her motion sensors fixed, then hugged her lungs flat before chasing her out of his office.

Pratt didn't have to remind her to be careful. Every day on the force was a day of taking risks, but coming across that creep in her own back yard had freaked her out almost as much as it had pissed her off. What she needed was a distraction.

She made a fresh pot of coffee and spent the rest of the morning poring over witness statements, interviews, and evidence reports, all while coaching herself to play it cool when Dix and Mo got back. If they'd found anything, she'd know soon enough. The sheriff put a kink in her plans by announcing that as soon as the guys got back, they'd all sit down to a working lunch to discuss their way ahead — in other words, to figure out what they were going to do with Drew Langford. Pratt volunteered Charity to handle the food run.

Usually he sweet-talked Brenda June into doing it. Apparently this time Dispatch had managed to resist his charms.

Jerzy's Shake Shack sat right off US 87 and attracted a fair amount of tourist business — mostly the outdoor enthusiast kind. Central Montana was flanked by mountains on one side and prairies on the other and bragged proximity not only to the Teton and Missouri rivers, but to popular national parks and forests like Glacier and Flathead. Hunters and fisherman especially appreciated the Shake Shack for its hearty fare and plain décor and Jerzy for his affable, life's-too-short-to-rush-a-meal manner.

But the local barbecue lovers were the restaurant's mainstay. When the long-ago fire destroyed eighty percent of the building, and afterward the fire inspector determined the cause to be arson, the county's residents had been first shocked, then enraged. Their fury had turned to grief when they'd learned Jerzy didn't intend to rebuild. Charity had never seen a man so heartsick.

Even after all this time, shame stalked her.

In the end, the town had taken up a collection and managed to convince Jerzy to change his mind about starting over. Thus began "Shack Part Two." Charity adored the chocolate shakes almost as much as she dreaded the stubborn memories. They weren't all bad, though, and Jerzy did make a kick-ass barbecue sandwich.

Which could help explain the mysterious shrinking syndrome currently plaguing her jeans and uniform pants. Between Jerzy's barbecue and the butter-laden waffles at the Good Dog, Bad Dog Café, only her yoga pants fit like they should.

Although the sugar-infused rainbow bits her breakfasts and dinners revolved around probably didn't help much, either.

Forget coffee. What she needed to give up was carbohydrates. Charity envisioned the fluffy rolls Jerzy used for his sandwiches and grimaced.

Or not.

She mounted the steps to the weathered-timber porch that fronted what was basically a one-story house. A stern mental talking-to did nothing to ease the automatic drag on her feet and probably never would. She tugged open the door, and a wave carrying warmth, chatter, and the thick, smoky aroma of roasted pork rolled over the threshold, beckoning her inside. Before she even reached the counter, Jerzy burst out of the kitchen, face beaming. His wide smile wasn't aimed at Charity, though. The restaurant owner headed away from her toward a table centered under the front window. She glanced at the occupants and dropped her keys. The jangling clatter as they hit the linoleum seemed especially loud.

So much for avoiding Grady the rest of his stay. And who was that sitting across from him?

"Grady West!" Jerzy thrust out his hand as Grady stood. "Welcome to Shack Part Two, my man. You're sitting in the wrong place, though. This your boy?"

Oh, dear Lord. His son. Grady's son was in Becker County.

133

8

CHARITY STRAINED TO HEAR the child's name. She'd never even asked, hadn't let Grady talk about him. But the jabber of voices, the cash register's beeping and a shouted "Order up!" from the kitchen drowned out Grady's response.

"Nice to meet you, young man." Jerzy shook the boy's hand, bent close, and pointed. "See that table way back in the corner? Every Friday night I served your father a mountain of French fries and a pair of chocolate shakes. Same night, same table, same girl. Way before your time, though. Turn-of-the-century type stuff."

Edith, the waitress, and Jerzy's longtime girlfriend, appeared beside Grady's table, a laden tray balanced on her hip. She whispered something.

Jerzy whipped around, his smile beaming brighter as his gaze settled on Charity. *Crap.*

"Well, speak of the angel," he said. "Sweet Charity, here to pick up her order. C'mon over here, girl. Have you had a chance to say hello to—" The grin slipped. "Well, of course you have."

She couldn't see Grady because Jerzy blocked her view. She could see the back of a sandy-blond head attached to a child's lean body. A head that took its time swiveling her way, revealing a sun-kissed face behind a mildly curious expression. That expression turned to a scowl when the kid got a load of her uniform.

Jerzy moved then, and she saw the way Grady stared at her. The vulnerability in his eyes reminded her of the way he'd looked the night Pratt had hauled her off to jail—part apology, part longing, part resignation.

It had to be a reflection of their surroundings, of what this place had once meant to them. If his watchfulness had anything to do with her reaction to his kid, they were both in trouble. Kids were not her strong suit.

Jerzy gave her a hug and held on tighter than usual. "C'mon up, angel, and get your order when you're ready. Tell Detective Dix I didn't get to the pecan pie today, but I packed up an extra-big slice of apple for him."

Dix and his notorious sweet tooth.

"He'll appreciate that," she said. And he would, especially since that meant Charity wouldn't be mooching his dessert. She'd never been able to stomach baked apples.

When Jerzy moved away, Charity saw Grady now stood beside his son's chair. The boy had twisted around in his seat, a French fry in one hand and a fork in the other. Ketchup dripped onto the thigh of his camouflage pants. She tried to smile, but her face remained cold and stiff.

"Grady." Charity poured as much neutral as she could into the word. "I'm glad you were able to make some time for Jerzy. Enjoy your lunch. I need to get back to the courthouse."

"Before you go, I'd like you to meet my son. Matt, this is Deputy Charity Bishop." He put his hand on the boy's shoulder. When the kid shrugged it off, Grady's eyes flickered. "Charity and I have known each other a long time," he said quietly. "Say hello."

The boy shoved the fry into his mouth. Charity managed a nod. He didn't have the West eyes, but he had Grady's stubborn chin and a way of holding himself that said, *take a good look, and tell me I don't deserve to be smug.*

"Matt." The naked word hung in the air, but what more could she say? *It's nice to meet you?* It hadn't been so far. *I've heard a lot about you?* She'd done her best not to. *I hope you enjoy your stay?* With his cousin under suspicion for murder? Not likely.

The kid glared at her, and his hand fisted around his fork. "Are you the one who put my cousin in jail?"

*   *   *

AW, HELL. THE MOMENT Matt spoke, an innate defensiveness rose within Grady, which was all kinds of screwed up because since he'd arrived in town he'd done nothing but question Charity and the way she did her job. Matt was scared, same as Grady. Same as everyone in their family. Grady knew Charity knew it, but she didn't let on. Even as conversation around them faltered and heads ducked and gathered, she regarded Matt with serenity.

"I am," she said. "The sheriff and the other deputies and I are all working hard to solve this case, and when we do, your cousin may not be in jail anymore. In fact, I'm here to pick up lunch so we can work while we eat." She started to back away. "Been to the Old Trail Museum yet?" Matt didn't answer. She didn't seem to care. "If you have time to explore, you should get your dad to take you there. Ask him to introduce you to the skeleton of Old Sol. He was a trapper, and you can tell how he died by looking at him. It's pretty gruesome."

Matt struggled to look disinterested. He finally noticed he'd dripped ketchup on his pants and grabbed a napkin.

"That's a great idea." Grady winced when the words came out sounding like he was doing a cheerleader impression. He cleared his throat. "What do you say, Matt?"

No response. When Matt finally lifted his head his expression had turned sly, and he aimed that craftiness at Charity. "My dad has lots of girlfriends back in Seattle."

Oh, Jesus.

The buzz around them turned into a babble. Charity shot Grady a glance, but all he could see in her hazel eyes was a grudging admiration for his son. Nothing for Grady. Not even the tiniest glimmer of jealousy.

"Great," Charity said brightly. "Thanks for letting me know. You two take care, now."

Grady caught up to her at the cash register. "I need to talk with you."

"This isn't the time." She snatched up her bags of food and a tray of shakes. "I have my hands full." She tipped her head in Matt's direction. "So do you."

He glanced over at Matt. The simmering reproach in his son's eyes pulled at him. Grady turned to say goodbye, but Charity was gone.

*   *   *

CHARITY CLIMBED OUT OF her SUV, caught the eye of the man waiting at the courthouse door, and almost climbed right back in. Damn it, she'd been smelling barbecue and onion rings for the past ten minutes and she hadn't had anything to eat since that chocolate chip cookie at Kate's. She was starving, but it would be childish to continue avoiding him.

Surely this couldn't be any worse than running into Grady and his son at Jerzy's. If looks could kill, that kid would have knocked her off ten times over. His own father wouldn't have fared much better. And she would not think about whatever it was that Grady wanted to discuss.

With a sigh, she collected the goodies from the passenger seat, nudged the door shut with her hip, and nodded at the other candidate running for sheriff of Becker County.

"Oliver."

"Charity."

Fifty-something state-trooper-turned-gun-shop-owner Oliver Bloom strode down to the end of the sidewalk to greet her, his muscle-bound body barely contained by an outfit she realized with a start matched the one Grady's son had been wearing. Black tee, camouflage pants, work boots. What she could see of his expression behind his shades was also identical — full-on petulance.

Here we go.

Oliver folded his arms and spread his legs in the classic convince-me-not-to-cuff-you stance. His hair, as black as Dix's but with random patches of gray, gleamed in the afternoon sun. With his cleft chin and power pose, he looked like he'd stepped right out of a military recruitment poster. Or an erectile dysfunction commercial.

He dipped his chin and peered at her over the top of his sunglasses. "How's the campaign coming?"

"I've been busy with the Sarah Huffman case. In fact, I don't have time to talk. We're working through lunch. Or we will be, as soon as I get this inside."

Oliver got to the door first, but instead of opening it, he held it shut. "You don't come to the gun range like you used to. When you are there, you're distant. Professional."

Charity's stomach started to feel greasier than the bottoms of the paper bags she cradled. "Since when is being professional a bad thing?"

"My wife thinks there's something going on."

"Between us?"

Oliver flinched at the squeak in her voice. "Is there? Something going on?"

"Don't you think you'd know?"

"What I mean is, do you still have feelings for me?"

Oh, dear Lord. "Oliver, we had three dates. Four years ago."

"Yeah and it was….well, it was…."

Oh, please don't let him do that channeling Meg Ryan thing again—

"…magic."

Charity's arms sagged, and she had to scramble to keep half a dozen rapidly-cooling lunches from splattering all over the sidewalk. This was the candidate favored to win the Becker County' sheriff's election. A power-tripping, regulation-happy he-man who quoted *Sleepless in Seattle* in the hopes of earning a free trip to panty land.

Then again, she ate her tuna sandwiches by nibbling away the pesky crusts first and had no hope of sleeping if her sheets weren't changed at exactly the seven day mark. Everyone had their quirks.

"I've moved beyond that," Charity said firmly. But she couldn't quite help the tiny catch in her voice—she was still dealing with way too much crap she hadn't managed to move beyond.

As she juggled the take-out bags, her fingers brushed the butt of her sidearm.

Oliver went rigid. "Tell me you're not...that you wouldn't hurt yourself."

Her chin dropped. The motion nudged one of the paper bags open, and the smell of barbecue wafted up to remind her she was crazy hungry while he was just...crazy.

"Where is this coming from?" she demanded. "Why are you suddenly convinced I'm pining for you?" *Pining.* She cringed at the word.

He didn't look happy with it, either. He yanked off his shades. "The murder investigation. I heard you're making mistakes. It's like you're trying to throw the election."

"You think I want you to win?"

"Do you?"

Do onion rings taste better when they're soggy and cold? "No. Now move or I'll call nine-one-one."

"You're still running for sheriff."

"I'm still running."

"And you're not into me."

"Not even a little."

He jerked his sunglasses back to his face, poked himself in the eye, and turned a pained grunt into a snarl. "You will lose. So you should start looking into a transfer because we both know we can't work together. Not with this...thing between us."

She took a step closer, and aimed a deliberate glance south. "The only thing between us is a hard-on you didn't get from thinking about your wife."

"Yeah? At least I have someone at home who can do something about my hard-on."

Bullseye. She sighed. "You're an asshole, Bloom, with a bad memory and sucky timing."

Surprisingly, he pushed away from the door and pulled it open. "Heard about you and Grady West," he said. He called after her as she launched herself into the dim quiet of the hallway. "Better get yourself an umbrella. It rains nine months a year in Seattle."

Charity delivered lunch to Drew and Justine, interrupting a half-hearted game of rummy. Afterward she slid a spinach salad onto Brenda June's desk—remembering the extra bacon bits was her way of taking the high road—and hustled into the break room, fully expecting to be hit with a barrage of complaints and not-so-good-natured insults. What she didn't expect was a strained silence shared by three grown men who refused to look her in the eye.

The sheriff leaned back against the sink, arms crossed, gaze locked on the linoleum while Mo and Dix hunched over the table.

Her arms went limp. Lunch landed on the scarred surface of the table with a rustling *thwop.* "What happened?" *Dear Lord, please don't let it be another murder.*

"We were just…catching up." Pratt looked as if he wanted to say more, then tugged at his goatee hard enough to make himself wince.

Dix tapped both sets of fingers on the table. Mo cleared his throat, and Charity frowned. Hard to imagine he could fit any more insinuation into that sound.

She glanced from Dix to Mo and back again. "Is this about—?"

Dix gave his head a quick shake. Not about his decision to leave, then. Her breath faltered. Had they heard about her visit from Grady last night? Pratt lifted his chin in an it-wasn't-my-fault gesture, and her heart tumbled.

"We heard from the commonwealth attorney with regards to Drew." He spoke over Mo's snort and pushed away from the sink. "She says we don't have enough to make a case."

So…not about last night? Her gaze locked on Pratt. "We're releasing Drew?"

"You sound surprised," Mo drawled.

"That's enough." Pratt reached across the table for a grease-stained bag and started passing out containers. "Let's eat."

"Enough what?" Charity passed a scowl around the table. "Tell me."

"Someone left a note on our windshield when we were serving the warrant on the Wests." Mo shoved to his feet. "I supported you. I ripped Dix a new one for not giving you the benefit of the doubt and then someone spots you in your front yard, smeared all over Grady West like sauce on a barbecue sandwich."

"Shit," Dix muttered, looking down at his lunch.

"Shit," Charity echoed breathlessly, and slumped down onto the bench. Panic writhed in her stomach. Who would do such a thing, and why?

"He was there last night," Mo ranted. "And you didn't say word one about it."

Ploink. Water dripped from the faucet into the sink.

Was someone spying on her?

She shuddered, and couldn't bring herself to look Pratt in the eye. *We didn't do anything,* she wanted to say to the others. But it wouldn't help. Besides, if the sheriff hadn't come along, who knows what she and Grady would have done.

"Where's the note?"

Pratt pulled a folded piece of paper from his back pocket. "I made you a copy." He tossed it across the table. "Consider yourself lucky they didn't get a photo."

Charity unfolded the laser-printed page and sucked air. *Anyone else see Charity Bishop and Grady West making out in her front yard last night? Someone needs to hose that bitch down.*

Oh, this was perfect.

Carefully she re-folded the note and tucked it into her shirt pocket. With one poor choice she'd endangered everything she'd worked for — the chance to be sheriff, the respect of her colleagues, the trust of the community.

Not to mention the sanctity of her murder investigation.

"It was a mistake," she finally said and raised her head, meeting head-on the disapproval coming at her from three different directions. "And I apologize if I've put you all in a tough position." The words *it won't happen again* dangled on the edge of her tongue, but she couldn't bring herself to let them go.

"If?" Mo demanded. "Who's going to trust how we handle the case now? And what the hell was West doing at your place, anyway?"

"You're right. He shouldn't have been there."

"That's it? That's all you have to say?"

"I apologized, Mo. What more do you want? I didn't invite him, if that's what you're fixating on."

"What more do we want? How about a guarantee we won't get another note?"

"How about you back off?" Dix growled.

"Let's cut the bullshit." The sheriff settled heavily onto the bench beside Charity. "I think we can all trust Deputy Bishop not to let any more...reminiscing interfere with the case, and maybe that'll keep the busybodies out of her yard. Now let's eat, so we can get down to business."

Mo muttered darkly while Dix poked at his onion rings. With one edge of her napkin, Charity swiped at the moisture coating the outside of her milkshake.

The note hadn't been about the election. Otherwise whoever wrote it would have arranged for a county official to find it. Dissension in the department ranks had been the objective.

Mission accomplished.

"Let's focus on the job, people," the sheriff said. "Namely, Drew Langford. We have no reason to hold him. We've already established he was at the scene, so the presence of the necklace is circumstantial."

"Sheriff." With a scowl, Mo brushed salt from his palms. "We found it under her body."

"We can't prove she didn't take it back, and we found nothing on the kid's neck to indicate our victim yanked it off him." The sheriff dipped his head and spread his hands in a what-can-we-do gesture. "And it's not the murder weapon."

Charity looked at Dix. "You didn't find anything at the house?"

"Nothing in Drew's room or the common areas. Then Roberta West gave us permission to search the rest of the house."

Pratt blinked. "Why would she do that?"

Mo raked his fork through his coleslaw. "Either she has the hots for Dix, or she was hoping we'd find some dirt on her husband."

Charity leaned forward. "Did you?"

"Yeah. We found evidence of more than one female using Hampton West's private bathroom. We bagged several samples, all pulled from the shower drain. Nothing in the bedroom or closet. That family has a crazy-industrious cleaning crew."

"Let's ID those samples as soon as we can," Pratt said briskly.

Charity raised her eyebrows at the sheriff. "You don't think one of those samples belongs to Sarah, do you?"

"You mean, do I think she was sleeping with all three generations of Wests?" Pratt stacked his hands on top of his head, mouth twisted with distaste. "I hope to hell not."

"Back to our most likely suspect," Dix drawled. "We do have probable cause to hold him. We have a witness placing him at the scene. We have motive and opportunity."

"But no physical evidence." Charity continued wiping at her shake container, no longer interested in the contents. She could feel them all looking at her, but just because she'd screwed up didn't mean she couldn't have a say. "What we have is circumstantial, and he's not the only one with a motive. Anyone in the family who knew they were sleeping together has motive. Then there's Keith Tarrant. He barely had his door open before he was demanding a lawyer."

With a disapproving grunt, Mo scrunched up his trash, making as much noise as possible.

Charity regarded him impatiently. "Is this how it's going to be? Every time I suggest we look into someone outside of the West family, you're going to give me attitude?"

"'Til I have a reason not to."

"Then I'll have to give you a reason."

"Give it your best shot."

Charity balled up her napkin and lobbed it across the table. "You know my best shot is pretty damned good. You still owe me a hundred bucks from the last time we went to the range, remember?"

"I told you, I got a cramp." Mo flexed his right hand. "Can I help it if I got a cramp?"

"You know what'll take care of that?" Brenda June appeared in the doorway, eyeing Mo's fist. "A girlfriend."

"Or better yet, try the other hand," Charity said solemnly.

"Jesus," Dix groaned.

"I need the other hand for this." Mo flipped Charity the bird.

"Feel better now?" she asked.

His trademark grin, as sly as it was infamous, lifted the corners of his mouth. "Yeah."

The knot in Charity's chest loosened.

"So we're all friends again?" growled the sheriff.

"Not all of us." Brenda June sniffed and avoided the sheriff's gaze. "The judge wants to know who's out on patrol today."

Dix gave her the name of one of the regulators. Dispatch nodded and turned to go.

"There a problem?" Pratt demanded.

Charity hid a wince. The sheriff's cluelessness about his dispatcher's feelings for him was truly pathetic.

Brenda June swung back around, face pale but placid. "No problem. The judge wants to make sure his house gets a drive by. Apparently he's afraid our vandal might escalate from junk cars to brand new luxury sedans."

"Hey." Charity jerked upright. "No dissing Clarabelle."

Pratt frowned. "Why doesn't he park in his garage?"

"Because then no one would see his brand new luxury sedan."

Mo nodded. "I get that."

Brenda June rolled her eyes and disappeared.

The sheriff rubbed a palm over his head. "Can we get back to work now?"

"Why does he need a drive by?" Dix eyed Charity's milkshake. "Doesn't he have an electronic gate? And security cameras?"

She pushed her shake across the table and snapped her fingers. "Cameras," she said. "The Wests have cameras. There might be footage showing who left the note."

"I'll look into it." Pratt slapped his palms down on the table. "Now. How about we get back to our murder?"

A thought hovered just out of Charity's reach. An important thought. *Crap.* Hand jobs, milkshakes, video cameras —

"Her phone," she blurted.

Dix thumped the end of the straw against the table until it popped out of the wrapper. "Whose phone?"

"Sarah's. She texted Drew, but we didn't find her phone."

Mo shrugged. "So he took it."

"Why didn't he take her purse?" Charity asked.

"Why would he?" Another shrug from Mo. "He was getting rid of evidence, not looking for something to steal. We ruled out robbery at the very beginning. And it's easier to get rid of a phone than an entire purse."

"Which means that if her phone was in her purse, he took the time to search for it. Because her purse was intact."

Dix's face was thoughtful as he pushed the straw through the cup's lid. "Logic versus panic."

Pratt's eyes narrowed. "Meaning?"

"Let's say Drew killed her." Charity blinked away the image of the teen's quivering chin and anxious eyes. "He strangled her, pocketed both the weapon and Sarah's phone, then pulled out his own phone and called his mother. Calling his mother indicates panic. The rest of it doesn't."

"He's a smart kid," Mo said. "Maybe he planned it that way."

Dix swallowed a mouthful of chocolate malt. "Uh-uh. The stretch of road that runs by the vet's is virtually deserted after dark. It wouldn't make sense to count on some random witness driving by."

"Except one did," Mo pointed out. "Anyway, he didn't need the witness. Once he admitted he was at the scene, his mother backed him up. That whole purse thing is bullshit. He didn't have to dump her purse because she had her phone in her hand when he got there. He attacked her, she dropped it, he picked it up. Doesn't prove a thing."

"It proves he had presence of mind. What's bullshit is thinking his panic was an act." Charity mentally kicked her own ass for letting herself get so invested in Drew's welfare. "The kid had motive and opportunity. He wouldn't risk a conviction without something stronger than the tone of his voice to save his hide. The prosecutor would say he called his mother in a panic because he'd finally registered what he'd done. How's that going to get him off the hook?"

Another *ploink* from the direction of the sink interrupted the silence. "We need her phone records," Charity said. "We need to compare the timestamp on Sarah's text to the time of her death."

"Because someone else could have sent that text." Mo ran both hands through his hair. "The ME hasn't established time of death. He had a case with a higher priority come in yesterday. I waited as long as I could, but he was never able to make time for Sarah."

"I'll give him a call. We need that autopsy. And that phone. Get the phone company to ping it." The sheriff turned to Dix. "Any trace evidence on the clothes Drew wore that night?"

"Red hairs on his jacket. Makes sense, since he was Sarah's lover. Also Mrs. Langford said her son was holding the victim's head in his lap when she pulled into the parking lot."

Oh, dear Lord. Charity swallowed around a sudden thickness in her throat. "When did she say that?"

"Later that night. I followed up on her statement while you and Mo worked the scene."

"Doesn't mean he's innocent," Mo said, stubborn to the end. "Could have been remorse."

"Whatever it was, his lawyer will have a field day with it. And the fact that he moved the body could explain why we found the necklace underneath it." Pratt squinted at Charity. "Maybe Mrs. Langford panicked and got rid of the phone."

Charity winced. She should have thought of that sooner. "We'll ask Drew if he noticed it at the scene."

"Maybe Mrs. Langford killed Sarah and decided to frame her own son," Dix suggested quietly.

"Yeah." Mo dragged out the word. "Because she knew it wouldn't stick."

Charity wagged her head. "Big Mike vouched for her. She was at the bar when Sarah was killed."

"Didn't I just say we don't have TOD?" Mo studied her. "You really don't want any of the Wests to be guilty."

"I really don't want the wrong person to go to prison. Too many people knew about the affair, Kate Young and Peyton Langford included. Besides, it might not have had anything to do with the murder."

"We can't hold Drew Langford forever. We either arrest him or we let him go." The sheriff pushed to his feet, and everyone else followed suit. "If we charge him, Owen Quinn will shred our case to pieces, and we'll have wasted a hell of a lot of time and money. We let him go and we can keep an eye on him. A close eye, people. We need more than conjecture to catch us a killer."

*   *   *

DREW SAT ON THE thin mattress, back to the cement, knees to his chest, gaze locked on the opposite wall and the *sucks to be you* someone had scratched into the paint. The food at the Shack kicked ass but he shouldn't have eaten that sandwich they brought him — even several hours later the sauce was burning a slow hole through his stomach and pancreas and spleen and whatever the hell else took up space below his ribs.

Nothing inside felt normal. Except for his kidneys. He knew his kidneys were okay because he had to take a piss, but after hours of playing it cool for his mom he was too damned tired to move. So yeah, it sucked to be him.

Sucked more to be Sarah.

He dropped his gaze to his socked feet, reached forward and tugged at a black thread dangling from a hole above his second toe. Who had hated Sarah so much that they thought she deserved to die? What kind of lowlife thought it was okay to squeeze the fucking life out of someone? Out of a *woman?* A woman who wouldn't even step on a frickin' spider?

His eyes burned. He should have known something was wrong. They'd been together a while, and they hadn't spent *all* of their time screwing. Why hadn't he noticed something was wrong?

Why couldn't he have saved her?

Maybe he deserved to be locked up.

Footsteps, and the jingle of keys. "Langford."

He leaned his head back against the wall and cut his eyes to the door. Chief was working the lock. Great. More questions.

He wanted to ask why they weren't all out there looking for Sarah's killer. But that's exactly what a TV killer would say.

Not that he'd actually admit to watching Lifetime.

"We have processed your release," the big man said. "We tried to get in touch with your mother. No answer on her cell. Since your lawyer is with a client in the city, I will drive you home."

Slowly, clumsily, Drew got to his feet. Whether he deserved it or not, that was the best news he'd heard since finding out he was actually going to pass senior English. Didn't matter what the badasses who spent time in juvie had to say—spending a night in lockup was scary as hell.

"This mean you know I didn't do it?" he ventured.

"Means we can't prove you did."

Drew heard the rest of it, loud and clear. *Not yet, anyway.*

Still. The suck factor had eased up just enough so he could breathe.

Chief handed him his shoes.

Drew put them on without sitting down. "What about my dad?"

"Board meeting."

Nice. Drew dropped his head, took his time tying his laces. Then he was out of the holding cell and pulling in a breath. He could always call Uncle Grady, but that would mean he'd have to wait. He'd rather catch a ride with Chief Ironlung than hang out in a place that smelled like piss, puke, and self-pity.

Besides, he'd never been in a police car before.

Half an hour later, it wasn't his grandparents' place Chief parked in front of. Drew had talked the deputy into a pit stop at Allison's. He had to man up. Apologize.

Make sure she was okay.

He walked up the driveway like he'd walked into the sheriff's department the morning before, with dread hammering so hard at his knees he could barely stand upright. Dusk had already stolen the light but he could still see the yellows and purples in the flowerbeds Allison's mom had always been so proud of. Last summer he'd gotten Allison in trouble by convincing her to go to the movies when she was supposed to be weeding. One kiss and she'd forgiven him.

It wouldn't be so easy this time.

Then again, it wasn't forgiveness that mattered.

He pulled in a breath and caught the rosemary-like scent of pine tree resin. When Allison's mom came outside he almost choked. She had on sneakers and black stretchy clothes and her face was splotchy. She must have just finished a workout, though she looked far from relaxed. More like she wanted to kick him in the 'nads.

What did he expect? He'd dumped the daughter for one of the mother's best friends.

"Mrs. Young." He stopped at the bottom of the porch steps, fingers itching for the insides of his pockets. "I was hoping I could talk to Allison."

She crossed her arms. "I thought you were in jail."

"I was. I'm out now, and I'm not going back."

Her face went slack. Judas Priest, what did she think he'd do, take her hostage? Did she not see the badass deputy parked at the curb?

"All I meant," he said tightly, "was that I didn't do it. I wouldn't hurt Sarah. I wouldn't hurt anyone."

Kate Young made a kind of humming noise and dropped her gaze.

She didn't believe him. She thought he was guilty.

Would everyone think he was guilty?

A cocktail of regret, resentment, and sissy-ass fear started up a party in the back of his throat. Damn, he needed a Coke.

He managed to scrape the words out anyway. "So may I? See her?"

"I don't think that's a good idea."

"Is she here?"

"That's not the point."

"I need to talk to her."

"You think an apology's going to help?" Kate Young stomped to the edge of the porch and glared down at him. "She's in therapy because of you. *Therapy.*"

"Oh, my God, Mom." Allison came out from behind her mother, wearing plaid flannel pants and a navy tee. She'd gathered her reddish-blond hair, the hair that always smelled like sugar cookies, in a high ponytail. She looked so young.

Or maybe it was just that he felt so old.

149

"Why would you tell him something like that?" she demanded.

Her mother reached out and smoothed her palm up and down Allison's arm. "He needs to understand what he's done to you."

"I did plenty to him, too." She motioned with her chin toward the front door behind her. "Mom. Go inside. This is between me and Drew."

Reluctantly her mother left them alone. Drew rested a foot on the bottom step, feeling like a dweeb in his wrinkled suit pants and polished shoes.

"You should take charge more often," he said. "It looks good on you."

"Are you really here to see me?"

"What does that mean?"

"You go for older women." Bitterness twisted her lips. "I figured Mom might be next on your list."

He sighed. "I never wanted to hurt you."

"But you did."

"Yes. And I want to apologize."

"For breaking up with me?"

Shit. Did she think he wanted to get back together?

"No," he said gently. "Breaking up was the right thing to do. We were spending more and more time apart. When we split neither of us really seemed to mind."

She gave a full-body flinch and stared down at her socked feet. "So what are you sorry for?" she asked huskily.

"I guess…just…this thing with Sarah. I'm sorry you found out the way you did."

"You mean you're sorry I found out."

"Yeah. Because you said you'd hurt yourself if I dated anyone else."

Her head swung up and her eyes went narrow. "And you wouldn't want that on your conscience."

"I wouldn't want that at all. We may not be going together anymore but that doesn't mean I don't care."

"If you really cared you wouldn't have made me look bad by dumping me for someone old enough to be your mother. Do you get that everyone's saying how sad it is, that I couldn't keep you satisfied? Do you even get how much that hurts?"

His fingers fisted at his sides. "Do you even get that she's dead?"

She stared at his hands, an odd light flaring in her eyes. "I'm not going to hurt myself. You're not worth it. Especially if you did it."

Her words ripped right through him. "You think I did it?"

"Peyton does. She said that no matter what, you should go to jail for what you did to me."

He didn't realize he'd swayed backward until he lost his balance and stumbled back a step. When had his own sister turned against him?

"It's not against the law to break up with somebody," he finally muttered.

"If you humiliate them it should be."

"You're upset about what everyone thinks, not about losing me."

"I'm upset about that bitch taking what was mine."

Drew stared. She'd spit that out in a tone worthy of one of those TV teens who went around being possessed by demons.

Her mom poked her head out of the house. "Allison. Time to come in."

Behind them, the tricked-out Tahoe started up. Allison shivered, and Drew hunched his shoulders.

"I have to go," he said slowly.

"Me, too." And she sent him a look that had him absolutely convinced she was anxious to get back to jabbing needles into a voodoo doll that looked exactly like him.

This time he was the one who shivered. He trudged back to the SUV.

Twenty minutes later, he was letting himself into his grandparents' house. All he wanted was to take a shower and crash for an entire week. But he heard voices—and the all-too-familiar *tink* of ice against crystal—coming from the living room. He should check in. Maybe someone was still sober enough to care that he was home.

Suit coat and tie flung over his shoulder, his free hand in his pocket, he trudged down the hallway. He paused under the arch that opened into the big-ass formal space he and Peyton had always steered clear of. Too many breakables. Stainables. Fuck-up-ables.

His grandfather hunched over the bar, fixing his grandmother a drink she didn't need. The gurgle of liquid, the rattling smack of a bottle returned not quite steadily to a metal tray—how many times since they'd moved in had he heard these sounds? His grandfather turned with a drink in each hand—one for his wife and one for Drew's mom—then turned back and poured himself a whiskey. Drew exhaled. They all looked rumpled and pale. Defeated. He opened his mouth to tell them to stop worrying, to let them know he was there. The odd expression on his mother's face stopped him. She was looking at his grandfather, who had his hand in his jacket pocket.

As she held out her palm, the old man produced a plastic amber bottle. He uncapped it, tipped it, and presented his daughter with a couple days' worth of oblivion. Drew inhaled. The need to yell, to kick, to hit, to smash every last bottle in the fucking house rose up inside him like foam charging out of a glass filled too quickly with Coke.

"Mom?" His legs wobbled as he stormed into the room. "What are you doing?"

She spun toward him, fist to her chest. "Drew! You're home!" She hurried toward him, relief drenching her eyes. "Oh, honey, it's so good to see you. Thank God. Thank *God*." Her forehead hit his chin as she wrapped her arms around him.

"Why didn't you call us?" His grandfather trailed drops of whiskey as he crossed the room. "We would have come for you."

"One of the deputies brought me home. And they did try to call." Drew pulled away, eyeing his mother's fist. "You didn't pick up."

"I didn't hear my phone ring."

"What are you taking?"

"Just a little something to help me sleep. Never mind that. What matters is you're back, safe and sound."

"What matters is Sarah is dead. Somebody killed her. What matters is those pills are fucking you up so much you believe your own son is a murderer."

His mother went white.

His grandmother slapped both palms to the diamond glittering against her chest.

His grandfather pointed at him with the hand holding his whiskey. "You watch your mouth, young man."

"That's not true," his mom said, her voice small and tight. "I know you couldn't hurt anyone."

"You confessed to protect me. Everyone knows it. You thought I did it."

"No. I wasn't thinking clearly. I panicked."

"You weren't thinking clearly because you'd been drinking. And popping those." He nodded stiffly at her pocket. "Can't you see what these are doing to you? To us? Mom, you've gotta stop."

"I...I can't," she said, and the despair in her voice took him right back to the desperate days after his father had moved out.

"Drew." His grandmother put a trembling hand on his arm. He shook it off. Wished he could shake *them* off. He rounded on his grandparents.

"So, what, you're her suppliers? Judas Priest, don't you care what you've turned her into?"

His grandfather made a harumphing sound and drew himself up. "You will *not* speak to us like—"

"Mom. You're an addict."

"Don't be ridiculous. You've been through a lot but that's no excuse for disrespect. I think you'd better go to bed."

"So you can be alone with your pills?"

His grandfather slammed his nearly empty glass down on an end table. "Don't give us that holier-than-thou shit, Drew Bartholomew," he said. "You had an affair with a woman twice your age."

"That sounds more like sour grapes than outrage," Drew said wildly. "At least I cared about Sarah."

"She certainly didn't care about you." His grandmother snatched up her husband's whiskey glass and drained it. "All the while she was sleeping with you, she was —"

"Don't you dare," his mom choked.

" —sleeping with your father."

Remorse replaced the triumph on his grandmother's face the moment she finished the sentence. Drew stared for a moment, struggling to wrap his mind around her words.

Dumbass. He really was a dumbass. Sarah was already seeing his father when she'd ended things with Drew.

At the moment he was too tired to care.

He stalked out of the living room. He'd reached the bottom of the staircase when his dad came in the front door, Peyton clinging to his arm. The surprise and relief on his dad's face when he saw Drew warmed him. Until he remembered what his grandmother had said. The warmth turned into freezer burn.

"You're supposed to wait outside," he snapped, dodging his dad's embrace.

Uncle Grady and Matt came in then. "Drew!" Matt shouted, and thrust himself forward. They exchanged the back slap that was the male version of a hug, then bumped knuckles. "Dad said you wouldn't be back yet. What was it like in jail?"

"Give him some space, Matt." Uncle Grady closed the door, gaze bouncing back and forth between Drew and Drew's dad.

With a scowl, Matt backed into the corner of the foyer.

"Matt and I took Peyton to dinner," Uncle Grady told Drew quietly. "Your dad had just pulled up when we got back." He held out a hand. "It's good to see you, kid."

Drew shook his uncle's hand and continued to stare darkly at his dad.

Finally realizing he wasn't going to get that hug, his dad dropped his arms. "Your sister invited me in."

"Yeah." Peyton shoved her takeout carton at Uncle Grady like she was thinking of throwing a punch or two. "What's the big deal?"

"I missed you, too," Drew said tightly.

"What'd they do to you?" his dad demanded. "What'd they say?"

Drew choked out a laugh. "So it is true. You'd already started seeing Sarah."

"What?" Looking like he'd gotten a whiff of the entire soccer team's laundry after a game, Uncle Grady tossed Peyton's leftovers on the hall table, ordered Matt upstairs, and rounded on his ex-brother-in-law. "Scott, what the hell?"

His dad had gone pale. "Let me explain."

He had to be frickin' kidding. But before Drew could tell his dad to go to hell, he heard the clacking scurry of high heels.

His mom rushed into the room and got right up in his dad's face.

Everyone except Uncle Grady took a cautious step back.

9

W HAT ARE YOU DOING here?" Drew's mom demanded. "You know damned well you're not welcome in this house."

"This is your fault," his dad growled at his mom. "My son hates me because that liquor-logged head of yours is so far up your advantaged ass you couldn't keep him from screwing a woman twice his age."

"You're busting *my* balls? Please. Sarah was two-timing you with your own son and you didn't have a clue. She must have figured out what I already knew — a teenage boy is more man than you are."

"What?" Peyton shrieked. "Dad and Drew were both — ? *Eww.*" She punched Drew in the shoulder. "What is *wrong* with you? You couldn't just let him have her? You had Allison. Why did you need anyone else?"

"Pey." He rubbed his shoulder with one hand and reached out with the other. She dodged him and ran up the stairs, legs pumping like a football player running a tire drill.

"Follow her," Uncle Grady urged, and Drew knew it was more about getting him away from his parents than getting him to make things right with his sister. Fine by him. Hearing his parents whale on each other always sucked ass.

"You sour little bitch." His dad's voice followed him up the stairs. "At least I had the pleasure of fucking something other than a puddle of gin for once. And you know what's pathetic? You're a better lay than you are a parent."

"That's *enough*," roared Uncle Grady. "You think this is over for him? It's not. Far from it. You're his parents. He needs you. Suck it up and be there for him."

His mom said something, too low for Drew to hear. Probably just as well. He paused outside Peyton's door, then barged in without knocking. Something else she'd never forgive him for.

"Leave me alone," she mumbled. She was tucked up against the headboard, forehead to her knees. No tears in her voice. He didn't know if that should make him feel better or worse.

He settled at the foot of the bed, glancing around at the ruffles and polka dots and purple sparkly junk that made Peyton's room uniquely hers. A unique and inviting trap. Just like his own room.

"It was a bad idea, moving in with our grandparents," he said. "They're only making things worse."

Her head snapped up. "What are you talking about? They look out for us. They love us. We have everything we need." She grabbed a round purple pillow and hugged it to her chest.

"They're not looking out for Mom. They got her started on those pills and now she's hooked."

"How can you talk about them like that? They're our *grandparents*."

"That doesn't mean they're perfect. C'mon, Pey. You're not stupid. You know Mom hasn't been right since we got here."

"She's been through a lot, what with Dad leaving and then losing her job. God, Drew, she was willing to go to *jail* for you. Why can't you cut her a break?"

"You love her, right? You want her to be around for a long time?" When she rolled her eyes he pulled his knee up on the bed and turned to face her. "She keeps this up and she'll die."

"You're trying to manipulate me. I hate that. I hate you."

He exhaled, and slowly got to his feet. He'd heard it before. Still it shook him. "Sometimes I hate myself, too," he said.

That shut her up, but only for a second. "Anyway, you're lying. Why are you trying to upset everyone? It's not our fault you were arrested."

"They didn't arrest me. Not yet."

Her eyes went round. "You think they will?"

"I'm their best suspect."

She opened her mouth, closed it, snatched up her iPod and slid onto her side, face to the wall. "Turn off the light on your way out."

He watched her untangle her ear buds. "Aren't you going to ask me?"

"Ask you what?"

"If I did it."

"Go away." She jammed the ear buds into her ears.

Once in his own room, Drew sank down onto his bed. He needed that shower but lacked the energy to undress.

Sarah had been screwing both him and his old man. When she'd broken things off, she'd told Drew she'd developed feelings for his father. Feelings she couldn't help. Feelings she'd wanted the space to explore. She'd said she wouldn't have felt right doing it while seeing Drew.

She'd lied.

Had that been some kind of kinky turn-on, taking turns with father and son? Hell, maybe she'd even hoped to talk them into a threesome.

Bile bubbled up into his throat. Joining the nausea was a savage resentment that lit up his chest like too much Tabasco on a chili dog. He lunged toward his bathroom, landed on his knees in front of his toilet and let loose. Minutes later, kneecaps throbbing, stomach sore, he staggered over to his mini fridge and snagged a soda, flipped the tab with shaking fingers and took a desperate swig.

Had he loved Sarah? No. But she'd made him feel good. Made him think he was special.

Made him forget the shit waiting for him at home.

He set the soda on his desk, dropped sideways onto his mattress, and pulled his knees up against his chest. Stared in the direction of his *Fast and Furious* poster and let loose a wave of dumbass tears.

* * *

In Full Force

AS CHARITY SLID INTO a back booth at Sweeney's, she snagged a French fry off Mo's plate. A bump of her hip forced Dix to the wall. "Thanks a lot for waiting, guys."

Dix had drunk almost all of what looked like a whiskey, and Mo was halfway through a beer and his fries. Charity reached across Dix and grabbed the pepper out of the caddy at the end of the table. She straightened back up, only to find Mo had spread both hands over his plate.

"My fries are fine the way they are. And we did wait for you. Appetizers don't count."

She rolled her eyes. "How about drinks?"

"Thanks." Mo brightened. "We're good for now, but you can get the next round."

"My ass."

Big Mike brought over an iced tea. She smiled her thanks. Once upon a time the bartender had figured big in her fantasies—so delightfully big. Who could blame her? With his bulky muscles, ocean-deep voice, and slow Southern drawl, the erotic dream version of Big Mike was the perfect orgasm donor. Dolan Sweeney, who co-owned the bar with his sister, wasn't half bad, either. And she still had fond memories of a local firefighter who'd been the most fun she'd ever had in bed.

But sooner or later, no matter who she envisioned as she writhed against her own hand, they always ended up wearing Grady West's face.

"Y'all ready to order?" Big Mike asked, and Charity cursed Grady West to hell when her thigh muscles didn't even quiver.

They ordered sandwiches, and Mo asked for another plate of fries. "You can pepper half," he told Charity.

She was distracted by Dix asking for a refill of his drink. At least he'd ordered something to eat. After Big Mike moved away from the table, she elbowed her lead detective.

Well, her lead detective for the next thirty days.

"I didn't think you were going to make it tonight." They'd planned dinner to catch up on the case and to make peace after the drama at lunchtime, but Dix's wife had needed him at home.

159

"Sheila has a migraine." Slowly Dix rotated his glass. "She said I was making too much noise."

"I'm sorry she's not feeling well. I'm glad you're here, though. Someone has to pick up the check."

Instead of giving her the half grin she expected, he raised his glass and drained it. She glanced at Mo, who shrugged and crammed two ketchup-coated fries into his mouth. Bless Riley Morrissey and his uncomplicated view of life. Seemed he really had decided not to hold that anonymous note against her.

"How'd it go with Drew?" she asked Dix quietly.

They'd released the teen that evening. Dix had ended up driving him home, since Justine wasn't picking up her phone, and Scott couldn't pull himself away from…whatever. Or whoever.

After a couple of beats Dix inhaled and looked up. There came the half grin. "Before he got in the patrol vehicle he asked for Mo. Guess I make him nervous."

Mo gave Charity a told-you-so nod. "See? Smart kid."

"Then he asked for Allison Young."

Charity sat back. "He wanted to see Allison before going home?"

"That took balls," Mo said grudgingly. "Did her mother let him in?"

"No. Allison did come out on the porch, and the two of them talked. And no, I do not know what about. Kid remained silent until we got to Pill Hill."

Mo leaned forward. "What'd he say then?"

"'Thanks for the ride, chief.'"

Charity winced.

Reddening, Mo scratched his neck. "Hope you set him straight."

Charity felt a swell of pride on Mo's behalf. Dix had set *him* straight the first time Mo had called him chief, explaining succinctly that the nickname was an incorrect label that trivialized the title held by Native American tribal leaders and reduced Dix solely to his race. Mo had taken the correction to heart.

Dix grunted a response that could have meant anything.

Charity poked at the lemon bobbing in her tea. "Drew really is afraid Allyson will hurt herself."

Silence. *Crap.* For what seemed like forever, Dix had worried the same about Sheila. Could she be any more insensitive? "Dix," she began.

"*Kayim,*" he said. "Don't go there." He spoke lightly, but it was obvious he was upset. It was the only time he used Cree.

More silence. Mo's gaze flicked from Charity to Dix, and he gave his empty plate a shove. "You two ready to tell me why we're here? 'Cause it's obviously not about the case."

Dix glanced at the bar, and Charity spotted the desperation in his gaze. Misery squeezed her heart. This was about more than not wanting to tell Mo.

Dix didn't want to leave Becker County.

"Fuck me," breathed Mo, when no one spoke. "You were sleeping with her, too."

Charity squawked a *No!* while Dix shook his head in disgust.

"I am married," he gritted.

Mo threw himself back against his seat. The booth trembled. "What, then?"

"Sheila and I are moving to the city," Dix said. "I have a month left with the department."

Mo's jaw went slack. "Didn't see that one coming," he said finally. "Didn't see that one coming at all." He ran his palm over his face. "Your wife is one lucky woman."

"Gee, Morrissey, I did not know you cared."

"Fuck you."

They all went quiet as Big Mike delivered their food.

"I hate change," Mo muttered.

"Speaking of which." Charity grimaced. "We need to talk about Oliver Bloom."

"No, we do not," said Dix, jaw as hard as the table beneath their elbows. Charity hesitated and glanced at Mo, who aimed a defiant glower across the table, as if daring Dix to crack a smile. Yes. Good. No wallowing allowed. There'd be plenty of time for that later.

Charity told them about her encounter with Oliver Bloom outside the courthouse. Ten minutes after that, she and Morrissey were laughing their asses off. Dix, on the other hand, remained stone-faced.

161

"Bet he can quote *Pretty Woman,* too." Mo saw their faces and flushed. "Hey, if watching ninety minutes of a chick flick means my dick will see some action, I'm all for it." He shook his head at Charity. "But Oliver Bloom? A little old for you, isn't he?"

"Father figure," Dix muttered into his whiskey.

"You still here?" Charity glared. "I thought you were leaving."

"I would like to finish my sandwich first."

"I'm sure Big Mike would be happy to wrap it to go." She picked at her turkey sub. "Sorry, Dix. I didn't mean to make this about me. But Mo, I need to let you know. If Bloom wins the election, you're on your own."

Mo choked on a fry. "What does that mean?"

"Means I can't work with the guy."

He took a deep pull of his beer and held the mug aloft, staring morosely at the few inches of liquid left inside. "Where does that leave me?"

"Easy enough." Dix pushed away his empty glass. "Pull your head out of Bloom's ass and help her win."

Charity stiffened. "You're backing Bloom?"

Mo's face flamed so fiercely she half expected to see steam coming out of his ears. "It's not personal. Bloom's older, has military experience, and was a state trooper for more than twenty years. He's better qualified."

"He's also an asshole," gritted Charity.

"No argument there."

"But you'd feel more comfortable working for him."

"Not for him. With him."

Gaze traveling to the curved bar that on Friday night would be stacked three customers deep, Charity lifted her tea and pretended to drink. Hurt, heavy and cold, crawled into her chest and pressed on her lungs as she automatically scanned the half-dozen barflies, cataloging their clothes, expressions, body language.

She knew she wasn't the popular choice for sheriff. She simply hadn't expected any of her own team to vote against her.

A loud *clack* and a rattle as on the other side of the bar someone started a fresh pool game with an overzealous break shot. Tea sloshed as Charity jerked in response.

A masculine chuckle sounded over her shoulder. "Jumpy, much?"

She shifted in her seat and looked up at Cal Brennan, the firefighter she'd been thinking about moments ago, and couldn't keep her face from heating. He gave her a wink and nodded at Mo and Dix. It didn't take him long to register the somber mood at the table, and his smile dimmed.

"Sorry for interrupting," he said. "You're probably discussing Sarah's case. We were all shocked to hear what happened."

His partner Nina Morales moved up behind him, tugging at the cuffs of her long-sleeved uniform shirt. "Sarah sold me my house when I moved here," she said. "If there's anything we can do, please let us know."

"Hey." Mo spoke in a loud and suggestive drawl, drowning out Charity's thank-you. "What have you two been up to?" He gestured at their wrinkled navy uniforms and tousled hair.

Instantly Nina's hands flew to her thick, dark ponytail and the band that seemed determined to escape it, while Cal scrubbed his fingers through his own short sandy hair.

"Screw you, Deputy," Cal said cheerfully. "I'll have you know that we just survived four hazardous duty hours as the after-school special. And we're not even on shift today."

"Can't tell you how many times we got in and out of our bunker gear." Nina offered a wry smile. "The kids insisted on timing us."

Dix grunted. "Middle schoolers?"

"They're brutal." Nina exaggerated a shudder.

"We'll let you get back to your meal." Cal pulled out his wallet. "This is on me. Everyone at the station appreciates what you're doing for Sarah."

Nina shot him a questioning look while Mo popped up and gave him a knuckle-bump.

Cal set some bills on the table and slid them toward Charity. "You look good, Char." His tone was sincere, and mostly free of flirtation. "Still living on coffee and Pop-Tarts?"

"You're one to talk. The slightest whiff of chocolate and you're reduced to a quivering, drooling mess. Am I right?" She looked to Nina for confirmation and that's when she caught it. The combination of envy and hurt that flared on the female firefighter's face.

Charity bit her lip. Crap. Nina Morales was in love with her partner. A man who could barely commit to the contents of his grocery cart before making it to the checkout counter. That had worked fine for Charity, but she could tell Nina was a different story. And her feelings were obvious, to anyone paying attention.

No one was paying attention.

Especially not Cal, who was craning his neck so he could catch the action at the pool table. Dix was frowning down into his empty glass, no doubt considering a refill, and Mo was checking out his sideburns in the chrome-plated napkin holder.

"I just spotted Sunny with Fee." Cal jabbed a brotherly elbow into Nina's ribs. "C'mon, partner. Let's go show them a thing or two about wielding a cue."

Charity watched them go, the acceptance on Nina's face a miserable thing to see, now that Charity knew what was behind it. Suddenly Cal whipped back around.

"Hey, congrats on the sheriff thing," he called. "You can count on my vote." With a grin he turned away again and followed Nina to the pool table.

Silence descended. Mo poked his beer mug. Dix muttered something in Cree.

More silence.

When Charity's cell jangled Brenda June's ringtone, her eyes burned with relief. Sixty seconds and a murmured conversation later, she was able to face her coworkers without crying like a baby.

"That was Brenda June, passing on a message from the ME. Sarah died roughly between ten and eleven p.m."

Mo pulled a face. "Doesn't help our case against Drew Langford."

Charity swallowed a smug retort. "We also have her phone records now, and Dispatch verified the timestamp on the text Sarah sent to Drew. Eight twelve p.m."

Mo sat up. "So Sarah did send the text."

"Or whoever has her phone did," Charity said.

Dix eased his elbows back and stretched. "No luck locating it?"

"Couldn't ping it. It's either dead, or whoever has it knew enough to take the battery out. And I've had no luck recreating her day." She sighed. "Drew wasn't with her, and her coworkers haven't been much help."

She really needed to know where Scott Langford had been Wednesday night. Kate, too. She also needed to set up an interview with Keith Tarrant and the ever-popular Lawyer Quinn.

As if she didn't already have enough paperwork.

"The service is Tuesday." Mo signaled for the bill. "Want to bet how many of Sarah's ex-lovers show up?"

"At least one," Charity said softly.

Mo looked away. "It could get ugly."

"I hope it does." Dix reached for his wallet. "We could use some fresh leads."

* * *

GRADY BACKED AWAY FROM the doorway of the upstairs den, where Matt and Drew were playing video games. His shoulder ached—he'd been leaning against the jamb for a while, watching what looked like World War II tanks take on some kind of Ninja zombies. All he knew was, he was way out of his league. What had ever happened to Mario Brothers?

On his way back to his room, he pulled his cell from his pocket. He'd been fighting the urge to call Charity since Drew had walked through the front door. Might as well give in to the impulse. Whether or not she'd pick up was another story.

She picked up.

He sank down onto the foot of the bed. His sweatpants were slick on the navy-and-maroon-striped comforter and he almost fell on his ass. "Hey," he said, thighs straining as he struggled back onto the bed. "It's nice to have my nephew home where he belongs."

On the other end of the phone, keys jingled, and a door opened and shut. A thud shortly after had him picturing Charity dropping her purse on the small table by her front door.

"I hope you didn't call to thank me," she said. "We didn't have enough evidence to charge him."

"I still want to help."

"I still have to say no."

He got to his feet and wandered over to the window. He pushed the drapes aside and stared out at the side yard, dimly lit from the spillover of the spotlights out front. "Rough day?"

"How did you know?"

The wary surprise in her voice made his lips twitch. "Something about your tone. Plus I was there when my son gave you a hard time, remember?"

"That was one of the nicer things that happened to me today." She sighed. "I found out Dix is leaving."

He let go of the drapes. Soundlessly they shifted back into place. "I'm sorry to hear that."

"I was, too." Bottles rattled and something thumped. She'd opened and shut her fridge. "I'll miss him."

He thought of the photos on her wall. "How much?"

"Don't you have some spreadsheets to update or stocks to annualize?"

With a chuckle, he turned and sat on the window sill. The curtain rod squeaked as the drapes pulled tight. "What do you know about annualizing?"

"Not a thing. I must have heard it on TV."

"I was wondering about something."

Moments passed. A gurgling sound — she was pouring herself a glass of something. Orange juice, probably.

"You do realize," she said dryly, "that you have me wondering what you're wondering?"

"Did you ever get a dog?"

Her refrigerator opened and shut again. "My hours aren't pet friendly."

He waited.

She made a little humming sound of resignation. "How about you?"

"Yeah." He stood, and began to pace. "Zeus. He's a mix, but he has a lot of black Lab in him. Matt's babysitter has him until we get back."

"I doubt Matt appreciates the word 'babysitter.'"

"He wouldn't appreciate her no matter what I called her. She's our neighbor, Mrs. Karpinski. Matt's always complaining she smells like salami."

Charity's throaty laugh rippled through him. "Does she?"

"She kind of does. Hey." He turned left at the door and paced toward the closet. The hand holding his phone was starting to get sweaty. "You know one of the things I've missed most about you? Your voice. It's like soft, warm sand. Naughty sand. Sand on a nudist's beach." He groaned. "Jesus, never mind."

Charity sputtered. "I didn't know sand had a sound, let alone a naughty one."

He grinned at the inside of the mostly empty closet, wondering when the hell he'd opened the door. "We'll be sure to hit the beach when you come to see us in Seattle."

She didn't respond to that. He hadn't expected her to, but still he lost the urge to grin.

"Tell me about it," she said brightly. "Seattle."

He shut the closet door and paced on toward the bathroom, which was bigger than his master bath back home. "It's a beautiful city." He flicked on the light, scowled into the mirror and gave his reflection the loser sign. "Crowded, though. Traffic can be a nightmare, which is one reason I work from home. The cost of living keeps getting higher." He turned off the light and backed out of the room. "But the parks are great, and there's lots of waterfront. If Matt and I aren't out on the water, we're kicking the soccer ball around."

"Do you have a house there?" Charity asked.

"Condo. We've done some house hunting off and on, but nothing's spoken to us yet."

"Matt seems like a good kid," she said, tentatively.

"He is." Grady finished his circuit of the room, and dropped back down onto the foot of the bed. He propped a hand on his thigh. "He's firmly in the rebellious stage, but I'm not going to give up hope that he'll eventually run out of reasons to resent me."

"I still can't wrap my mind around the fact that you're a father."

"There are days I struggle with that myself." He switched the phone to his other hand and dried his palm on his thigh. "Tell me something. What did you resent most about your mother?"

Charity inhaled and exhaled. "Grady, what are we doing?"

"Catching up."

"Because?"

"This time when I leave, I'd like for us to at least be on speaking terms."

She blurted an uneven laugh. "How am I supposed to argue with that?"

Grady heard a clattering sound, and Charity said something from a distance. More muffled sounds, followed by her voice back in his ear.

"Sorry about that," she said. "I dropped the phone." She cleared her throat. "Okay, here goes. When I was Matt's age, I suppose I resented not having a father. I used to fantasize that if he were still around, he'd always side with me, and raise the odds to two against three."

"You have the resources to find him now," Grady said. He bent forward, staring at his socked feet as he swept them apart and together, apart and together over the plush carpeting that was so clean, it looked brand new.

Hell, knowing his mother's fondness for redecorating, it probably was brand new. "You were never tempted to track him down?"

"He left when I was four, and not once has he contacted us. He made it clear he was done."

"You haven't talked to me in twelve years. And no, leaving a voicemail saying you forgive me but please don't call again doesn't count." Regret almost shoved the words back down his throat. "Does that mean you're done with me?"

"Hold on while I get rid of my rig." A pair of *thunks* as she put down first her phone then her duty belt. "We live completely separate lives hundreds of miles apart. We were done with each other, until you came back to help Justine."

"So when the investigation is over, that's it?"

"What about all those girlfriends back in Seattle?" she teased.

"Char."

She let out a breath. "I promise not to avoid you the next time you come to town."

Grady gritted his teeth. *Thanks a whole hell of a lot.*

"So what about you?" The double thud of her boots hitting the floor and the rustling on her end made it pretty obvious she was readjusting pillows and settling back against her headboard. "What did you resent most about your parents?"

"When I was Matt's age?" Grady scooted backwards, his socked feet digging into the comforter until his spine rested against his own headboard. "I guess I'd have to say the expectation that I'd be the best at everything. School, soccer, swimming, Scouts, even tending bar for all those booze-fests they called fundraisers."

She inhaled sharply. "You never told me about that."

He shrugged, though she couldn't see it. "You and I had a pact. We agreed we'd never touch the stuff. I didn't want you to know I wasn't holding up my end."

"You weren't drinking, you were mixing. And they're your parents, so it's not like you had much of a choice. Though I can't believe no one reported them for having a minor mix their cocktails."

Grady grabbed a round throw pillow, tossed it up into the air and caught it again. "You should have seen my father's face when I told him I had no intention of going to medical school. His cheeks were the color of grenadine."

Charity snorted. "You should have seen my mother's face when I told her about the police academy. Her cheeks were the color of crème de menthe."

"You sound like you know your liqueur."

"I had a boyfriend who was a bartender."

Grady chuckled. "I miss this."

"I have to go."

He closed his eyes. "I know."

"Good night, Grady."

"Good night, Char." He ended the call and hurled the pillow across the room.

* * *

THE FOLLOWING AFTERNOON, CHARITY'S fingers shook as she scrolled through her recent calls. When she landed on Grady's number, she jabbed at first the send, then the speakerphone buttons, and slapped the phone onto her thigh.

This conversation would be nowhere near as civil as the one they'd shared last night.

Two and a half days. Two and a half days since Drew Langford had discovered Sarah Huffman's body in a public parking lot, and Charity was no closer to finding the killer than she was to calling it quits with coffee.

Hence the jumbo-sized takeout cup currently warming the insides of her thighs.

She banged the side of her fist against the steering wheel. She'd expected sadness. Curiosity. Wariness. Maybe even a little resentment for the badge and the questions it gave her the right to ask. What she hadn't expected from the people of Becker County? Hostility. If they didn't believe she wanted to clear Drew so she could get back together with Grady, they believed she was trying to frame Drew to punish Grady for the breakup.

They could remember prehistoric teenage drama but couldn't remember the stop sign at the corner of Springfield and Butternut?

Her anger had started out as annoyance when Sarah Huffman's banker, hair stylist, and mechanic had all refused to answer her questions. It had turned into full-fledged fury after she'd stomped out of Scott Langford's townhouse not ten minutes earlier. It kept her sitting in her SUV in front of said townhouse because she knew better than to drive. Lord only knew how many stop signs she'd take out before she worked the bitterness out of her system.

The phone continued to ring. When he finally answered, her stomach clutched. The low timbre of his voice carried a cautious pleasure, but she refused to let herself get sidetracked from her fury.

"Hello?" Grady said.

One woman had accused her of being in bed with Grady — literally. Charity had decided to ignore how hypocritical it was to act outraged when she'd spent more than one sleepless night thinking about that very thing.

Although now her fantasies had everything to do with wrapping her hands around his throat and nothing to do with wrapping her legs around his hips.

Well, nothing much.

"If this is supposed to be a crank call," he drawled, "you need to breathe harder."

"What are you doing?" she demanded.

"You're supposed to ask what I'm wearing."

Her thighs tightened, and coffee seeped out from under the plastic lid. Hot liquid soaked through her pants and she hissed in a breath.

"You're picturing me naked, aren't you?"

"Spilled my coffee." Charity gritted her teeth. She set the cup in the holder and swiped at the widening splotch with a napkin. The one advantage to her uniform's unflattering color? Stains rarely showed.

Shouts sounded in the background. Grady grunted like he'd shoved something, and someone yelled "Aww, man."

Curiosity got the better of her. "What *are* you doing?"

"Watching a soccer game. From inside the goal. Made you spill your coffee, huh? You all right?"

She mentally elbowed aside memories of cheering him on from the sidelines during high school games and reminded herself why she'd called. "Want to know what I'm doing?"

"Besides sucking at phone sex?"

"I just finished taking a statement from Scott Langford. Funny thing. He's under the impression you're helping with the investigation."

"You don't sound like you think it's funny."

171

His nonchalance was the last straw. "You want to compromise everything we've done so far? You want to hand Drew over to the county prosecutor? Then you continue playing detective."

"Afraid I'll show you up?"

"Back. Off."

"We still talking about the investigation?"

Charity didn't say anything. She didn't need to.

"What are you going to do, come after me full force?" Another grunt, a muffled *thump,* and a cheer in the distance. Grady exhaled. "Isn't this the kind of thing you should be telling me in person?"

"I tried."

"Were you going to tell me about your intruder the other night?"

Brenda June. Charity wagged her head in disbelief as her fingers crept up to the scratches on her shoulder. What was the saying? Silence is golden, but duct tape is silver?

"Char?"

"No," she snapped. "And you're not putting this back on me."

"You could have been hurt."

"I face that possibility every day." When Grady didn't respond, she added, "I have a weapon and I'm trained to use it." Still no answer. "Are you going to back off, or am I going to have to lock you up?"

"I worry about you. Have since the day we met."

"There's no need."

"Why were you taking another statement from Scott?"

Deep breath in, deep breath out. "His property was vandalized. I handled the call, and he spent the entire time ranting about being questioned a second time. By you."

"What'd they do?"

"Trashed his front porch. Spray-painted the columns pink and coated the steps with dog doo." Charity sipped at her coffee, hating herself for playing along. For not being able to bring herself to end the call. "He said he told you where he was Wednesday night. How'd you know he refused to provide an alibi?"

"Idiot got himself kicked out of my father's house after starting a fight with Justine. Guess he figured he needed to prove he was a badass."

"Yeah, well, I need to know where that badass was Wednesday night."

"And I need to be in on this case."

She dropped her forehead to the steering wheel. She got it. She did. He wanted to clear Drew's name. Get back to Seattle. Get back to his life. She wanted all of that, too, even more than he did. She had an election to win. And so damned much to prove. Unfortunately, Grady was having an easier time of proving it.

He was showing her up.

"Why won't people talk to me? Don't they want Sarah's killer found?" Suspicion bloomed. "You asked them not to talk to me, didn't you?"

"Right. Just to prove a point, I'm willing to let the killer who's trying to frame my nephew go free, so I slogged door to door and advised all of Becker County not to talk to you."

Hilarious. "Where are you?"

"The middle school. Drew and Matt needed out of the house, so we decided to kick some balls around."

"I like that idea." She smiled when he made a noise somewhere between a grunt and a whimper. "I'll be right there."

Fifteen minutes later, she was parked where she had a view of the field behind the school, feeling like a pervert as she watched Grady and Drew play keep-away with four boys all about the age of Grady's son. She spotted Matt right away. The kid had skills, like his dad. She also spotted a number of parents on the sidelines and thought twice about confronting Grady in public. The last thing she needed was to fuel the gossip fire. Although considering what had happened the last time they were alone together, confronting him in private might prove just as flammable.

Charity reached for her phone.

"Not like you to avoid a fight," he said when he answered.

"Tell me what Scott Langford said to you."

He signaled for one of the boys to take his place. He turned to face the parking lot—to face her—and ambled to the edge of the field. "I'm not leaving town until Drew's in the clear. You might as well let me help."

"You won't be much help to anyone if you've been charged with obstruction or I'm thrown off the case."

He sighed. "What'll it take?"

"Won't happen. You're a West. And an ex-boyfriend. So tell me what I need to know." Charity could feel the intensity of his gaze across the shamrock-green field.

"Is there a boyfriend in the here and now?"

She hated that she was tempted to tease him. "No." She hated even more that his quiet exhale gave her a thrill. Hated most of all that she couldn't leave it at that.

"I don't do long-term," she said. "And short-term gets you labeled a slut."

"Your mother might have had something to do with that."

"My open bedroom door policy might have had something to do with that."

An inhale this time. Grady went rigid, then flicked his free hand in a *fuck it* gesture. He knew she was punishing him. "Scott was at a job interview. He wants out of the hospital and away from his in-laws. He's smart enough to know if my parents find out, they'll ruin him."

"Can he prove he was there?"

"He gave me a number and asked that you be discreet."

Charity thumped the heel of her hand against the steering wheel. "He couldn't give it to me this morning?"

"He said he didn't know whose side you were on."

"I'm on Sarah's side."

"That's what I told him."

One of the mothers, a slim blonde, all hair and legs, sidled up to Grady. He held up a finger, and she pouted prettily, arms under her chest, hair cascading over her shoulder as she tipped her head. He moved a few steps away.

"One last thing," Charity said.

"Yes, I still wear boxers. Yes, the clingy kind."

A husky, feminine laugh. Charity scowled through the windshield. The blonde had followed Grady and was listening in. Talk about clingy. Charity started her Chevy.

"Those two boys Matt's hanging with? You don't want to encourage them."

"Because you don't want my son getting attached to Becker County?"

"Because you don't want your son getting involved with the wrong crowd. They're troublemakers, Grady."

He went quiet, and she could see from the set of his shoulders that she'd said the wrong thing.

"You know," Grady said finally. "My parents once said the same thing about you. See you around, Deputy." He disconnected and turned back to the blonde.

Her cell rang. Numbly Charity answered, still watching Grady flirt with the blonde. A solemn-sounding Kate started apologizing before Charity could say "Hello."

"Please let me explain about this morning. I know I came across as bitter toward the West family, Justine included. There's a reason for that. I mean, I was in a bad mood anyway because the bank turned me down for a home renovation loan, and how the hell am I supposed to afford a new roof without it? But that's not what I called to tell you." A clinking sounded on Kate's end, followed by a gurgling rush—pouring herself a cup of coffee? Or something stronger? "When I was a senior in college, my mother was killed by a drunk driver. She worked her butt off to help pay my tuition then never got to see me graduate."

Well, damn. "I'm sorry, Kate. That must have been terrible."

"It was." Kate swallowed audibly. "Anyway, I know a little bit about what you're dealing with, with your family. I'd hate to see you continue the cycle by inviting even more addiction into your life by getting personally involved with the Wests. I know we're not really friends, but we…we could be, couldn't we?" She was weeping now. "I miss Sarah so much."

Charity propped her elbow on the door, rested her temple against her knuckles, and said a few consoling words. She wished she could feel more compassion than impatience. Unfortunately, she sucked at friendship pretty much the same way she sucked at the whole boyfriend-girlfriend thing. She'd stopped hanging out with anyone but Brenda June. Her job led to too many last-minute cancellations—never a good thing when everyone was counting on you to be designated driver. Only Brenda June understood. The guys, too.

But now Dix was leaving, and if Bloom won the election, Charity would be, too. The department, anyway. Which meant she wouldn't only be out of a job, she'd be out of a social life.

Not that it mattered. What mattered was the case.

She tuned back in to Kate, who was saying Allison had decided on community college after graduation, instead of trying for Stanford. Not only did she want to avoid Drew, who'd been accepted to Stanford, but she wanted to stick close to home for a while. Quite a sacrifice for the teen to make, giving up her move to California. Then again, Allison was only a junior—she had a year to change her mind about being a lawyer. Kate seemed eager to talk about it, so after turning away from the Adventures of Grady and Soccer Barbie, Charity hunkered down to listen. She was in no hurry to get back to the station and start her report on Scott Langford's poop-smeared porch.

Except...Charity inhaled sharply, and scrambled upright. Kate's voice faltered.

"Is something wrong?" she asked.

"You don't want to be friends," Charity said. "You want to know if I know you're sleeping with Hampton West."

After a few awkward beats, Kate sighed. "How'd you find out?"

"Hair samples from his shower drain. We haven't ID'd them all, but considering you work together at the hospital, I should have figured it out sooner."

"It's not for money, I can promise you that," Kate snapped, then gentled her voice. "You won't tell anyone, will you?"

"He's your alibi, Kate, and vice versa. That information has to be part of the case file. At this point, it doesn't need to go any further than that."

"I appreciate that, Charity. I-I have to go now."

"I'll see you at the funeral." But Charity was talking to dead air.

So much for being besties.

*   *   *

GRADY HAD LOOKED FORWARD to hanging out with Matt, Drew, and Peyton that night after dinner, maybe play some poker or team up for ping pong. Whatever it took to get his mind off a certain stubborn, badge-happy blonde. And all the things he'd like to do to her. Again and again and again —

Dammit. He pushed away from his laptop and the underperforming stock portfolio he couldn't care less about. He needed some air and wanted nothing more than to go for a good long run, despite the cold. In fact, he wouldn't mind a little brain freeze so he could stop thinking about Charity.

She'd meant to shock him. Scare him off, even, with her supposed promiscuity. But though she hadn't been a virgin when they'd started dating, she'd been far from easy.

Okay, yeah, he was jealous.

He scrubbed a hand over his face. He needed to pound the pavement and jog these juvenile thoughts out of his head, but he wouldn't saddle Drew with the responsibility of keeping an eye on Matt, who was in his room grudgingly catching up on reading for his English class, pissed at Grady for enrolling him in the local elementary school despite all his talk about staying in Montana.

Grady's father had gone back to the hospital to catch up on paperwork, and his mother was out with her Council for the Beautification of Becker County, on the hunt for something to beautify. She must have taken Justine with her. Peyton was holed up in her room on speakerphone with one of her friends while they watched a movie "together," and her brother was...

Grady frowned. He didn't know what Drew was up to, but the kid had to be feeling neglected. He'd just gotten out of jail, for God's sake. He'd disappeared after dinner, but maybe now Grady could talk him into an hour of lifting weights in the basement gym.

It took him twenty minutes to track his nephew down. When he did, he didn't know whether to yell or cry. What he did know was

177

that he was one self-involved son of a bitch. Maybe he wasn't so different from his father, after all.

Soundlessly Grady walked across the darkened living room and dropped to his haunches. Drew was tucked into the corner, between the baby grand and a butt-ugly one-armed sofa. He sat with his back to the wall, legs spread, hands boneless in his lap as he stared down at the half-empty bottle of Scotch on the carpet between his thighs.

Frustration burned the backs of Grady's eyes. "Drew?"

The teen raised a bloodshot, bleary gaze. "Don't get it," he mumbled, the thickness of his words making it clear he'd done more than stare at the bottle. "What's the big deal?" He swept out a hand and would have toppled the Scotch if Grady hadn't grabbed it.

Grady had been around enough drunks to know now was not the time to ask questions. He helped the teen to his feet. "Time for bed, big guy."

"I feel sick," Drew moaned. "Why'd anybody want to feel sick?"

Shit. If Grady didn't get them to a bathroom right the hell now, he'd be scooping puke off the carpet.

"Dude," choked Drew. He stumbled, and drove them into a wall.

Grady winced as his shoulder smashed against the wood trim. He got them both upright again and steered them toward the bathroom.

"I'm fucked up." Drew raised a hand to his head. "Dizzy. Judas Priest. Why's he give her pills? Who needs pills on top of this shit?"

Grady froze. "What pills?"

Drew frowned, concentrating, then his face went gray.

Grady shoved the toilet seat upright and stepped back. "Let it out," he said grimly. "Let it all out."

After the worst was over, Grady dispensed aspirin and water, tucked Drew into bed, and marched into Justine's room. He slapped on the light to find his sister splayed out on her bed in a crumpled skirt and blouse.

She pressed a palm to her eyes. "Time for dinner?" she asked groggily.

"You slept through dinner," Grady shouted.

Her face crumpled, and she worked her eyelids as she struggled to push herself upright. "Why are you yelling?"

"Because while you were up here sleeping yourself sober, your son was downstairs getting drunk off his ass."

"Drew?" Justine staggered to her feet, brushing at the wrinkles in her clothes. "Is he okay?" When Grady didn't answer, she raised her head. "Don't look at me like that. This week has been…" She gave up on the wrinkles and jammed her feet into her shoes, holding on to the edge of the bureau for balance. "I could go to jail, you know. For making a false confession."

"Right. And that's so much worse than going to jail for murder." Her eyes appeared bruised, but he'd be damned if he'd apologize. "Show me the pills."

After confiscating four bottles of sedatives, Grady put Matt to bed, warned Justine to stay put, and slammed out of the house.

When every other person in the hospital elevator eased back to hug the rear wall, leaving Grady alone in the front, he realized he'd better make an effort to smooth the rage from his face. Otherwise he'd find himself tranquilized and on his way to the psych ward.

He walked off the elevator at a slow, deliberate pace, while his heart continued to punch an angry rhythm. Outside the door to his father's office, Grady paused and worked air in and out of his lungs. Didn't help. He pushed inside.

The reception area was empty. He stalked past the plush leather seating, rounded the corner, and stopped when he saw his father had company. A trim strawberry blonde, looking like a vet's assistant in aqua scrubs printed with mint-colored kittens, hovered at his father's side. They were both standing behind his desk and frowning toward the doorway, no doubt finding it hard to believe anyone would dare disturb the great Hampton West at work.

"Dad," Grady bit out. "We need to talk."

While the red in his father's cheeks deepened, something speculative flickered over the woman's face. She tucked her hands in the front pockets of her smock and came around the desk, spotless white sneakers whispering across the carpet. She spoke to his father but kept her gaze on Grady's face.

Hoping for an introduction? Grady wasn't in the mood.

"I'll see if I can find that file, Dr. West," she said. "Excuse me."

His father didn't respond. He was too busy glaring at Grady. "What brings you here at this time of night?"

Grady waited for the outer door to close. "I want to know what the hell is wrong with you. Drew told me about the drugs. About how you're dealing to your own daughter."

Hampton drew himself up. The action wasn't as intimidating as it used to be. "I don't deal drugs, I prescribe them. Even before Sarah's murder, your sister was under a lot of stress. She takes antianxiety meds. That doesn't make her an addict." He picked up a pen and threw it back down. "Who do you think you are, anyway? Come home to visit maybe once every couple of years and still think you have the right to make these kinds of accusations?"

"Whether you like it or not, I'm part of the family, at least enough to know Justine's an alcoholic. She needs counseling, not another fucking prescription."

"You're the one who doesn't seem to like being part of the family."

Grady stilled. Something odd, almost desperate, had latched onto his father's voice. Charity's words came back to him. *He's scared. I may not like it, but I won't judge him for it. Who knows how I'd act under the same circumstances?*

She was right. For his own sake, he needed to dial down the whole judgmental thing, because there was more than fear in his father's voice. There was loneliness.

As much as Hampton and Roberta West bickered, Grady had always believed they loved each other. What if that wasn't true anymore? Was that part of Justine's problem?

"Dad," he said, clawing for patience. "You don't think it's a conflict of interest? Prescribing a narcotic to a family member? A family member with a drinking problem?"

Hampton sat down and picked up a file. "You can talk to me about family when you start acting like family."

Grady sensed movement behind him.

The blonde gave her throat a gentle clearing. "Dr. West? You asked me to remind you about your meeting with Dr. Stephens."

His father jumped up out of his chair and charged out of the room as if he were late for a life-saving surgery.

The blonde held out a hand. "Grady West. I finally get to meet you."

Grady couldn't help the skeptical edge to his words. "My father talks about me?"

"Not often. I'm friends with Charity Bishop."

"Does she talk about me?"

"Do swear words count?" She arched an eyebrow. "You two used to be an item. Are you here to try to…?"

"I'm here to try to keep my family out of prison."

"Isn't that what the sheriff's department is for?" She said it almost fiercely. "Charity doesn't have the greatest reputation around here, and she's trying to fix it so she can win an election. You hanging around, demanding to help, sends the message she's not qualified to be sheriff. If you really care about her, you'll go back to Seattle and let her do her job."

Grady lifted an eyebrow. "Are you trying to defend her or condemn her?"

"Defend her, of course." She ran her eyes over him. "What are you trying to do to her?" When he didn't answer, she flipped her hair over her shoulder. "I'm Kate Young. I'm a temp here."

"You're Allison's mom?"

"So Drew told you about Allison. That surprises me."

No way he was going there. "Tell me, Kate. Did my dad really have a meeting?"

She merely smiled.

Grady merely left.

He drove to Charity's neighborhood but resisted the urge to park in her driveway and knock on her door. She was probably still pissed at him, and he wasn't thrilled with her, either.

Not to mention, her lights were off.

He cruised up and down her street a couple of times, then cruised every street that formed her block. Failing to see anything suspicious, he finally parked in front of the house across the street behind a minivan. If he slid over to the passenger side, he had an excellent view of her property.

He adjusted his seat as far back as it would go and settled down to wait. If her intruder showed up again, the son of a bitch was going down.

*   *   *

THE NEXT DAY WAS Monday, and it should have been a day off for Charity since she'd spent all day Sunday on the Huffman case. But there was no way she could sit at home. She didn't even want to take time to hit the range. Sometime today, though, she had to snag some groceries—she was getting dangerously low on milk and cereal. Too bad that meant meeting face after face in aisle after aisle, admitting again and again she'd failed to solve Sarah's murder.

She tapped her signal indicator and turned down Judge Purl's road. While she took her turn at patrol, Dix was back at the station, scouring the murder file for a motive. Mo was sweet-talking the two real estate agents who'd worked with Sarah, hoping to glean some personal details. If anyone could do it, he could, considering both agents were female. Meanwhile Pratt was working the vandalism cases and trying to figure out why Brenda June wasn't speaking to him.

The SUV juddered along the dirt road as Charity squinted through the pine trees bordering the judge's property. Judge Purl had elected against a manor on Pill Hill so he could buy a rundown farmhouse a good twenty minutes outside of town. Instead of putting money into his house, he'd put it into a "pond"—a ten acre lake he'd stocked with trout. Pooh-poohing the river that bordered Pill Hill, he claimed he preferred to fish in waters only he could pee in.

Despite the dust, Charity lowered her window. The sweet smell of pine, the bright twinkle of sun on water, and the flurry of spring air helped fend off the funk brought on by her last conversation with Grady.

"Unit Four, this is Dispatch." Brenda June's husky voice brought the radio to sudden, startling life, and Charity jumped. "I have a ten-seventy-five with the owner of Lady Luck Liquors."

Great. Perfect. Charity grabbed her radio. "Again?" That made the fourth time in eight days. "I'll head over there now."

"Buy me a lottery ticket while you're there, babycakes."

The liquor store owner's request was simple: he wanted his gun back. The same gun Hank Bishop had stolen from behind the counter while their mother pretended to have a seizure in front of the Jamaican rum display. Somehow Eve Bishop's blouse always ended up half-unbuttoned during these attacks. Her chest was nowhere near as scrawny as the rest of her and was usually good for a few seconds of distraction.

Charity had to explain—again—that the sheriff's department needed permission from the county prosecutor before they could release any evidence. The impatient shop owner took his frustration out on Charity by assuring her he'd start stocking those "fruity ass wine coolers" before he voted any Bishop into public office. Her purchase of a king-sized candy bar failed to smooth things over.

She was halfway to her Tahoe and already gnawing on her chocolate when a maroon sedan rolled into the parking lot and pulled alongside her. Grady. He got out of the car, looking grim. All kinds of hot, too, in his faded blue jeans and thermal shirt. But noticing his hotness would only get her into more trouble, so she focused on the grim.

"You don't get to be mad at me," she said. "I'm still mad at you. You withheld information. That's at least another seventy-two hours' worth of mad."

He took off his shades. "Everything okay?"

"Fine. Why?"

"You look upset."

Charity gestured with her candy toward the liquor store. "This isn't the first time someone's told me they're voting for Oliver Bloom for the sole purpose of keeping me from getting elected."

Grady's gaze shifted from her to the store and back again. "What else did he say?"

The shop keeper had made a good point. How could the people of Becker County be certain she wasn't running for sheriff so she could aid and abet her family?

When she failed to answer, Grady scowled. "I'll ask him myself."

"Don't." She grabbed him before he could turn away and at the same time took a moment to marvel at his instinct to jump to her defense. "You'll make it worse."

"I'm damned tired of hearing that." He watched her hand as it lifted away from his arm. "Isn't there anything I can make better?"

Charity gave a high-pitched, hiccupy sort of laugh as need sizzled to flaming life.

10

G RADY SUCKED IN A breath. "You look at me like that, and —"
    "Don't." Charity practically gave herself whiplash shaking
    her head. "Don't say it."

"Because?"

"I might want to hear it, and that could get us both in a lot of trouble."

When his gaze dropped to her mouth she took a step back. She folded the wrapper over the remains of her candy bar and tucked it into her pocket. "Where's Matt?" she asked brightly.

Grady shot her a look chock-full of reproof. "Earth science." He pulled out his phone and checked the screen. "Make that gym."

"You enrolled him in school?"

"I'm not ready to go back to Seattle. He's not ready to go back to Seattle. We have eight weeks 'til summer break. Easy enough to spend them here. All I had to do was get my lawyer to overnight a copy of my custody papers."

"What about your job? Your condo? And Matt — didn't I hear he's on a soccer team? If he's anything like you, he'd sooner wear a skirt to school than miss practice."

His lips twitched. *Mad*, she reminded herself. *I'm supposed to be mad at him.*

"My clients are used to dealing with the virtual me, and our home is in good hands. As for soccer, Matt was impressed with the group we scrimmaged with yesterday. He's hoping to join their team." Grady frowned. "I heard about the anonymous note."

"Let me guess. Dispatch told you where to find me. What are you, BFFs now? And by the way, those boys, Turbo and Will? You should know I caught them drinking at the public dock a month or so ago, and there are rumors of drug use."

"Rumors aren't facts or you'd have arrested them. Don't change the subject." His frown got down and dirty, and he shook his head when she opened her mouth to blast back. "You've been spied on, vandalized, and threatened. What's Pratt doing about it?"

"Pratt is letting his investigators do what they do best. Investigate. And if you don't start following his lead, one of us is going to end up behind bars. You for obstruction, or me for grievous bodily harm."

He shook his head slowly. "I left you that night. I shouldn't have."

Charity fought the thaw and backed toward her SUV. "You don't need to apologize."

He followed her. "I'm not here to apologize."

"Then why are you here?"

"That's what I want to ask you." Loose gravel scraped under his feet as he jerked to a stop. "Why the hell do you stay?" he demanded. "You like your job, and the people you work with. I get that. But your family gives you nothing but personal and professional heartache. You don't date for fear of feeding a reputation that doesn't have shit to do with how you do your job. Twelve years ago you wanted nothing more than an apartment in the city and the opportunity to live where no one would know you or your family. Where no one would judge." He aimed a pointed glance at the liquor store. "So tell me, Char. What's holding you here?"

She swung away and marched around the front of the Tahoe. "I don't have time for this."

"Make time."

"It's none of your business."

"It's not about becoming sheriff. Otherwise, you'd say so."

Charity yanked open the SUV's door, then whirled to face him. "It is about that. My family has been crapping on this community for more than thirty years. The least I can do—"

"They'll be crapping on it for thirty more. Nothing you can do to change it."

"You're right. I like the people I work with. More than that, I feel a connection with them. I stay because I doubt I could find that anywhere else." She staved off his response with a shake of her head. "I know you understand. You're struggling to reforge a bond with your son. Connecting with him means a lot to you."

Grady's eyes went bleak. "Noticed that, did you?"

"Yes, and I can't help but think that connecting with me, if only physically, is supposed to be some sort of consolation prize."

Silence. Charity tried but failed to break free of his solemn gaze. Some part of her registered the crunch of wheels over crumbled pavement, the heavy thunk of a car door, the gruff greeting followed by a flat electronic tone announcing entrance to the liquor store. She moved her chin in a belated response to the *How ya doin,' Deputy?*, but her eyes never left Grady's.

"I take it back," he said. "I am here to apologize."

She faltered. "For?"

"For the way we handled things after the fire. The way *I* handled things."

"No. We're not going there."

He ignored her. "I apologized for getting you arrested. It's way past time I apologized for talking you into leading Pratt astray. Earlier Jerzy and I had a chance to catch up while Edith showed Matt the fine art of making a milkshake. Jerzy said people never believed our story about accidentally setting fire to his place. He said they assumed you'd done it and I was covering for you. He said it made things tough for you. Especially after you were arrested for vandalizing my mother's car."

Why did he persist in dusting off memories better left on the shelf? Beneath her hat, Charity's scalp started to prickle. She forced a lazy posture, but the fingers of her right hand curled within her pocket, slowly throttling her keys.

"They didn't believe our story because we sucked at lying," she said.

He must have caught the edge in her voice. "You think we made a mistake."

"I think my brothers should have been punished for what they did, no matter what that would have meant for me and my chances of getting into the academy."

He made a noise, a soft grunt, like he'd taken an elbow to the gut. A rogue breeze lifted a dark tuft of hair above his right ear. Charity caught a whiff of cotton, realized breathing eased the ache in her chest, and inhaled again.

"We don't know one of your brothers did it," Grady said gruffly.

Charity snorted.

"The lie was my idea," he said. "It doesn't matter that I was right, that they tried to get Jerzy for fraud. What matters is that I left and you were stuck with the consequences."

"We did what we had to do. Without the lie, Jerzy would have ended up in jail. All's well that ends well."

"You don't believe that any more than I do. Here I am, telling you to go get yourself a life, and meanwhile I'm part of the reason you're still here."

"Speaking of which…" Sacrificing grace for speed, Charity scrambled into her seat and reached for the door handle.

Grady got in the way, and she ended up handling his abs instead.

She yanked her hand back. "Get out of my way, West."

He leaned in close enough that she could see the amber banding the dark blue of his eyes. "You don't even realize, do you?" His gaze drifted from her mouth to her nose to the brim of her dorky hat. Seconds passed.

"Realize what?" Charity prompted. Dear Lord, why did her voice have to sound as if she'd gone without water for a week?

"No one's in your way but you."

She was damned tired of hearing that from him. "What are you, Seattle's answer to Confucius?"

"Why don't you visit some time and find out?"

Her brain sputtered. Since it wasn't the first time he'd made the suggestion, she had to assume he was serious. She took off her hat, threw it at the seat beside her, and struggled to cold-shoulder the cautious glee zinging through her veins. "That's not going to happen."

"Why not?"

Before her brain could even try to draft a response, he leaned in, and lightly grazed his teeth along her earlobe.

Grady chuckled when she shuddered. "All I'm asking is that you keep an open mind."

"It's not my mind you want open." She shoved at him. "Sex is one thing. Friendship's another. Anyway it doesn't matter. The job comes first."

"The job?"

"My job." Charity finger-combed her sweat-streaked hair.

He followed the motion. "Why'd you cut it?"

The change in subject startled her. Relieved the crap out of her, too. Her shoulders bounced. "Self-preservation. Gives the scrappy ones less to grab on to. How about you? Why'd you cut yours?"

"Same as you. Image. Clients prefer their personal asset managers with tidy hair."

"Tidy hair, tidy profits?"

"Something like that."

"We're not the same people," Charity blurted. "It wouldn't be the same."

Grady's mouth took on a seductive curve, with more than a hint of smug. "I'm happy to report my...reflexes...aren't as hair-trigger as they used to be. I can guarantee it would be better."

Her pelvic muscles gathered, but memories of all the ways he'd once looked out for her had started to overlay the visions of lusty, sweaty sex, and if she didn't get her ass out of there, she'd end up blubbering all over the man.

"I have to go," she said, unable to keep the desperation out of her voice.

His eyes narrowed, but he moved out of the way. As she jammed the key into the ignition, he pushed her door shut and stepped back, the need in his expression giving way to speculation.

Her body sagged under the weight of self-disdain. They'd once been so honest with each other. Slowly she opened her door, and climbed back down to the pavement. Grady watched her, body braced, sunglasses dangling from his right hand.

"I am grateful for your help with Scott Langford despite the fact that your interference could have had me pulled from the investigation. I don't need that kind of press. Winning the election means a lot to me." Charity licked her lips. "That said, those eight weeks you mentioned? It's awfully tempting to let ourselves enjoy each other for as long as you're in town."

Grady's body jerked, and his navy eyes went black. She finally realized the source of the faint drumming she'd been hearing — a sporadic rain had started. A drop chilled the tip of her nose, and another slid down her cheek.

Grady didn't even blink as the rhythm increased, working to flatten his hair. He stared at Charity. "What's stopping you?"

"Besides the investigation?" She choked out a laugh and swiped her palms across her cheeks. "That connection thing we talked about? I don't want you to leave now. After eight weeks of sleeping together, I'd be clingier than syrup on a waffle." She lurched forward, rose up on her toes, and kissed his mouth.

Lord, the man tasted good.

His arms came up, but she managed to step back before he could touch her.

She bent her head. "It would be too hard to say goodbye."

Grady didn't say anything more. Didn't try to stop her. She climbed back into the SUV and drove slowly out of the lot, the rainfall on the windshield inviting tears she refused to shed.

Seconds later Charity's phone chirped with a text from Grady.

If you're the consolation prize, I hope to hell I never win.

*   *   *

GRADY DIDN'T THINK HE could be any prouder of Drew. At the same time he was seriously tempted to wring the kid's neck.

His nephew was determined to attend Sarah Huffman's funeral. Grady understood that Drew wanted to pay his respects. He even understood Drew's desire to make it clear to all of Becker County that he had no reason to hide. But Grady knew that ugly looks and even uglier words were inevitable, and he knew the kind of damage they could do.

The only other person who knew it better was Charity Bishop.

He spotted her the moment he stepped into the sanctuary and out of the snow. Yeah, snow. How foolish they all were to be thinking about spring when it wasn't even May yet. A pissed off sky was spitting some serious flakes at the mourners as they funneled into the church. At this rate they'd have six inches by nightfall. As Grady followed Justine and Drew down the center aisle, a mass of flakes at the back of his neck melted and trickled downward.

Damn, that was cold.

The sight of Charity warmed him.

She stood in front of the first pew, deep in conversation with the blond deputy and an older couple who had to be Sarah's parents. Their faces were drawn, their postures weighted with grief. Grady gave a slow exhale and allowed his gaze to slide back to Charity. Like her fellow deputy, she wasn't in uniform. She wore a pale blue sweater and slim black skirt, and her hair had been slicked back from her face. He'd never seen her look so...elegant.

It would be too hard to say goodbye. Her words had haunted him all night long, which meant he hadn't gotten much sleep. Ironic, considering he'd hired a guy to keep watch over Charity's house at night so Grady could pass the wee hours in his bed instead of his car.

A lot of good that did him.

"Everyone's staring," Justine muttered and pinched his arm. "Including you."

Grady blinked and glanced around, noting expressions that ranged from sympathetic to suspicious to downright hostile. And the murmuring had started. Justine and Drew had already settled into a pew. Grady gritted his teeth and sidled in beside them. He turned to face front and saw they'd captured Charity's attention. Her eyes were on Drew, and she looked startled. A moment later, her gaze connected with Grady's, and something secret and sweet flickered over her features.

He sat too quickly and almost ended up with a face full of pew. Charity looked beyond him and went still. He followed her gaze. Kate and Allison Young had arrived, and with them was Peyton, who'd refused to ride with her family to the church. Justine had been on the verge of ordering her daughter to stay home, but Drew had intervened. Peyton hadn't thanked him. She could barely look at her brother.

Reluctantly Grady had left Matt at home with the good doctors West. He'd been relieved to hear an Uno tournament was planned, and his parents had both pledged — albeit sourly — to remain sober.

The organ music ended, and the pastor approached the pulpit. *God, please get us through this.*

Justine spent the entire service vibrating with tension. Whether from the attention they were receiving or the absence of alcohol in her system, Grady had no clue. Drew sat in rigid silence, hands clasped tightly between his knees. Grady had lost track of Charity, but he swept the crowd only once in search of her. Just as well she wasn't in his line of sight, because he wouldn't have been able to keep his eyes off her, and the town had enough to talk about.

After the service, mourners left the church in solemn, silent clumps. The flakes had slowed, but not enough. As the procession of vehicles headed for the cemetery, car after car swung out of line. Only a couple dozen people trekked through the inch or so of powdery snow to rim the gravesite.

Charity stood directly across from Grady under an umbrella held by the deputy who looked like he'd rather be hanging ten off the coast of Oahu. The deputy grabbed for his phone, frowned down at the screen, and whispered something to Charity. He handed her the umbrella and walked away, phone to his ear. A sharp elbow to Grady's side scolded him for staring again. He drew in a breath and focused on the pastor's words.

* * *

SHOWING UP AT SARAH Huffman's funeral had been a given. Even if Charity hadn't been involved in the murder investigation, the real estate agent had been a friend. A friend with a whole hell of a lot of secrets, but who didn't have a secret or two?

She wrenched her gaze away from Grady and scanned the rest of the mourners at the graveside. Shivering, she blinked a snowflake out of her eye. No unfamiliar faces. Not surprising, considering how small the turnout. Had the killer decided to skip the service? Or was he—or she—already here?

This hadn't been a crime of passion. The murder had been deliberate. Planned. Carried out by a careful mind. But what possible motive could one of these people have for committing murder?

Once they figured out the why, they wouldn't be far from the who.

Between Grady and Justine slouched Drew. He'd stood tall in the church, but his obvious grief—and no doubt all the speculation—had gradually molded his shoulders into a hunch. Beside him, Allison and Peyton, both in ridiculously high wedge heels and short, black skirts, leaned against each other. Something was definitely going on with those two. Each somber sentence intoned by the pastor had Peyton edging farther and farther away from her brother. The greater the distance between them, the grimmer Drew's face, and the more palpable the tension among the rest of the crowd.

Peyton's expression remained condemnatory, but Allison's wavered between sad and uncertain, and she kept sneaking glances at her ex. Peyton finally gave her a hip bump, and from that point on, Allison kept her gaze trained on the snow-coated grass at her feet.

A hand touched Charity's elbow. She allowed Mo to pull her aside.

"We have the weapon," he said, sotto voce. "They found an ear bud cord buried at the scene."

Her pulse began to pound. "Sarah's?"

"Maybe. We didn't find any electronic devices. But remember we're looking for a pair of straps, one with a thicker segment? The cord they found has a break in the wire, up near the connector. Someone used duct tape to repair it."

"Is something like that strong enough to…" She couldn't say it. Not here.

"The ME will tell us for sure." Mo shifted closer. "Thing is, it has a pattern on it. Butterflies."

Charity glanced over at Drew and saw, to her chagrin, that most of the mourners were looking their way. "Butterflies aren't very masculine, are they?" she whispered. "I'll meet you back at the station. See if you can find the owner of those ear buds."

By the time the service was over, the whispering had resumed. Again Charity expressed her sympathies to Sarah's pale-faced parents, promising to keep in touch. Then she made a beeline for Peyton Langford, slowing when she overheard Drew talking to his uncle.

"I shouldn't have come," the teen muttered. "Everyone was talking about me instead of remembering her."

Charity paused long enough to say, "That was the bravest thing I've seen in a long time. Sarah was lucky to have you for a friend."

Drew's eyes glittered, and he nodded jerkily.

Before she could turn away, Grady spoke. "I expected to see you in uniform."

She was grateful he couldn't see her goose bumps. The last time she'd seen him in a black suit was at their senior prom. He'd never admitted it, but she'd known he hadn't worn a tux because he hadn't wanted to advertise the fact that unlike her, he hadn't had to rent his outfit.

Grady had been a hottie then. Now his good looks were edged with maturity and strength, and he was so damned male it hurt to breathe.

Charity had spent the entire night regretting her words. *It would be too hard to say goodbye.* What good had it done to admit what she felt?

"We talked about it," she managed. "Whether or not to suit up. In the end we decided that would put the focus on how Sarah died, rather than how she lived. We didn't want to do that to her family."

"That was nice," Drew blurted.

Grady murmured his assent. Charity's cheeks prickled with heat. Dear Lord, how long had it been since she'd actually blushed?

She took a step back and noticed Justine several feet away, arguing with Peyton. *Back on track, Bishop.* She watched mother and daughter, their slim builds, long, jet hair, pale skin, and fierce expressions making them mirror images of each other. Peyton finally crossed her arms and turned her back on her mother. Fists at her sides, Justine heaved a long-suffering breath and spun toward Grady and Drew.

Not anxious to get caught up in family dynamics — or to deal with Justine and her caustic comments, thank you very much — Charity gave Grady's sister a wide berth and headed for Peyton. She'd only taken two steps when Scott Langford marched up, sun-reddened face tight with the promise of battle. He pushed a palm at Charity and scowled at Justine.

"What are you doing here?" he demanded of his ex-wife.

"I could ask you the same," Justine drawled.

"I asked first."

Justine tipped up her chin. "She was my friend. I forgave her."

Scott snorted. "I was your husband. You can't forgive me?" He wrapped a fist around his gray silk tie. "Or do I have to be choked to death first?"

"That's enough," Grady growled from behind Charity. "Remember where we are."

Charity's backbone tingled from the warning that lurked beneath his tone.

"Everything okay here?" Cal Brennan and his buddy Sunny appeared on either side of Scott. They wore dark suits and even darker expressions, but neither Justine nor Scott paid much attention. They were too busy staring doom and gloom at each other.

Charity quickly introduced the firefighters to Grady. "We'll be fine, guys, but thanks for checking."

A stern-jawed Grady nodded at the pair before they turned away and headed for the parking lot, shoulders rigid, heads close in conference.

Charity mentally rolled her eyes. It was a wonder none of the men were grunting and groaning under the strain of lugging all that testosterone around.

Justine poked a finger at her ex. "I could probably find my way to forgiving you for what you did to me. I'll never be able to forgive you for what you did to your own son."

"You and me both," Scott said fiercely, and everyone shut up. No sound broke the silence but the whisper of flakes sliding from the sky and the occasional brush of cloth as someone shifted position. Scott stared over Justine's shoulder at Drew, who remained apart from the group, eyes on the coffin that had been lowered into Sarah's grave.

With a growl that sounded more damp than irritated, Scott turned to Charity. "The bastards who trashed my house—know who they are yet?"

"We're working on it, Mr. Langford."

"Not hard enough." This from a cultured female voice that harbored more bitter than a lemon grove.

With a sigh Charity turned to face Oliver Bloom and his wife, a thin woman with pitch-black, pixie-cut hair and a natural prettiness, despite too many worry lines.

"These vandals have become a huge problem in Becker County. And they're getting away with it again and again." Janet Bloom stared fixedly at Charity. "Last month our mailbox went missing. And just the other day, someone egged our front porch."

"Better eggs than dog shit," Scott muttered.

"I'm sorry to hear that, Mrs. Bloom. Mr. Bloom. Can we talk about this later, down at the station?" Charity cast a pointed glance around them. Investigating Sarah's murder was one thing. Airing civic complaints at the woman's funeral was something else entirely.

Janet raised an eyebrow, along with her voice. "So you are protecting someone."

Charity kept one eye on Peyton Langford. She really did need to talk to her before Kate whisked her away. "Did you report these incidents?"

"What would be the point? And please. Mr. Bloom? I know he's Oliver to you. Though you'd better get used to calling him 'sir.' You're letting a killer go free, and soon my husband will be sheriff. When he is, he'll make damned sure every victim gets justice."

Charity knew she should defend the department, even though Janet's attack was meant solely for her. But she was distracted by Grady, who'd moved to stand stiffly beside her. She turned her head and indulged in a slow brush of crystals from the right sleeve of her wool coat, breathing in the warmth of his ocean breeze scent.

"It's clear you're not on the side of justice, Deputy Bishop," Janet continued.

"I'm due at the range," a red-faced Oliver said loudly. He tugged his wife toward the few remaining parked cars. "Let's go."

"That's right," she tossed over her shoulder at Charity. "It'll be you, working for him."

Grady moved into Charity's line of sight, his expression tight. "What's going on? Why'd Deputy Morrissey hightail it out of here?"

"You know I can't tell you."

"Something to do with the case? With Drew?" When she didn't respond, his eyes narrowed. "And that little set-to with Bloom's wife? Wait, you know what? Never mind. Some things I can figure out for myself." He swung away, gathered up Drew, who looked sick, and Justine, whose eyes were cartoon-character wide, and strode away toward his rental.

Charity rolled her shoulders under a jacket that had gone heavy. The sting hadn't been quite so fierce when it was Brenda June who thought she'd had an affair with a married man.

Footsteps creaked through snow. The ocean breeze smell was replaced by the scent of vanilla. Kate joined her in staring after Grady.

"I hereby retract my question about you two getting back together. You really don't get along, do you?"

Charity angled her body away from the roadway. The other woman's eyes were red-rimmed and tired. "I'm glad you're still here," Charity said. "I need to talk with Peyton."

"I heard you found the weapon."

Damn it. "Where'd you hear that?"

"Have you seen Allison? I turned away for a moment, and she was gone."

"Tried her cell?" Charity ground her back teeth. How the hell had word about their discovery spread so quickly?

"I wouldn't let her bring it." Kate peered around anxiously, the tip of her ponytail sweeping snow from the back of her faux-fur collar. "How about while you're talking to Peyton, I drive around the cemetery? See if Allison wandered off to look at headstones."

Kate hurried away before Charity had a chance to comment. Charity glanced at the two men from the funeral home who hovered at the graveside, waiting for everyone to leave before they summoned workers to backfill the opening. Swallowing a fresh surge of regret, she made her way over to Peyton, who sat perched on the aged stone wall that snaked through the cemetery. Her head was bent toward the phone she cradled in both hands. Considering her only protection from the weather was a zippered purple blazer with the sleeves pushed up to her elbows, a thin silk shirt, and the black miniskirt, it was no wonder the girl was shaking.

Or did Charity make her nervous?

"I thought Kate put a ban on cell phones today," Charity said lightly.

Peyton shrugged without looking up. "We muted 'em."

"So Allison has hers? You know her mom is looking for her. Is she the one you're texting?"

Peyton's thumbs stopped, and she hefted a sigh. "I'm not texting with her." She lifted her head. "And I shouldn't be talking with you."

"Don't you want to help us find Sarah Huffman's killer?"

Another shrug. Her thumbs started moving again.

"Peyton. I need to know about you and Allison."

"We're friends."

"Best friends, right?"

"Yeah," the teen said slowly.

"Can you tell me about your arrangement?"

"I don't know what you mean."

Charity blocked the phone's display with her hand. After a pause Peyton raised her head, brown eyes more wary than annoyed.

"Allison told me about what you two decided together," Charity said quietly.

"She told you? About the pact?" Peyton's hands collapsed into her lap. "I don't believe you. She wouldn't have done that. We swore."

Charity held her breath, torn between excitement and dread. Close. So close. "She would, Peyton. She would if she knew how much was at stake."

Moisture pooled in the girl's big brown eyes. "We didn't mean for anyone to get hurt," she whispered.

Oh, dear Lord. "Why don't you tell me what happened?"

* * *

CHARITY WOULD RATHER GIVE up waffles for life than do what she was about to do. She stood on the porch, eyes gritty, muscles longing for the uncomplicated comfort of her bed. The night that pressed against her back tempted her, tugged at her, while the mumbling rush of the river beyond the house mocked her hesitation. Why hadn't she arranged for someone else to handle this?

Easy. There was no one else.

With clumsy fingers she adjusted her hat and stabbed at the doorbell. Seconds passed. She winced. Yes, it was past midnight, but she'd hoped someone would still be up. A handful of moments after she pressed the bell again, the foyer light went on, and the door swung open.

Roberta West pushed her over-permed hair out of her eyes and squinted at Charity. She smelled like alcohol and coconut. "You," she said. She wrapped her gray knit cardigan tighter around coral silk pajamas and gave a harsh, throaty laugh. "Who're you after this time? Me? My husband? How about the housekeeper? Hell, why don't you drag us all down to the station? Or better yet, instead of harassing the law-abiding citizens of Becker County, why don't you track down your other brother and lock him up? Your mother, too, while you're at it. Lock 'em up and throw away the key. Save us all a lot of – "

"That's enough." Grady appeared behind his mother, in sweatpants and a T-shirt, hair disheveled, eyes alert. "Jesus, Mother. Did you bother to ask her in?"

His mother ignored him, her spite-filled gaze never leaving Charity. "This is payback, isn't it? You've been waiting for your chance to settle the score ever since we called the cops on you that night. It won't work, you hear me? I'll call the sheriff. I'll tell him all about you. This is harassment."

Charity sighed. Roberta sounded remarkably like Eve. She focused on Grady. "My business is with you."

His jaw went tight. Gently he pushed his mother out of the doorway. "Go back to bed." He ignored her sputtering, stepped out onto the porch, and closed the door behind him. Wisely he didn't try for a smile that neither would buy. "Just like old times."

"There weren't that many times you met me at the front door." When a shadow crossed his face, she held up a hand. "That wasn't me being passive-aggressive. We both got a kick out of sneaking in and out of this house."

Dammit. How had they gotten so far off track?

"Come inside," Grady said.

"I'd rather not."

His chest rose, then fell. "You're here to arrest Drew."

"No. I'm here because —"

"I'm sorry. About today, at the cemetery. I was an ass. I have no right to —"

"Grady. Here's the thing." The metallic taste of regret coated her tongue. "Matt's in trouble."

THE HARSH LINE OF Grady's shoulders eased. "Is this about those so-called delinquents again? Or is this about wanting to see what I wear to bed these days?"

"I'm serious. I'm here to take you to your son."

"Take me—what are you talking about? He's upstairs. Asleep. Which is where I should be."

"Grady. He's in the hospital."

His face went white and he grabbed at her. "What happened? How is he?"

"He'll be all right. Come with me. I'll take you to him."

He let her go and backed away. "He was upstairs. Last I knew, he was upstairs in bed. He turned in right after dinner because he..." Grady closed his eyes, swore, and ran a hand over his face. When he opened his eyes, they held nothing but weary resignation. "He was with those boys, wasn't he?"

She nodded. "He sustained minor injuries when he ran from Deputy Morrissey."

Grady flinched. "I'll get my jacket."

In less than a minute, he was back. The scent of leather chased Charity down the stone steps, which had been swept free of snow and treated with salt. The crystals crunched under her boots.

Grady jogged to catch up. "What kind of minor injuries?"

"His nose is broken. When I left, they were getting ready to take X-rays." She paused at the passenger side of the SUV. "You need to know. Once he's been treated, we'll be taking him to the station."

"He'll be under arrest?"

"Yes. Destruction of public property, trespassing, fleeing the scene. I'll fill you in on the way."

"You can't—you're going to keep him? Overnight? Char, he's eleven."

The devastation in his voice liquefied her knees. "He's asking for you."

"Right." He shoved trembling hands through his hair, and it was all she could do not to pull him into a hug. Instead she concentrated on opening the passenger door—the rear passenger door. Grady looked from her to the door and back again.

"So this is how it's going to be."

"I've been trying to tell you. This is how it has to be."

*   *   *

GRADY WATCHED AS CHARITY made her way around the front of the SUV. Son of a bitch. This kept getting better and better. He shook his head, climbed into the back seat, and swallowed the panic and bile churning up into his throat.

They were a mile down the road before he trusted his voice. The steel partition between the front and back seats served as more than a physical separation between driver and passenger.

He stared at Charity's profile through the metallic lattice, finally leaned forward, and managed two words. "Tell me."

She kept her eyes on the road. "Deputy Morrissey was out on patrol when he noticed activity at the school bus depot. He discovered three juvenile males vandalizing the buses. He called for backup, jumped the fence, and informed the boys they were under arrest. They ran. Will and Turbo managed to get over the fence, but Matt didn't make it. He fell into the gravel, face first. Not enough snow to cushion his landing."

Grady winced and pulled in a breath. "All right. Matt fucked up his face. What'd he do to the buses?"

Charity glanced in the rearview mirror. "Slashed tires and upholstery, broken windows, gas tanks filled with dirt and gravel."

"Jesus." He let his forehead drop to the screen.

"The depot manager is there now, making repair assessments. They'll be significant, Grady."

This was unreal. Dammit, he should have hustled Matt's ass right back to Seattle. "I can't believe you're going to keep him." His gut twisted as he imagined his young son, alone in a jail cell. It had been hard enough on Drew. "What about bail?"

"There is no bail for juveniles. But we'll go through the process as quickly as we can." Charity braked at a stoplight and turned in her seat. "He won't be alone. I don't just mean he'll have Turbo and Will with him. I mean we'll be with him. The officers on duty. We won't let anything happen to him. I promise."

Anger surged. Unfair, unfounded anger that fired up a rolling riot through his veins. "I don't need your promises," he gritted. "I need my son."

"You'll see him soon," she said, her voice careful.

Grady couldn't have cared less if he'd hurt her feelings. Matt was everything. Matt was all he had.

The light changed and the engine revved. Grady fell back against his seat. "Shit," he muttered. "He's going to have a record."

"He's a first offender." Charity hesitated. "Isn't he?"

"For God's sake!"

"Good. That's good. If he cooperates with the judge, he may end up having his record expunged."

"What about the other boys?"

"I can't discuss their cases."

"Can you tell me if they were hurt?"

"I don't know if Mo's caught up with them yet." She pulled into the emergency room parking lot. "We're here."

Grady hadn't been in the ER since Matt was seven, when he'd sprained his wrist falling off his skateboard. The incessant beeping, the muted slap of padded shoes, the whispering huddle of nurses, the jingling whisk of curtains pulled back—all the same. Like the panic pulsing in his chest.

Except this time he could have kept his kid out of the ER. This time the worst wouldn't be over once Matt was discharged. If only Grady had listened to the deputy beside him.

Jesus, this was surreal.

A nurse in mint-colored scrubs led them to the glass-front cubicle they'd assigned to Matt. A heavy-set deputy stood outside the room, shoulders hunched, expression morose. He was eyeing an empty chair at the nurses' station across the hall.

Son of a bitch. "You put a guard on my kid?"

"It's procedure. Plus we thought he'd appreciate having someone within shouting distance until you got here."

Fair enough. While Charity checked in with her coworker—Flunker, she said his name was—Grady stepped into the cubicle.

Matt sat propped up in bed by a mass of pillows, head back and eyes closed. A faded hospital gown exposed one thin shoulder. Grady swallowed, and fought a sympathetic groan when he zeroed in on his kid's face. Cuts and bruises peppered his cheeks and his upper lip was split in two places, but there was no bandage on an obviously swollen nose.

"Dad." Matt blinked up at him.

Grady couldn't refrain from touching him. He squeezed the boy's foot, patted his leg, ruffled the bristles of his hair, and had to swallow again before he could talk. "Doing okay, buddy?"

Matt didn't complain about the nickname. He was too busy trying to blink back tears. "I'm sorry, Dad."

"Are you? What the hell were you thinking?"

"I wasn't. Okay? I wasn't thinking."

Grady made a conscious decision to focus on the words instead of the attitude behind them. "That's not good enough," he said.

Matt started to speak, then his lower lip trembled, and Grady experienced an overwhelming need to fold him into a hug. At the same time he wanted to kick the kid's bony ass. Where had this reckless, secretive boy come from? What had happened to the sunny child who'd once awakened Grady at three in the morning to ask permission to snag an ice cream sandwich out of the freezer?

"You're lucky you weren't hurt worse. You get that, don't you?" He ran a hand over his face. "Do you understand how serious this is?"

A simple nod had Matt flinching.

Grady relented. For the moment. "They give you something for the pain?"

"Yeah." Matt stared down at his legs, shifting them under the blanket. "I just wanted to do something on my own. Something…you didn't have control over."

And how's that working for you? Grady fought to keep his voice even. "It's my job as your dad to watch over you, to do my best to keep you out of harm's way." And Christ, had he fucked that up. "You know that, right?"

A tiny shrug moved the slight shoulders under the gown. "Am I going to jail?" Matt whispered.

Grady hesitated. "I'll see what I can find out." He started to turn away.

Matt shot upright. "Are you coming right back?"

Grady nodded. "Hang in there, hambone."

Charity waited alone in the hallway, an oversized cup of takeout coffee in hand. "Don't judge," she said, but neither of them smiled.

"You can't release him into my custody?"

"It doesn't work that way. I know that's not what you want to hear, but—"

"Dammit, he's eleven."

"Grady—"

"You're going to have to arrest me, too, because there's no damned way—"

"Shut it," she barked. When he did, she took a gratified swig of coffee. "I talked to the doctor. He agreed it would be best to keep Matt under observation. So he'll be staying the night here, and you can keep him company."

* * *

CHARITY WATCHED AS SURPRISE flashed across Grady's features. Good. That was good. Things would go a lot smoother if he considered her a hard-ass.

"Thank you," he said, and eyed her coffee.

She moved it out of reach. Hard-asses didn't share caramel macchiatos. "Don't thank me yet. He's in trouble, Grady. If we prove Will and Turbo are the same vandals who've been plaguing

Becker County for months now, the judge will land on them like a Buick dropped from a ten-story building. On Matt, too. You need to talk to Quinn."

"Quinn. Right. I still don't believe this, I—" He broke off, staring hard at the middle finger on the hand that held the cup. The finger she tended to tap when she had something on her mind. A lot about her had changed, but a lot had stayed the same, too. "What aren't you telling me?" he demanded.

Charity sighed. What did she have to lose, but her career and her self-respect? "Still interested in helping me solve Sarah's murder?"

Grady's eyebrows shot up. "What?"

"We know what killed her. Someone strangled her with the cord on a set of ear buds."

"Jesus." He paled. Then his eyes went narrow. "There's more."

"They belong to Allison Young."

"You don't think…"

"She doesn't have an alibi. Supposedly she was home alone while her mom spent the night with…her lover." If Grady didn't know about his father's extramarital affair, he sure as hell wouldn't find out from Charity. "And she has one hell of a motive."

"But she's a smart kid. Why would she plan everything so carefully, only to leave evidence like that behind?" Grady rubbed a hand over his jaw. "Unless she wanted to frame Drew."

"He would have had access to those ear buds, too," Charity said carefully.

"Yeah, and he's as smart as Allison." Grady swung away, scratched the back of his neck, and swung back. "Isn't this the worst possible time to join forces?"

"I need this case closed. People won't talk to me. Keith Tarrant, Scott Langford, others. They will talk to you. The sooner we get this thing figured out, the sooner Drew can go back to being a graduating senior. The sooner I can go back to my campaign. And the sooner you can go back to Seattle."

He nodded once, and she almost rolled her eyes at the inevitable pang of disappointment. Had she really expected he'd regret leaving?

"So what's next?" he asked.

"Next I remind you this partnership will be strictly confidential. Not to mention professional."

One side of his mouth jerked upward. "You sure know how to take all the fun out of a murder investigation."

Charity grunted. No argument there.

"This mean you can tell me what you and Peyton were talking about at the cemetery?"

She drained her coffee and tossed the cup. "Seems when she and Allison were freshmen, they both liked the same guy. Things got ugly, there was a lot of hurt involved, and it nearly put an end to their friendship. So they made a pact. No more hurting each other. And if a guy did the hurting, they'd shut him out. Hence Peyton's treatment of Drew."

"Peyton's a suspect, too." It wasn't a question.

"I'm an investigator, Grady. It's my job to investigate."

He scrubbed his hands over his face, and when he dropped them again, her heart squeezed at the exhaustion pulling at his features.

He tipped his head at the room behind them. "What's next?"

"I spoke to Judge Purl. Here's the deal. Since this isn't the first juvenile justice case Will and Turbo are involved in, they'll be required to attend a formal hearing. Matt's can be informal. He meets with the judge tomorrow at one."

Grady blew out a breath. "Good. That's good."

"This doesn't mean the judge will be any more lenient when it comes to sentencing."

"I understand. He screwed up. He will make amends." He took her hand. "Thank you. I owe you."

Charity tugged free. "Helping me put Sarah's killer behind bars will be payment enough."

"I still owe you an apology for how I acted today." He reached out again, but she was already backing away.

"Apology accepted," she said briskly. "See you tomorrow at the hearing."

*   *   *

THEY STOOD IN AN awkward triangle on the front steps of the courthouse, hands in pockets, shoulders hunched against the chilly prod of the afternoon wind. But the sun was strong, and the snow from the day before had long since melted. Outside the thrift store on the other side of the street, a kid pounded on a toy piano, the tinny notes sounding like they belonged in a low-budget horror. A cluster of hot-pink tulips in a nearby planter quivered accordingly.

Grady nudged Matt with his elbow. "Is there something you want to say to Deputy Bishop?"

Matt kept his eyes on his shoes. "Thank you," he muttered.

"For?" Grady prompted.

"For talking to the judge about me."

Charity resisted the urge to glance around for anyone within earshot. "All I did was remind him you'd never been in trouble before. You did the rest by acting respectful and showing true remorse."

No response. She looked at Grady and couldn't help a swell of sympathy at the disappointment in his eyes. She was sure to see worse in Pratt's face when he found out Purl had put her in charge of overseeing Matt's community service. Once he did, she'd be handling the lunch run for the next six months.

She really needed to solve Sarah's case and get these West men on a plane back to the coast.

Grady's phone rang. He held up a finger and stepped aside. Charity met Matt's malevolent stare and suppressed a shiver. Guess now was not the time to tease him about his black eye. The skin over the kid's right cheek was a swollen, reddish-purple mess. She doubted he realized how much worse things could have been.

"Ready to start paying your debt to society?" she asked.

"Whatevs," he mumbled. "You can make me wash windows or mop the floor or junk like that, but you can't make me like you."

Later she would break the news about toilet duty. "I didn't talk to the judge on your behalf so you'd like me. I did it because from what I've heard, this kind of behavior is unusual for you. Yes, you gave in to peer pressure. Yes, you made a poor decision. Several, in fact. You can still turn this around. You can be proud of yourself again."

Matt turned a wince into a sneer. "So this community service is going to be all, like, sappy lectures over milk and cookies and stuff?"

Eleven? This kid sounded more like sixteen. "I don't reward bad behavior."

"You sound like my dad." His eyes turned wary. "So you don't care if I don't like you?"

"I didn't say that. Your father and I were once good friends, and I'm sure I'd enjoy being friends with you, too. But it'll mean more if you decide to like me on your own."

"That's not gonna happen."

"Whatevs. You still don't get any milk and cookies."

Matt rolled his eyes, but some of the hostility had eased from his expression. "You and my dad. You're not friends anymore?"

The air went still. The piano prodigy had disappeared, and the wind had settled. The only sound was the remote masculine murmur of the voice on the other end of Grady's call.

"Not like we used to be," Charity managed. "We haven't seen each other since before you were born."

"Did you know my mom?"

Grady moved back to Matt's side, saving Charity from having to answer.

"I need to get back to work," she said. "Any more questions? About how you'll be spending your afternoons?" she added quickly.

"What about Will and Turbo?" Matt asked.

"They were transferred to a juvenile facility. They'll probably be there through the summer."

"They're going to think I narced on 'em." The kid's voice rattled with panic.

Charity resisted the urge to smooth a hand over his thin back. "No. They know we have them on video."

Grady squeezed his son's shoulder and tugged him toward the parking lot. "I'll bring him back after we grab something to eat."

With a scowl, Matt freed himself and speed-walked toward the car.

Grady hesitated, pulled his wallet from his back pocket and walked back to Charity. "I've been meaning to give this to you." He handed her a square of paper and watched as she unfolded it. "It's a price quote from J.T. Muscoe's, on a security system for your Camry. I talked him into giving you a top-of-the-line system for a basic price."

Charity stared down at the pale yellow paper. She could actually afford this. She could have Clarabelle so wired that no one would dare come within five feet of her. She inhaled. His gesture had caught her unawares, and left her feeling off balance. "Thank you," she said, looking up with a smile. "This was very thoughtful."

His cheeks darkened and he shrugged. "Thank you for looking out for Matt and Drew. Justine, too. And for putting up with me."

"You're welcome."

He snapped his wallet closed and started walking backward, toward his car. "We need to talk," he said. One side of his mouth edged upward. "Partner."

"I'll call you when I get home tonight." She watched him turn and walk away, admiring the strength in his shoulders and the clever fit of his expensive suit.

"What'd the kid get?"

Charity jumped, and aimed a grimace at the courthouse entrance. Brenda June peered around the edge of the heavy door.

"Restitution. Mandatory curfew. Community service." She stuffed the paper from Muscoe's in her pocket, marched up the steps and sidled past Dispatch into the quiet dimness of the building. "Under my supervision."

Brenda June shut the door behind them, her slick ruby lips forming a capital O. "Pratt's going to shout this place down."

"You know it."

The dispatcher patted her cheek. "Dix is looking for you. He went to Kate Young's house to talk to Allison and no one answered the door. Allison wasn't in school today, and Kate took a sick day from the hospital."

"Did Dix spot either of them inside the house?"

When Brenda June shrugged, Charity set off for Judge Purl's office. The dispatcher kept pace, kitten heels clacking an urgent rhythm along the tiled floor, oversized turquoise sweater swirling around her like a cape.

"I'll get the judge started on a warrant," Charity said. "Meanwhile I'll try to get Kate on the phone. Tell Dix to start calling Allison's friends, starting with Peyton Langford."

*   *   *

EYES SQUEEZED SHUT, HIP braced against the kitchen counter, Charity chugged another glass of water. She really needed something stronger, because once she grabbed some dinner and put on a clean uniform shirt she was headed back to the station, but damn it, she was determined not to cave to caffeine again. Even if her head did feel like she'd slammed it in a car door. But dear Lord, how many painkillers would it take to get rid of that incessant knocking?

Oh. *Try the back door, dummy.* Someone stood on the cement porch—someone tall and dark—and her midsection started to vibrate. *Grady.* He'd decided not to wait for her call. With an embarrassing amount of eagerness, she lunged at the door and swung it wide. Her visitor turned to face her.

She put her fists on her hips and inhaled, smelled lilacs and smoldering leaves and all kinds of trouble. "I don't know why you're here," she said grimly, "but it's a very bad idea."

12

DREW LANGFORD WAS ALL wide-eyed innocence. "Can I come in?"

"No, you can't come in. You're a person of interest in my murder case. What in God's name are you doing here?"

He eyed her unbuttoned uniform shirt and the white tee she always wore underneath. "You coming in or going out?"

"Both. Why are you here?"

"I'm here for the truth."

"About?"

"Did you really forgive Uncle Grady for getting you arrested?"

Charity gaped. "Seriously? You're standing on my back steps, in plain sight, risking my career and your own criminal defense because you want to know about something that happened a dozen years ago?"

"I want to know if you're setting me up to get back at him."

Her skin went cold, and it took her two tries to find her voice. "Your grandparents have about as much common sense as a bag of dirt."

"They didn't send me. By the way, the longer you make me stand out here, the greater the chance someone will see us."

"Oh, this is perfect. This is great." She stepped aside. "Come in."

She shut and locked the door and turned to find his gaze lingering on the meal she hadn't gotten around to—a bright yellow bowl and a box of Lucky Charms. When he caught her eye, his expression turned sheepish.

"I haven't felt like eating with the family lately."

She gestured at the chair opposite hers. He sat, and watched as she fetched a second bowl — this one orange. Ceramic clanged, and the cabinet door banged shut. She yanked open a drawer, scrabbled for a spoon, and hit the drawer with her hip. Silverware jangled. She fetched the milk out of the fridge and slapped the door shut. Bottles clinked. Finally she snatched the cereal box off the counter and thumped it down in front of Drew. Magically delicious marshmallows and bits of toasted oats rustled.

His grin was half desperation, half defiance. "You sure make a lot of noise when you cook."

She dropped back into her chair, picked up her spoon, set it back down, watched her guest as he emptied half the box of cereal into his bowl — damn, she'd have to settle for oatmeal for breakfast — shoved the box across the table, and frowned at the jug of milk.

"Skim," he muttered. "I don't suppose — "

"Take it or leave it."

He shut up and poured. For ten minutes they concentrated on eating, the only sounds in the kitchen the close-mouthed crunch of cereal and the rhythmic plunk of spoon meeting milk. When Drew's pace didn't slow as he reached the bottom of the bowl, Charity got up and put two slices of bread in the toaster.

His expression was grateful. His words were not. "So are you? Setting me up?"

She held on to his gaze. "You don't know me. You have no reason to trust me. But I have too much respect for the law, and my profession, to be anything less than honest, on or off the job."

"So when someone asks you a question, you always provide an honest answer?"

"If it's a question I can legally answer, then yes."

Drew watched her with those too-damned-perceptive Grady West eyes.

She pushed away from the counter in search of knife, plate, butter, jelly. "Unless it's a question I don't want to answer. In that case I say nothing at all."

213

His gaze lowered to her cheeks, which she could feel turning pinker than the marshmallow hearts sitting abandoned in her bowl. Drew nodded.

"Do you think I killed Sarah?"

One by one Charity set the items on the table, then turned her back to her guest as she waited for the toaster. Her fingers shook. What a question. And one she shouldn't answer. Then again, Drew Langford shouldn't be in her kitchen eating Lucky Charms.

"No," she said.

"Do you think someone's trying to frame me?"

She thought of the leather necklace. "Yes."

"Anyone you know?"

"I don't know who it is, so I don't know whether I know them or not. I do know it's no one in the sheriff's office."

Bit by bit Drew's shoulders eased downward. He ate his toast as Charity rinsed out his bowl. When the kitchen was quiet again, Charity sat back down.

"I'm not going to let you go to jail for something you didn't do," she said.

He angled his head. "Why do you care?"

Charity started to say, *it's my job*, but realized that wasn't the entire truth. "You remind me of someone."

He smirked around a mouthful of strawberry jam. "You really expect me not to know you're talking about Uncle Grady?"

"I really expect you not to be a smartass when you're sitting in my kitchen eating my food."

Drew ran a napkin across his mouth and stood, keeping the smirk while handing her his empty plate. "Now I'm not doing either. Thank you for feeding me."

"You have his eyes. And his ego."

"You ever going to forgive him for what he did?"

"I forgave him a long time ago."

"So what don't you forgive him for?"

"Getting married." When Drew's gaze sharpened, Charity managed a wheezing sort of laugh. "So soon after we split, I mean."

"You should forgive him. For Matt's sake."

"Matt?"

214

"He says you're mean to his dad."

"Does he?" She considered. "Maybe I should kick mean up to brutal."

"How come?"

"He's still mad at his dad for the divorce. If I give him someone else to resent then maybe—"

"He'll back off Uncle Grady." Drew's expression turned speculative, but when he spoke, it was only to say, "Thanks for letting me in."

He opened the door and stepped out into the chilly dusk, paused, and looked back. "Allison's not returning my calls. Do you know if she's okay?"

They were looking for Allison, too, and Charity had a very bad feeling about the reason she was making herself scarce.

"I'll look into it," she said. "And Drew—" the butter dish clattered as she pushed to her feet "—you know we'll need to bring you in tomorrow. For more questioning."

"Okay if I stop in after school?"

She gave him a nod. "Do you mind if I ask, are you still planning to go to Stanford in the fall?"

With a shake of his head, Drew fastened the snaps on his letterman's jacket. "I wouldn't mind being near Uncle Grady. But I'm going to stick close for a while. See what I can do about getting my mom back out on her own. Living with my grandparents...it's not good for her."

"Kate Young told me Allison had opted for community college instead of following you to California."

"I don't think she was ever serious about Stanford. Heck, she's not even serious about high school. Anyway, she doesn't have the grades for a scholarship."

Translation: she couldn't have afforded Stanford otherwise. It must have been wishful thinking on Kate's part.

Drew braced his palms on either side of the doorway and leaned in. "Let me know when you talk to Allison, okay?"

"Absolutely."

He hesitated. "My dad wants to see me."

"Do you want to see him?"

He gave his head a shake. "Does that make me a bad person?"

"You know it doesn't."

"Think I should forgive him?"

Charity crossed her arms against the chill that sidled through the open door. That one question was, without a doubt, the entire reason behind this visit.

"Forgiveness is a very personal thing," she said, "so I can't answer that for you. At some point, though, you'll realize it takes more effort to hold onto a grudge than it does to forgive. So you have to ask yourself, how much will you lose between now and then?" She shrugged. "Maybe it won't matter. Maybe it will. No one else can decide that but you."

Frowning, he mulled over her words. Then he slapped the door frame twice and took off.

Charity moved forward and watched his tall form lope around the corner of the house. A ridiculous swell of sadness tugged at her shoulders. She snatched up the hem of her T-shirt and pressed it to her face. Breathed in and out, through cotton gone suddenly soggy.

*   *   *

KATE'S HOUSE REMAINED DARK. Charity walked the perimeter twice, flashlight playing over every window, every exterior door. No sign of movement, no hint of forced entry. She circled back to the front porch and dropped down onto the top step, wincing as the bricked edge bit into her thighs.

What the hell? After the judge granted a warrant that afternoon, Dix and Mo had searched Kate's home. No signs of a panicked departure. Empty suitcases remained stacked in an upstairs closet. But neither mother nor daughter would answer her phone.

Charity clicked off the flashlight and sat in the deep black of the night while she concentrated on the weight of her phone in her jacket pocket. With a not-quite-steady sigh, she pulled it out, and dialed Grady.

"I'm sorry to call so late," she said when he answered.

"It's only ten. Besides, I'm used to you keeping me up at night."

A delicious awareness buzzed through her veins. "I…don't know what to say to that."

"Say you'll make it up to me."

"What happened to keeping this professional?" *What happened to understanding that I'm not up for another episode of loving and leaving?*

His turn to sigh. "That mean I'm not next on your to-do list?"

A sweet, sudden heat pulsed between her thighs. She shifted on the steps, this time welcoming the scrape of the bricks against her legs. "How about you talk to Sarah's coworkers in the morning?" she suggested briskly. "Then see what you can get out of Keith Tarrant. I need to track down Allison."

"You worried about her?"

"Not yet."

He paused. "You'll need to talk to Drew again."

A sweep of headlights sent Charity to her feet. Kate was back.

"We'll talk tomorrow." She stuffed her phone back into her pocket and waited.

Ten minutes and a pocketful of tissues later, an emotional Kate admitted Allison had gone into hiding. "I know she's with one of her friends, but none of them will own up to it. I've left message after message. She won't return my calls. She felt so guilty after your visit the other morning. She said she shouldn't have dumped on Drew. I know I told you she was handling the breakup okay, but she really did love him."

"We need to talk to her, Kate."

"About the ear buds, right? I realize that makes her look guilty, but she wouldn't hurt Sarah. She wouldn't hurt anyone. She lost those ear buds. I haven't seen them in forever. I don't know how they ended up…you know."

"We'll need the names of her friends. Anyone she could be staying with."

"Of course. Come in, and I'll get those for you. I should go and work a few hours at the hospital. I really can't afford to take any more leave. But I'm so tired." Kate pushed to her feet. "I guess you told your colleagues about Hampton and me."

"I had to, Kate. I explained that." No way Charity would repeat what the sheriff had had to say about it. "The only way it'll come out is during someone's testimony."

The other woman nodded curtly. "Someone mentioned they saw you and Grady looking cozy in the liquor store parking lot. Since you were supposedly trying to avoid him, I take it he finally talked you into working together?"

Kate's words carried an understandable bite, but Charity had no intention of going there. She asked why Kate couldn't stay home and rest. As the other woman listed all the expenses involved with raising a teenager, Charity struggled to concentrate on the moment Kate had pulled into her driveway. A second vehicle — an extended cab pickup — had driven slowly by the house at the same time.

Dark blue? Black? She'd seen that truck before.

Now she just had to remember where.

*   *   *

CHARITY JUGGLED HER BACKPACK, her keys, a bottle of water, a plastic sandwich bag of almonds, and a travel cup filled with instant hot chocolate — was she really willing to let a handful of Colombian beans get the better of her? — as she maneuvered through her front door and onto the porch. She tucked the water under her arm, shoved a corner of the snack bag into her mouth, and locked the door. A warm awareness drifted down her spine, and she turned to find Grady standing at the bottom of the steps, a paper bag in his hand and a sleepy smile on his face.

The almonds hit the floor of the porch with a rattling *thwap*. "What are you doing here?"

"Good morning to you, too." He looked askance at the almonds and hefted the bag. "I brought breakfast."

Charity heard the words, but they barely registered. All her senses were too busy admiring the fit of the jeans and turtleneck he wore beneath a short, black wool coat. His thick, dark hair was rumpled, his jaw unshaven, and she prayed he didn't yawn; the fact that the door to her bedroom was maybe twenty feet away would make it much too easy to suggest he slide back between the sheets. With her.

"Charity?" Grady rattled the bag at her. "Tell me you haven't already eaten."

The sweet scent of maple syrup wafted her way. "Pancakes?"

"Waffles."

She moaned and turned back to the door. "Follow me."

Somehow she managed to lead him past her bedroom door. Once she'd gotten a whiff of those waffles, it wasn't that hard. They took off their jackets in the kitchen. Grady poured juice into mismatched glasses—he'd ignored her one coordinating pair—while she set out plates, forks, knives, and napkins. They settled at the table, and Grady handed her a container from the Good Dog, Bad Dog Café. The Styrofoam cracked and creaked under the weight of a golden Belgian waffle, three links of sausage, a plastic container of butter, and another of heated syrup.

"Thank you," she said reverently, holding the container in both hands and giving a mighty inhale.

Grady winked and reached again for the bag. Together they transferred the food to their plates, and Grady lifted his glass.

"To partnership."

They locked gazes over the orange juice. Charity sipped loudly, set down her juice, and grabbed her fork. They ate in silence for several moments, until she looked up and caught him watching her.

"I thought we agreed to divide and conquer," she said.

"The kind of conquering I have in mind requires togetherness."

Her fork clacked against her plate. "Flirt all you want. I have a lot riding on this case. You won't distract me from it."

"I have a lot riding on it, too. I don't want to distract you, I want..." Grady leaned in. "Drew told me he was here last night. I want to thank you."

"For?"

"Believing in him. He's been having a hard time."

Charity could imagine. Still she couldn't help feeling deflated as she gazed down at her waffle. "I like the way you express your appreciation."

"A simple thank-you for who you are, not for anything you've done." He leaned closer, letting her feel his heat. "When you're ready for a more in depth expression, you let me know."

Tiny spasms of need flickered up and down her backbone. It took everything within her to swallow the words that hovered at the back of her throat. Absently her gaze traveled from her plate to his. Slowly she raised her head. "Grady?"

"Yeah?" His voice was deep. Raw.

Charity licked her lips and smiled when his body jolted. "You have syrup all over your shirt."

*   *   *

GRADY LOOKED DOWN. SURE as hell. He'd pressed right into his plate.

He leaned back, tossed his napkin aside and willed his body to loosen and deflate. "So." He picked up his juice glass and pressed it to his forehead and each cheek, enjoying the husky, delighted sound of Charity's laugh. "What's on the agenda for this morning?"

"You mean after you clean the syrup off your shirt?"

"Yeah." He pushed away from the table and helped himself to the dishrag.

She stood, but instead of gathering their plates, she stared down at them. "First we need to find Allison. I've put out some feelers, but no one's talking."

"And once we find her?"

"We set her mother's mind at ease, then pay a visit to Keith Tarrant."

Grady glanced over his shoulder as he rinsed out the dishrag. "Should I bring my Taser?"

"I'm certainly not going to let you borrow mine."

Five minutes later they were on the road. Grady had been prepared to argue against taking separate cars, but Charity didn't say a word when he climbed into the passenger seat of her SUV.

Never underestimate the power of a waffle.

He buckled himself in. "When do you get your Camry back?"

"Clarabelle?" She grinned, and bounced in her seat. He turned a groan into a cough. All that vigorous jiggle, wasted on a car. "J.T. promised someone would drop her off today or tomorrow."

"Planning a party?" he mocked.

"What I'm planning," she muttered, "is an ass kicking."

They didn't talk much after that. They drove from address to address, slowly crossing out the names on the list Kate Young had provided. Charity had timed the visits well, catching the girls before they left for school, but none of Allison's friends would admit to knowing where she was, which meant Grady's plan to show Charity what a kick-ass team they made was crashing and burning.

They stood beside the SUV, watching as the last name on the list left her driveway in the passenger seat of a compact car. Charity's handset came to static life, and she turned away to check in with the dispatcher. Grady's gaze followed as she paced the sidewalk, her frustration apparent in the stiffness of her posture. The morning sun glinted off the hair she'd tucked behind her ears. She'd swallowed the last of her hot chocolate before they'd knocked on this final door, and she still had a small stain at the corner of her mouth. He looked away.

In the liquor store parking lot, he'd thrown out that suggestion about her visiting Seattle. Now that the idea was out there, he couldn't stop thinking about it.

Charity signed off the radio and strode back to his side. "Brenda June forgot to tell me earlier. We won't know for sure until the lab verifies it, but Mo didn't find any fingerprints on the duct tape used to repair Allison's earbuds."

Son of a bitch. "Somebody *is* setting up Drew."

"That text he received the night Sarah was killed does make it look deliberate. Any idea who could be holding that kind of grudge? Besides Allison, I mean?"

Grady shook his head. "We'll have to ask him." But the first face that popped into his mind belonged to Drew's own father. *Christ.* "Wait. Couldn't someone have followed Sarah, not knowing Drew would show up, too?"

"It's possible," she said slowly. "That's a coincidence, something cops don't usually like, but it's something to keep in mind." She squinted at him. "You're already earning your keep."

"My pleasure. Now what?"

"Now we go see Tarrant."

Grady nodded. Charity had told him that despite laying on the charm, Deputy Morrissey hadn't managed to get much more information about Sarah than what he'd learned while dating her. Her coworkers were being closemouthed. Charity said she couldn't help wondering if it was more about self-preservation than respect for the dead. She also said she hoped Grady's last name would loosen some lips. For her sake, he hoped the same.

"I'll drive." He lifted a palm in anticipation of a key toss.

Charity twisted her lips. Yeah, it was a smirk, but it was better than the scowl she'd been wearing. "In your dreams," she said.

But Tarrant wouldn't be in that day, according to the only agent in the office, a woman with short, slicked-back hair wearing a too-tight pantsuit the color of dead leaves. She—Claire—had been nervously licking her lips since the moment Grady and Charity walked through the double glass doors. It took some time, but after Grady's name-dropping, Charity's unashamed play of the guilt card, and an offer of four tickets to the next Pill Hill fundraising gala, Claire agreed to talk.

"But not here," she said. "The other agent should be back from showing properties in about an hour. Why don't you meet me at my house for an early lunch?" She recited an address on the outskirts of the county, and her expression turned sly. "Maybe you could bring something from Jerzy's?"

Back in the SUV, Grady raised his palm for a high five. "Told you we'd make a good team."

Charity smacked at his hand and started up the Tahoe. "Let's hope what she has to say will be worth the cost of lunch."

Chaos reigned inside the Shake Shack. Apparently Jerzy had popped the question to his girlfriend Edith, who was bouncing from table to table, showing off her left hand. Customers crowded the restaurant, laughing and clapping and shouting their congratulations. It took Grady and Charity fifteen minutes to navigate the twenty feet to the counter.

"My favorite couple!" Jerzy greeted them then looked abashed. "I mean, besides my wife-to-be and me. Whatever you want, it's on the house. And help yourself to some cake."

They congratulated him, Charity with a hug and Grady with a slap on the back. After placing their order, they moved out of the way. A beaming Edith maneuvered sideways through the crush, gave them each a chance to admire her ring, then pushed on to the next batch of well-wishers.

"Deputy Bishop."

Charity turned toward a short, plump woman wearing feathered earrings that dangled to her shoulders. She grabbed for Charity's hand and shook it. "You helped me out last month when I crashed my car after swerving to miss a deer. I wanted to thank you for all you did. I was a wreck—literally—but you helped me keep it together." She giggled self-consciously. "Thanks for the ride home, too. My little boy still talks about the time he got to sit in a real police vehicle."

"I'm glad you're all right."

"Good luck with the election." The woman smiled and started to move away, then retraced her steps. "By the way, I work for the library, and every month we host a career night. We'd love to have you as a guest speaker sometime."

"Th-thank you," Charity stammered. "I'll let you know."

As the woman disappeared into the crowd, Charity turned back to Grady, her expression dazed. "That…doesn't happen."

"What? Getting thanks for helping someone out?"

"People don't usually just come up to me. Unless they're angry, drunk, or trying to take my order."

"Maybe you seem more approachable today. You do tend to be tense." He bent down, and let his lips brush her hair. "I could help with that, you know."

Charity stepped aside to let someone pass, and didn't step back. "For eight weeks," she said stiffly.

"For eight weeks," he agreed. Eight weeks he'd have to convince her they deserved more. But his evil plan didn't stand a chance in hell if she kept pushing him away.

"So I asked myself." Jerzy held aloft a plate of cake as he spoke above the noise of the crowd. "What am I waiting for? Life is short!"

Charity jolted, then swung toward the counter, but Grady hadn't heard them call her name. Long minutes later she was back, a bulging paper bag hugged to her chest. "Ready to go?"

"Always."

She shot Grady a dirty look and led the way to the SUV. He opened the door to the back so she could tuck the food behind her seat.

"You ever think of settling down?" he asked.

"As in, marriage?" Charity hesitated, then pushed an eyebrow upward. "Why, because it worked so well for you?"

"Because I'm curious. Where do you see yourself in five years?"

She rolled her eyes. "This sounds like a job interview."

"Never mind." He stepped back. "We have an informant to feed." He rounded the back of the SUV, calling himself all kinds of asshole. A flash of white caught his attention and he stopped. Someone had tucked a note in the rear wiper.

Shit.

Grady swung around and scanned the parking lot. "Uh…Charity?"

Forty five minutes later, after the note had been bagged, Charity had taken a photo of every license plate in the parking lot, and Mo had arrived to canvass the area and switch vehicles so he could dust Charity's for prints, Grady and Charity were on their way to the real estate agent's house for a not-so-early-after-all lunch.

"Any ideas?" Grady asked, hating the silence but hating the half-pissed, half-hurt jut of her jaw even more.

What he hated most was that he'd been with her and still hadn't managed to protect her.

Charity's shrug looked forced. "Someone's taunting me, but I doubt it's the killer. He—or she—wouldn't have risked getting caught leaving love notes in such a public place."

Some love note. *Think you always get your man? Think again, bitch.*

The urge to smash in the face of whoever was harassing Charity rose up inside him, unaccompanied by even the slightest twinge of guilt.

"Or it could be that someone's jealous I'm hanging out with you," she said stiffly.

Grady considered. Maybe it was time for a conversation with his parents.

Claire wasn't pleased they were running late. She was even less pleased with her lukewarm barbecue sandwich. Still she provided two fascinating pieces of information. One, Sarah and Keith Tarrant hadn't been getting along. And two, there were rumors involving Tarrant Properties and a big-money deal gone wrong. Claire was able to give them the name of the investment group, but she couldn't identify the individual investors.

Charity prepared to back the SUV out of Claire's driveway, caught Grady staring, and frowned. "What?"

He shook his head, never looking away. "You really love this, don't you?"

She had a glow to her, like she'd just come in from a brisk walk in the sun. "My job?" She checked her mirrors and merged onto the highway. "Yeah, I do. Though there are times I wish I was better at it."

"You need to stop beating yourself up about this case. You'll crack it. Besides, you're doing the best you can. No one can expect more."

"I wonder if you realize the same applies to you."

Grady lifted his head from the seat back. "What does that mean?"

"It means you're constantly beating yourself up over Matt. But you have to know you're a good father."

He cleared his throat. "Where are we headed now?"

"To the courthouse, to see if we can get a list of Tarrant's investors." She smiled over at him tentatively. "I can't tell you how much I appreciate your help."

Aw, hell. Grady turned his head to look out the window, barely registering the brilliant blues, greens, and golds as the Montana landscape flashed by.

Her voice had practically shimmered with excitement. And why not? She'd found out she had a fan and got a solid lead in Sarah's murder, all in the space of an hour.

Oh, yeah. He was helping her case, all right—her case for staying in Becker County.

*   *   *

CHARITY ENDED UP HAVING to send Grady to the courthouse on his own. They were five minutes away from the county seat when every uniform was called in to work a ten-fifty-eight on Interstate 191. An auto accident with fatalities. Brenda June's voice had quivered over the radio. Charity dropped Grady off at his car, and swung back toward the highway.

Hours later, when she was finished working the accident, she dragged herself home for a shower. She stood under the hot spray of water, too drained to cry, too tired to relax. Too bad she had to go back to work, but Grady would be dropping off Matt at the station in half an hour and she still had a butt-load of paperwork to finish.

After she got dressed again she called Grady, reveling a little too much in the sexy stroke of his voice. What he had to say distracted her from her sadness, her hormones, and her fatigue.

"Meet me at Red Top," she told him, and scooped up her keys.

*   *   *

GRADY TURNED INTO THE lot, tires grinding over gravel.

Matt's eyes rounded when he spotted the "Red Top Range" sign on the building's scarlet metal roof. "A gun range?" he asked breathlessly. Not only were the words the first he'd spoken since he'd slammed into the car, he sounded like a little boy again.

Grady's heart pinched. "Sure is," he managed. He parked beside Charity's SUV. When she got out, and Matt saw she was wearing her uniform, he jerked his arms across his chest.

"What, does their floor need sweeping, too?"

Grady eased a breath in and out and unfastened his seatbelt. "Let's ask."

Matt huffed a beleaguered breath before shoving his way out of the car while Grady hid a grin. When he got a closer look at Charity's face, he lost all sense of amusement. Her jaw was tense, her skin pale, her eyes full of shadows.

Grady moved closer, barely resisting the urge to touch her. "Rough afternoon?"

"It was definitely more than a fender bender." She glanced at Matt and away, sending a clear signal.

Subject not fit for young ears.

Grady shoved his hands in his pockets and swung toward Matt. "Didn't you have something you wanted to ask Deputy Bishop?"

"There was an accident? Did someone die?"

Grady winced. "I mean about what we're doing here."

Calmly, Charity answered Matt's question. "We had two casualties, yes. Both thrown from their vehicle. If the victims had been wearing their seatbelts, they probably would have survived."

"Are you just saying that so I'll wear my seatbelt?"

Charity moved abruptly to the rear of the Tahoe. "I'm not just saying it, no. It is a good lesson. What else did you want to ask?"

Matt watched Charity closely as she opened the hatch and tugged at a duffel bag. She zipped it open to reveal a collection of guns, and the kid sucked air.

A moment later he backed away, eyes back on Charity, expression unfriendly. "Is this supposed to make me like you?"

Christ. "Matthew Thomas West," Grady growled. "Adjust your attitude or we'll call it quits right here."

Charity didn't seem fazed. "Like me or don't like me, it's up to you. Bringing you with me to the range was your dad's idea. If I had my way, you'd be back at the station, cleaning out the break room fridge. But you're not completely off the hook. We will have to pick up after ourselves. It's bad form to leave empty casings on the floor."

Matt offered up a solemn nod while practically shuddering with excitement.

Grady moved to Charity's other side and leaned in. "I know what you're doing."

"Glad someone does." She turned back to Matt.

Grady lingered, breathing in honeysuckle. He must have breathed a little too loudly, because she took a step back and let her heavy-duty assault boot grind his toes into the gravel.

Son of a bitch, that hurt.

"Okay, Matt." Charity still sounded exhausted, but at least she sounded happier about it. "Before we go inside, I need to tell you the rules of the range, and I need you to listen."

Matt's head bobbed on his neck.

"The first rule is that you never take a loaded weapon into the range. In fact, you never carry a loaded weapon at all. I've already checked my guns, but I'm going to check them again." She drew her spare service weapon from its holster. "This is a Sig Sauer three fifty-seven caliber automatic pistol." She dropped the magazine and racked the slide. "Not loaded." She put it back into her holster, reached into the duffel bag, and pulled out a revolver.

"This is a forty caliber Smith & Wesson." She flipped open the cylinder and showed Matt it was empty, then set the gun aside. She reached once more into the bag. "And this is a nine millimeter Beretta automatic." As she did with her service weapon, she released the magazine and pulled back the slide. "See? No rounds." She reversed her actions and repeated them, demonstrating how he needed to keep his hand away from the ejection port to prevent a serious pinch. Again she reversed her actions, and offered the weapon to Matt. "Want to try?"

He fumbled a bit, replaced the magazine, tried again, and slapped that sucker in like a pro. Grady didn't know whether to be proud or concerned.

Matt grinned up at Charity. "Will I get to shoot this one?"

She bounced a shoulder. "You can fire all three, if you'd like. As long as you follow the rules."

Earnestness replaced the delight on Matt's face. "You never told me the rest of 'em."

Charity fought a grin, and Grady fought the urge to wrap his arms around her. "The second rule is to wear eye and ear protection at all times," she said. "We'll talk about the others inside. Ready?"

Grady hadn't been inside Red Top in years, but it hadn't changed much. Same lopsided glass-top counter, same peg-boards jammed with goggles and ear protectors and cleaning kits, same dusty shelves crowded with rolls and rolls of paper targets. Same muffled gunshots still loud enough to startle.

"Grady West. It take you this long to get over that last shoot-off with Charity Bishop?"

Same wiseass behind the counter.

"Neely Allan." Grady shook the outstretched hand. "Good to see you."

The old man's grip wasn't as strong as it used to be, but his tobacco-stained grin was wider than ever. "Wish I could say the same. You've gotten ugly in your old age."

"Always did want to be just like you." Grady could feel Matt staring up at him in shock. He clapped him on the shoulder. "Neely, meet my son. Matt."

"Now that's one good-looking kid. How'd that happen?"

Charity snorted.

Grady winked down at Matt. "Just lucky, I guess."

Neely leaned over the counter and offered his hand, gaze briefly scanning Matt's injured eye. "Bet you can out-shoot your dad with one eye closed. Hell, one's already halfway there. Hope the other fella got it worse." He was too smart to expect a response. He pulled his hand back and smoothed it over his sparse gray hair. "Ever been to a range before, Matt?"

"No, sir." Matt stared at the glass vestibule that separated the range from the storefront. The more thumps and cracks that echoed within the glass, the more Matt's upper body leaned toward the noise.

Grady looked at Charity and smiled. Warmth gathered in his belly at the answering curve of her lips.

"Well, you listen to the deputy here," Neely said to Matt. "She'll tell you all you need to know. You want to learn to shoot, you watch her. Like your old man—he never could take his eyes off her. Not that it helped his aim any."

Charity pushed up to the counter. "All right, Neely, time to start earning your pay. Give us two sets of ear protection, three targets, and fifty rounds each for my nine millimeter and my revolver."

"Done. But Matt here's gotta fill out some paperwork first. And you all need to sign the logbook."

Charity nodded, ignoring Matt's groan, and reached for a pen. "Bloom around?"

"He's out runnin' errands. Should be back within the hour."

While Neely helped Matt fill out a waiver Grady would have to sign, Charity pulled Grady off to the side. "Tell me what you've got before Bloom gets back."

Peering through the glass at the contents of the cases, Grady slowly led Charity back toward the entrance. He paused at a dusty bookshelf taller than he was, and thumbed through stacks of paper targets. Circles, torsos, squirrels, prairie dogs, buck silhouettes— Neely's stock hadn't changed much. Charity moved around to his right, and sidled in close. He enjoyed the sense of solidarity.

He enjoyed even more the brush of her breast against his bicep when she braced her hands in the small of her back.

"Sarah Huffman was involved in something shady," he said, "but only because she wanted to do the right thing. An elderly woman was about to lose her home. This woman went looking for Sarah, who'd approached her before and had told her if she ever wanted to sell, Sarah could get her a good price." He turned away from the targets and wandered over to a wall display of scopes, Charity right behind him. "The woman ended up signing with one of the other agents when she couldn't find Sarah. Six months later they'd shown the house twice. One couple was interested, but the agent talked them into buying a different property. The old lady was forced into a short sale."

Charity turned away from the scope she was checking out. "Meaning she sold the house for less than what she owed on it?"

"The mortgage company agreed to eat the difference. It's not a great solution, but it's cheaper than foreclosure for both parties."

He leaned closer to a glassed-in riflescope to double-check the price. "Twenty one hundred dollars?"

"It's a Swarovski." Charity eyed it like...well, like Grady eyed her. "It's waterproof, fog proof, and scratch resistant."

Grady looked from her to the scope and back again. "Should I leave you two alone?"

She snorted, and crouched to examine a different scope, one that looked like it belonged in a Bond movie. Her uniform pants stretched taut across her ass. He remembered her skin being just as taut and before he could get fully lost in the memory, he gave himself a mental shake and got back to the subject at hand. "Anyway." He cleared his throat. "Guess who bought the old lady's house?"

Charity straightened, her expression suddenly fierce. "Tarrant?"

"One of his investment groups."

Her eyes went cold. "They sold it for a profit?"

He pushed at a metal peg jutting from a circular display of gun cleaning supplies, forcing the rack into a lazy spin. "After some basic repairs, they sold it for a significant profit."

"Assholes. What did Sarah do when she found out what her boss had been up to?" Charity plopped her hands at the small of her back again. Jesus. Didn't she realize what that did to her chest?

Grady distracted himself with a quick calculation of semiannual compound interest on three-year bonds then glanced over at Matt, who was still bent over his paperwork.

"She went ballistic," he said. "She tried to convince Tarrant to make it right with the homeowners. When he refused, she threatened to contact Phil Smiley."

Charity cocked her head. "But Tarrant already has a negative rep. And even though what he did is far from ethical, it's not illegal. So why would he care if Smiley trashed him in a small-town paper?"

"Maybe he didn't."

Her arms dropped to her sides as she considered that. "Are you saying you know someone who would care?"

231

He pushed the display rack into another spin. "Guess who's a member of the investment group."

She moved in closer, and stared up at him. Her eyes were looking less haunted than they had out in the parking lot. "Bloom."

"He has a lot of money tied up in his campaign."

Charity jammed a hand into her hair and gripped her skull. "You put all of this together by visiting the courthouse?"

He put out a hand to shush her, and glanced again over his shoulder. "I caught up to Sarah's other coworker. When she realized how much I knew, she was willing to fill in the blanks."

"But we already questioned those two." She shook her head in disgust. "Doesn't anyone trust the police anymore?"

"I may have given the impression I was in the market for a house."

"Great. Perfect." She slapped her hands onto her equipment belt. "Which means word will be out on the street that you and Matt are staying."

"What?" Matt popped out from behind Grady and gazed up at him, wide-eyed. "What's she talking about?"

"Easy, bud—uh, Matt. We're just kidding around. Anyway, I thought you wanted to stay."

"With Peyton and Drew, yeah."

Out of the corner of his eye, Grady caught Charity's flinch. And his kid was only eleven. What the hell would thirteen be like?

He exhaled. "How about we drop this for now and focus on the reason we're here."

"Good idea." Neely came around the counter, a set of protective muffs in each hand. "A man's gotta make a livin,' so you three need to be shootin' more than the shit."

*   *   *

CHARITY LEANED BACK AGAINST the grill of her SUV and stared across the dusk-shrouded plain. A faraway trio of lodgepole pines stood silhouetted against cushiony twilight layers of navy, purple and orange. Wheatgrass rippled under the stroke of a night wind that smelled of sage. Tree frogs exchanged growly chirps and a hoot owl —

No, wait. That would be her phone.

"You should be in bed," Grady said when she answered.

With you? she wanted to ask, but that wouldn't be wise in any way, shape, or form.

"With me," he added.

She shivered. Hot, naked skin sliding over cool, silky sheets, hard muscles, and soft laughter, and Grady's gorgeous mouth —

"Thanks for working with Matt at the range today," he said.

She swallowed. "You're welcome, though I don't think he's eager to repeat the experience. He said he'd rather take shooting lessons from his social studies teacher, who spits when she talks and smells like old potatoes."

"He's eleven."

"He's good at it." She flinched. Crap. Had she really just quoted Bloom's favorite movie? "He has an alibi," she said.

"Matt?"

"Bloom. He has an alibi for Sarah's murder. Tarrant, too."

"Maybe they hired somebody."

"This seems more personal than that."

Brenda June's nine-hundred-number voice sounded at Charity's shoulder. "Unit Four, we have report of a ten-one-oh-six at the elementary school."

She turned her back on the view. "Grady, I have to go."

"What's a ten-one-oh-six?"

"Suspicious person. I'll call you later." She hung up with Grady and pressed push-to-talk on her mic. "Ten-four, Dispatch. Ten-seventy-seven, twelve minutes. And for God's sake, Brenda June, is your sister Trudy ever on duty?"

Charity parked one street over from the school, planning to approach through the trees. This call made the sixth or seventh trespassing report this year. She doubted Turbo or Will had had anything to do with the earlier calls — none of the deputies had ever spotted any damage. And since the boys were still in juvie, they definitely weren't involved now. If there really was something going on besides the occasional spike in old Mrs. Glammeyer's imagination, Charity intended to find out what it was, once and for all.

She called in her position, grabbed her flashlight, and eased out of the SUV. After gingerly shutting the door, she checked her weapon. Five steps into the woods, there was no denying she'd come up with a sucky plan, since she was making enough noise for seven people. And the flashlight didn't do her stealth factor any favors.

A killdeer gave her a high-pitched scolding as she stepped out of the woods. She played her Maglite over the side of the school and froze. This was not an old woman's imagination. This was a hot mess.

Mo answered on the fourth ring.

"Sorry to disturb you," she said.

"No, you're not."

"All right, I'm not. Can you meet me at the station? I need to see tonight's security footage for the elementary school."

His are-you-fucking-kidding-me pause didn't last as long as she'd expected. "What's up?"

Whispering sounded in the background. Someone giggled, and Charity winced. She was going to owe him, big time.

"Let me put it this way," she said. "I also need you to Google how to clean paint off brick."

"Shit." A flapping sound came across the line, as if he'd thrown the sheets back. "I'm on my way."

Charity emerged from the woods and was halfway to her vehicle when she spotted a silver compact idling at the entrance to the parking lot. The car was too far away to make the plates. That couldn't be her vandal...could it? She hopped into her SUV, knowing as soon as her engine turned over, the other driver would peel out and she'd have to make a decision about pursuit. Only...the compact never moved. Even when she pulled up behind it.

In the glare of her headlights, she saw the driver—a tall, beefy dude—hold up his hands.

What the hell?

Five minutes later she was handing back his license, wavering between fury and a reluctant appreciation. "If Grady West hired you to watch over my house at night, why are you here?"

Beefy Dude, aka Leon, shrugged. "He called, said you were on your way here, and asked me to check on you. I was just getting out of the car when I heard you coming out of the woods. I knew if I took off you'd be right behind me."

"Thanks for the save on gas," she said wryly. "I don't suppose you sometimes drive a dark-colored truck?" When he shook his head, she sighed. "How long are you supposed to watch my house?"

"As long as it takes, is what he said." He scratched his head. "You know he got someone to fix your motion sensors, right?"

"I do now."

* * *

MO SAT HUNCHED OVER Charity's computer while she stood behind him eating the second Pop-Tart from the two-pack they were supposed to share. Ten o'clock, and she should have been off duty hours ago. But Dix had needed time to handle a situation with his wife, and if Mo wasn't complaining about being yanked away from what he'd alleged had been celestial sex, then Charity certainly shouldn't complain either.

Okay, screw that. She hadn't had sex in months, which meant she had every right to complain.

"Hey, what are you doing back there? Because it sure as hell ain't listening." Mo swiveled around in the chair and scowled up at her. "You're eating my Pop-Tart."

"You ate my cinnamon bun."

"That was like, two months ago."

"No statute of limitations for cinnamon buns." She peered down at the screen. "Get anything?"

He sighed at what was left of the Pop-Tart and scooted back around. "Looks like we have only one tagger." He pointed at the screen. The image was dark and grainy and the camera's angle far from ideal, but there was clearly only one figure spraying the side of the building. The slim silhouette emptied two cans of paint before disappearing into the same section of woods Charity had tromped through.

"Any way we can get a height on him? Or her?"

Mo shrugged. "I'll play with it tomorrow, get some footage of someone else and do a comparison. What's unusual is we have only the one tagger. Generally they work in crews. Pairs at the minimum. One to be the lookout while the other works the cannon."

"I assume 'cannon' is another word for spray paint can?" she asked dryly. "How old are you again?"

"Hey." He swiveled around again, and snatched what was left of the Pop-Tart out of her hand. Ignoring her squeal, he jammed the square of pastry into his mouth. "It's not all about the ladies," he said, his mouth full. "I make time for a book now and then."

"Let me guess. You keep your books in a basket by the toilet."

"Milk crate. Baskets are girlie." He turned back to the computer. With a few clicks of the mouse, he brought up the pictures Charity had taken.

"We've already agreed the message looks like an adult trying to set up a kid." Mo traced the string of bubble-type letters with the tip of his finger. *I want to go to the zoo!* "Obviously a response to the cutbacks. But kids are all about four-letter words. Like the graffiti at the bus yard. Fuck, shit, prick...words that make 'em feel badass."

"Right. There's no shock value here. Almost as if the tagger didn't want to upset the kids. Which pretty much puts my brother Lucas in the clear."

Mo grunted. "Something like 'Where's my fucking fieldtrip?' would sound more like teen speak. Then there's the bible reference." He gestured at the JOB 4:8 dangling off the end of the sentence. "What kid adds a bible reference?"

Charity read the passage off her phone. "'Even as I have seen, they that plow iniquity, and sow wickedness, reap the same.'"

"'You reap what you sow.'" Mo leaned back in his chair. "A message for the school board?"

236

Charity tucked her phone back into its holder on her belt and perched on the corner of her desk. "Maybe it's a kid smart enough to know how to throw us off."

"I don't think so." Mo gestured at the screen. "Whoever's responsible for this throw-up is pure toy."

Charity sputtered a laugh. "Now you're just showing off."

"A throw-up is a quick, easy piece, usually two colors like this one — one for the outline and one for the fill."

Charity slid off the desk and bent forward to squint at the computer. The letters of the message were outlined in black, and had a lime-green fill. "And what does toy mean?"

"Inexperienced writer."

"A rookie, huh?" Charity rested an elbow on Mo's shoulder and turned her head toward his. The piece of toilet paper stuck to his freshly-shaved neck would have earned a smile if she hadn't known how much it would offend him. "How can you tell?" she asked.

"See the drip marks? The uneven patches of paint? Even in a hurry, that doesn't happen to the pros." He shifted in the chair, and she straightened. Mo slid his wallet out of his back pocket, stood, and plucked out a dollar bill. "Soda?"

She shook her head, eyes back on the screen. "But not all kids are automatically experts at graffiti."

"True." He backed toward her office door. "They learn faster, though. My gut's telling me an adult did this."

"I respect your gut." Charity rounded her desk, reached for his arm and squeezed. "Thanks, Mo. For everything. Could you please pick this up again tomorrow? See if you can find any similarities between this and the damage done to my car and Scott Langford's front porch?"

He nodded, brandished the dollar bill and turned to leave.

"Wait." When he turned back, she bit her lip. "I appreciate you coming in like this at the last minute. Tapping into the surveillance network is something I've never had to do. On my own, I mean."

"One of the regulators could have handled it for you."

"You're right. I thought of you first." Charity glanced back at her desk, and the empty Pop-Tart wrapper topping a stack of files.

"I didn't even feed you like I promised. I'll fix that tomorrow. And, listen, calling you in tonight doesn't have anything to do with politics. You know that, right?"

Mo grunted. "What I know is your Camry got trashed and you're looking for vengeance."

"True." Did her smile look as pathetic as it felt? "When you find the culprits, let me know. I'll be waiting with a bucket of flamingo paint."

Mo left to get his soda, and Charity started the list of local truck owners she'd meant to put together after spotting the pickup outside Kate's house. Brenda June appeared in her doorway, her face nearly as white as Mo's teeth.

Charity's lungs crumpled. "What's happened?"

"Allison Young." Brenda June jerked at her bubblegum sweater, wrapping it tighter around her waist. "She tried to kill herself."

13

FOR THE SECOND TIME in as many days, Charity found herself in the emergency room at Twin Rivers Hospital. She rounded a corner, and her heart dropped to her knees. Kate sat doubled over in an armless chair, head down, arms wrapped around her shins, the ends of her stringy blond hair grazing the floor.

Oh, no. Oh, please.

"Kate?" Charity touched the other woman's shoulder. "Is she all right?"

Slowly Kate sat up, and stared at Charity out of bleary eyes. "They pumped her stomach."

"But she'll be okay?"

"They said yes."

"That's good." Charity exhaled, and sank down onto the chair beside Kate's. She squeezed Kate's hand, but let go when the other woman stiffened.

"I know what you're thinking," Kate said. "This is not that. This could never be that."

Charity wasn't so sure. She nodded at a passing nurse and shifted sideways in her chair, keeping her gaze trained on Kate's face. "Can I get you anything?"

Kate shook her head.

"Can you tell me what happened?"

Kate drew in a trembling breath. "She took Demerol. Ham — Dr. West prescribed it after my knee surgery last year. I never thought about getting rid of it. I never thought it would be a problem. I didn't even know she'd come home."

Charity waited until Kate had finished blowing her nose. "Did she leave a note? Any indication of what made her take those pills?"

Another shake of Kate's disheveled head.

"Drew said he talked with Allison the night he got out of lockup. Did she seem upset afterward?"

"Yes, but she feels things so strongly. I don't...this isn't Drew's fault."

Charity had an unhappy feeling Drew would see it differently. "What happens now?"

"They assigned a staff member to sit with her. There has to be someone within six feet of her twenty-four hours a day. They searched her and...said they couldn't give her sharp utensils to eat with." Kate covered her face with her hands.

"Would you like me to stay with you a while?"

"No." Kate's head came up so quickly, Charity reared back. "This is something Allison and I need to work through together. I won't repeat my mistake of not paying enough attention. We don't need anyone else."

Charity fought a ridiculous surge of envy. If only her own mother had felt the same.

Not about you, Bishop.

There was no sense in telling Kate there would be a number of people involved in this situation. Especially if it turned out Allison had had something to do with Sarah's death.

"If you need anything, or if you think of anything else we should know, please call." Charity stood. "As soon as Allison feels up to it, I'll need to talk with her."

Kate had resumed staring at the floor.

Charity had her cell in her hand and was dialing before she'd even cleared the hospital doors. When Grady answered, relief sapped the strength from her knees. She plopped down onto a nearby bench.

"About time you called me back," he growled. When she didn't—couldn't—respond, his voice went up an octave. "Char? You okay?"

"Yes." Then her throat went thick, and she barely managed a "Hold on" before squeezing her eyes shut and forcing her lungs to do their thing. In, out. In, out. The cold air sharpened the ache in her throat, but gradually the hot grip of misery loosened. When she figured she could talk without blubbering, she spoke again. "I'm at the hospital."

"*Why?*"

"It's not me," she said quickly, ashamed by the thrill his worry gave her. "It's Allison Young."

While she explained what had brought her back to the hospital, she found herself yearning for the steady warmth of Grady's arms.

"Christ." He was silent for a while, then, "You don't think she did it, do you?"

"I don't know. I don't *know*." She got to her feet and started lapping the bench. "It could be despair over Drew. Or guilt because it was her property that was used as the murder weapon."

"What can I do?"

Behind her, the hospital doors swished open. A lanky old man sauntered out, gave her a weary smile and lit up a cigarette. She smiled back, wondering if he realized how much he resembled a pool cue after it had been chalked. Tan shoes, tan slacks, tan jacket—all topped with a powder blue driving cap.

"Charity?"

She walked along the sidewalk, into the darkness, away from the cigarette smoke and the pain on Kate Young's face. "There's nothing you can do, but thanks for asking. Really. I'm sorry. I shouldn't have bothered you."

Silence, as they both digested the fact that she'd reached out to him.

"You're blaming yourself," he said. "I can hear it in your voice."

Well, yeah, because what if suspicion alone had been enough to send Allison over the edge?

She paused beside a shaggy pine tree, leaned back, blinked up at the stars. Her vision was too blurry to appreciate them. "She's just a kid."

"She's in the right place to get the help she needs."

"I know." She straightened, reached for the tree with her free hand and pinched off several needles. Rolling them between her thumb and forefinger released a sharp, sweet scent. "I need to get back out on patrol."

"You're not done with your shift?"

"I'll be fine." She sprinkled the pine needles onto the sidewalk. "Besides, it seems I have a guardian angel."

A long pause. "You met Leon."

"I met Leon." Charity headed for her SUV.

"You don't sound mad."

"I was at first." She pulled out her keys and pressed the unlock button, and found herself cheered by the vehicle's answering tones. "Then I decided it was kind of nice, having someone look out for me. Until he gets in my way, that is. Besides, I'm betting it was enough of a challenge for you, settling for requesting a quote from Muscoe's instead of having J.T. go ahead and install that security system."

"You have no idea."

She climbed into the driver's seat, leaned back, and closed her eyes. "Still, I don't suppose it'll do any good to ask you to call Leon off."

"You know me well."

"I used to," she said, too tired to regret the wistfulness in her voice.

He went silent, then, "I don't hate Christmas anymore."

"Where did that come from?"

"I'm helping you get to know me. You remember how much I dreaded Christmas, right? My folks stayed wasted the entire month of December. Matt changed all that. I even learned how to make those cornflake and marshmallow things. You know, dyed green to look like holly? You're supposed to put those cinnamon candies on top, but Matt insists we use red M&Ms."

"That's sweet," she said. She couldn't help a smile, even as she pressed a thumb and forefinger against the burn behind her eyelids. "I'm glad for you."

"Your turn."

She bit her lip. She didn't like this. Didn't like sitting in the cold, quiet dark, sharing an intimate conversation with the man she'd once given way too much power to. A man whose strength and heat she missed even more than Pop-Tarts Crunch, a cereal that should never have been discontinued.

"What are we doing?" she whispered.

"Distracting you."

She huffed a silent laugh. Hadn't he distracted her enough?

"Char?"

The hope in his voice did her in. "Fine." She thumped the back of her head against the headrest as she considered. Oh, right. "I learned how to ride a horse."

"You what?" Grady's amazement came through, loud and clear. "You were terrified of horses. Whenever I took you by the stables, you'd stay in the car."

"Pathetic, right? But I made friends with this guy at the police academy whose family owned a ranch. The guy who broke my nose, actually. When he found out I couldn't ride, he insisted on teaching me, as an apology. I was too stubborn to tell him the idea scared the crap out of me, so...I learned to ride. But only well enough to use my knees to stay on instead of my hands wrapped around the saddle horn."

"You always were strong. You had to be. But that...that's fucking formidable. I'm proud of you, Char."

The earnestness of his words warmed her like a full-body hug. "Thank you," she managed. She sat up, and started the SUV. "I have to go."

"I'm glad you called."

"I'm glad you picked up."

"Good night, Char."

"Good night, Grady. And thank you. For Leon, and for...making me feel important."

He cleared his throat. "You are important. And not just to me."

She was starting to think she could believe that. She thought back to the lady who'd thanked her at Jerzy's. Maybe she had a chance of winning this election, after all.

If she could solve Sarah's murder.

"Good night," she said again. She stared down at her phone for a long time before turning on the heat and dialing Brenda June.

*   *   *

BY SIX THE FOLLOWING morning, Charity was practically whimpering at the thought of her bed and all the crisp, cozy percale goodness it promised. She'd just finished inspecting the holding cells and high-fiving herself because toilet duty was so much more pleasant if the toilets weren't actually being used when Sheriff Pratt caught up with her.

She smiled a wary good morning. "You're here early."

"I wanted to catch you before you left."

"I updated the murder file and put it on your desk. Dix questioned Drew Langford yesterday. He recognized the ear buds as belonging to Allison but didn't know they'd been missing. Our biggest lead is a real estate scam Sarah planned to expose. Dix is out double-checking a couple of alibis." She faltered.

Pratt wasn't looking impressed. In fact, he was looking downright mean. He motioned for her to follow him into his office, and shut the door.

The longing for her bed increased, but now she wanted to hide under it. "What's up?"

"I need you back here at four. You're scheduled to appear before an investigative panel."

"I'm what?" She needed a chair. She settled for leaning against the door. "What for?"

"The fact that you don't know is a big part of the problem."

"Does this have anything to do with the election?"

"The election?" He laughed, and it was a jarring, miserable sound. "You'll be lucky if they don't ask you to turn in your badge."

Oh, dear Lord. "This is about Grady West."

"It's about the entire goddamned West family. You bring Grady West into the investigation when there's an obvious conflict of interest, you speak to Judge Purl on Matthew West's behalf — hell, you even get yourself assigned as the kid's community service mentor — you don't bother to charge Justine Langford with the DUI she deserves, and you buy her son milkshakes and question him at his own convenience while managing to ignore he's a person of interest in a murder investigation."

She didn't know what to say. There was nothing she could say.

"And the last goddamned straw? Your bullshit paperwork skills are setting a felon free. A felon who just happens to be related to you."

That jolted her upright. "What?"

"Your arrest forms for Hank. Incomplete. The deadline passed. Know what that means? It means he can't be charged with possession of a stolen firearm. It means you've successfully saved your brother from serving time in a maximum security prison. It means if this becomes public knowledge, you've blown the election. That's on top of ruining the department's reputation."

"Clarkson." Charity's chest and throat were on fire, her head dizzy with horror and shame. Nausea writhed in her belly and her vision blurred. *How?* How could she have made such a mistake? "Sheriff, I don't know what to say, I...oh, damn it, damn it...I can't believe I..." She crossed her arms and dug her fingers into her biceps, praying the pain would distract her from a hot surge of tears. She swallowed hard. "What can I do to fix this?"

Pratt shook his head, his disappointment so much worse than his anger. "The panel convenes at four in my office." He turned away, reaching for something on his desk, dismissing her. "Don't be late."

*   *   *

SHE DIDN'T EVEN TRY to sleep. Her head spun as she considered over and over the countless implications of the biggest fuck-up of her life. Hank would get away with felony theft, and once he'd served time for the DUI, he'd be back behind the wheel, and maybe this time he'd kill someone. Dix, Mo, Flunker, and Tim and the other regulators — no one, not the public or the courts or other law enforcement agencies would trust their judgment from here on out, and they'd end up paying again and again for her mistake. Bloom, too, because Sheriff Pratt would be retiring in disgrace.

Brenda June may never speak to her again.

Worst of all, Pratt would realize he should never have taken that risk on Charity's behalf all those years ago when she'd been caught slashing Roberta West's tires. He should have pursued the charge of vandalism and let her serve her time in jail.

No. Wait. There was something worse. Grady would see her for the loser she really was. But hadn't that been inevitable?

I'm proud of you, Char.

With a groan, Charity set aside her orange juice and stood up from the kitchen table. Enough already. Pity wouldn't get her anywhere but back in her pajamas with cookie crumbs clinging to her chest. If Pratt and his panel ended up putting her on suspension — and she didn't see that they had any choice — then she might as well get as much work done as she could beforehand. Dix would be working the murder today, so she'd work on running herself down a vandal. She'd start with Lucas. It was doubtful her brother had anything to do with what happened at the school — why should he care about field trips to the zoo? — but he might know who did.

After a quick call to the hospital to check on Allison — the nurse said she was doing as well as could be expected, thank goodness — and a belated call to Grady to let him know what had happened — with more time spent thanking her good fortune that he didn't pick up — Charity headed for her bedroom and a change of clothes. Her uniform was not popular with the rest of the Bishop family.

Twenty minutes later, she stood on the porch of her childhood home. Lucas must have found time to make repairs, because the floor no longer sagged, but the rest of the house seemed to droop like a Jell-O salad left under a picnic sun. There was more clutter than grass in the yard, and the chickens apparently spent a lot of time on the front walk.

The sharp smell of fresh paint was oddly cheering, until Charity's mother answered the door, expression scrunched with anger. "They let Hank go yet?"

Charity jammed her hands in the pockets of her jeans to keep herself from shaking Eve Bishop into sanity. Solemnly she regarded the woman who stood before her, gray hair bobby-pinned out of her face, thin hands clasped at the breast of a housecoat dotted with cigarette burns.

"He's not going to get out for a while, Eve." Though a hell of a lot sooner than he deserved.

Her mother sagged against the jamb. "What am I going to do without him?"

Charity didn't get it. What did Hank do but eat Eve's food, smoke her cigarettes, and steal crap so he could afford to gas up the pickup he shouldn't be driving?

"You have Lucas," Charity said. Neither of them expected her to offer up herself as a means of comfort.

"Dumb as dirt," her mother grumbled. "And half as fun as Hank." She reached back inside the house and snatched up a beer from the table by the door.

As she tipped it back, Charity noted with shock the fat tears catching on the wrinkles in her mother's cheeks. Eve never cried. Screamed, raged, begged and bullied, but tears?

When Charity was a kid, she would have felt jealousy. Now she couldn't even drum up pity. "Where's Lucas?"

"What do you want him for?"

"Do you know where he is?"

Eve shook her head at her beer. "Like I would tell you, priss."

"Why do you hate me?" Charity regretted the words the instant they tumbled out of her mouth, but she let them loiter in the cigarette-scented air, too curious to retract them.

Her mother shrugged. "You always thought you were better than the rest of us."

"It has to be more than that."

"Does it?"

Charity pulled her hands from her pockets and stood tall. "When Lucas comes home, please tell him I need to see him."

"Yeah. Sure."

Charity hesitated. She really wanted to make headway, so she'd have something to tell the sheriff's panel.

"I said I'd tell him. You want it in writing?" Beer sloshed as Eve spread her hands. "You want I should sign some kind of contract?"

Charity continued to stare wordlessly, even as a startled satisfaction began to take root. *A signature.*

Eve gusted a sigh. "Why you think you're any smarter than your baby brother, I'll never know. Get off my porch, priss."

*   *   *

CHARITY SNATCHED UP HER phone the instant her butt hit the front seat of her Camry.

"I don't have anything for you yet," Mo said when he answered. "Call him crazy, but Dix seems to believe our murder case has precedence."

"Forget about taking new footage. Here's what I need instead." She explained.

He cursed. "Are you kidding me?"

"If you have a better idea, let me know."

"Why can't you do it?"

"Because Judge Purl has to okay this, and I'm not his favorite person right now."

Mo growled in protest. "What if I promise to vote for you?"

Charity bit back the urge to tell him it could be a moot point. "Riley Morrissey. I would never ask you to compromise your integrity like that."

"No, you'd rather I compromise my dignity by making me pick up dog shit."

"For a noble purpose. I have a strong suspicion the DNA results will crack our graffiti case. Anyway, I haven't forgotten I owe you. I'm doing a bakery run on my way in this afternoon. What's your dignity worth?"

"A dozen red velvet cupcakes, the shift change of my choice, and you never tell a soul what I'm about to doo-doo for you."

Charity disconnected, chuckling in spite of herself.

*   *   *

SHE STEPPED INTO PRATT'S office two minutes before four, legs feeling graceless and heavy. Somehow she managed to keep her hands open and relaxed at her sides. No way she wanted these people to see her squirm, because on a scale of one to ten, the smug factor in the room had to be eight hundred. Standing in a grim semicircle in front of Pratt's desk were Judge Purl, two local business owners, and County Commissioner Ruth Lyle, a short, plump woman with mustard on her cheek and glee in her eyes.

Beside Ruth Lyle slouched Phil Smiley. Apparently the sheriff wasn't concerned about having this go public after all.

But an even bigger head-banger stood beside Phil. Oliver Bloom.

Oh, hell, no.

Glaring at Pratt, Charity tipped her head toward Bloom. "How does it make sense for him to be here?"

"Phil's here as a business owner, not a reporter. Nothing we discuss is for public consumption."

"Not him. *Him.*" She pointed at Bloom, who actually flashed a grin. A *grin.* Too bad she wasn't carrying that umbrella he'd recommended. She could think of a place she'd like to pop it open, and it wasn't Seattle.

Bloom must have guessed what she was thinking because his face went slack and he promptly sat on the edge of Pratt's desk.

"How is it ethical to have him here?" Charity asked, striving for calm.

"You're hardly in a position to judge someone else's ethics." This came in a pompous tone from Judge Purl.

Did he not remember he was the one who'd helped her with Matt in the first place?

Pratt nodded in agreement. "We're here to ask questions, not defend our process." He passed her a thin stack of eight by tens. "Can you explain these?"

There were four color photographs, all taken in the evening. The first showed her talking with Drew Langford on her back steps, the second ushering him inside her house, the third eating cereal with him at her kitchen table—Smiley must have finally invested in a zoom lens—and the fourth showed her lifting her tee high enough to reveal the bottom band of her bra.

That she'd been photographed pissed her off to no end, but...wasn't this supposed to be about her screw-up with Hank?

She raised her head and caught Phil Smiley's eye. He winked at her. Well, then, no need to guess who took the pictures. And no way she'd admit she'd been using her shirt to mop up tears.

She turned her frown on Pratt, whose gaze gave nothing away as he skimmed his thumb along the edge of the small notepad he held in his hand. *Zzzzu-lipp.*

"Why am I under surveillance?" she demanded.

"We're asking the questions," Ruth reminded her crisply. Someone must have pointed out the mustard smear, because it was gone.

Phil spoke up. "Someone e-mailed those to the newspaper. The message referred to you as a cougar. There were also a few X-rated comments about you keeping it in the family."

Oh, for God's sake. Charity curled her fingers into her palms and squeezed hard. "Someone?"

Phil's shrug oozed self-righteousness. "A lot of our best leads come from anonymous sources."

Anonymous, my ass. How had Leon missed Smiley lurking in her back yard? Then again, she couldn't expect the poor guy to watch the front and the back of her house at the same time.

The sheriff motioned at the photos. "Drew Langford is a person of interest in a homicide. Why was he inside your house?"

She stared. What the hell was going on? Surely Drew's visit didn't warrant this kind of attention. Why weren't they discussing her brother's paperwork? Pratt refused to meet her gaze, instead played his notepad like it was a musical instrument. *Zzzzu-lip, zzzzu-lipp.* Bloom cleared his throat. Pratt ignored him.

Were they merely warming up before going in for the kill?

Charity lifted her chin. "Drew Langford came to see me because he wanted to know if I was framing him for Sarah Huffman's murder."

One by one the members of the "panel" turned to glance at the next person in line. It was all Charity could do not to laugh out loud when Bloom sent a disbelieving look over his left shoulder and there was no one there to receive it.

"What did you tell him?" the sheriff asked.

"That someone is trying to set him up, but it isn't me."

Pratt tossed the notepad on his desk, his expression pained. "So you discussed the investigation."

"No. I answered his question. Then he left."

"After you fed him."

"He was hungry."

"Are you sleeping with him?" This from a wild-eyed Oliver Bloom.

"No." Charity gritted her teeth. "I am not. And I am beyond offended that you would suggest such a thing."

"Poor form, Ollie," the judge muttered. "Poor form."

"She lifted her shirt." Oliver pointed a righteous finger at the photo on top of the stack. "She exposed her belly."

Oh, dear Lord. "The kid had already left, and I didn't know there was a Peeping Tom in my yard." Enough already. "Maybe the best thing would be for me to—"

"I think we're done here." Pratt plucked the photos from her hands and opened his door. "We'll be in touch."

Charity blinked. "I'm not suspended?"

"You have a killer to catch." Judge Purl peered at her over the top of his glasses. "When you've done that, we'll talk suspension."

Dazedly Charity walked out of the courthouse. Somehow she'd won a stay of execution. So why wasn't she happier about it?

Because she damned well didn't deserve it.

She stood on the sidewalk, under a cherry tree adorned with bright green buds, and watched a string of cars make a beeline for the parking lot's exit. She wouldn't mind going home herself, but she had work to do. Mo and Dix were right. The murder investigation had to take precedence. Someone had to pay for what they'd done.

Someone they hadn't considered yet? Possible, though strangulation was a passionate form of murder. Most cases were personal.

She turned and made her way back to her office, grateful for the quiet corridors. She shut her door and collapsed into her chair, leaned back, and propped her Oakleys on her desk.

Who had the most to gain not only from Sarah's death, but from setting up Drew? Allison may have hoped to get her boyfriend back, but that would be difficult with him in prison. Did she hate him that much for breaking up with her?

Peyton certainly seemed to. At the funeral she couldn't have made it any clearer that she didn't want anything to do with her brother. Did the pact she'd made with Allison involve something a hell of a lot more sinister than ghosting?

Her stomach rumbled, probably because her office still smelled like the burrito she'd had for breakfast. Her belly could grouch all it wanted. Food was the last thing on her mind.

She didn't consider Justine a suspect at all anymore. Not unless she had exceptional acting skills—she'd been clueless about how her friend had died. Kate and Hampton served as each other's alibi, and anyway they had no reason to conspire to kill Sarah. Neither had been on the list of real estate investors Grady had provided. Yes, relationships had ended, but with nothing more at stake than teen heartbreak.

Could Tarrant or Bloom have hired someone to do their dirty work? Someone who went out of their way to provide the police with a convenient suspect?

Or was that convenient suspect, aka Drew Langford, guilty after all?

Charity's boots hit the floor and she stared down at a jagged, six-inch scratch that marred the surface of her desk.

Drew was a smart kid. But smart enough to frame himself and make it look like someone else had done it?

She shuddered. Dear Lord, she hoped not.

* * *

MUCH LATER THAT EVENING, after she'd finally dragged herself home and managed a few hours' sleep, Charity was pulling black stretch pants up over hips that hadn't seen any yoga action for far too long and at the same time waffling between poached eggs or cold cereal for dinner — and as usual, that which required the least effort would win out — when her phone rang. After fastening her bra and grabbing up a cardigan, she headed for the table in the hall where she'd left her cell. She bent over the screen. She didn't recognize the calling number.

Two seconds later, she wished she hadn't picked up.

"What can I do for you, Dr. West?" she asked warily.

Roberta West didn't mince words. "You can stay away from my son."

Charity sighed, and slumped back against the wall that separated the hall from the kitchen. The way the good doctor struggled with her words, it was clear she'd been drinking.

"I'm off duty, Dr. West. If you have something you'd like to discuss, please call me tomorrow at the station." Or not.

"I know what you're up to. I know the two of you went to that hole where they serve that overcooked, overpriced pig, and then according to my grandson, you all went shooting together. How cozy." Roberta started to sniffle. "But soon Grady will go back to Seattle, and don't think he'll be taking you with him." A muffled sound came from her end of the call. She blew her nose.

Charity shook her head at the phone. She was starting to feel like Jane Austen's Elizabeth Bennett squaring off against Mr. Darcy's condescending aunt. Only her story would not enjoy the same happy ending. But like Lizzy Bennett, and despite Roberta West's obvious unhappiness, Charity refused to give the snooty old lady the satisfaction of a guarantee.

"This is none of your business, Dr. West," she said firmly. "If there's anything else you'd like to discuss, please call tomorrow during business hours."

Roberta was still reciting an impressive number of synonyms for slut when Charity ended the call.

She closed her eyes, tipped her head back, and thumped it against the wall. If only she was getting half the sex everyone thought she was. She pushed away from the wall. The half that didn't include Drew Langford, of course.

Her cell dinged. An incoming text. She braced herself for more name calling and lifted her phone.

Back door. Don't shoot.

She spun, and squinted into the darkened kitchen. A moonlit shadow stood patiently on the other side of the door. Damn, she'd never realized before how thin those curtains were. Even before she registered the sudden thrum of anticipation deep in her belly, she was already moving toward the door, faster when her bare feet hit the cold linoleum. She caught a white flash of teeth at the same moment she realized she still carried the sweater. She yanked it over her head and reached for the door.

Wait. *Wait.* What was she doing? What was Grady doing? Wasn't she in enough trouble?

She shook her head at the door, turned her back and sent a text. *Go away.*

An instant later, she received his reply. *Make me.*

Okay, well, that was mature. Still her thighs had started to tremble.

Her phone dinged again. *Leon gave the all clear.*

Charity sucked in a breath. No stalkers, and no Phil Smiley — he was busy covering Keith Tarrant's annual spring charity event. Charity knew that because Phil had asked the sheriff to send a couple of deputies to Tarrant's house to make sure the unwashed and uninvited didn't sneak in. The sheriff had declined, less than politely.

Her free hand tugged at her cardigan and she glanced over her shoulder. Then there was the whole stay-away-from-my-son lecture she'd just received from Roberta.

Make me.

She turned and opened the door.

Grady came in smelling of spearmint and pine, his leather jacket rustling as he shut the door behind him. He set a basket on the counter and turned in the dimness to face her.

"I liked you better without the top."

She fingered a small plastic button on her sweater. "And I liked you better on the other side of that door." But she said it without any heat. The man had come bearing food, after all. Charity wrenched her gaze away from the basket. "Why are you here?"

"Your message. You sounded upset. I called back but you didn't answer."

"I was sleeping."

"That explains the bed head." Grady lifted both hands and slowly combed his fingers through her hair. For the first time ever, she regretted cutting it short.

"Have you been crying?" he asked quietly.

"Rough day." She gave a disgusted grunt and backed away. "God, listen to me. A teenaged girl put herself in the hospital and I'm the one complaining."

"Drew talked to Kate, and she assured him Allison will be okay. Physically, anyway."

Charity nodded, relieved.

Grady waited.

She sighed. "Yes, you're right, there's more, okay? Not about Allison. We're still working that, though we did check her location history. If she went out the night Sarah was killed, she didn't take her phone with her."

Her stomach clutched at the thought of confessing to Dix and Mo what she'd done. "No, the trouble is I fucked up and it's not a good feeling."

"You're talking about when Drew came by?"

"It's bigger than that." Charity winced at the shame that slurred her words. She turned away.

Grady palmed her shoulders. "We all make mistakes."

"I don't." She swung back to face him, dislodging his hands. "I can't afford to."

"I'll go, if that's what you need." In the dim light of the kitchen, she could see his half-grin. "I promise I won't take the sandwiches with me. Or I could stay, eat one of the sandwiches, and save you some serious heartburn."

Her taste buds perked up. "Meatball?"

"With provolone and mozzarella." When she hesitated, he raised his palms. "Hands off, if that's the way you want it. We'll eat and brainstorm about the case. What do you say? Feel like a picnic?"

"It's dark outside." He'd had her at *provolone*. Okay, really he'd had her at *Don't shoot,* but he didn't need to know that.

He shrugged out of his jacket. "Grab a blanket and meet me on the living room floor." He saw her expression and raised his palms again.

They ate meatball subs and dill pickles while sitting cross-legged on a beach towel. She hadn't thought she could eat, considering the crap day she'd had and the decisions that faced her, but she couldn't resist a meatball sub. Twice she had to go back to the kitchen for more napkins.

When she finally came up for air, she brandished the remains of her dill pickle spear. "This is the only vegetable I've had in days, not counting French fries."

Grady shot her a look as he packed away their trash. "I'll give you a thousand dollars if you promise never to say that in front of my kid."

Instead of jumping up and announcing she had work to do, and could he please show himself out, thank you very much, she wrapped her arms around her legs and settled back against the sofa. She knew better. By inviting him to linger, she was begging for heartache, but putting off unpleasant things was so much easier than facing them.

But it would be so nice to forget, if only for a little while, the unholy mess she'd made of her career.

"Speaking of Matt," she said, "what's he up to while you're here plying me with comfort food?"

"Homework. He won't be doing any more late night wandering, that's for sure. I lectured him for an hour, then grounded him."

"Change the alarm codes?"

"You bet I did."

She smiled. "Tell me about him."

Grady crawled over the basket and sat beside her. "He's a good kid. He resents me, though, and I can't seem to stop giving him reason to. Like traveling out here to handle a family crisis and leaving him behind. No wonder he thinks I don't care. At the same time, he's constantly complaining that I 'hover.'" He lifted his hands to make air quotes.

"I get the impression," she said slowly, "that he thinks you're keeping him away from the rest of his family."

"He's right. Everyone but Peyton and Drew is an addict."

"Does Matt know that?"

"What do you mean?"

"Maybe he thinks you're keeping him away because of something he's done. Maybe he thinks you're ashamed of him."

Grady stared. "Why would he think that?"

She shrugged, and struggled for a way to explain, a way to make him understand how it felt to never be good enough. But those weren't the words that came out of her mouth.

"I've been fine for years." She spoke through clenched teeth, fingernails digging into the legs she held tight against her chest. "Never minded coming home to an empty house and eating across from an empty chair and curling up in an empty bed. Having flings instead of relationships because nothing could measure up to the memory of us. Then you came back to town and....I hate you for making me remember what I'm missing, Grady West. And I hate you for making me wish I could have that with the man you are today."

For an instant he sat without moving, his expression dazed. Then he reached out, and his reaching was her undoing. Her tears fell so fast they began to choke her. The raw sounds escaping her throat were as shocking as they were humiliating.

"Shh." He unfolded his legs and tucked her up against him, her back to his chest. He shoved the remainder of the napkins at her, then wrapped his arms around her and pressed his lips to her neck. The heat of his mouth on her skin kept her in shudders.

Long moments passed. A crease in the terrycloth towel bit into one heel, and the backs of her knees began to ache. But the steady sound of Grady's breathing and the rhythmic stroke of his thumbs on her biceps made her wish they could hold this position forever.

When her tears finally slowed, he kissed her neck and leaned back, settling his chin on her head. "It's not always a good thing, having someone waiting at home for you," he murmured. "Not if you don't love them."

Charity tensed, expecting him to spill on his ex.

"I missed you," he said instead.

"I missed you, too. So much it hurt." She swiped her palms across her cheeks. "And what did I do about it? I slept with any man who showed interest."

"Exaggerating much?"

"Not too much."

Grady's chuckle sounded forced. "So when did you find time to do anything else?"

"Is that supposed to be a compliment?"

He exhaled. "It makes me sad you were so determined to forget what we had."

"It wasn't about forgetting. It was about making sure you'd never want me again."

"I think it's obvious that didn't work."

"Which is frustrating, considering how much effort I put into it."

He grunted. "Can we move on?"

"It bothers you."

"It bothers me. But it doesn't change how I feel about you."

Enough with the feelings. Time to nudge the conversation in a different direction.

The inevitable direction.

14

CHARITY STRETCHED, PRESSING AGAINST Grady. She let her head drop to his shoulder and raised a hand to the back of his neck. The motion lifted her chest. She tangled her fingertips in his hair, desperate for him to touch her, and not in a sympathetic or soothing way. She wanted to be grabbed and squeezed and kneaded.

He groaned. Had she said that out loud? She must have, because his hands scooted up over her waist and palmed her breasts. He squeezed and plucked and she writhed, reveling in the sensual overload provided by the hard grip of his hands, the softness of his hair in her palms and the hot, heavy cock prodding her ass.

"Grady," she moaned. Dear Lord, even her earlobes were tingling. How could he take her to the edge in mere seconds?

His right hand moved to her jaw and tilted her face toward his. He took her mouth while his left hand slid down to her sex. He cupped her, then began to stroke her, and her trembling turned violent. She whimpered against his lips and arched into his touch. Close...she was so close...

"Jesus," he breathed. "We're both ready to blow." Despite her protests, he eased her forward and twisted her around so she faced him, her thighs propped over his. He kissed her again, deeper, and reached for the hem of her sweater. "I need you naked."

Even as his words sparked panic at the thought of revealing a body that had aged a dozen years since he'd seen it last, she was wrenching his shirt out of his jeans. When she nearly had the tail free she hesitated, and covered his hands with hers.

He groaned. "Charity —"

"Wait." She squeezed his hands. "Full disclosure."

His shoulders went rigid. "No details, please."

"Not that kind of disclosure. Your mother called me tonight."

His shoulders collapsed, and he gave a long-suffering sort of chuckle. "Which explains why you let me in the door."

She trailed a finger along the buttons on his shirt. "Not entirely."

"First the sheriff, and now my mother." He found her mouth again and bit at her lower lip. "Why don't they know better than to warn you away from something? It only makes you more determined to do it."

While his hands slid under her sweater, her fingers busied themselves with opening his shirt. "But you do know better."

"I do." He gave up trying to tug her sweater over her head and started on the buttons instead. "Which is why it's for your own good when I tell you that under no circumstances do I want you touching my zipper."

She chuckled as she pushed the two halves of his shirt apart, then dropped a hand to his lap.

He gave a choking growl of protest. "I'm being serious here, Bishop. Do not put your hand in my pants."

She eased his zipper over his erection with one hand and squeezed with the other, loving the way he surged and rubbed against her touch. She slid her fingers under the waistband of his boxers, brushed up against ribbed heat, and watched his stomach flex as he struggled to breathe.

"Like this?" she murmured. "Don't touch you like this?"

"Exactly like that."

She gripped him hard.

His hips jerked. "Condoms," he panted. "Back pocket of my jeans."

Reluctantly she released him and reached around him. They moaned in unison as the movement pushed her core against his cock. While she frantically searched the back of his jeans, Grady worked her yoga pants and her panties down over her hips. His hands roved over her bare ass as he pressed open-mouthed kisses to her breasts, and she almost forgot what she was looking for.

"I can't find them," she cried.

"Yours," he breathed. "We'll use yours. You must have plenty —"

She froze.

His hands flexed on her hips, then slid slowly away. "Hell."

Slowly Charity lifted up and eased her pants back into place.

Grady swore again, and let his head drop back against the couch. "That didn't come out right," he said raggedly.

She slumped down onto the floor between his feet. "Suddenly this doesn't seem fair to you." She pulled the sides of her sweater together while he zipped himself back into his jeans.

"I had you. I almost had you, and I fucked it up." With shaking hands, he ran his fingers through his hair.

Charity's cell rang. She pushed stiffly to her feet. "It's Dispatch." She strode into the darkened kitchen and scooped up her phone, her chest feeling cold and tight. So cold she barely noticed the chill of the linoleum beneath her toes. "Bishop."

Twenty seconds later, she ended the call and gently set the phone back on the counter. A hot mass of misery clogged her throat. She struggled to swallow, fought to breathe.

Grady moved up behind her and cupped her elbow. His fingers warmed her skin through the thin sleeve of her cardigan. "What is it?"

She turned, looked up into his handsome face, and found herself scrabbling for what little control she had left. The genuine concern in his navy gaze tempted her to fall into his warmth, to burrow into his arms, to surrender all responsibility.

But her department needed her.

"For God's sake, Char. Tell me what happened."

Charity pulled in a soggy breath. "Dixon Ironmaker just found his wife. Dead."

"Aww, hell."

She saw the question in his eyes. "Suicide."

"Shit."

"Exactly." She straightened her spine, scooped up her phone and her keys, and slid her bare feet into a pair of boots.

"No uniform?"

"I'm not on duty, I'm just...I need to be there." First Allison, then Sheila. Except Sheila had done a better job of it, damn her.

The despair they must have been feeling... It made Charity want to crawl into bed and sob into her pillow. But that would be selfish. It wasn't her pain to feel.

Grady followed her outside to her SUV. He held the door open as she buckled herself in. "Don't forget your jacket."

Charity stared down at her duty jacket and watched her own hand reach out and take it. He must have grabbed it on his way out of her house. Such a small gesture kicking off such a massive tangle of emotion: confusion, resentment, wistfulness.

None of which she could afford. She couldn't afford emotion, period.

Grady leaned in. "I'm sorry about this. Please. Call me if there's anything I can do."

"We've got it covered. This is what we do."

"Charity. I mean if there's anything I can do for you."

"You shouldn't want to." She reached for the door handle, forcing him to step back. "I was using you."

He shook his head. "It's too late to pretend what we have is casual, but we'll work that out later. Right now your friend needs you. Drive safe."

In the rearview mirror Charity watched him watching her as she drove away.

*   *   *

LONG HOURS LATER, CHARITY sat at a rigid angle inside her Camry, arms stacked on the steering wheel, windows a wide open welcome to the sharp, pine-scented chill of the midnight air. She was exhausted, but sleep was the last thing she wanted. After leaving Dix's house, she'd driven home, but her own house had felt far too lonely. Still in her yoga pants and cardigan, with her bare feet jammed into her boots, she'd waved at Leon, switched vehicles, and headed back out again.

A plastic bag and a roll of duct tape. That's how Dix's wife had killed herself. Not the most popular method among women, but there wasn't any question of foul play—Sheila had videotaped her own death, no doubt to make sure her husband suffered for it as much as possible.

Dix had been stoic, but there was no missing the shattered look in his eyes. Charity had watched the EMTs load his wife's body onto the stretcher while Dix stood by, the massive weight of his guilt evident in the droop of his shoulders and the nothingness in his expression. He'd refused to leave the scene. In clipped, quiet tones he'd thanked the sheriff, Charity, and Mo for being there, when not one of them would have considered being anywhere else.

His restraint and the misery struggling to break through it had made Charity ache on his behalf. It had also made her realize that not everything could be fixed. That sometimes in the fixing, you ended up breaking yourself. That maybe the best thing you could do was cut your losses and walk away.

Which was why she'd decided to pull out of the election. The sheriff's department deserved better.

She did, too. Despite how badly she'd messed up with Hank.

There were too many shadows in her life. She wanted to laugh again. She wanted to love again. She wanted Grady. And he'd wanted her, despite her past. He'd always made her feel lighter. Freer. And she'd never laughed with anyone like she'd laughed with Grady West. That hadn't changed.

What had changed was how he'd become both harder and softer. He no longer took any crap from his parents, and he fought for his sister and her son like a bulldog. At the same time, he'd learned to relax his own rules—no more bans on holidays, or reluctance to so much as talk to his parents. He would obviously do just about anything for his son.

And even though they hadn't seen each other in years, he'd known her.

Known how much she loved waffles and meatball subs, how kids made her nervous, how injustice frustrated the hell out of her.

He'd known her, yet still wanted to know her better.

She liked that.

She needed that.

She needed him.

She stared through her mud-speckled windshield at the massive brick house at the top of Pill Hill. Stately Wayne Manor, Grady used to call it and, with a teen's casual malice, had dubbed his mother's private garage the Bat Cave. Charity had seen it only once, and its dust-free, concrete coldness had given her the creeps, much like Roberta West herself, who would surely have ordered the house fumigated if she'd known an undesirable like Charity Bishop had been let loose in the place.

Undesirable.

Grady had never found her so.

Despite her sadness, a combination of satisfaction and sizzle managed to work its way beneath her skin. She refused to feel guilty about it. Not after seeing what their lead detective was going through. He'd done all he could to make his wife happy, to make things work, but so much had been beyond his control.

Like so much was beyond Charity's control. There was plenty she did have final say in, though. Thing was, she no longer liked a lot of what she'd been saying. That was about to change.

She was going to sneak into Stately Wayne Manor.

She reared away from the steering wheel and pushed back against the seat, arms locked, palms slick. Nearly an hour had passed since she'd parked. No movement inside or out, no lights on or off.

No more stalling.

She grabbed her flashlight, scooted out of the car, and gently shut the door behind her. The tricky part would be avoiding those pesky cameras. She could only hope their location hadn't changed since she'd last run this gauntlet more than a decade ago. If they had, she'd simply have to seduce Grady into erasing the footage.

Her stomach wobbled as she crept to the edge of the property. She tucked the flashlight under one arm, hugged herself, and scanned the spooky collection of statues and shrubs spotlighted by well-hidden fixtures. So well hidden that as a teen Charity had tripped over more than one. One particularly nasty fall had earned her four stitches in her chin.

She exhaled, and rubbed her palms up and down her arms. Some of the neighbors considered the Wests' front lawn a year-round monument to too much money and too little taste. But what did Charity know about good taste? She ate Cocoa Puffs for dinner, told dirty jokes, and drove a crap car. *No offense, Clarabelle.* The only thing "designer" she owned was an unopened packet of Vera Bradley pencils Brenda June had given her one Christmas.

Unless you counted her Oakley boots.

Besides, the Wests' front yard was a damned sight more attractive than her mother's. When the Bishops stepped out on their front porch with their morning coffee, they were greeted with rusted out tractor rims, stacks of mismatched lawn furniture, a baby blue toilet Hank had promised two decades ago to turn into either a planter or a barbecue, a cinder block fire ring, and a faded, green-striped couch they'd attached with rope to the thick limb of an ancient oak tree to create a swing.

Charity jumped as a hoarse series of yips sounded in the distance. A fox? Her gaze roved the grounds and her knees went slack. Was she seriously going to do this? What if she got caught? She never had as a teenager, but it would be a gazillion times more embarrassing now. For Grady, too. His son was in there. Justine and her kids. Grady's parents. As much as the Wests despised Phil Smiley, they'd have him here in a flash if they discovered Charity sneaking into their house. She could see the headline now.

Redneck Sheriff Hopeful Stalks Wealthy Ex-Boyfriend

Except...she wasn't running for sheriff anymore. And though she was still a cop, wasn't it a little late to worry about professionalism and propriety?

Way to rationalize, Bishop.

Tonight she wasn't a cop. Tonight she was a woman. A woman who'd finally realized life was too short to hold on to ancient grudges and convenient cowardice.

A horny woman hauling ass across the street.

She headed for the border of trees to the left of the house. A crawl past the pair of two-tier, pineapple-topped fountains, a duck walk through the alley of pink and purple azaleas, and a dash past the koi pond should keep her out of camera range and get her to Grady's window.

Minutes later she was there, leaning against the rough brick exterior, breath hustling in and out of her lungs. She couldn't help an exhilarated laugh. She'd had to scale a wrought iron fence she hadn't remembered and made far too much noise stumbling through a bed of decorative gravel. Still, it had been easier than she'd expected.

Brushing the dirt off her palms, Charity pushed away from the wall, tilted her head back, and studied the second story window that was her target. She had no difficulty remembering the hiding location of a spare key. So, yeah. She could get inside.

But she had to draw the line somewhere.

A quick, fortifying inhale. Flashlight heavy against her armpit, she plucked her cell from her pocket and thumbed a few buttons. Before she got the chance to wonder if Grady would even pick up, he did.

"Char. You all right?"

Pathetic how the sleepy concern in his voice made her feel like she'd slipped into the caressing warmth of a Jacuzzi. She leaned her forehead against the brick. The sharp ridges dug into her skin, but she couldn't bring herself to care.

"Thanks for picking up."

"Why wouldn't I?"

"I basically told you to leave me alone."

"You were upset." A beat of silence filled the air. "Charity?"

"You said to call if I needed anything."

"Name it."

"I need to see you."

He didn't hesitate. "I can't be gone long. I don't want Matt to wake up and find me missing."

"You're a good dad."

"I try." A rustling sounded in the background. He must be getting dressed.

A warm tingling erupted at the base of Charity's spine. Did he still sleep naked? On his belly, with one arm under his pillow and the other hanging off the side of the bed?

On the rare occasion they'd spent the night in the same bed, she'd slept tucked up against him on her back, which had made it oh so convenient for him to slide her beneath him whenever he'd jerked awake in the middle of the night with a hard-on neither would dream of letting go to waste.

"I'll see you in fifteen," Grady said.

It was all she could do to attach meaning to his words. "Wait." She pushed away from the wall and rubbed her forehead. "I'm not at home."

"Still at Dix's? Text me the address."

"No, I'm here. Outside your window."

Charity heard a sharp inhale, then nothing. It took a second to realize he'd disconnected. *Here we go.* Panic and anticipation poked at her skin with hot, tingling jabs. She slid her phone into her sweater pocket, hugged herself and stared up at the window, watching it so intently she started to see spots.

More nothing. No *shirr*ing sound to signal the sash sliding upward, no movement behind the glass. She blinked, and sank her teeth into her lower lip. Had he changed his mind? Had he decided he didn't want to deal with a psycho ex who couldn't decide whether or not she wanted to have sex?

Movement at the back corner of the house had her jerking her chin to her left. Grady came out of the shadows, his hard physique backlit by the muted glow from the lights that lined the path to the pool. He wore sweatpants, and a not-quite-tight-enough tee, feet bare, hair crazy.

Charity sagged against the wall and barely registered a distant thump as her flashlight struck the ground.

Want.

No, not want. Need. A raw, militant, mindless need that hit her like the business end of a blackjack. Her bones shook from the force of it.

He moved toward her, footsteps whispering over the damp, neatly trimmed grass. She couldn't see his face, couldn't tell from his posture what he was feeling, so she stood there, rigid and trembling, weighed down with equal parts doubt and desire.

He stopped a few feet away, looked from her to the second story window and back again. "I feel like I just stepped through a time warp, finding you here." He motioned with his head at his bedroom window. "Good thing you didn't throw any rocks. That's Drew's room now."

Oh. Oh! Thank God she hadn't let herself in. Though being inside would be so much smarter than staying out in the open. She was certain she hadn't been followed, but there was no sense in taking chances.

She gestured for Grady to follow her into a copse of trees and waited for him to ask why she'd gotten him out of bed in the middle of the night. Instead he muttered something sympathetic and folded her against him. He inhaled, slowly raised his hands, and stroked his fingers through her hair. She closed her eyes and relaxed against his hard, sleep-warmed length, breathing in the faint bleachy scent of his T-shirt and melting into the pleasure of being soothed.

She bit down on a whimper as a heavy tension settled between her hips.

"I'm sorry." Grady rested his chin on her head and skimmed his hands down her back. "So sorry. For what I said earlier."

"I'm sorry for being defensive."

"You realize I'm jealous."

Charity turned her face into his neck and tasted him. He shivered, but not in a sexy way.

She looked down at his feet. "I can't believe you forgot shoes."

"I was in a hurry. I thought you might leave."

Dear Lord. What was she waiting for?

She tangled her hands in his tee and yanked. He let loose a startled chuckle as his mouth bumped hers. Bumped, then settled. The kiss was fierce, searing, and heady as hell. Her knees went soft, and she sagged against him.

He moaned, a sound that echoed in her chest and shimmered down her spine. His lips coaxed then commanded, caressed then consumed, sending her fingers scrabbling for the hem of his shirt.

As his tongue flirted with hers, she found bare skin and the hard, ridged plane of his belly and let her grateful hands roam.

So warm. So hard.

So hers, if only for the night.

She reached around his waist and slid her hands up his back to clutch at his shoulder blades. Overwhelmed by the raw, reckless need she felt only with him, only for him, she broke off the kiss and buried her face in his neck.

"I never did thank you for the picnic," she whispered raggedly.

"Is that what this is? An expression of gratitude? I'm okay with it, I just wondered."

She smiled against his skin. "Why do you smell like oranges?"

"The soap in the guestroom."

She sucked at his neck. "You don't taste like oranges."

"What do I taste like?"

"More. You taste like more."

He groaned again and slid his hands down to her ass. She whimpered when he began to knead, and he hissed in a breath.

"We can't do this out here," he said tightly. Reluctantly he moved back, then held out a hand. "We'll need to keep the noise down."

"I suppose that's aimed at me." Charity's snort came out sounding more like a hiccup as she ignored his outstretched hand. "What about Matt?"

"He's asleep. I'll double-check when we go in. My door does lock."

"Can't we use the pool house?"

Grady breathed a quiet, tortured laugh. "As much as I'd enjoy reliving some of our adventures there, we don't have that option. It's closed for repair."

This time he helped himself to her hand, and she shivered at the contact.

"Come with me." He turned toward the house. "And I mean that in every possible sense of the phrase."

Her brain popped and sputtered like the failing light bulb in her fridge as he led her to the back of the house. The laundry room, maybe twice the size of her kitchen, smelled like warm starch.

Without letting go of her hand, he shut and locked the back door, backed her up against the wall, and dove in. His fingers tangled in her hair, and his greedy mouth roved her lips, her cheeks, her neck. When he started nibbling, she couldn't restrain a delighted squeal that bounced off the appliances and danced in the shadows. They froze, staring at each other as they gobbled air and waited for someone to come running.

Long seconds passed with no sound but the rasp of their breathing and the tick of the clock above their heads. Charity relaxed against Grady, resting her forehead on his chest.

"What was that all about?" she whispered.

He pulled her away from the wall. "Building anticipation."

"Twelve years isn't enough anticipation for you?"

"Keep it up and you'll give me performance anxiety."

"You're the one who has to keep it up."

"Aaand now I have it."

Charity rolled her eyes and nudged him toward the door that led to the kitchen. He held up a finger and started opening cabinets.

Oh, dear Lord, they were so going to get caught. "What are you looking for?"

"Something to use as a gag."

"Hilarious," she muttered, and stripped off her cardigan.

Grady went still. She smiled and drew in a long, deliberate breath.

"Touché," he choked, and fumbled for her elbow.

Charity draped her sweater over her shoulder and trotted alongside him, free hand clapped to her mouth to stifle the giggles. She was almost dizzy with the sense of déjà vu. Somewhere overhead a door shut, and that was the end of the urge to laugh. Grady tugged her behind him and locked every muscle. She hovered at his back, eyes squeezed shut, hands on his shoulders. *Please don't let anyone catch us.*

It wasn't the embarrassment she dreaded, it was the interruption. She wanted sex. Serious sex. Hot, sweaty, how-many-times-can-we-make-each-other-come sex. With grown-up Grady.

Her belly tingled, even as she held her breath and listened. No running feet. No strident voices. No sinister shuck of a pump action.

A toilet flushed. A door again. Then silence.

Grady reached around and squeezed her hip. Charity pressed her face into his back and bit down. His muscles gathered. He twisted around and reclaimed her hand, the gleam in his eyes promising retribution.

Bring it on.

He led her to the stairs off the kitchen and up to the second floor. She hadn't seen the inside for over a decade but remembered it all—the high ceilings that dripped ornate chandeliers, the gleaming marble floors bordering plush carpet, the dust-free cherry furniture crowned with exotic flower arrangements, the glass-front zoos of figurines and sculptures and fine china—and it all still intimidated her.

Bare feet sinking into the carpet, Grady steered her down the hallway to the right. The closer they got to the end of the corridor, the faster he moved. He jerked to a halt, pointed to a door behind them and put a finger to his lips. Matt's room.

He pulled Charity through the set of double doors at the end of the hall, shut and locked the doors behind them with one hand and tugged her back against him with the other, trapping the heat of their need between them. It was ridiculously tough to entertain second thoughts with Grady's ragged breathing in her ear, not to mention his erection plastered against her ass. Yet she couldn't completely tune out the voice in her head that had picked up the chant *you don't belong here.*

He must have heard that voice, too, because Charity barely had a chance to register the white-blond furniture and king-sized bed before he turned her around to face him and dipped his head. She leaned away and tossed her sweater toward the nearest flat surface. A muffled thud sounded as her phone landed on a chest of drawers. She slid her hands up his arms and around his neck, her gaze snagging on the erotic promise of his mouth.

"What are the chances Matt will come knocking?"

Grady reached back without looking and hit the switch. "A lot lower if the light's off."

She blinked in the sudden dimness. "Grady."

"Don't worry. The kid's a sound sleeper."

"Glad to hear it."

He lowered his head again. His lips, tongue, and teeth seduced her until every muscle in her body trembled with mindless want. He swung her around, walked her backward, and sandwiched her lower body between his hips and the wall. The heated press of his thick arousal against her belly had Charity moaning into his mouth.

Grady's tongue tangled with hers as his hands skimmed up over her ribcage and trailed inward to cup her breasts. The sensation robbed her of air, and her nipples went tight with need. He rubbed her with his palms, and she bucked against his hips. She must have made too much noise because he shushed her.

"Oh, no you didn't," Charity whispered fiercely and pushed him away.

He grinned and stripped off his tee. Through the gaps in the heavy striped curtains, the moon scattered beams across hard, heaving muscle.

"Touché back atcha," she said thickly. Her thighs started to shake, and every nerve ending below her waist coiled tight. With a moan, she reached out and yanked him back. "I missed you."

His sudden intake of air signaled he knew she was referring to more than the past ten seconds. "I missed you, too." He nipped her chin, and stroked a fingertip down her nose. He gathered her close again, the stubble on his jaw a delicious scrape against her temple. "I worry about you."

"I like the way you show it." Charity shoved him away again, but with her hands gripping his waistband, he could only go so far. She kept her eyes locked on his as she dropped slowly to her knees, pulling his sweatpants out and down as she sank to the floor.

His cock, long and thick and quivering, leapt at her face, and she whimpered as she remembered the feel of its rigid, relentless stroke. She pressed her thighs together, deliberately let her head fall back, and licked her lips.

Grady exhaled a slow, trembling breath. "You're determined to make me embarrass myself," he said gruffly, even as his hands cradled her skull.

"Trying to tell me you're only good for one go?" Charity gave him a lick, making his hips jerk. "My, how times have changed."

"Was I the only one listening when we talked about performance issues?"

"Tell me again." She gripped him with one hand and touched her tongue to the damp tip of his shaft.

Grady didn't answer except for a tortured moan when she scraped her teeth across the head of his cock. The sound of his pleasure shimmered through her, and she got busy, licking and laving and nipping. When she finally sucked him into her mouth, noises rather than words erupted from his throat. His head went back, his fingers tightened, and his hips began to thrust as she worked him with her palm and with her lips, the fingers of her left hand alternately stroking and gripping Jake and Elwood, his "boys."

It wasn't long before Grady's thighs went rock-hard and his hands pushed at her head. She knew he didn't want to finish, knew he wanted to see to her first, but she couldn't stop, couldn't wait to watch him lose the control he'd always prided himself on. She gripped his hips and took him deeper, reveling in his frenzied thrusts.

"Charity," he begged, and exploded in her mouth.

She sucked him dry, holding him through the aftershocks, and couldn't help a grin as he collapsed to his knees in front of her. She licked his shoulder, loving that she'd made him sweat.

"Jesus," he panted, and pulled her into a hug. "Guess I won't be wearing that Olympic silver condom after all."

Charity laughed. "You'll make it up to me."

"So confident."

"So determined." She winked. "I'll be right back." She pushed to her feet, kicked off her boots, and let the moonlight guide her to the connecting bathroom.

15

B Y THE TIME CHARITY came out of the bathroom, Grady had managed to haul his ass off the floor but only barely because his legs had misplaced their bones. His cock, too, until he registered that she'd taken off the rest of her clothes. She walked — Christ, make that bounced — toward him, a glass of water in one hand, her other hand full of luscious, ivory-colored hip. His junk snapped so straight it was a wonder he didn't pull a muscle.

She'd lost some of her confidence, though. He could see it in the tilt of her head as she approached, the slight hunch of her shoulders, the twitch in her arms as she resisted the urge to cover herself. God knew she had no reason to be insecure.

Still he understood. It had been a long time.

"Christ, Charity," he said. "You're more beautiful than ever."

She must have heard the sincerity in his voice because her shoulders straightened. She dipped her head and handed him the glass, the gesture demure but the gleam in her eyes all brashness.

He gulped half of the water, his gaze roving the moonlit wonder of her body. Slowly she reached for the half-empty glass he held, mouth a teasing curve, generous breasts jiggling, hips slowly flexing toward his. He dodged her hand and tipped the water over her tits.

With a gasp, she crossed her arms over her chest. Grady let the glass thud to the carpet. He leaned forward and kissed her hard. He tugged her arms away from her body, guided her backward to the bed, gave her a push, and followed her down onto the satiny comforter. With a siren's smile, she slid her arms over her head, arching her back and offering up the rosy, rigid tips of her breasts.

An offer he had no intention of refusing.

He worked her tits like she'd worked his cock, sucking and tugging, using his tongue and teeth and fingers until she was sobbing his name.

"That feel good?"

"Good. Great. Perfect. *Grady,*" she begged in a strangled whisper. "Please." She squirmed beneath him, entreating him with the wide spread of her thighs, the rhythmic surge of her hips.

"Shh." He abandoned her breasts to kiss his way down her belly to her sweet-smelling center.

The tally was already zero-one, advantage home, and Grady had every intention of evening the score. But his lips had barely grazed hers before she was yanking at his hair, gritting his name and bumping him with her hips in a frantic attempt to scoot him upwards.

"For God's sake, Grady, fuck me already!"

His cock swelled painfully, and he lunged for the bedside drawer.

Twenty seconds later he was sheathed in latex and stretched above her, thumbs stroking her jaw line as he gasped into her mouth. Charity's fingers dug into his hipbones, spurring him to prod at the entrance to her pussy. She was slick with want but tight, so damned tight. She made him work for it. He eased in, eased out, eased in again, further this time, sweat coating his chest and plastering her gorgeous tits to his skin. When he was finally balls deep, he nearly blew from the pulsing squeeze of her muscles and the mewling sounds she made as she writhed beneath him.

Slowly he pulled all the way out and thrust back in. She let loose a growling sob, reared up, and clamped her teeth on his shoulder.

Greed. It blanked out all thought, governed every instant of their ferocious coupling. He thrust, faster and faster. He couldn't get enough of her, couldn't slow the pace if his life depended on it. She smelled like honeysuckle, tasted like sugar cookies and coffee and sex. Her sighs echoed in his ears and sparked his hips into a grinding frenzy.

It was too fast, he knew it was too fast, but Christ it felt amazing, and she wouldn't let him slow but urged him on with both hands clamped tight on his ass. He lifted his mouth away from their kiss and sucked air. Stared down at the bliss on her face. How the hell would he live without her?

He tried to hold back, wanted her to come first, knew fast didn't have to mean selfish. Then the quivering began, and he thrust faster, the explosion seconds away. He should slow down. He should wait...dammit! He'd make sure she came, he'd use his tongue —

The thought pushed him over the edge. He bucked against her, shuddered into her, the blast breaking all records when Charity cried out his name and joined him, her hips melded to his, her inner muscles squeezing him in ecstasy.

For long seconds, they shuddered against each other.

Grady let his chin fall to his chest as he gasped for air, overwhelmed by the ecstatic violence of his climax and an overpowering sense of belonging. The tremors lessened, and he sank down onto his elbows, keeping his hips pressed tight against hers. He nuzzled her ear, and she started to laugh.

"I feel like I've been Tasered," she gasped. "Only in a good way."

Grady grinned. "Thank God everyone else is at the opposite side of the house, or they'd be banging on my door." Her expression gave him pause. "What?"

"That was..." Charity's hips surged up against his as she shook her head in wonder. "I like it when you take charge, Grady West." Her smile turned wicked. "I also like it when you lose control."

"Yeah? I like that thing you do with your finger."

She licked his chin. "Maybe next time I'll use two."

He winced. "Let's not get carried away."

"Really?" She offered a knowing smile. "That certainly lets me off the hook."

He considered that, and sighed. "Guess I backed right into that one."

Laughing, she stretched out an arm, grabbed a pillow, and aimed for the side of his head. He dodged the pillow and lifted away from her. She scowled and reached both arms toward him. He dodged those, too, and got out of bed.

"Hold that thought," he said.

He got rid of the condom and returned from the bathroom to find her snuggled under the comforter, one pillow under her head and the other hugged tightly to her chest. He snatched them both. Outraged, she jackknifed into a sitting position and grabbed, but he held the pillows out of reach.

"Trade you a pillow for a joke."

All the while she pretended to pout, a smile tugged at her lips. "Fine." She settled against the headboard and patted the mattress beside her.

He snuggled close, handed her a pillow, and dipped his head so she could hit him with it. She did, then stuffed it behind her back, comfortable again in her nudity, as she'd been when she was a teen. Comfortable, and sexy as hell.

God, he'd missed this woman.

"An old farmer bought a new pair of boots," she began. "When he got home he tried to get his wife to notice them, but she didn't pay any attention. So he went in the bedroom, took off all his clothes, and came out wearing only the boots. 'Notice anything?' he asked his wife. 'All I see is a limp dick,' she replied. 'Yeah, but look what it's pointing at. My new boots.' 'I see,' she said. 'Next time, buy a hat.'"

Grady chuckled. He scooted down, and pulled her over on top of him. They kissed for long moments until the alarm clock on the nightstand snagged her attention.

"I should go," she said.

He rubbed his hands over her back, then followed her spine down to her ass and caressed her just this side of rough. She began to move with his hands, eyes gleaming with sudden need. Her damp heat penetrated the sheet, and his groin caught fire.

"Maybe," he managed, "you should come before you go."

Her hips rocked more insistently. "You mean maybe you should come before I go."

"I like the way you think," he said. "But you first." He flipped her underneath him, and kissed his way down her body, his cock so hard it hurt as she rasped his name over and over into the shadows.

*   *   *

CRAP.

Charity sighed up into the moon-spattered darkness. She'd promised herself she wouldn't regret it. As she'd gone against every last one of her cop instincts by trespassing on West property, she'd pledged to appreciate this chance to reconnect with Grady. She knew their time would be limited, and she'd vowed to cherish it.

Fuck that. She wanted more. She wanted all the time. She wanted beyond the murder case. And she couldn't have it.

She inhaled and pressed her palms to her eyes, already feeling the heaviness of tears gathering in her throat. They'd fallen into their old pattern so effortlessly, so comfortably, that the enormity of what she'd sacrificed all those years ago was like the weight of a thousand black sins on her soul. She stared up through the shadows at the lazy spin of the ceiling fan, Grady sprawled on his stomach close beside her, his muscled arm flung over her waist, his breath puffing warmth against her shoulder.

She stifled a sob. He groaned, arm flexing as he started to tuck her beneath him. Dear Lord, she had to get out of there before she started begging him again. Only this time, to stay in Becker County.

She'd already decided she wouldn't be spending the weeks before summer with him. She'd never be able to survive his leaving at the end of it.

She shifted to the edge of the bed. "I have to go."

Grady groped under the sheets and tangled his fingers in hers. "Stay."

"I can't."

"Stay."

"Grady..."

He pushed up and rolled onto his side, pulled her close, and kissed her temple. "Having second thoughts?"

She smiled despite herself. "Seconds and thirds."

"You counting the time we fell off the bed?"

"Fine. Fourths."

Grady breathed in through his nose and brushed the backs of his fingers along her cheek. "I missed you."

"Missed me? Or missed this?"

"You're already doing it." Gently he traced the outline of her lips. "Pulling away."'

Enough already. "Because I have to go." Charity kissed his finger, slid out of bed, and collected her clothes. She counted herself lucky when she discovered her phone was still in her sweater pocket. Grady hesitated, then got to his feet, grabbed his sweatpants, and pulled them on. He paused, T-shirt in hand.

"Will we be doing this again?"

"I certainly hope so," she said lightly, and swung to face him. "Wait, you mean with each other?"

"That's not funny." He lunged, and she tried to run, but she didn't get far. A mock spanking turned into a quickie against the wall. When she could breathe again, Charity finished dressing.

"I'll walk you to your car," Grady said.

"Please don't. I can manage."

He hesitated. "You pulling a shift today?"

"Eight to four. Why? You up for a ride-along?"

He gave a mock groan. "You at least going to feed me first?"

"Seriously?" Charity was too surprised to hold up her end of the banter. "You want to come with?"

"I do want. But I can't." He reached for her hand. "I have an appointment I can't reschedule."

She frowned. "Something to do with the case?"

"Would I do that without telling you?"

She snorted.

He grinned. "Now that we're partners, I mean?"

She pressed a quick kiss to his jaw. "Call me when you get a chance."

"Listen, when I get back, how about you and me and Matt do something together?"

Like a family? Something greasy uncoiled in her stomach. "That's an idea," she managed.

He slid his fingers through her hair and gave it a gentle tug. "I know you have to go. But give me a minute. I want to tell you about my ex-wife."

"Grady—"

"Please." He leaned back and snagged her gaze. "There isn't much to it. I got drunk at a party, went home with a girl, and got her pregnant." He grimaced. "When you're drunk, you can't feel anything. And when you're fucking drunk...you know, fucking while you're drunk...you can pretend the chick you're with is the only chick you've ever loved. But you have to know—"

She jerked away from him. "You're blaming me."

"What?"

"You're saying it's my fault. That you were drunk when you fucked Valerie. Too drunk to practice safe sex. You're saying your marriage, Matt, everything that went wrong with your life is my fault."

Grady froze, and even through the gloom she could see the ice in his eyes. "Nothing about Matt is wrong. He was unplanned, yes, but the best damned mistake I ever made."

Charity's shoulders slumped. "I'm sorry. I didn't mean that. I know he means everything to you." She put out a hand but dropped it before she touched him. "He's fighting for your attention. At the same time, he resents the hell out of you for giving it."

"Sounds like someone else I know."

She turned away.

Grady followed. "Please tell me you know I'm not blaming you. For anything. I'm my own man, Char. I make my own decisions."

"I really do have to go," she whispered.

"Wait." He turned her to face him, and stroked his thumb across her chin. "There's something else I need to tell you."

"Did I mention I have to go?" Charity suppressed her cop curiosity and patted his cheek before crossing quickly to the door. "Call me when you can. We can talk about the case."

"The case. Right."

All the way home, she pictured the grim disappointment on his face as she'd shut the door behind her.

*   *   *

CHARITY WOULD ALMOST RATHER French kiss a rabid elk than tell the sheriff her decision about the election. Scratch that. There was no "almost" about it. So she decided to put it off. And for good reason. Mo had sent her a text while she was in the shower, and now she had an arrest to make. Nothing like a clean, solid arrest for boosting one's self confidence.

Providing one remembered to fill out the paperwork afterward.

She tipped her cereal bowl and swallowed her regret along with the last of her Trix-flavored milk, reminding herself she had to reimburse Mo for the DNA test he'd arranged. She headed for the bathroom and a quick brush of her teeth, all the while trying not to wonder how many more times she'd get to see Grady West naked before he headed back to Seattle.

And trying hard to forget she'd promised herself she'd stay away.

Outside Oliver Bloom's house, she checked in with Dispatch, grabbed her hat, and hopped out of the SUV.

He was on the front porch before she'd set foot on the flagstone path. He had a mini cooler in one hand and his keys in the other; she'd caught him on his way to the range, which opened early on Saturdays.

"Well, if it isn't my opposing candidate. Come to concede?"

"No," Charity said flatly. "Is your wife home?"

"What do you want with Janet?"

"I have a warrant for her arrest."

Blue eyes bulged. Even the bristles of his buzz cut seemed to quiver. "What the hell for?"

"Will you bring her out, or would you rather I go in and get her?"

They stared at each other, Bloom's face getting redder every second. Finally he turned his head and spat into the azaleas. "This is bullshit, Bishop."

The door behind him swung open. "No," his wife said. "It's not." She stepped out onto the porch and studied Charity, her thin face serene but pale. "I'm guessing that warrant says something about destruction of private property?"

"Yes, ma'am, and damage inflicted on a public school."

"Then it's not bullshit."

"Janet." Bloom fell back against the black iron balustrade, and it protested with a long, low-pitched squeak. "That was you? But why? What were you thinking?"

"That you deserved to be sheriff. And that she deserved a reality check." She gave Charity the once-over. "How'd you figure it out?"

"Don't say anything." Bloom put a meaty hand on his wife's shoulder, only to have her shrug it off. "Janet. Not without a lawyer."

"A DNA test proved the feces on Scott Langford's porch came from your dog." Charity nodded at the Irish setter that had his face pressed up against the glass on the storm door. "As far as the graffiti on the exterior wall of the school, you added your initials." Charity moved away from the path and motioned Bloom's wife to the SUV. "J-O-B. Janet and Oliver Bloom. At the last minute, you changed your mind about signing your work and added chapter and verse for misdirection."

Janet Bloom took her time joining Charity in the driveway. "You going to cuff me?"

"I don't think that'll be necessary." Charity really wasn't up for a tussle on the lawn, and Janet Bloom looked like she was spoiling for a tussle.

Her short black hair stood up in indignant spikes. "I intend to tell the sheriff all about your dirty affair with my husband."

Charity sighed and opened the back door. "You do realize our 'affair' lasted all of three nights before you two even met?"

"Oh, fuck. Oh, shit." Head in his hands, Bloom sat slumped on the cement steps. "My campaign. What'll I do about my campaign?"

"Here's an idea," his wife yelled from the back seat before Charity had a chance to shut the door. "Shove it up your adulterous ass."

As Charity backed down the driveway, her passenger congratulated her. "Looks like you're about to be sheriff."

Charity shook her head. "I'm pulling out of the race."

"Why?"

"I made a mistake."

"I'll say you did. Oliver has more hang-ups than a telemarketer. You're welcome to him."

"Not that kind of mistake. And by the way, you were wasting your time following me around. I am not hooking up with your husband."

"I haven't been following you around."

Charity frowned into the rearview mirror. "You're not the one who's been writing anonymous notes?"

"Not unless you count the one on the side of the elementary school."

Janet Bloom could be lying, but Charity wasn't getting that vibe.

Crap. How many enemies did she have?

She braked at a stop sign, turned in her seat, and glared through the steel partition. "How about my Camry? Was that you?"

"Oliver always said it was worse than ridiculous, how attached you are to that car."

Charity forced a casual smile. "I hope you enjoyed it, Janet." She turned back around and pressed on the accelerator. "Because it's going to cost you."

"What? Community service? Big deal."

"I bought that car used, did you know? The man I bought it from sold it only because his wife insisted. He's almost as fond of Clarabelle as I am. Want to guess what his name is?" She glanced into the rearview mirror.

Janet was finally starting to look uneasy. And for good reason.

"Clarkson Pratt," said Charity, and grinned all the way to the station.

*   *   *

CHARITY WAS FINISHING UP Janet Bloom's paperwork when a dour-faced Pratt stepped into her office doorway. "Can we talk?"

How ironic. He was going to fire her before she had a chance to tell him she was no longer running for sheriff.

Her stomach shuddered, but she lifted her chin. Might as well get it over with.

"Come in," she said, then raised her eyebrows when one of the regulators stepped into the office behind the sheriff. It was Tim, who'd booked her brother Hank and his buddy the night Drew had found Sarah's body. The lanky regulator kept his gaze averted, his clenched fists and sweat-slick forehead revealing he'd rather be anywhere else. What the hell? Slowly Charity got to her feet.

"Tim has something to say," prompted the sheriff.

The regulator cleared his throat. "I'm the one who followed you and took those photos. I left the notes."

"You?" Charity's gaze traveled from Tim to the sheriff and back again. "Why would you do that?"

He shrugged. "I got paid."

She clamped her arms across her chest. "You stalked a fellow officer for money?" She thought about what he'd put her through, the night she'd spotted him in her back yard, and it was all she could do not to let loose the outraged shriek building in her chest.

His cheeks had gone ruddy. "It wasn't just the money. I got hired as head of security at the hospital."

Oh, they did not. "Who hired you?" Charity demanded. "Hampton or Roberta?"

"Roberta," he said sullenly.

Oh, Grady.

Pratt slapped his hands against his rig. "I assume you want to press charges."

Charity hesitated. "The publicity won't do the department any good. But neither will cops who can't trust each other." She gave a curt nod. "Press away."

Pratt jabbed a thumb at the door. "You heard her. Clean out your desk and turn in your badge to Dispatch. Deputy Morrissey will get you processed."

Charity waited until the door closed behind the regulator before walking around to the front of her desk and slumping onto the edge. "How'd you find out?"

"Finally got my hands on that security footage for the West house." Pratt tugged at his goatee. "We're going to be a little shorthanded. I'll have to see if any of the other volunteers can put in more hours. Maybe we should have a drive. See if we can bring in some more warm bodies before the shortage becomes your problem."

A hot, prickling itch attacked the back of Charity's throat. *Here we go.* She swallowed. "About that…"

Three minutes later Pratt stared at her, stunned. He'd flopped down into the chair in the corner the moment she'd used the word "withdraw" and he hadn't twitched a muscle since. His throat worked, and he pinched the bridge of his nose, dislodging his black-framed glasses. He pinched so hard the tips of his fingers turned white.

"I hate to see this happen," he finally said, in a wispy shadow of his usually booming voice.

Regret sliced through Charity's chest. She slid off her desk and stood as tall as she could. "I fucked up. I appreciate that you're trying to protect me, but it needs to come out. Everyone on that panel and everyone in the department needs to know what I did." She was itching to take him to task over letting Bloom on the panel, but it wouldn't change a thing. In the end, the decision had belonged to the County Commissioner.

"Before I can even think about running for sheriff," she continued, "I need to prove I won't make that kind of mistake again. 'Respect the badge and it'll respect you.' That's what you're always saying. That's what I need to do. That's what I *didn't* do."

With a stiff nod, Pratt pushed up from the chair. "I'll let the election board know. So much for retirement."

"I'm sorry about that." If her guilt were any sharper, her insides would be in shreds. "I'm hoping to convince Dix to run. He was always the better choice, anyway."

Pratt plucked a tissue from the box on her desk and turned away, ostensibly to clean his glasses.

Charity swallowed hard. "By the way," she said, then had to clear her throat and try again. "That night you came by my house and chased Grady away? You said that something had happened, and you wanted to talk about it. But we never did."

He kept his back to her, and took his time fitting his glasses back onto his face. Afterward he made a harrumphing sound. "Brenda June asked me out. On a date. I thought maybe you had something to do with that."

Charity didn't know whether to cuss or cheer. "Forget cleaning those glasses. I think you need a new pair altogether."

He swung around. "What's that supposed to mean?"

"It means she's been wanting to ask you out for a while. Please tell me you said yes."

His scowl provided the unhappy answer. Before Charity could try to talk some sense into him, someone rapped twice on the door.

Mo poked his head in. "Good. You're both here." Oblivious to the tension in the room, he pushed the door wide and flapped a piece of paper. "We got the results back from the samples we collected in the West house. Some of the hair we bagged from Hampton West's shower drain is a match to Sarah Huffman."

Charity collapsed back against her desk, ignoring the stack of folders that slapped against the floor. *Finally.* Solid evidence. But why did it have to lead to Grady's father?

The sheriff grabbed the report and looked it over. "Drew Langford. Does he use that shower?"

Mo shook his head. "There's no DNA evidence that he's ever been in the bathroom, let alone used the shower. Same with everyone else in the family."

"Are you suggesting," Charity asked slowly, her pulse a deafening thud in her ears, "that Hampton West killed Sarah Huffman?"

"Either that, or they were lovers."

Charity stared at Pratt. "You seriously think he was sleeping with Kate *and* Sarah?"

Mo banged a fist against the wall. "More likely that he killed Sarah and carried strands of her hair in with him when he showered afterward."

"But he was at the hospital that night. We checked the security footage. Since he was messing around with Kate, I'm betting she shared his shower more than once, and considering Sarah and Kate hung out all the time, it makes sense that she'd have Sarah's DNA on her. Unless…could there be something wrong with the footage from the hospital?" Charity rounded on Pratt. "We need to check additional security tapes from the West house. See if Sarah was a regular visitor."

Pratt bobbed a nod, his head heavy on his neck. "Okay, people. I'll go see the judge. You bring Hampton West in. Let's figure out what the bloody blue blazes is going on."

"You take the house," Mo said to Charity. "I'll take the hospital." Jiggling his keys, he hurried out to the parking lot.

Charity followed without arguing. If he wanted the high-profile arrest, he could have it. She couldn't help it. She didn't want Grady's father to be guilty of murder.

She yawned as she merged onto the highway. Her incredible night with Grady was about to cost her dearly. If they did end up making an arrest, sleep would not be something she'd be getting anytime soon. She might even have to resort to ODing on caffeine.

She frowned. OD. Overdose. *Drugs.*

She hit the brakes, skidded to the side of the road, and gripped the steering wheel as her heart floundered in her chest. The night Justine was arrested, Hampton West had shown up at the station barely able to walk, let alone manage a straight line. Could he have been drugged?

Her breath lodged like a stone in her throat. What was it she herself had said to Drew about Justine? *Mothers can be fierce when their children are threatened.*

She heard Kate's voice in her brain, loud and clear, when she'd admitted to having an affair with Grady's father. *It's not for money, I can promise you that.*

And Stanford. Kate had told Charity that Allison had changed her mind about Stanford because she wanted some distance from Drew. But Drew had said Allison didn't have the grades.

Allison, who the morning Charity had questioned Kate had acted equally as dazed as Hampton West had on the night of the murder.

They'd found Sarah Huffman's hair in Hampton West's shower drain.

Charity scrabbled for her cell phone, practically chewing a hole through her lip as she waited for Pratt to pick up.

"Pratt here."

"We need to bring in Kate Young." A scalding sense of urgency shot through Charity's veins. "She and Hampton met for sex in his office, and she drugged him so he wouldn't know she left to meet up with Sarah."

"Hold on." She heard the scrape of skin against skin as he ran his palm over his head. "You're saying she killed her best friend?"

"Sarah ruined Kate's plans for an alliance with the Wests. That was how Kate planned to fund tuition for Allison at Stanford. By having her marry into a wealthy family." And hadn't Kate said something about needing a new roof? But money hadn't been the reason she'd seduced Hampton West.

She'd needed him to provide an alibi.

Brenda June was in the background, talking quickly.

Pratt came back on the phone. "The hospital called. They can't find Allison. Kate threw a fit, started ranting about payback, and took off. Hit three cars on her way out of the parking lot."

"When was this?"

"Half an hour ago."

Oh, dear Lord. Charity checked her mirror, jammed her boot on the accelerator, and swerved back onto the highway. "Send someone to Kate's house. I've got the Wests.' Sarah's not the only one who ruined Kate's plans."

Drew.

Last night Grady had said Drew and Matt would be home alone today.

Oh, God. Oh, Grady.

Charity flipped on the takedown lights and prayed.

*   *   *

JUDAS PRIEST. WHO'D HAVE thought?

Rehab. His mom was going to *rehab.*

Drew wandered into the house from the garage, still in a daze. He'd just rolled out of the guest bed at Ethan's when his mom had called and told him he wouldn't be hearing from her for a while. Uncle Grady, apparently, was driving her to a rehab facility in

Billings. Drew had stayed up until two with Ethan, shooting pool, so he wasn't sure he'd been hearing his mom correctly and asked her to say it again.

Yep. *Time to get sober,* she'd said.

At first Drew had been hurt. Why couldn't *he* drive her? Then she'd asked him, haltingly, to explain things to Peyton, and he'd realized.

She was embarrassed. Justine Langford. The woman who was so drunk she'd stabbed him in the cheek while pinning the boutonniere on his Homecoming suit. Then she'd thrown up all over him. *Then* she'd taken a picture and posted it on Facebook.

He snagged an apple from the bowl on the island, slung his backpack over his shoulder and started up the stairs. Things were looking up.

Now if only they could find the psycho bastard who'd murdered Sarah.

The bite of apple went bitter in his mouth. He forced himself to swallow, then sighed. He'd dump his stuff, find Matt and see if he wanted to play some pool. Drew needed the practice 'cause Ethan had wiped the floor with his ass. Anyways, Uncle Grady had asked Drew to keep an eye on Matt—his grandparents were both working today and Peyton had gone to the mall with a friend. Uncle Grady had said Matt would be okay for a while—he'd left him playing video games in the family room—but he didn't want him left alone for long.

No sweat. Drew liked to hang with his cousin. When the kid wasn't dissin' his own dad, anyway.

Drew opened his door and tossed his backpack at the bed. Blinked when it smacked into Matt, hitting him squarely in the chest. Belatedly Matt raised his arms, and ended up hugging the pack.

"Dude. Sorry about that." Drew set the apple on his bureau and crossed over to the bed, retrieved his pack and dropped it in the desk chair. "If you're done with *Call of Duty,* are you up for shooting some pool?"

Matt sat unmoving, face pale and strained, eyes as wide as frisbees. Drew frowned. "What's up with you?"

The kid looked at something over Drew's shoulder. Drew turned, and came face-to-face with Allison's mom. She stood with her back against his door, a smug expression on her face and an automatic pistol in her hand.

What the *fuck?*

Her hands were shaking, just like his, but that didn't make him feel any better. She looked like she knew what she was doing, with her left hand cupped under her right, and her finger hovering where he figured the safety must be. She didn't look crazy at all. Her hair was all slicked back in a bun and she was dressed like she was on her way to…

To a funeral. Black suit, black shoes, pearl earrings.

His stomach tumbled, over and over. Shit, were they about to *die?*

Behind him Matt whispered something, and Kate Young's eyes got squinty.

His mom. Peyton. *Dad.* He should have told them all he loved them.

Drew forced his gaze up and away from the gun and tried to swallow, but there wasn't a drop of spit in his mouth.

"Mrs. Young," he croaked. "What's going on?"

"It's payback time, that's what's going on. I'm tired of being screwed over by you and your family." She reached behind her without looking away and locked the door. "She left. She *left,* and it's all your fault."

"Allison's out of the hospital?"

"*Don't you say her name,*" she yelled, jabbing at him with the gun, while behind him Matt groaned. "*You don't get to say her name.*"

Matt was making grunting, choking sounds as he tried not to cry and the noise made Drew's chest ache. He wanted to start wailing himself, and his legs shook like he'd been running laps all morning. But he had to man up. Matt was scared enough for both of them.

Drew put out his hands, palms down. "I'd like to talk about this," he said, his voice scratchy like sandpaper. "I'd like to find out what you need, but how about you let my cousin go? Then it'll be just you and me —"

"No!" Kate Young shouted. She grimaced, then shook her head. The tiny pearls dangling from her ears quivered. "No," she said more calmly. "This isn't just between you and me."

"But Matt doesn't even know All—your daughter. He's just a kid. He doesn't have anything to do with this. Please. Let's send him downstairs. I'll stay. If you do that I promise I'll stay."

"You'll stay because I locked the damned door. And of course he has something to do with this. He's a West, isn't he? And you Wests are all alike. Liars and cheaters and thieves."

Drew was staring at her, mesmerized by her words. He'd known she was pissed at him, but this was over the top. He glanced at his backpack, but it was too far away. He'd never get to his phone before she had a chance to use that gun. And he couldn't leave Matt alone on the bed.

Why hadn't he left his pack where it was?

"I had plans for you," she was saying. "Big plans."

"What kind of plans?" He had to keep her talking. Weren't you supposed to keep them talking? Except...his grandparents wouldn't be home before dinner. Uncle Grady wouldn't be back for hours. And Peyton—

Oh, shit. What would happen when she got back from shopping? Sweat trickled down between his shoulder blades and fear kicked in his gut. Then he realized. Peyton was Allison's best friend.

He drew in a breath. "What about my sister? Don't you think this would scare her? Don't you think she'd want you to let Matt go so you and I can talk this out?"

Kate Young shook her head, and her eyes glistened. "She's just like my Allison. She'll hate me too when she finds out what I did."

"She won't hate you. Not if you put the gun down. Not if you let us go."

"Why would I let you go? You promised my daughter the world, then threw her over. For a woman old enough to be your *mother.*"

Matt was curled up in a ball on the bed, breathing hard into his knees. Drew flexed and unflexed his fingers. He had to figure something out. He had to get them out of the house. Think, dude. *Think*.

"I didn't let Sarah get away with it," she drawled. "Why should I let you?"

"I didn't mean to hurt her," Drew began, and stopped. It registered, then. What she'd meant. What she'd already done.

He couldn't move, couldn't breathe, as if someone had stuffed his lungs with dryer lint.

"Sarah," he choked, and instantly wished he hadn't. Because Kate Young's eyes lit with an eerie glow at the mention of the dead woman's name. Her cupped hands trembled, and Drew knew she'd use the gun. He had to get it away from her. He had to get it away from her *now*.

I love you, Mom. He gathered his muscles. But Allison's mom was ready for him. She took two steps to her right and aimed the gun at the bed. At Matt.

"You. Come here."

Drew threw out his arms, blocking his cousin. "Leave him alone."

"Get that kid over here or I'll shoot you both in the head."

16

A N AWFUL, EARNEST DREAD slithered through Charity when she spotted Kate's Volvo parked on the street two houses down from the West property. Her heart thundered against her breastbone as she swung into the driveway. She braked in front of the house and launched herself out of the SUV. At the front door she paused, her breathing too fast, too heavy. *Easy, Bishop.* She pulled her weapon free of its holster and tried the front door. Unlocked.

Gently she pushed it ajar. A yell had come from upstairs. Drew's room? Lifting her Sig, she eased up the carpeted steps, back to the banister, eyes locked on the hallway above her head. She should have caught it. Why hadn't she caught it? The big plans when there was no money. Kate's coyness when it came to her lover. The bias against Grady...

Kate hadn't wanted them to work together. That's why she'd advised Charity to steer clear.

She reached the top of the stairs and a chill dragged down her spine. She could hear Kate's voice now, high and hard, followed by Drew's, tight with fear. She crept down the corridor, toward Grady's old room. The door was shut. And locked?

She flattened against the wall outside the room, heard someone hyperventilating. Matt? Her heart squeezed.

Dix. Mo. Where are you? Kate had to have a gun or some sort of weapon. Otherwise Drew would have taken her down.

"Why would I let you go?" Kate was saying. "You promised my daughter the world, then threw her over for a woman old enough to be your *mother*."

Good job, Drew. Keep her talking.

"I didn't let Sarah get away with it," Kate said. "Why should I let you?"

"I didn't mean to hurt her." Drew went quiet.

Charity knew, she could *feel,* the moment he registered Kate's meaning.

"Sarah," he choked, and Charity's heart squeezed at the anguish in his voice.

"You," Kate snapped. "Come here."

Charity heard rustling sounds and pictured Kate positioning her hostages. Away from the window? A movement to her right had her head jerking around, her weapon snapping up. Mo moved stealthily up the stairway, right hand holding his gun at the ready, left hand gripping Charity's tactical vest. Her shoulders went lax and she nodded at his wordless scolding. She holstered her weapon long enough to shrug into the vest.

"Get that kid over here, or I'll shoot you both in the head." Kate's threat was followed by the unmistakable hiss and *clack* of a semiautomatic's first round sliding into the chamber.

And that answered the question about whether Matt was in there, too.

Charity swallowed a hot wave of nausea and stared at Mo with wide eyes. He stood on the opposite side of the closed door, mirroring her pose with his weapon pointed at the floor. Charity had to sweet-talk her way in, and she had to do it fast, because Kate's voice had been rising steadily.

Hang in there, boys.

She wrenched her thoughts away from Grady and how frantic he'd be and knocked lightly on Drew's bedroom door. "Kate? It's me, Charity. Can we talk about what's going on in there?"

A shaky laugh came from the other side of the door. "I'm pretty sure you've already figured out what's going on."

"I'd like to talk about it. I'd like to help. How about you send Matt and Drew out and let me come in?"

"Drew Langford is the reason I'm here. Allison and I were depending on him and he let us down. I'm sure you know what that feels like."

Charity exchanged a frustrated glance with Mo. "How about Matt, then? He's only eleven. He doesn't have anything to do with this."

"He's a West."

"He's a kid. Come on, Kate. Help me out. I'm the only one here who can make things happen for you."

"I'm not too happy with you, either. Why couldn't you leave well enough alone? Why couldn't you just let this loser take the fall?"

"We almost did, Kate. You had a good plan, but it didn't work, and now you need to let those boys go. Don't make this any worse. What do you say? Do we have a trade?"

In the silence that followed, Charity struggled to recall the layout of the room. It was a big space with a built-in desk on one side, a walk-in closet on the other, and a full bath between the closet and the outside wall.

Charity motioned Mo forward and whispered in his ear. "Find out if the curtains are closed and whether the bathroom window is locked. And the closet — does it have attic access?"

Mo nodded and disappeared down the stairs.

Charity took the opportunity to dry her palms on her pants. She shifted her weapon back to her right hand and faced the bedroom door. Still no answer from inside. "Do we have a deal, Kate?"

"I'm not an idiot, Charity Bishop. You're trained law enforcement. You get in here and you'll find a way to get hold of my gun. As a matter of fact..."

Drew said something. Something thumped, and thumped again. Charity's pulse began a rabid pound. What the hell? Matt squealed, Charity's muscles jumped, and she barely refrained from lunging at the door. Instead she hauled in a breath and held it. She placed her left palm on the wall and hung her head.

"Everything all right in there?" she asked as calmly as she could manage.

"Whatever you're planning," Kate said breathlessly, "you should know I have Matt right here beside me. No unexpected guests, all right? FYI, we locked the doors and windows and lowered the blinds."

At that same moment, Mo came up behind her, and handed her a piece of paper. *No attic access. Blinds closed. Fire department's checking bathroom window.*

Below that, *Allison's here.*

Charity stuffed the note in her pocket, gave Mo a nod, and they took up their positions again.

"What can we do for you, Kate?" She winced at the quiver in her voice and focused on Mo, who gave her a thumbs-up. "There must be something you want. Something we can do for you in exchange for letting those boys go."

No answer.

"Kate?"

Nothing.

She licked her lips. "Allison's here, Kate. She's worried about you. If you won't talk to me, will you talk to her?"

Charity and Mo both jumped when something hit the door. The murmur of Drew's voice sounded again, right before Kate yelled, "Shut up!"

Charity's breath quickened. She bounced on her toes. With every fiber of her being she wanted in, wanted to wrench Kate's gun away from her and hustle the boys out to their families and slap cuffs on the woman who'd strangled her own best friend. Every cop instinct told her to wait, to have patience, until Kate got less volatile. By now, Pratt would have called in a trained negotiator.

Charity could only hope Kate kept it together until that negotiator arrived.

"No. I won't talk to my daughter." At last Kate's voice drifted out to them. "But there is something you can arrange for me."

Outside the house, a woman yelled. Roberta West. Fear laced her strident tone, and Charity whispered a prayer of thanks that Pratt was out there to handle her hysterics. Her husband wouldn't be far behind.

"You know how this works, Kate," Charity said. "I'll do whatever you want, but you have to show us a gesture of good faith. Let the boys go. I'll come in. You'll have me." She ignored Mo, who was poking a finger at her and giving her the don't-even-think-about-it glare, as if he knew what was coming. "I'll come in unarmed."

Mo threw out his hand in a *what the fuck?* gesture and Charity straightened, prepared to hand over her weapon once she got the word.

"All right," Kate said, and Charity squeezed her eyes shut in a brief prayer of thanks. "You can come in, as long as you don't bring your gun. But I'm only sending out Matt. Drew stays with me."

Damn it. Damn, damn, damn, damn, damn. Charity sighed and shrugged at Mo. He held up a finger, as if to say, *we got one. One's good.* And he was right. One was better than none.

But she'd get them both out alive, if it was the last thing she did.

After long, agonizing seconds, the lock clicked. Slowly the door swung open enough to reveal Matt's pale, tortured expression. *You poor baby.* He stared at Charity with half-horrified, half-hopeful eyes, and she gave him an encouraging nod.

"It's okay," she said softly. Her arm was extended at her side, her Sig resting against her leg. "Open the door all the way."

Matt pulled the door wide, giving Charity a clear view into the room. Kate stood with her back to the wall between the bathroom and the closet. Drew knelt in front of her, facing outward, hands laced at the nape of his neck, Kate's pistol pointed at his head. Charity tensed. Kate had left her head and upper torso vulnerable; Charity could take her out with a well-placed shot, but Kate's finger rode the trigger of her own gun. No way Charity could risk Drew's life by taking the shot. Her gaze dropped.

Drew's stare was steady, but his lips were folded in and his shoulders twitched, as if preparing for movement. Charity's thighs locked and her stomach slid. She stared him down, hoping he got the message. *Don't move. Don't you* dare *move.*

She lifted her gaze to Kate, who wasn't looking as smug as Charity had expected. "Hold it right there, Matt," she ordered and tipped her chin at Charity. "Get rid of the gun."

Matt's body quivered as he hovered in the bedroom doorway, wide eyes fastened on the weapon at Charity's side. She lifted her arm to the right, straight out, signaling for Mo to take her piece. A thumping sound to her left had Charity jerking her head to the side. Allison ran down the hallway, hair a tangled mess, face wet with tears.

"Mom?" she yelled. "Mom!"

Dix was right behind her.

"Close it!" Kate screamed and gestured frantically at the door with the nose of her gun. "Close the door!"

Drew looked up at Kate, saw the gun no longer pointed at him and dove to the floor. Charity brought her weapon up and aimed as Mo flew past her knees and tackled Matt. Charity fired, slamming Kate back against the wall.

"Mom!" Allison launched herself through the doorway at the same instant Kate hit the wall and her gun went off.

Charity's brain reverberated with the double blast. White noise plugged her ears and gunpowder stung her nostrils. Weapon extended, she stepped over Mo, moved quickly to the nine millimeter and scooped it up. Keeping an eye on Kate, she dropped the magazine, shoved it into a pocket and tucked the pistol in her waistband at her back. She pulled out her cuffs. Kate stared up at her with an astonished expression, tears leaking out of her eyes and onto the carpet, blood welling around the bullet hole in her shoulder. She'd live.

Charity rolled her over and cuffed her.

Despite the thick ringing in her ears, she could hear Mo shouting for the EMTs, and heavy footsteps on the stairs. She finally registered the agonized groans of someone behind her. *Drew.* She swung around and out of the corner of her eye saw Mo hand Matt off to Dix and rush through the door. Drew sat slumped against his bed, moaning, staring down at the blood smeared across his palms. But the blood wasn't his.

Allison lay across his outstretched legs, eyes closed, face whiter than the petals of a meadow daisy.

* * *

CHARITY MADE HER WAY across the Wests' yard, this time aiming for the massive front door. She was exhausted, but Grady had begged her to come by before she went home for the day. If he hadn't begged her, she'd have begged him.

When she stepped up onto the front porch, she texted him instead of ringing the doorbell. It was after ten; no sense in waking everyone up. Grady texted back that the front door was open, and she should come on up. Tucking her phone back into its case, she eased inside the house and made her way upstairs to Grady's room. He stood in the doorway, in gray sweatpants and a hoodie, one hand outstretched. Once he'd tugged her close, she wrapped her arms around his waist and pressed her face against his throat.

She allowed his steady heartbeat to soothe her, then pushed gently out of his embrace. "How's Matt?" she whispered.

He nodded over his shoulder at his bed. In the dim light that spilled from the open bathroom door, she could make out a lump in the center of the mattress. "All right, thanks to you. After Deputy Morrissey took his statement, my parents both insisted on checking him over. Justine made him some warm milk and he was asleep after the first sip. It was my idea and not his, by the way, having him in here with me. You know, in case the subject ever happens to come up."

She smiled. "I would never question his courage." Her mouth went flat. "Especially after today."

"I couldn't bring myself to let him out of my sight." Grady stroked a finger along her jaw. "I didn't get a chance to thank you earlier. Not properly."

They hadn't had a chance to talk much at all. Grady and Justine had made it halfway to the rehab facility before Pratt called them back. When they'd arrived home, the West house had been in chaos. Paramedics, deputies, regulators, and family members had rushed in and out while neighbors milled around the statues and topiary, gawking. Cal and Nina and the rest of their shift had lingered beside the ladder truck, ready to render any assistance at a moment's notice. Phil Smiley had wandered from room to room snapping pictures, and the Wests' cook had served coffee and biscotti to everyone, including the crowd outside. Justine had screamed at her parents to lock the alcohol away, and Peyton had alternated between apologizing to Drew and sobbing that he'd gotten Allison shot.

"I called the hospital before coming over," Charity said. "The surgery went well. They're not thrilled they had to take Allison's spleen, and she suffered some damage to her ribs, but the doctors said it could have been so much worse."

Grady nodded, took her by the hand, and led her into the room. They settled on the padded bench under the window. She smelled Ivory soap and coconut shampoo, and pictured Grady hovering outside the bathroom door while Matt showered warmth back into his bones. She snatched up a throw pillow and plucked at the fringe.

"I wish I could be with you tonight," Grady said gruffly.

She looked up, and in the shadows watched his jaw flex. "I don't think Matt would go along with that."

"He might, after today."

"I wouldn't want it that way. I wouldn't want anyone to like me because I did them a favor."

"A favor? You saved his life."

She shook her head. "Drew's the one who deserves the credit for that. You should have heard how he kept Kate talking. How he tried to keep her calm. I suspect Pratt will see he receives a citation."

"That would be great. Especially after what he's been through." Grady reached out, and slid his fingers through her hair. He watched it spill softly against her cheek, and did it again. Her skin tingled.

"How did Allison find out her mom killed Sarah?" he asked.

Charity caught his hand and clutched it against the pillow on her lap. The whole thing still seemed so unreal. "Allison told Pratt she got suspicious when she heard about the ear buds, since the last time she saw them, they were in her mom's purse. She had assumed her mom was going to buy her a new pair, then suddenly they're the murder weapon. She started snooping and found Sarah's phone."

"Which is why she tried to kill herself."

Charity nodded. "Not only because she was appalled by what her mother had done, but because she didn't know how she'd face anyone once the truth came out. And she couldn't envision her own life with Kate in prison." She twined her fingers with his.

"I should have known," she whispered. "Kate was too calm after Allison's suicide attempt. She was too adamant about not blaming Drew. Of course she blamed him. She blamed you all. In a situation like that, parents usually blame themselves. Not Kate."

She pulled her hand free, set aside the pillow, and got to her feet. Arms wrapped around her waist, she stared over at Grady's sleeping son.

"She had it all figured out. She planned to marry off Allison to Drew so she could live what she saw as the good life. She was tired of working two jobs, tired of not being able to pay her bills, tired of being tired." She ran a palm down her face. "But dear Lord, she was convincing. I could have sworn all those tears were real."

"So what was my father? Plan B?"

"He was her alibi. She was especially proud of that. When we took her statement, she must have said half a dozen times how tickled she was that the great Hampton West almost helped to frame his own grandson for murder." Charity sighed, and settled once more on the bench, lifting her knee to provide a much needed buffer between her and the man she needed so badly she ached. "It explains why he showed up at the police station barely able to function. She'd drugged him."

Grady grunted. "Probably with something he himself gave her. My dad's a little too free with the prescription pad."

Oh, the irony. "I think she may even have been experimenting on her own daughter to figure out the right dosage." She shook her head. "Anyway, Kate told us she and Hampton often stayed late at the office to have sex. The night of the murder, she spiked Hampton's drink so she'd have time to meet up with Sarah, kill her, and get back to the hospital before he woke up. Surveillance footage confirms it. She was determined to set Drew up for it, which is what the text message and the planted necklace were about. I don't know how Kate got hold of Sarah's phone beforehand — we're guessing they met earlier in the day, maybe for lunch, and Kate snagged it then. She probably set up that second meeting on the pretext of returning the phone. As far as the necklace, she wouldn't have had any trouble getting hold of something Drew owned — her affair with your father meant she had access to the house. All she had to do was wait for everyone to be out."

"Christ," Grady muttered. "That is one diabolical bitch. What I don't understand is why she didn't just blackmail my father for the money. He'd have paid."

"It was about more than the money. She wanted the prestige of your family name." Charity dry-washed her face. "I should have followed up on her alibi sooner. It would have saved a hell of a lot of heartache."

"Stop it. You did your job, and you did it well." He tugged her knee out of its bend and slid her close. Her equipment belt creaked as he moved her. He pressed his mouth to her temple. "No one died here today."

She leaned into him. "There is that." Then she sobbed an inhale, dug her fingers into his sweatshirt and clung. By breathing through her mouth, she fought the overwhelming urge to weep, but she couldn't ward off the trembling. Grady tucked her under his chin and let his palms rove her back, rubbing and squeezing, warming her skin.

"Is this reaction?" he murmured. "Or something else?"

"I could have gotten him shot," she whispered brokenly. "Your son could have died."

"It didn't happen," he said. "It won't happen."

She pushed away, embarrassed to see she'd left a circle of drool on Grady's hoodie.

He didn't seem to notice. He sighed when she yawned. "It was selfish of me, asking you here. You're wrecked. Go home. We can talk tomorrow. The future kick-ass sheriff of Becker County needs her sleep."

Charity pushed upright. "I withdrew from the election."

"You what?" He cringed at the volume behind his words and glanced at the bed. Matt didn't stir.

"I've made too many mistakes," Charity said. "I can't...it wouldn't be fair. To the department, or to the county."

"But this is all you've ever wanted. After today, especially —"

"I told you. I want respect, not appreciation. And I certainly don't want credit for something the entire department made happen."

He was watching her closely. "You don't sound too upset."

"I'm disappointed, though I don't have anyone but myself to blame."

"Not even me?"

"Not even you. I'm my own woman, Grady. I make my own decisions."

"Touché," he whispered, and leaned in for a kiss. Almost immediately he pulled back. "Does this mean we can go on a real date?"

Charity's stomach tilted. "Don't you have to get back to Seattle?"

"Not for a while. I don't want to make Matt switch schools again. Not now. It'll be good for him to hang with his cousins. And I think it'll be very good for me to hang with you. Starting tomorrow. You deserve a day off. What do you say?"

She braced against a shudder. "Your back pocket's beeping."

"Nope, that's yours."

"Oh. Sorry." She pulled her cell free of its case and peered at the screen. "I have to take this," she said softly. "Be right back."

She walked quickly down the hall, more to gain distance from Grady than to keep from waking Matt. She spoke quietly with Brenda June, who only wanted to check one last time that Charity was okay. After ending the call, Charity leaned over the balustrade and peered down at the sleek marble floor of the foyer. No one stirred. The heat kicked on. Overhead the glass droplets of the chandelier tinkled, and Charity stared at the muted prisms on the floor.

Full circle. After twelve years she'd come full circle, and she didn't have many more options now than she did then.

Her throat was suddenly parched. Before she could change her mind, she headed downstairs. She'd grab a drink from the fridge.

One for Grady, too. Pretend she had a mission other than avoidance.

She was pushing at the stainless steel refrigerator door with her right elbow, a bottle of sweet tea in each hand, when she heard footsteps behind her. She turned, but it wasn't Grady who stood in the kitchen doorway.

Roberta West wore the same coral pajamas and gray cardigan she'd had on the night Charity had driven Grady to the hospital. Same disgruntled expression, too. Charity watched silently as the other woman found a glass, filled it with water from the sink, and settled back against the counter.

"I suppose you think I should thank you," Roberta drawled. "Even though you were only doing your job."

"No, Dr. West. Thanks is the last thing I expect from you."

"Nevertheless, I am grateful." The other woman produced a smile. It was flimsy, but genuine. "Thank you for rescuing my grandsons."

"On behalf of the Becker County Sheriff's Department, you're welcome."

"I know you did this in part for my son." Roberta set the glass on the counter with a clack. "He deserves better than you."

Here we go. "I've always thought so."

"But you're going after him again." She gestured at Charity's chest. "With everything you've got."

Barely resisting the urge to hug the plastic bottles close, Charity didn't bother to correct her. She let her arms dangle at her sides.

Roberta frowned. "I looked up the statute of limitations on arson."

Charity went motionless. "Because?"

"Because before I confessed, I wanted to make sure you couldn't arrest me."

"Wait. What?" Charity's tongue was suddenly five times too big for her mouth. "You're saying *you're* the one who burned down the Shake Shack?" She stumbled to the granite-covered island between them and let the plastic bottles tumble to the surface. "Grady and I agreed to let everyone think we'd done it because we were afraid Jerzy would take the fall. All these years, I assumed one of my brothers set that fire." She struggled to process what Roberta West was telling her. "What did Jerzy ever do to you?"

"You two practically lived at Jerzy's. Anyone who ate there saw you together. It was humiliating. Jerzy had no right, encouraging you like he did."

"So to punish him, you burned down his restaurant?"

For the first time since she'd walked into the kitchen, Roberta looked uneasy. "I decided that if you two didn't have a place to hang out, you wouldn't spend so much time together."

"But, why now?" Charity choked out. "Why tell me this now?"

"Men keep secrets." Roberta's throat worked. "That's just what they do. You should know. Husband, son, lover, doesn't matter. That's what they do."

Grady came in then, and Charity turned slowly toward him. "It was you," she whispered. "You're the one who financed Shack Part Two."

"What the hell, Mother?" He scowled at Roberta, wrapped his hand around Charity's upper arm, and led her out into the hallway. When he released her he pushed all ten fingers through his hair. "Dammit, I wanted to be the one to tell you. I tried, the night you came to me after Dix's wife died."

She remembered. She'd cut him off, terrified he'd wanted to talk about his feelings. "Why didn't you tell me twelve years ago?"

"I didn't know then. I didn't figure it out until after you left that message, asking me not to call again. By then, the damage was done." He jerked his head toward the kitchen. "And she'd promised to go to rehab."

"Did she?"

The regret in Grady's eyes belied the wry twist of his lips. "It didn't take. Either time." Something clattered in the kitchen and Grady frowned over his shoulder. "Look, can we just…" He shepherded her into a room to their left…a library, or a study…flicked on the light and shut the door. The room smelled like lemons, and old books.

"Char. I'm sorry. About all of this. I have a feeling if I hadn't come downstairs to find you, you'd be halfway home by now."

Charity was tired. So tired and dizzy. "You lied to me. We swore we'd always be honest with each other and you lied. You let me think Hank or Lucas had done it."

"I've been wanting to make it right with you. At the same time, I dreaded telling you. Giving you one more reason to resent me." He moved closer, and smoothed his palms up and down her arms. "Please tell me you understand."

A sense of betrayal welled up inside her, so bleak and heavy it nearly forced her to her knees. She jerked away from him, stumbling back until her hip bumped the arm of a brown leather recliner. "You used me. You used my family to keep your mother out of prison."

"No. Not at first." He reached out. When she pushed her shoulders back, and rested her hands on her rig in "official capacity" mode, he let his hand drop. "I wanted to tell you."

"But you didn't. Which means I agreed to sucker the sheriff for nothing. And not only Pratt, but the fire chief, too. The old man hasn't been able to look me in the eye since." She shook her head, chin sliding back and forth in denial. "The other day, outside the liquor store… Why didn't you tell me then? I told you things…and all the while you knew…" The thickness in her throat threatened to choke her.

Grady stood stock still in front of a wall of books, the track lighting above highlighting his grim mouth and helpless expression. Charity gulped in a breath and pictured the teenage version of him grappling with turning his mother in for a crime she'd only claimed she committed—a crime they had no proof of. Struggling to make that decision must have been hell.

But…he'd lied.

"You know what?" she whispered, and let her arms drop to her sides. "I do get it. She's your mother. And in the end you made it right with Jerzy." She held up a shaking hand when Grady took a step closer. "I understand, but I can't forgive."

"Then tell me what I have to do so you will forgive me," Grady said. "Because I love you, and I want to take you home with me to Seattle."

17

As GRADY WATCHED THE shock and rejection seep into Charity's eyes, the inside of his chest pulsed with a sudden panicked need for air. Dammit, he never had timed these conversations right with her.

Didn't mean he wasn't going to see this through.

He approached her slowly, encouraged when she didn't back away. Then again, at the moment she looked barely capable of breathing, let alone moving. He cupped her shoulders, slid his hands down her arms, and threaded his fingers through hers. "I love you. I never stopped loving you. We're getting a second chance here. Come back with me. Be with me."

She stared at him mutely.

He lifted an eyebrow, forcing an unconcerned expression. "You're not convinced. That's okay, I'm a convincing kind of guy. Let's start with how you can't live without me. How I can't live without you. How my kid can't live without you, even though he doesn't know it yet."

"Grady, I can't. I can't be with you."

The words Grady had dreaded slammed into his chest, like he'd belly-flopped into his parents' pool. He couldn't breathe, and it hurt like hell. "Why not?"

"You know why not," she said in a choked whisper.

"Tell me."

Her throat bobbed. "I'm established here. I have a career. Now that Bloom's out of the running for sheriff, I have no problem serving as undersheriff. In fact, I need to serve as undersheriff. I have some mistakes to make up for. Anyway, I like it here. I don't want to live in the city. You were the one who couldn't wait to head for the coast." She sidled around him and headed for the door.

He followed, and braced a palm against the door. "Is it really about the city? Or is it because twice now I've had my head up my ass and made life miserable for you?"

"It's everything," she said to his hand. "We don't belong together. We especially don't belong together in the city."

"You haven't tried living in the city."

She turned, and leaned her left shoulder against the door. "I went to police academy in Great Falls. I lived there for six years."

Heat flushed through his body and he wanted to kick the goddamned door. He started to point, made a fist of his left hand instead and jammed it in the front pocket of his hoodie. "You're not in Becker County because you enjoy the country. You're here because you're serving penance. You wear your martyrdom like you wear that damned badge. You're trying to make up for every single time one of your brothers hotwired a pickup or beat someone up for beer money. But you're never going to be able to do enough. How long 'til you figure it out? You're too good for this place. You don't belong here."

"I do." She launched upright. "And anyway, that's not for you to decide."

"Jesus, you're stubborn. It's almost like you don't think you deserve—" Realization doused him like a bucket of cold water. Shit. He noted the guardedness in her expression, and his head went into a slow bob. "That's it, isn't it? You can't believe you deserve anything more. You probably don't think you deserve what you have. That's why you pulled out of the election." And he'd bet it was the reason behind her predilection for casual sex, too. His hand on the door fisted. "Christ, your family's done a number on you."

"Forget my family. I have my own mistakes to make up for. That's why I pulled out of the election. Because the county deserves a trustworthy sheriff. Stop making me sound like a victim."

He bounced his fist off the door. "Stop acting like one!"

Eyeing his hand, she angled her chin. "Is this invitation to leave Becker County more about wanting me in your life, or wanting me to stay safe?"

He couldn't deny he had a protective streak, especially where she was concerned. "Can't it be both?"

"I'm a cop, Grady." She rested her palm on the butt of her service weapon. "I can take care of myself, no matter where I am."

"So take care of yourself in Seattle."

"I belong here. And you can't tell me that if I went with you to Seattle you wouldn't try to talk me out of joining the force there."

He might. As proud of her as he was, he just damned well might.

With a growl of frustration he swung away, paced to the recliner and back. "All right. You don't want to move? Fine. Matt and I will move to Becker County." They'd figure something out. If it meant he could have Charity in his life, he'd deal with having his parents close by. It didn't have to mean Matt would end up a drug abuser.

And Sarah Huffman's murder aside, Becker County was a hell of a lot safer than Seattle.

Charity's chin quivered, but her posture remained rigid.

He wasn't getting through to her.

"You love me," he said steadily. "I know you love me. We deserve this. Both of us. All of us. We can make it work."

She shook her head again, and desperation grabbed hold of Grady's throat. He grasped her arms, less than gently. "You're scared. Scared that one day I'll wake up and decide I don't love you. The truth is I love you more than I ever have. I love the person you are *now,* and there's nothing you can to do make me stop." He leaned in and spoke with his lips pressed to her forehead. "Say yes. You and me and Matt — we'll be a family."

"The department is my family."

His throat burned like hell. He closed his eyes and swallowed. "You're saying there's no room for anyone else."

She didn't deny it. Her wet, broken breaths told him she was hurting, too, but she was so caught up in punishing herself for her family's faults, she couldn't see the life she deserved to lead. Couldn't realize — or didn't care — that she was punishing him, too.

He released her shoulders and stepped back. Watched in aching resignation as she fumbled to open the door. "I shouldn't be surprised," he said, his voice a shredded mess. "Someone had to die before you'd admit you wanted me. God knows what it'll take to admit you love me."

* * *

THE MOMENT HER OWN front door closed behind Charity, she dumped her duty belt and yanked off her uniform shirt. She staggered to her bed and collapsed onto her knees, somehow found the energy to turn herself over and unlace her boots. Her fingers were on their own, since she couldn't see through the tears she'd held back all the way home.

Grady.

Sobbing, she kicked off her pants. Why couldn't he see that he and Matt were better off without her?

Why couldn't *she* see she'd done the right thing?

She crawled up to her pillows, crying harder when she couldn't find the strength to peel back the covers. Finally she gave up and rolled herself in the top blanket. She spent the next ten hours envisioning Grady as he sat across from her at her kitchen table, going all smoky-eyed and intense until she'd pointed out the syrup on his shirt.

Saying goodbye had been a hell of a lot harder the second time around.

* * *

GRADY AND MATT HAD the upstairs den to themselves. They sat on the soft suede couch, their feet on the coffee table, a bowl of popcorn tucked between them as they watched *The Simpson Movie.*

Matt hadn't said a word when Grady had skipped past The Military Channel and a Schwarzenegger movie. They'd both had enough of guns for a while. Grady had made an appointment with the hospital's resident child psychologist for the morning, and once he got back to Seattle, he'd find someone else Matt could talk to, in case he needed extra help dealing with what he'd been through.

Maybe Grady should find someone for himself.

"Dad?"

"Yeah?"

"You really going back to Seattle without me?"

Grady fished for the remote and hit the mute button. "I thought that's what you wanted."

"It is." Matt scooped up another handful of popcorn. "I just didn't think you'd do it."

"Doesn't mean I won't worry about you."

Matt leaned his head back and rolled his eyes. "What are the chances I'll be held hostage again before you get back?"

Christ. "That's nowhere near funny."

"Drew's got my back."

"I know he does." Grady grabbed his own fistful of popcorn. He should have been there for Matt. Drew, too. Thank God Charity had been.

"You don't like my grandparents, do you?"

Grady swallowed his popcorn before he'd had much of a chance to chew it. He coughed, thumped his chest, and scooted around to face his son. "I do love them." He coughed again, fist against his mouth. "We just don't have a lot in common."

"You don't have a lot in common with Charity, either."

Slowly Grady lowered his hand. Matt's voice had been surprisingly free of hostility. He waited.

"But you love her."

Smart kid. "You may not think we have a lot in common because she knows all about guns and how to make a J-turn and never had a decent oyster sandwich. But we're the same where it counts."

Matt turned his head back toward the TV. "You mean like you're both against drugs and injustice and stuff."

"We both had tough childhoods, so that gives us a special connection. And speaking of connections." He pointed the remote at the television and pressed the power button. Matt heaved a sigh and flopped his arms in protest. Grady leaned forward and poked his thigh.

"When parents split up, the kids suffer the most. A lot of times the kids will latch on to the remaining parent, terrified they'll lose him or her, too. I know you've seen it with some of your friends at school."

"Da-ad." Matt scowled. "I'm not the clingy type."

"I know, but I am."

That got Matt's attention. "You were afraid I'd go live with Mom?"

"I was afraid of losing our connection. You know how much I love you, right?"

Matt ignored that. "You're not afraid anymore?"

"I'm still nervous, but I realized I was helping to make it happen."

"By hovering."

"Yeah. By hovering." Grady lifted his socked feet and pressed against Matt's hip and thigh and shoved, scooting him farther down the couch. "But I'm working on that."

Grinning, Matt lunged for the popcorn bowl and yanked it out of reach. Popcorn bounced onto the coffee table and the rug beyond and Grady winced. They'd have to break out the vacuum cleaner later.

"Is Charity going to live with us in Seattle?"

Grady's throat seized. *Where the hell did that come from?* He brushed popcorn off the remote and shook his head. "I wanted her to."

"But she doesn't want to leave?"

Grady shook his head again.

"Maybe she'll change her mind."

"And you'd be okay with that?"

Matt bit his lip, then tried to cover his flash of vulnerability with an exaggerated shrug. "She was pretty cool. About everything that happened, I mean."

"Yeah. She was pretty cool." Pretty fucking awesome, as a matter of fact. "But I don't think she's going to change her mind."

Grady turned the television back on and they sat in silence for a while, watching Homer steer a motorcycle up the walls of the see-through dome that isolated the town of Springfield from the rest of the world. There was some kind of parallel to be found there. But Grady was too damned tired to think it through.

And it was hard to concentrate when his chest ached like a son of a bitch.

"Dad?"

"Yeah?"

"It's okay if you hover sometimes."

"Thanks."

"But you still can't call me buddy."

"Understood." Grady stretched out a hand. "Pass the popcorn, would you, princess?"

*   *   *

THREE DAYS LATER, CHARITY sat sprawled in an Adirondack chair on Dix's front porch. Head back, eyes wet with unshed tears, she stared up at the blurry spread of glittering stars overhead. The scent of cinnamon reached out to her. She groped for the mug of hot tea on the timbered floor beside her, dislodging the woven throw that warmed her lap.

She blew on her tea, sipped, and leaned her head back again. "It really was a lovely service," she murmured.

"Sheila would have enjoyed all the black." Dix was slumped in a twin Adirondack on the other end of the porch. The weary smile in his voice heightened the burn behind her eyes.

She sipped her tea and prayed Dix's wife had finally found peace. The service had been brief, with Dix saying little, but the photos and tokens he'd put on display had expressed what he could not—that once upon a time, his marriage had been filled with joy.

Since Dix's sister was still recovering from the flu, Brenda June had handled the meal at his cabin, which meant desserts ruled the table. No one had complained. Charity had stayed to help Brenda June with the cleanup, and so had Sheriff Pratt, which Charity had found fascinating, and the dispatcher, nerve-racking. The sheriff and Brenda June had left an hour ago, but Charity lingered. She and Dix both needed the company.

"Want to talk about it?" Dix's quiet words drifted across the dark. "It makes me sad to see you so miserable."

His words reminded her of Grady and what he'd said the night Dix's wife died. *It makes me sad you were so determined to forget what we had.*

He'd left for Seattle the day before. He'd be back, though; Matt had stayed behind to finish out the school year, and Grady had promised he wouldn't make Matt travel home alone. Or so Drew had told her when she'd run into him at the Good Dog, Bad Dog Café that afternoon.

It took her a moment to realize she was smiling up at the sky. There was hope for Matt and Grady yet, if Grady had realized he needed to grant Matt a little free rein. That Drew refused to leave his cousin alone with their grandparents probably had something to do with it.

"You should follow him," Dix said.

Charity caught her breath. "It's not that easy."

"It is when you realize what's at stake."

"Which is?"

"Your happiness. You deserve to be happy. Let Sheila's death serve a purpose. Let her remind you life is short."

"He deserves better."

In a flash Dix was up and out of his chair. He strode across the porch, his footsteps a harsh staccato thud as he approached. He dropped to his haunches in front of her, took her tea and set it aside, and enfolded her hands in his. "*Katawasisiw,*" he growled. "That is enough."

She stared into the angry glint of his eyes, the rest of his features mere shadows in the dark. "Dix?"

"You say that not because it is true, but because you've believed it for so long. Besides, I could not love someone who is undeserving."

Silence. There must have been sounds all around them—the wind through the trees maybe, or the call of a night bird—but all she could hear was the *whump whump whump* of her own astonished pulse.

"Dixon," she whispered. Her heart ached under the weight of her freshest regret. "I didn't know."

"Better you did not. I don't tell you to dishonor my wife. I tell you because you're smarter than to punish yourself for something you did not do. Self-pity should be the exception, not the rule."

Charity huffed, but she couldn't bring herself to break her physical connection with him. "I think you just called me a martyr. That's what Grady accused me of."

"Maybe he deserves you after all."

The thought stunned her. That someone might consider they didn't deserve *her*. She knew what it was to feel unworthy. The last thing she wanted was for Grady to feel that way. Had she perpetuated that sense of not being good enough all these years because it was familiar? Safe?

Grady was right. She was scared. Still she knew, had always known, that if she took Grady up on his offer, he'd be there for her. She wouldn't be going it alone. But she had so much that remained unsettled here, and he and Matt had established a life there.

How would they get around that? Could they get around that?

"I told him I couldn't forgive him," she whispered.

"Can you?"

"He lied to me."

"Ten years ago."

She gave one shoulder a bounce.

Dix rose out of his crouch. "If you can forgive him, and you do not tell him, that is also a lie. If you cannot forgive the boy he was for trying to protect his family, you must ask yourself why."

"You think I'm jealous."

"I think you're scared."

"I think you're psychic," she muttered. She peered up at him. "You still planning to leave Becker County?"

"You're deflecting."

"You're right."

With a sigh, he leaned back against the porch railing. "I have a job lined up. An apartment. There is nothing for me here."

It was Charity's turn to spring out of her chair. "Are you kidding me? You have Pratt and Mo and Brenda June and the whole damned community. And me. Dix, you could be sheriff. You deserve to be sheriff." At his snort, she tipped her head. "You're not scared, are you?"

For long moments he said nothing. Then he offered a flash of teeth. "*Ka pakwâciyetohk.* Do you know you are a pain in my ass?"

* * *

CHARITY STARED INTO THE bedroom closet she had absolutely no energy to organize. She reached out, and poked at the purple sleeve of a hip-length sweater she should have packed away — it and all of its cable-knit cronies, considering it was almost May — and idly watched the sleeve swing, back and forth. She sighed, backed up a step, and slumped onto her bed. She'd already scrubbed the bathtub, dusted all the blinds, and cleaned out the refrigerator, which involved eating two handfuls of olives for breakfast because she was *not* going to throw those puppies away. At least she was down to one jar now.

The problem was, she had too much time on her hands. Too much time to think. She collapsed onto her back and stared up at the ceiling. A mistake, because her nose clogged right away. A side effect of this on-again, off-again crying jag she'd been battling for a week.

And she had another three weeks of her suspension to go.

Another three weeks of watching the light go out of Grady's eyes as she prepared to walk out on him.

She choked out a cough, rolled onto her left side, and stared at the box of tissues on the nightstand. The nightstand that seemed oh-so-far away. She reached out, but the box didn't get any closer. Oh, dear Lord, she was such a loser.

What she needed to do was get out. Get some sun. Go to the range, maybe, and blast this ridiculous self-pity right out of her brain.

But that would mean getting dressed. Which demanded energy she didn't have.

316

She rolled onto her back again, and started breathing through her mouth.

When someone knocked on the kitchen door, she whimpered, and closed her eyes. *Drew.* He'd come to nag her again about calling Grady. She knew from experience that ignoring him didn't work. He'd only knock louder.

The good news was, she didn't have any cereal left, which meant he wouldn't stay long.

With a groan, she rolled out of bed, pushed her feet into her flip-flops, and shuffled out to the kitchen. But it wasn't Drew staring at her through the glass.

It was his mother.

Charity smoothed both hands over her hair and opened the door. "Justine."

"Charity." Justine strode into the kitchen, high heels clacking across the linoleum, and set two bulging grocery bags on the table. She turned back to Charity, hand on hip, and gave her the onceover. "You look like hell."

"Anyone would, next to you," Charity muttered. Seriously, in her leaf-green blouse, black skirt and heels, and with her curly hair gathered neatly at her neck, the woman looked like she was ready for her walk-on part in *The Good Wife.* "Where's Drew?"

"Grounded, for failing his mission. And here I figured if anyone could talk you into changing your mind about dumping Grady, it would be Drew." She gestured at the grocery bags. "I hope you don't mind, but I threw a couple of boxes of raisin bran in along with the boxes of sugar-coated, circus-colored bits and pieces Drew says you've been feeding him."

"That wasn't necessary," Charity said stiffly, "but I appreciate it." She glanced at the bags and bit the inside of her cheek. "I don't suppose you brought milk."

"I know what's going on here." Justine crossed her arms and leaned back against the counter, her coordinated elegance out of place in Charity's mismatched kitchen.

"Breakfast, as soon as you leave me to it." Charity shuffled over to the cupboard where she kept the bowls. Justine got there first, and slapped a palm against the cabinet door to keep it closed. The gesture reminded Charity of Grady, trapping her in his parents' study, and it pissed her off.

"Back. Off," she growled.

"It's one in the afternoon," Justine said calmly.

"Which explains why I'm hungry."

"You're not hungry, you're mourning, and since there's absolutely no reason for it, you need to snap the hell out of it."

Charity jerked her spine straight and stared down her crooked nose at Justine. "This is between Grady and me."

"Exactly. So why aren't you in Seattle?" Justine shut Charity up with a palm in the air. "I know what it's like to think you'll never measure up. To believe you'll make five mistakes for every one thing you get right. You don't think Grady ever felt that way? You don't think he's feeling that way now, after you told him he wasn't worth rearranging your life for?"

Charity jerked her head left and then right. "That's not what I told him. I told him we don't belong together."

"But what you meant was, you're too scared to try." Justine snorted in disgust. "And this from the woman he called badass."

Charity swallowed, lurched backward, and dropped into a chair. Her elbow hit one of the grocery bags and a box of cereal hit the floor with a rustling slap. She stared at Justine as nerves started to party in her belly. "It rains nine months of the year in Seattle," she said breathlessly.

"Well, then. You'd better invest in some umbrellas so your family doesn't get wet."

Justine blew her a kiss and disappeared through the back door. Came back in long enough to rustle through one of the bags, pull out a gallon of milk and stash it in the fridge. When she banged out of the door again, Charity stared at the space where she'd stood. One word echoed in the tiny kitchen.

Family.

She and Grady and Matt. A family?

Grady had suggested the same thing. He had believed in her, and she'd refused to return the favor. Had refused to forgive him.

Her gaze traveled to the cereal box on the floor. The same cereal she'd shared with Drew when he'd come to her for advice about forgiving his father. She was the last person he should have asked about that. Or maybe that had been his point?

With a grimace she recalled telling him he should consider how much he could lose by holding onto his grudge. And here she was, about to sacrifice the best thing that had ever happened to her because it was easier to hold a grudge than to face her own failings.

Failings Grady already knew about. Failings that didn't keep him from loving her.

A sad, crazy, wonderful, miserable, terrifying realization took root. She drew in a breath, and held it 'til her lungs burned. Slowly she exhaled, and plucked at the flannel of her Hello Kitty pajama pants.

What would a badass wear to the airport?

*   *   *

SIX HOURS LATER, CHARITY stood in front of the door to Grady's condo, fist raised to knock, heartbeat so insane it was a wonder she didn't pass out. She dropped her hand and concentrated on breathing while wondering what the hell Grady had been thinking, calling her formidable. When a door opened down the hall to her left, she whirled so fast, she almost fell headfirst into the wall.

And wouldn't that make for a graceful reunion.

A plump, sixtysomething woman wearing a black and pink flowered apron and carrying a casserole dish in her hands bustled toward Charity. The closer she got, the wider she smiled.

"You here to see our Grady?" She didn't wait for an answer. "You'll save me some trouble." She pushed the red enamel dish into Charity's hands and tut-tutted at the closed door. She pulled a key from her pocket, unlocked the door and shooed Charity inside. "Better you than me. Man's been sour as month-old milk since the day he got back. You'll find him in his office. That's where he spends all his time when his son's away. Don't say I didn't warn you." The skin beneath her chin trembled as she nodded once, then shut the door in Charity's face.

Charity stared at the closed door, wondering if she'd just met Matt's least favorite babysitter, the infamous Mrs. K. The woman had seemed nice enough, and she hadn't smelled a bit like salami. More like—Charity lifted the casserole and took a whiff—tuna. *Oh, Lord.* Her already unstable stomach curled up and whimpered.

Slowly she turned and faced the interior of Grady's condo. No sign of the owner. Her shoulders relaxed, and she loosened her death grip on the casserole. But considering the sweat coating her palms, and the state of her stomach, she'd better put the dish down, pronto.

She crossed to the edge of the polished oak platform she stood on, descended two steps, and hesitated at the border of Grady's living room, which was about the size of her entire house. The palette was a masculine, relaxing mix of browns, blues, and lime green, the furniture cushy, the clutter minimal. To her left a spacious kitchen extended behind a curved island fronted by four stools, all covered in lime green fabric, and backed by a weathered brick wall. The far left corner was reserved for the dining room, a space dominated by a heavy rectangular table under a chrome chandelier. Charity looked straight ahead again and swallowed.

The entire wall she faced was made up of windows overlooking Lake Washington, with a hazy, cloud-draped view of Mt. Baker.

Thank you, Google.

"Wow," she muttered, and seriously considered backtracking. She knew Grady had done well for himself, but this...this was downright intimidating.

All at once this seemed like the worst idea in the world. She shouldn't be here, in his home, without his knowledge. She should go. Not home, necessarily. She could get a hotel room. Give him a call in the morning. Get a feel for how he'd react if he knew she was in town...

Her reflection in the window gave way to Justine's disapproving scowl and Charity flinched. She straightened her shoulders, and suddenly registered they'd started to ache. She carried the casserole over to the kitchen and with a huff of relief set it on the counter. As she pressed against the edge of the island, she felt a wet spot, and looked down to see the casserole had leaked onto her cardigan. Great. Perfect. Of course it couldn't have leaked a little lower, onto the black skirt that would have hidden the stain.

With a glance over her shoulder, toward the hallway on the other side of the living room — a hallway she assumed led to the infamous office — she hurried to the sink, scooped up a dishrag, and started scrubbing. After all the soul searching she'd done, and all the miles she'd traveled, she'd be damned if she'd face him not looking her best.

A scrabbling sound had her whipping around. A big, black dog headed her way, tongue lolling out of the left side of his mouth, a thick piece of knotted rope hanging from the right. He trotted right up to her, nudged her knee with his nose and backed up, clearly inviting her to play.

"Hello, boy," she said softly. "You're a cutie, aren't you? I'm sorry, I've forgotten your name."

He nudged her again. Oh, what the hell. She tossed the dishrag at the sink and grabbed the free end of the rope. Instantly the dog backed up, with a strength that caught Charity by surprise. He pulled her off balance and she stumbled forward. She tripped over the edge of the living room rug and fell to her knees behind the couch.

Ouch. And crap. And ouch.

Thinking it was all part of the game, the dog bounced around in front of her, wagging the rope, then disappearing around the end of the couch. He barked, daring her to chase him. Charity pushed up onto all fours, wincing at the rug burns on her palms.

Footsteps thumped down the hall and into the living room and she froze.

"Zeus? What the hell are you up to in here?"

Oh, God, oh, God, oh, God. She hadn't seen Grady in a week yet it seemed like a year. As many hours as she'd spent psyching herself up for this encounter, she still felt far from ready. Of course, that could have a little something to do with the fact that she'd been spritzed with tuna juice and smeared with dog hair.

Slowly she rose to her knees and peered over the top of the sofa. Grady was on the other side of the living room, in front of the fireplace, crouching down as he rubbed his dog's head. He was barefoot, and wore a faded pair of jeans and a white tee under an unbuttoned, long-sleeved shirt the color of moss. His face was relaxed, his hands gentle as he tussled with Zeus. She could watch him forever.

But she had to come out from behind the couch sooner or later. She certainly couldn't sleep back there. Right?

Suck it up, Deputy. She pushed to her feet, her breathing patchy, her fingers digging into leather. She cleared her throat, and Grady's head snapped up.

"What the—" Navy eyes wide, he jerked to his feet. "Charity." His gaze bounced around the room. "How did you get in here?"

"Your neighbor let me in."

He swallowed, and his eyes narrowed. He took a step toward her. "Why didn't you come find me?"

"I was—" she jerked a thumb over her shoulder, gestured helplessly at her sweater, then huffed out a chuckle and shrugged. "Busy," she finished lamely.

He crossed the room, bare feet soundless on the carpet, and stopped on the other side of the couch, jaw clenching and unclenching. "Why are you here?"

He smelled so good. Like ocean and air. His hair was rumpled, his jaw shadowed, his open shirt an invitation to wrap her arms around his waist and snuggle close. If there weren't a couch between them, anyway.

A couch, a long overdue apology, and a distinct lack of welcome in his eyes.

"Why are you here?" he repeated.

"I missed the housewarming?"

She saw it, then. The slightest twitch of his lips, the merest hint of warmth in his gaze. She relaxed her hands. Her fingertips tingled as circulation returned.

"Did you bring me a present?" he asked.

"I brought you an apology."

He didn't look impressed. He backed up and sank into a chair, gesturing at the couch she stood behind. "Let's hear it, then."

As Zeus settled at Grady's feet, Charity rounded the end of the couch. Grady's gaze dropped to her legs, taking in the heels she rarely wore, but his expression remained unmoved. She bit back a sigh and sat.

Zeus panted into the silence.

"I'm sorry I let you down," Charity finally said, and twined her hands in her lap. "I'm sorry I let myself down. You were right. We were given a second chance, and I-I was too scared to take it."

"Was?" he asked, and though he sat slouched in his chair, his pose seemingly casual, his left leg had started to bounce. Like Drew's had in interrogation, Charity realized.

Grady was as nervous as she was.

Lord, he was adorable. For the first time since she'd walked in the door, she thought she might actually have a chance.

She stood, and smoothed her palms down the front of her skirt. "I'm not prepared to leave Becker County," she said. His knee stopped bouncing. She kept going. "At least, not until I can train a replacement. I'm not prepared to ask you to leave Seattle, either, but I don't want to be without you anymore."

By now he was leaning forward, gaze riveted on her face, fingers digging into his thighs. "Go on," he said hoarsely.

"I don't know how we'll work this out, but I know we can, if we want it badly enough. And Grady, I want it badly. So badly. Please give me another chance." She licked lips she suddenly couldn't keep steady. "I love you so much," she whispered.

Before she even finished that last sentence, he was standing in front of her, the wariness in his expression giving way to a relief so profound, it made her dizzy.

"I've waited a long time to hear you say that again." He caught her up against him and kissed her with an enthusiasm she had no trouble matching.

By the time Grady lifted his head, sweat dampened his neck and desire tugged at his eyelids. He rested his forehead against hers and stroked a finger over the bump on her nose.

"It's been killing me, not getting to see you. Touch you. Hear you. I wanted to call so badly, but I thought maybe you needed the space. All bets were going to be off when I flew back to get Matt, though."

"Yeah?"

"Hell, yeah."

She shook her head. "I couldn't have waited that long."

"Thank God you didn't." He slid his hands under her sweater, smoothed his palms over her back and lowered his mouth to her neck. "Char?"

"Yeah?"

"Why do you smell like tuna?"

She huffed a laugh against his ear. "I'm wearing part of your dinner."

"We should get you out of these dirty clothes."

"I like the way you think." Suddenly her eyes went liquid, and she latched onto his shirt as if her knees had disappeared. "I'm so sorry I put you through this."

"We've been hard on each other. But, hey. We'll figure it out." He lifted his head and stared a promise. "We can stay in Becker County until you're ready to leave the sheriff's department. Then we can come back and give Seattle a try. Or Denver, or DC, or wherever you want to go."

"We can't yank Matt around. He needs stability."

"He'll have us. As long as we're together, we can make any place our home."

"I always envied you your escape, you know."

Grady stilled. "Is that what I am to you? An escape?"

Charity framed his face with her hands. "You always have been. An escape from dishonesty and greed and addiction and loneliness and insecurity. You make me feel special. Like I matter. Like I can make a difference without even trying." She wrapped her arms around his neck and scraped her teeth across his chin. "I love you."

He palmed the backs of her thighs, lifted her up, and swung toward the hallway. "I love you, too."

In his room at the end of the hall, Grady laid her on the bed and followed her down, elbows bracketing her head. He frowned when her skirt kept him from settling between her hips, and lifted away again.

He smoothed a hand down her hip. "As hot as you look in this, I'm not a fan."

Charity rolled her eyes. "There is an easy solution." She kicked off her pumps, lifted her hips, and pulled the hem of the skirt up to her waist.

The amusement left Grady's face when he got a good look at her barely-there panties.

"That's more like it," he growled. He positioned himself between her open legs and dipped his head to hers.

Charity stopped him with a hand to his chest. "Did you hear about the man who joined a nudist colony?"

Grady urged her legs up around his hips and spoke against her mouth. "Tell me."

"The first day was his hardest."

He chuckled as he worked her sweater up over her ribs and her bra up over her breasts. "I don't know how I ever managed without you." He shifted his hips against hers, rousing a hot, rippling need, rendering her breathless.

Her head fell back against the pillow. "Tell me something," she gasped.

His murmur was incoherent. Understandable, considering his mouth was full of nipple. She gathered herself and rolled, pushing him onto his back. He snarled when the motion tugged her breast from between his lips. She straddled his hips, yanked her cardigan over her head and let her bra slide down her arms and off her hands. She planted her palms on his pecs and began to rock.

"What is it with men," she panted, "always having to be on top?"

"No idea," he groaned. Rearing up, he slid his hands down her back. He worked his fingers past the edge of her panties and squeezed her ass. "But they don't know what they're missing."

*   *   *

Thank you for reading IN FULL FORCE! I hope that Charity and Grady kept you entertained. :-)

Want a peek into their future? Subscribe to my mailing list and get instant access to an exclusive IN FULL FORCE bonus scene!

You can subscribe on my website (www.kathyaltman.com) for access to the download (ebook only), or scan this handy dandy QR code:

Interested in helping other readers find this book while earning my endless gratitude? Please consider leaving a review. I would love it so much if you did. Thank you!

To find out about upcoming releases, including the next book in the Badges of Becker County series, check out my website at www.kathyaltman.com.

ACKNOWLEDGMENTS

Heartfelt gratitude goes to super-talented writer friends Robin Allen, Toni Anderson, Carolyn Crane, Rachel Grant, and Jenn Stark, for encouraging me to give this self-publishing thing a whirl. You ladies are my kind of crazy. I miss you all!

I also wish to thank narrator Kayla Torrison, who did a glorious job with the audiobook and was a dream to work with. Looking forward to doing that again, Kayla!

ABOUT THE AUTHOR

Author, wife, cat mom, hardcore chocolate chip cookie fan, Kathy Altman prefers her chocolate with nuts, her Friday afternoons with wine and her love stories with happy ever afters. Her contemporary romance and romantic suspense books are an award-winning, feel-good blend of the heartfelt, the humorous, and the seriously sexy.